and its a

on and plan to stay up late, ... this is a scavenger hunt from hell that you won't want to miss!"
  MyBookishWays.com

"A very taut extremely fast paced novel that drags the reader into the spinning world of a psychopathic serial killer and doesn't let up until the very last pages. *Scare Me* is a book that readers will finish in one sitting and end up exhausted from event after horrifying event coming one after another. Excellent read and masterful fleshing out of people forced to comply with the dictates of lunacy, and this includes the motives of the killer explained at the book's ending."
  BookBitch

"From the opening it's a plot that will have its readers gripped and pulled headfirst into its globe-trotting internet-controlled macabre treasure hunt as Will Frost rushes from one crime scene to the next, his sole desire to rescue two people who he holds dear to his heart, whilst his life around him begins to shred and tatter. With a sadistic and creative killer in its midst and the nagging fear throughout as to what in the Frost's family's world could have brought the events upon them, *Scare Me* is a thrilling ride. If I dare quote Lady Penelope here: 'Parker...Well done!'"
  Book

ALSO BY RICHARD PARKER

Stop Me
Scare Me

RICHARD PARKER

STALK ME

EXHIBIT A
An Angry Robot imprint
and a member of the Osprey Group

Lace Market House,
54-56 High Pavement,
Nottingham,
NG1 1HW,
UK

www.exhibitabooks.com
A is for Assault!

An Exhibit A paperback original 2014
1

A catalogue record for this book is available
from the British Library.

UK ISBN: 978 1 90922 303 5
Ebook ISBN: 978 1 90922 305 9

Set in Meridien and Franklin Gothic by Argh! Oxford

To my lovely niece, Erin, who won't be able to read this for another fourteen years. Or, if she's like me, another four.

CHAPTER ONE

The only element of Beth's last glimpse that didn't seem to shatter was the windshield. Every other component of her reality fractured and splintered as if a pickaxe had swung and embedded itself at its centre.

She'd checked the road ahead was clear before turning to Luc, but didn't see the stationary brown camper van tucked just beyond the curve of beech trees. Luc was in the passenger seat looking at his iPhone and something that clearly amused him. Her reflexes were good; she would have hit the brakes and they would have suffered nothing worse than whiplash. But her eyes were on Luc's and as he'd turned to meet her gaze they'd hit the camper full on. It was the last time she ever saw him smile.

It was the smile Beth couldn't believe had been directed at her the day he first spoke to her outside the athletics track and that she'd seen thousands of times since, but the crash wiped it from her memory never to be retrieved.

After the impact, it was as if time had continued onwards and left Beth briefly suspended in a vacuum. Then her vision was flooded white, and momentarily she couldn't draw in air through her nostrils or mouth.

She could hear the sounds of panic trapped in her head and the membrane of whatever was trying to suffocate her pressing tight against her face. Her skull was aching, not as if it had been traumatised, but as if it were being pumped up. Her personality had momentarily ejected itself from the vehicle. Seconds passed as she tried to remember who and where she was.

With a great effort, she swung her neck back to fill her lungs, away from whatever was smothering her. It was the deployed airbag, and the sound of her erratic breathing bounced around its interior as its concentrated plastic smell filled her nostrils. She turned her head towards her passenger and heard bone grate with the action. Seeing Luc like that made her remember who she was.

Luc had his face in his airbag, eyes closed and almost serene. She'd helped him shave his head close that morning and momentarily focused on the tiny nick she'd accidentally made with the razor in the top curve of his left ear. Her identity and situation snapped back at her as if it had been on elastic, and the impact of that seemed worse than the crash. His chin tilted upwards and a tear of blood appeared at his nose. It didn't drop into his lap but rose to the ceiling quickly followed by more thick droplets.

"Luc…" Her voice sounded strange, as if it were bottled.

They were upside down and Beth could feel the pressure of her throat working against her jaw and making her ears chime. She could smell petrol. Until that precise moment, it had been an aroma she'd always liked. They both had to get out quickly. As her circulation overfilled the veins in her head, she listened for signs of other drivers, people who might be running to help. But all she could hear were the hard rain thudding on the bottom of the car and the motor of the twisted wipers repeatedly grinding like a sluggish, rusty countdown.

Beth's fingers scrabbled for the buckle of her seatbelt. Her weight was jamming it tight, and it was constricting her lungs. The pad of her thumb pressed weakly against the solidity of the button as she bent and kicked her dangling legs against the pedals in frustration. One of her backless high heels dropped to the ceiling.

The belt released and her scalp was suddenly slamming hard against padded metal, her sapphire blue dress falling over her like a parachute. The rest of her body toppled and her spine took its weight, her legs angled against the side window. She slid her shoulders from under the pile of herself and tried to reach across to Luc.

"Luc." Her constricted windpipe barely twisted out the word. Beth shifted closer to him.

He hung above her, blood continuing to trickle from his nose into a pool beside her. He moved suddenly and she heard a strangled breath escape him.

"I'm free. Don't move. I'm going to try and get out." She reached past the headrest and gently touched the back of his head, but he didn't respond.

Where was her mobile? She slid her hands about her trying to locate the tiny black tassel shoulder bag she'd brought to the restaurant. It wasn't anywhere in reach.

She slid herself to her door and tried the handle. It wouldn't budge. Was it locked, or was the metal warped from the impact? Try the window. There was no button for it on the door. She dragged herself back and stretched up between the two inflated airbags to the console above her. Which one was it? The buttons and icons were upside down. She tried a few, stretching her arm higher and feeling a sharp rush of pain in her spine.

Beth heard the soft whirr of the window and scrambled back to the door. The glass was rising in front of her like a stage curtain and she crawled through on her hands and knees into dim daylight, cold rain suddenly penetrating the skin exposed by the V at the back of her dress. She couldn't rise, couldn't stand. She felt the stones in her kneecaps and the icy droplets on her legs, saturating her tights and her knickers where her dress had ridden up her back. Darkness started soaking through her vision.

She moved herself forward and expected to see her own blood pouring from her face and spattering the backs of her hands. It felt like every part of her had ruptured, that everything inside her body was broken and loose. She pulled herself all the way out, her knuckles butting an unidentifiable piece of metal. She realised the warped obstacle in front of her matched the silver body of their Nissan Pathfinder.

Faint gravel-hissing footsteps. She couldn't work out which direction they were coming from. Was it somebody looking for survivors?

She angled her body away from the metal and pulled herself towards the sound. The rain intensified and she found herself crawling through a deep puddle, the impact of the heavy droplets splashing about her ears. She couldn't keep her head up, and it hinged forward so she was breathing the dirty water through her nostrils. She tasted oil and mud at the top of her throat and spluttered as she lifted her face back out.

Beth tried to look up and along the curving road, but her aching spine only allowed her to raise her vision enough to glimpse the bottom half of the skewed camper in front. The chocolate-brown back doors were mangled and the French licence plate lay in the other debris that had been smashed from it, but the vehicle was still the right way up. In the gap between its underside and the road, she could see a pair of feet moving. Dark navy trousers and black boots. Somebody was the other side of it.

She cried out, not recognising the mournful howl that emerged from her, but hoping it would be loud enough to attract their attention. Her face dropped into the puddle a second time and she had to blow a few bubbles of air into the water before she could raise her head again.

Beth fought unconsciousness, and when she cracked her eyes and blinked the water from them, somebody was standing beside her, a smudgy black silhouette against the failing daylight. She opened her mouth, fighting oblivion to alert them to Luc's predicament. Their foot swung back and kicked Beth squarely in the face. Before the impact embedded her deep into unconsciousness, she heard the squeak of her teeth and a flat crunch as her jaw fragmented.

CHAPTER TWO

Ferrand squinted through the coach's wall of windshield, as the wipers struggled to shift the rain obscuring his view of the narrow forest road ahead. Many of the circular mirrors on the bends had been smashed, so he spent much of the route blowing his horn to warn any oncoming motorists of his presence.

Mercifully, the handful of American exchange students were quieter than they'd been on the outward journey to Le Mans. Another ten or so minutes and he'd be at the drop-off point and they were again the responsibility of the families foolish enough to give them lodgings.

They were all about eighteen but seemed very immature to Ferrand. Their two chaperones, Kelcie and Ramiro, seemed to be only a few years older. Now that they were all spread out in the seats and wired up to their handhelds, however, the only noise was the engine and the rain battering the roof.

He ran his hand through his thinning hair, blew his horn at the next bend and peered through the waterfall of the windshield. He needed an eye test but knew his worsening myopia was likely to soon rob him of his licence. He'd been putting it off month after month. But his grown children and grandchildren had just moved back in with him and he was the only person bringing money into the house.

Ferrand was just rehearsing the conversation he might have

with his wife if the tour company took his keys off him, when the crash site swung into view. Two vehicles lay smashed on his left, a junked camper and a silver car farther away at the edge of the trees, on its roof. It was difficult to see through the rain, but he could ascertain there were no police present. The wreckage definitely hadn't been there on the journey out. He immediately pulled the coach onto the right-hand verge and switched off the engine. He could hear the students asking Kelcie why they'd stopped and then their awed reactions to the spectacle.

Ferrand pulled the door handle on the dash and the doors hissed open. He got out of his seat and walked down the steps. As he dropped down onto the grass, the rain soaked into his shirt. He checked there was no oncoming traffic and walked across to the buckled brown camper.

When he reached the other side, he heard voices from behind him. He turned to find the students climbing off the bus and was about to tell them to get back on, when dumpy Kelcie and hungover Ramiro came down the steps.

"Everyone stay away from the road," Kelcie said without much effect.

Ferrand left her corralling them and took a few more paces so he could survey the damage and look tentatively through the window of the buckled camper. If the bodywork was anything to go by, it was likely the occupants would be just as bashed out of shape. His stomach shrank at the thought of what might be slumped and bleeding in the seats.

He was relieved to find only a scattering of broken glass there. Perhaps the emergency services had already been. Why were the vehicles still in the road, though? He walked towards the upside-down car that was about ten yards away at the edge of the trees. He'd only gone one pace, however, when he saw the woman lying on her back outside the silver Nissan.

He scrabbled his phone out of his shirt pocket and quickly dialled 112.

Beth opened her eyelids against moisture and blinked it away. She was looking up at stars in a night sky through bare branches and watched rain droplets dilate at the end of them and then plummet towards her. Wind blew them sideways before they could land on her face, but a finer spray blurred her vision again.

Beth observed this for a while, mesmerised and waiting for her conscious fragments to gradually cluster and tell her why she was lying there. A vanilla hint of the Shalimar she'd sprayed on for the evening was still in her nostrils. She rarely wore scent. There were mumbling voices nearby, including a male's on a radio. She could only hear them through her right ear. The severity of her situation lurked at the periphery of her memory. She was injured and instinct told her not to move. But she needed to take in her immediate environment, and as soon as she turned, Beth was looking at Luc.

He was lying on a trolley next to her, red and blue lights skimming over him. His eyes were open and his soundless words punched a hole through the black patch of congealed blood coating his mouth and chin. His blue eyes were faded to grey, as if the exertion of trying to speak to her was gradually sapping him.

A warm hand was rested on Beth's forehead, repositioning and restraining her skull so she was looking at Luc through the corner of her eye. She tried to twist her neck, but the fingers holding her increased their pressure and squealed against the movement. They were clad in surgical gloves and she could feel their adhesion as they readjusted their grip.

"Let me up." But the plea emerged as shapeless babble and something scraped at her eardrum. The interior of Beth's mouth felt as if it were fused around her tongue, a useless and swollen bung of flesh. She rolled her eyes upwards and saw a few loose dreadlocks about the features of the black female paramedic holding her in place. She was looking from side to side, seeking assistance. She mumbled under her breath and

Beth could smell the spearmint and cigarettes on her warm breath as it fell on her face.

"*Ne bougez pas!*"

Her forehead was released and the paramedic disappeared from her field of vision. The rain fell harder on her face and she had to briefly close her eyelids again and exhale from her nostrils and swollen lips.

She turned slowly back to Luc. His eyes were screwed tight against the pain, teeth gritting and fresh blood flowing from his nostrils. Luc had a nosebleed every other month but nothing like this. He opened his mouth to try to speak to her again, but a movement beyond him caught her eye. She squinted hard at the blue blobs on the opposite side of the road.

Beth could see a crowd gathered there, their faces illuminated by the emergency vehicle lights. There were about fifteen or so people. A length of luminous yellow tape segregated them from the crash site. They were all craning to look at Beth and Luc.

Luc moved and came back into focus. He was still muttering deliriously and said her name but it sounded like an exclamation of agony. His lips parted and his voice cracked in his throat. "Sorry..."

Beth frowned a response. "Lie still," she tried to say. But the words came out mangled, and it felt as if she had gravel in her mouth.

"Sorry..." he repeated, and then his head fell back on the stretcher, and its impact seem to release the tears from his eyes. He clenched them tightly shut and a red bubble formed at his nostril.

Beyond him, Beth could see some of the crowd had their arms in the air. A handful of them had their phones raised. Surely they weren't recording her and Luc as they lay injured in the road?

Beth hinged her body so she was sitting up on the trolley. Her whole spine throbbed once and she felt her heart pulse irregularly in her jaw. She could see all the way across the road. Paramedics and police weaved around each other, but

Beth saw no other casualties. She felt hot and cold adrenaline course through her. The phones were aimed directly at them.

Beth swung her feet off the trolley and back onto the road. It felt as if she had been lying there for days. She reached over to Luc and clasped the icy hands that lay balled at the centre of his chest. He responded, but she knew it wasn't to her touch. He was convulsing. Was he bleeding internally as well?

"We need help!" She forced the words out through the tiny gap around her tongue, but they didn't emerge with the volume of urgency she wanted. It felt as if she had shards of broken glass piercing her gums. She tried to rise from the trolley, but her legs failed and her knees smashed into the gravel. Luc didn't turn to her when she touched his cold, wet face. Another spasm extinguished his recognition of her. He didn't know she was there.

"*Couchez-vous!*"

Beth turned to the paramedic whose hands were on her and forced out two mashed words. "Help him!"

"I will. Lie down first." The woman's English was crystal clear.

Beth felt the paramedic's hands hook under her arms, helping her up. When she was shakily standing, Beth found herself looking straight at the crowd. They were filming. They were capturing every second of the worst moment of her life. Luc could be dying, and they were casually recording it to show to their friends.

She shook off the paramedic and marched unsteadily forward, a concentrated rage she'd never experienced overwhelming her.

Beth didn't feel as if she were walking across the road. Sound ceased with the pain, and it seemed as if she were gliding to the row of faces on a conveyor belt.

She could hear the screaming in her head and discerned some of it as hers. The crowd was suddenly dispersing, scattering before her waving fists. But even though they retreated, one young guy wearing a blue camouflage bandana impassively stood his ground and held out his phone as if it were a talisman to ward her off.

She lunged forward to strike him, her shoulders tensing painfully as she heaved her fists. The yellow tape was gone but they were all recording her from further back.

Her hair undulated as if animated by her fury. A potent gust of wind was at her back and blasting her scalp. It was accompanied by a frenetic buzz overhead. She looked skywards and saw the helicopter shakily descending, the branches of the trees violently billowing as its blades whipped up the loose leaves from the road.

Beth could feel them scratching her face as she returned her attention to the crowd. They'd retreated, seeking safety from her attack and the barrage of energised air. They now had their phones pointed upwards to capture the air ambulance's entrance.

Hands were about her and she turned to see another paramedic being joined by two male gendarmes as she was gently restrained. The aircraft's engines whined in her head, and under its high-pitched whistling, she could hear her own unheard scream grinding in her throat. As the helicopter touched down, Beth's overwrought emotions short-circuited her and she blacked out.

CHAPTER THREE

The young, pretty nurse silently left the room as soon as Beth woke, and in that moment, she knew Luc was dead. A slim, middle-aged female doctor with glasses on a chain and puckered smoker's lips entered a few minutes later. The draught of her arrival smelt of nicotine and antiseptic hand wash, and her grey hair was clipped untidily to the back of her head. Was she to be the messenger?

When the doctor gently put her hand beside Beth's head, she wanted to sit up but felt as if every one of her muscles had seized. Was she paralysed?

"Good morning, Mrs Jordan, I'm Doctor Falconer." Her scrutiny played around Beth's face but she didn't meet her eye. "A nurse will be in shortly to make you a little more comfortable."

"Luc?" she enquired, but it hurt to say his name. Pain locked itself tight to the left-hand side of her face, and her mouth filled with saliva. She didn't want the preamble. Didn't want to delay the revelation by being told that she, at least, was going to live.

"You're going to be in this position for at least another couple of days. Your jawbone was in fragments. You had titanium plates inserted to hold it together."

"Luc," she repeated flatly. She could feel the resistance of the dressing around her cheek.

The doctor met her gaze, blinked slowly and nodded as if

acknowledging her wishes. She swallowed quickly and Beth watched the moment between ignorance and confirmation bounce in her throat. "I'm afraid your husband didn't survive the crash."

She'd hoped her instincts were wrong, that she was girding herself for words that wouldn't come, but the doctor's sentence was a thick blade thrusting into her sternum.

"I'm so sorry."

There were too many implications to absorb. She knew the reality of Luc being gone was something she couldn't begin to acknowledge, but it was the immediate certainties that were overwhelming. She hadn't been there. Luc had died without her. She'd been oblivious. "How?"

"His neck was broken." The doctor put her hot hand on Beth's wrist and it felt like it would scald her. "He didn't regain consciousness during the flight in the air ambulance and died before they reached the hospital. He didn't feel any pain."

Beth remembered tenderly touching the back of Luc's head in the car and his agonized expression as he lay on the stretcher. The doctor's features blurred, the tendons in Beth's neck hardening as she attempted to sit up.

She put her other hand gently on Beth's chest. "I know how difficult this must be, but please try to remain still. You've been transferred to the UK. You're now in St Andrews, Wandsworth."

"How long have I been here?"

"You were in a coma."

Beth felt panic stampede through her. "How long?"

"Just over eight weeks. You woke briefly last night and then fell into a deep sleep."

Beth needed to rise but couldn't; the blade felt like it was thrusting in deeper, pinning her to the mattress.

When she looked up, she caught the doctor slyly glancing at her watch. Her pale green eyes returned to Beth's, and they were briefly devoid of emotion. They softened in sympathy again. "Nobody was able to predict how long you'd be in the coma. I'm afraid arrangements had to be made in your absence."

Beth tried to see past the euphemism and quickly guessed what it meant.

"Your husband's funeral had to go ahead..."

Husband? She hated that label. She was talking about Luc, but Beth was trying to remember whether he wanted to be buried or cremated. He couldn't be gone. Not just like that. How could everyone who had known him but her have said goodbye to him? Buried or cremated? "When?"

"I don't have the exact date."

"Find out!" The painful vibration of the outburst travelled down her body and her bones amplified it. Buried or cremated? She imagined his body in a coffin under the earth. Saw it burst into flames. "What date is it today?"

"Today? The 9th... of March."

How long since Luc had been–

"We've notified your family; your brother's on his way. You mustn't upset yourself."

Buried or cremated? The doctor's words were losing their meaning.

"If you want, I can get somebody to sit with you." Just sounds about her wrinkled lips.

Beth closed her eyes.

"Can I get you some water?"

She kept her eyes sealed until she heard the doctor leave. She lay there, listening to the floor polisher in the corridor outside. She wanted her world to sound different somehow: vacant and inhospitable, not full of trivial background noise. It didn't. It just didn't have Luc in it any more.

For hours she just lay looking at the spotless white ceiling, waiting for tears that didn't come.

CHAPTER FOUR

When she was fit enough to leave St Andrews, Beth was picked up by her younger brother, Jody. As he slowly wheeled her in a chair past the garish artwork in the hospital corridor, she was still unnerved by how such a catastrophic episode in her life hadn't rippled the world around her. It just sounded small, like she was listening to everything through a tinny speaker.

In her head was the same circuit of thought she'd woken with. She'd been driving. That much was certain. Was Luc's death entirely her fault? Why had he been whispering "sorry"? Did he feel he was to blame? She had no recollection of how they'd ended up in the wreckage. However much she tried to negotiate the solid block of darkness lodged between their setting off for the restaurant and their being suspended from the ceiling of the car, it remained immovable. Was she deliberately blocking out the trauma to avoid facing her responsibility for it?

But she couldn't understand how Luc had broken his neck when his airbag had inflated. The police had said he hadn't been wearing his seatbelt. But he'd been hanging in the car as she had. If he'd released himself, it didn't seem possible he could have sustained the injury with such a short fall. Would he still be alive if the driver from the brown camper had helped instead of assaulted her? Why had he kicked her? Was it because they'd struck him? Had he also attacked Luc?

During their visits, Jody and her parents had relayed everything that had occurred while she was oblivious, did their best to fill the other void between the French roadside and waking in St Andrews.

Beth visualised her unconscious self being wheeled from the first casualty department, where the doctors had worked on her, and flown to the ward at home, and at the same time Luc's lifeless body being transported to the morgue, the undertaker's and then to the Rouen crematorium near his mother's house. She tried to imagine what she might have read for him if she'd been at the service but found it impossible to even project herself there.

Luc had been cremated. Even though they should have just moved into their new home together, he was now in an urn at his mother's. She'd taken charge of the ashes in Beth's absence and they were now in Quincampoix. His father had died before their wedding, and Luc had been estranged from his mother because of the handful of men she had chosen to make his interim stepfathers. He had plenty of friends and work colleagues to grieve him but no other family.

The holiday in the Forêt domaniale de Lyons had been their escape from solicitors, paperwork and an attempted mugging that had been the reason for their move from Edgware to Wandsworth. The move date had been delayed and had made them both fractious. They'd spent the fortnight prior to it living out of boxes, sitting on telescopic chairs and yelling at each other. The rows had always come back to the same issue.

They'd decided to abscond and rent their usual holiday accommodation, Gîte Saint Roch, a converted timbered barn in Luc's favourite corner of Normandy. It was in one of the most beautiful European beech forests, and it was where she'd proposed to him three years earlier. She'd beaten him to it by one day.

Luc had delayed asking her while he'd waited for the perfect conditions. When the sun shone through the slender trunks, it was like being inside a natural cathedral. But Tuesday had been overcast so he'd decided to wait.

They'd both known it would be a race to that question on that first holiday. The time had felt right. He'd produced the citrine ring after she'd proposed. Citrine was her birthstone and it had still been on her finger as she'd watched her hands dragging her body away from the car wreck.

It was Beth who'd suggested the last-minute January getaway. If she hadn't, they would now be safely ensconced in their new house. Everything waited for her, boxed and in storage. She thought about the two of them wrapping up their life in newspaper and how she'd never conceived she might have to unwrap it alone.

It seemed like a premonition now. Luc had been ruthless when they'd emptied out the memory chest as they'd packed up in their Edgware home. Most of its contents had gone to the dump. All their cards to each other, birthday and otherwise, all the mementos they'd kept from restaurants they'd eaten at and postcards from places they'd visited – they'd all been disposed of, and she'd felt a pang as they'd tipped them into bin bags. It was almost as if he'd been preparing for what happened. All those ephemeral keepsakes took on a new significance now. She supposed they'd been covered over in some landfill or incinerated as Luc had been.

Jody wheeled her out into the car park's cold morning air and opened the passenger door of his muddy tungsten Golf Mk7. She delicately climbed in. He'd been doing his best with the clichéd platitudes. Beth acknowledged how difficult it must have been for her younger brother to comfort her when their communication from childhood had always steered clear of any displays of emotion.

"You hungry?" Jody broke the silence as they pulled out into the main road.

"Not really."

"Sorry, I'm fucking famished. Do you mind if we stop somewhere?"

"Sure." She looked through the window at the grey sky mirrored in the tower blocks on either side of them. Her own reflection barely registered behind the bright white squares of the remaining gauze plasters around her mouth. She glanced down and found she had a tissue-wrapped bunch of canary-yellow lilies in her lap. She vaguely remembered Jody handing them to her in the ward. Cars beeped behind them, and Beth realised Jody was driving deliberately slowly. It had barely occurred to her she was back in the front seat of a car.

They stopped off at a down-at-heel burger bar that smelt of stale cooking oil. Beth seated herself in the window seat and examined the smudges on the glass while Jody ordered. After a few moments she noticed a young couple in the car park having an argument while they loaded up their car with shopping. She wondered how many times she and Luc had fought and how much time it had accounted for – days, months? Their last major quarrel at home had been pretty intense. The fallout from it had hung about like a bad smell for days afterwards.

Jody dropped onto the red plastic chair opposite and his arms trembled as he raised the meat-stacked bun to his mouth. Beth noticed they were the only customers. What time of the morning was it, anyway? She glimpsed his watch and saw it was just after 11.

He chewed robotically, and a string of melted cheese undulated on his ginger beard. A closely cropped crown of the same colour circled the sides of his bald head. Beth had seen him like this plenty of times. Low blood sugar turned him into a zombie. He'd put on a lot of weight since last year. That was the last time she'd seen him prior to the crash. Her mother had told her he'd developed type 2 diabetes. Good to see he'd modified his diet. She decided not to point out that he'd bitten off a corner of the wrapper as well.

Jody swallowed a lump of ground beef and briefly closed his eyes to savour the moment like a much-needed fix. He breathed with difficulty past his adenoids and then continued munching with his mouth open, sucking in air so he didn't have to stop eating. When he opened his eyes, there seemed to be more of his personality present. "Sorry, but I would have keeled over."

"Thanks for picking me up... and sorry they made you wait so long."

Jody nodded, but his gaze left hers. He was uncomfortable with anything that wasn't a joke or a statement of fact. Fortunately, it suddenly started raining hard and they both sought refuge through the pane. The couple got in their car to resume their squabble and thick rivulets poured down the window as if the burger bar were going through a car wash.

"Your swelling has gone down."

Beth found Jody studying the bottom portion of her face when she turned back to him.

"Looks much better now." He took another bite, not shifting his eyes from her mouth.

"Considering..." Beth knew she didn't need to elaborate.

Jody had listened to her account several times and didn't appear to want to hear it again. For a moment it looked as if he was going to use his chewing as an excuse not to answer. "They're still saying your airbag didn't deploy properly?" He knew they were.

"It deployed. Both of them did. And before you quote the accident report again, we both had our belts on. We were hanging from our seats by them." She could see Jody's eyes glaze. He'd been understanding but had been trying to persuade her that constantly analysing an incident she could only partially remember was going to drive her crazy. She repeated her version of events anyway. "I only undid mine to crawl out of the car. Luc probably removed his after I blacked out. Why does nobody believe that?"

He examined her injured face as if it were explanation enough and then looked back out at the couple again. "Like they say, maybe your memory is still dealing with last year's mugging."

"I know what I saw. There's no connection between what happened at the roadside and what happened in a car park five months ago." But even though they were becoming less frequent, Beth still had her own nocturnal flashbacks to the first incident.

She had been watching Luc put the groceries in the car when she saw the shadow of the hoodie with the baseball bat on the concrete wall. She'd turned and lashed out at them and her fist had connected with their mouth. She'd felt it wet on her knuckles and their teeth had left several dents in them. The attacker had run off, leaving them both unharmed but shaken. The police had done little even though CCTV had captured the incident.

"Luc was still depressed about it. He needed the trip to France more than I did. I knew it was because he felt he should have protected me. If that hadn't happened, we wouldn't have been on that road."

"You can't think like that."

She knew he was right, but the idea of one trauma leading to another had occupied her thoughts the whole time she'd been recuperating. "I told him we couldn't run from violence. Look where it got us. We left muggings and drug culture and moved to a neighbourhood targeted by the East Hill Sniper."

The sniper had hit the news while they were still waiting for the keys to the house. The gunman had taken random shots at wealthy residents from a high-rise block less than half a mile from where their new home had been built.

"I've been told you either live amongst it or in a place that invites it."

It was what one of her witnesses had said to her. Even having spent six years as a victim-support counsellor, she'd still rejected it. Now she wasn't so sure.

"But I didn't expect to find it when I crawled out of our car."

"Every doctor who examined you said your injuries were sustained in the crash."

"I know the man who attacked me was real, Jody. Luc was the one still troubled by the mugger."

"Your brain took a real knock. I'd be surprised if things didn't get all shook up."

"Then why did the other driver flee the scene?"

"The camper was unlicensed." Jody closed his eyes to relate the fact to her once more.

"Maybe he thought he could rob us first."

"But from your account, he could have done that very easily, without any resistance from either of you. And nothing had been taken from your bag or... the wallet."

Beth realised he was avoiding mentioning Luc's name. "Perhaps he was disturbed when the coach arrived..." but she didn't continue. There was no point sustaining a conversation she'd already had with him and the police a dozen times over. She hadn't been able to alert them to the assault until after she'd emerged from her coma. By then there were no longer any palpable leads to the vanished driver or his trashed camper. It had been scrapped weeks after it had been towed from the site. Plus the Normandy police had barely hidden their suspicion that the assault story had been an attempt to cover up the fact she and Luc had been less than safety-conscious in the car.

Jody looked out at the car park again. "Our guardians are still on their Med cruise until Sunday night." Jody always called them that. It was a joke, but also his way of reinforcing the distance he felt towards their parents. It was one of the few things she had in common with him. "So you're welcome to stay at mine."

She'd never been invited to her brother's pad before. Had no idea what sort of place he lived in. Her father had texted the night before, apologising for not being back for her return, but saying that Jody would give her a key to the house and to make herself at home in the meantime. She'd dismissed their offers of cancelling their holiday when it was unclear when she would be discharged from hospital. They hadn't taken much persuasion.

"Thanks for the offer..." She examined Jody's face for a reaction. Was he just saying it because he felt he should, or was it a genuine gesture? Jody at least appreciated that the last place she wanted to be was in an empty house, whether it was their parents' or a new home with stacks of boxes to unpack.

He looked down into his fries without meeting Beth's eye on the way. "I mean it. There's a box room; you can have some private time. If you need to get away from all the shit." He prodded his food around the carton.

"That's really kind…" Beth didn't mean to say it the way she did, leaving the sentence hanging as if she couldn't think of an excuse to say no.

Jody rose, closing and stacking his food cartons. "I'll eat the rest of this on the way." He shuffled awkwardly out of the fixed seat, his belly dragging along the loose salt at the edge of the brown tabletop.

They moved to the exit and stood in the doorway looking out at the rain.

Jody covered his shaved head with an old Gentleman Jack baseball cap. "Ready?"

"It would be good not to have to deal with the shit when they come back."

"I'm not just talking usual parental stuff. They've had reporters calling at the house."

"Why?"

Jody didn't turn. "Those clips of you on the Internet; you're an online celebrity."

CHAPTER FIVE

When she'd been in hospital, Beth had asked Jody if she could see the newspaper obituary Luc's mother had placed, as well as any records that would help her authenticate the events she'd been absent from. The impersonal eulogy had been barely two column inches.

Beth's mother had never hidden her disapproval when she'd married Luc, but she'd dutifully attended the ceremony in Rouen. She'd given Beth the funeral service pamphlet she'd retained and a copy of *Ouest-France*. . Much of the newspaper's space had been given to a cover story about the French Ecology Minister, Christiane Vipond, having had a heart attack. The crash had been relegated to a space smaller than the local obituary.

The scant details had only reinforced how Beth had felt about her presence within the collision. But just as she'd been feeling as if Luc's passing had barely intruded on the world he'd inhabited for thirty-three years, it now appeared the incident had made a media ripple of the very worst kind after all.

Jody had tentatively informed her about the accident site clips having been posted on YouTube, but it had only been on the journey home to his rented home in Stockwell that he'd told her they'd actually gone viral.

There'd only been thirteen spectators on the exchange-student coach that had stopped at the roadside, but the five phones that had recorded the aftermath meant hundreds of thousands of people had been privy to Luc's last moments.

While Beth had been comatose, people had watched it all over the world, searched for it on their PCs and handhelds to relieve boredom during lunch hours or when there was nothing better on TV. Their suffering and her violent outburst had been entertainment for scores of the curious and the morbid. Celebrity? It had been a repulsive joke. Jody had said under YouTube's privacy policy, the clips could be potentially removed within five days. They'd already been out there for months, but he'd said he hadn't taken any action yet because he thought when she was ready, she might want to see them before they were taken down.

After scaling the steps at the front of the Edwardian property, and then another flight to his first-floor flat, Beth was trembling. She didn't know if it was the exertion or what she'd just been told.

Jody carried her bag into the tiny box room with the single bed in it and placed it on the rug. "It's more a cupboard, but it's at the back of the house so it should at least be quiet. I'd give you my room, but you wouldn't thank me for that. I'll let you unpack." He left and carefully closed the door behind him.

Unpack? Beth seated herself on the single bed and lifted her tiny case, containing her handbag from the crash site, a few clothes, toiletries and the new pyjamas her mother had brought to the hospital, onto the duvet. She didn't usually wear anything in bed with Luc, but she took them out now and laid them carefully across the pillow.

She tried to remember exactly what she'd worn for their last night out. They'd both showered together after the make-up sex they'd had following their brief foray into a familiar argument. They'd washed each other and Beth had started to respond to his touch again, but they'd had a reservation at Oubliez Demain and they'd already been late.

They'd never made it, and now she imagined the candle lit at their table and the chairs empty for the entire evening.

It had been the first time they'd stayed at the cabin in the winter. The January air had been chilly. She knew she'd put on her sapphire blue knitted dress with the empire bodice. She could remember slipping on her black tights and suede heels but couldn't recall if she'd taken a coat. The clothes had probably been cut from her in casualty.

Her last vivid memory of Luc before the crash was of him looking meditatively at her in the mirror while she applied her eyeliner.

She heard Jody turn on the TV in the lounge and hurriedly tidying up while he waited for her to come out. When she did, he told her to sit down in one of his leather armchairs and said he'd order them some Chinese food when she was ready. She said OK, but that she had to pee, and headed to the bathroom even though she didn't need to.

She wanted to put off the moment of them both sitting through some junk soap like nothing had happened. Standing in front of Jody's tiny, toothpaste-spattered mirror, Beth painfully peeled off the last gauze plaster and surveyed her new appearance. The area suddenly exposed was a wrinkled, swollen and anaemic square on the left-hand side of her chin. She touched it lightly with her fingertips and the skin prickled. Victim-support counsellor? She barely knew where to begin with herself.

She'd been told the swelling would go down and that the lacerations would partially fade – particularly if she applied cream and massaged the scarred area. She couldn't work out which of the crescent wounds had been caused by the crash and which by the insertion of the plates.

Her curls that she'd had cut boyishly short and dyed a deep raspberry shade for their trip looked similarly lifeless, a faded, barely pink tinge as her light brown hair had grown out. It now lay in a low fringe over her dark eyebrows and hung in uneven fronds down to her shoulders. It was distressing to imagine herself lying insensible while it had got so long. It was even more distressing to feel as if she'd seen Luc less than a week ago.

Everyone said that she could have come off a lot worse. That she was lucky to be alive.

She looked different. Not just physically. She saw something absent from her hazel eyes as they reluctantly caught themselves in her reflection. The doctors said there was no discernible brain damage, but Beth wasn't the person that had left the UK with Luc anymore. However, although her appearance alarmed and upset her, she was almost glad the crash hadn't left her unscathed.

There had to be some physical manifestation of Luc's removal. Some side effect of being fleeced of the life she'd known. It was like another mugging, only this one was more brutal than any physical assault. It had made off with everything that was valuable to her.

Stalled feelings were locked away so deeply they didn't register anywhere in her expression. She still hadn't processed what had happened like everyone else had. They were months ahead of her. As far as she was concerned, the crash was a very recent memory. She was outside of the people she knew, dislocated, and didn't know if she would ever feel part of their world again.

CHAPTER SIX

It was a couple of days after Jody had told Beth about her Internet presence that she finally plucked up the courage to look. Her brother's tablet had been on the coffee table since she'd moved in, and she'd been eyeing it askance every time they'd sat together in the lounge.

She wasn't sleeping, had done enough of that. Her limbs felt weak but twitched when she tried to relax them. The bed was tiny and ice-cold even when Jody turned up the radiator. It was March but Beth knew it was nothing to do with the temperature.

Jody's dated and dusty place was modest but didn't need to be. Much to Beth's surprise, her brother had turned out to be something of a success story, albeit a covert one. And she thought that his days with the keyboards were over. He used to play for a variety of semi-professional indie bands. Like bassists, keyboardists were always in more demand than guitarists, drummers and vocalists. It appeared he'd harnessed his skills and was now composing music for computer games and earning a very lucrative living. He even had a timeshare condo in LA that he offered her if she needed to get away. He had to be doing OK.

Jody had never been very ambitious, never seemed to try hard at anything. He'd done effortlessly well at school and in college when he'd seemed to spend all his time smoking marijuana and drinking beer. He was just one of those people that didn't need to strive but had things land in their lap. His life seemed to consist of the odd meeting, lots of TV watching and the occasional trip to the tiny recording studio next to his bedroom.

Beth got the impression the music and money made no odds to him. His life was simple and it was just a way to get by. He'd lived in the same place for over a decade and had no plans to upgrade. He'd always struggled with his weight but now he seemed resigned to it. He took no exercise except for his wheezing assaults on the stairs.

Her mother and father had returned from their cruise and visited. When they'd attempted to get her to re-engage with the myriad financial demands she had to deal with, and Beth had asked them to put the newly acquired property back on the market, they'd told her she shouldn't make any rash decisions.

She got that they were trying to plug her back into her life by reminding her of her commitment to Avellana, Luc's company, but she couldn't yet face his colleagues, go to the house or anywhere she was meant to be with him. She would have to sooner or later, but Beth didn't feel any desire to "move forward" as her mother had suggested when it still seemed as if he would walk back through the door.

She still hadn't cried. Not once. Not even since she'd woken in the hospital. When it finally hit her that he really was gone, she knew it was going to feel like being in another car wreck. She waited for that impact to come but it still hadn't. How much longer would it take?

She knew shutting herself away was exactly the wrong thing to do. She had to inhabit the past backdrops of her life with Luc and allow herself to contemplate his absence. She was being a coward, and she recognised her parents were right, even if their motives weren't entirely admirable.

Her mother had never cared for Luc, and the feeling had been mutual. She was waiting for her to mention Adam. It would be coming. Her childhood sweetheart was still single, and her mother had it in her mind that they should have married and made things convenient for her. After all, he was the son of their dearest neighbourhood friends. Surely even she wouldn't be as crass as to try and put them back together so soon after Luc's funeral. She was already getting angry about it in advance. And her mother still insisted on calling her Bethany. She was the only person who did.

The media attention had ebbed and her father had told her nobody was calling at the house, and that they only had the occasional call from the newspapers. Would she like to come home? She'd looked at Jody and said she'd got herself settled for the moment. He didn't make eye contact during her reply but appeared to be pleased with her decision to stay with him.

But even hiding out at his place, Beth still had a gauntlet to run. What she was about to watch at just after three in the morning was going to be excruciating, but perhaps seeing it would be the catalyst she needed for her postponed grief.

Unlocking Jody's tablet, she touched the Google icon but didn't want to put her name into a general search. She didn't care about her own, but Beth didn't want to see unexpected photos of Luc appear.

She opened YouTube and entered the name of the clip that Jody had scribbled down for her: "French Crash Victim Assault." He told her to brace herself for the names of the others.

He'd suggested she view one at a time. She touched "search" and the clip plus the others related to it loaded up. She swallowed as she took in what was displayed before her. All were represented by low-grade night shots of the crash site – day-glo paramedics from a distance and the familiar overhanging beech trees. Her eyes skated instinctively but reluctantly about them and their titles. She saw the words "whack job", "psycho" and "bitch".

Someone called "thatTODdude" had uploaded the clip she was about to watch. Beth suspended the tip of her finger half an inch over the clip but couldn't touch it. How could she subject herself to any of this? She stalled, quickly opened another window and logged into her Facebook account.

While she'd been in hospital, she'd given Jody her password and had told him to keep anyone who had posted on her wall updated on her progress. She hadn't been ready to interact with any of her friends – their friends – and still wasn't. At his next visit he'd said there had been too many messages to respond to, so he'd just posted that she'd be out of hospital soon.

Perhaps the grief of the people they knew was what she needed to see now. She scrolled through them. Scores of reactions going right back to the crash date. Most of them were from mutual friends. Some of them she didn't even know. Everyone was "so sorry". Some users had even "liked" the condolences; thumbs-up to grief and RIP. One woman she'd never heard of had sent her some virtual flowers.

It was a joke. She just wanted to type WTF, tell them all she was sorry if she'd taken up five seconds of their precious time. But she saw faces she knew there. Faces attached to people who had sent cards to her in the hospital. She didn't want to look at the page anymore, though.

"What's on your mind?" the box asked.

She typed:

Thanks so much to everyone. You'll understand if I don't log in here anytime soon. Please take time to remember Luc and what he meant to you. I love him like he's still here.

She touched "post" and looked dispassionately at the words on her page, waiting for her own reaction to what she'd typed. Sitting atop the stack of facile sentiments, it was as if somebody else had written them.

WTF indeed. And "what the fuck" could trivialise events more than she'd just seen. She logged out.

When she clicked back to the YouTube page she registered the clip had been viewed 3,348,104 times. It had 48,922 thumbs-up and only 62 thumbs-down. It was one minute and forty-three seconds long. She didn't allow her eyes to dip to the comments beneath it. Beth swallowed dryly and wondered if she really was ready to see a replay of the event she'd barely physically recovered from. Before she could have second thoughts, however, she hovered her finger over the play symbol, then stabbed it.

Her finger slipped and nothing happened. She wondered if it was a sign. She stabbed it again.

The clip counter rotated in front of her and a commercial began. Beth was dumbfounded. It was for injury at work claims. Somebody was actually making money from hits on the clip. A slate-suited woman asked if she "was suffering but didn't know where to turn". Beth felt revulsion solidify and spotted a countdown that would allow her to skip the commercial. She poked the screen like it was something dead.

Seconds later the black square became a familiar night-time roadside. It was focused on a parked ambulance.

The accident report stated that the single ambulance had been sent back after it was decided the helicopter could get them both to the hospital faster. Luc had died on board. She vaguely recalled the black straps dangling above her from the ceiling of the helicopter while she'd been drifting in and out of consciousness.

The camera panned left to their inverted car, and it felt like a screw was being tightened in her chest. Gendarmes were on the scene. The clip jump-cut to Luc and Beth lying on the stretchers about twenty feet away. Her stomach hardened and she felt herself turning cold in the seat of the chair.

She hit pause, suddenly aware of her own uneven breathing. She got up from the armchair and staggered to the bathroom, kneeling in front of the toilet. But no liquid came up as her throat pumped. She drank some water from the tap, then padded back to the box room and got back into bed. Twenty minutes later, she seated herself in the armchair with the tablet again.

She clicked the play button and the action resumed.

CHAPTER SEVEN

The crowd was loud but incoherent, excited comments buffeting against each other. Wind boomed against the tiny mic. A man lit by strobing red and blue smoked a cigarillo right of foreground. The phone took in the scene in a leisurely fashion, panning left from him and getting Beth and Luc on the trolleys centre of frame. Beyond them was the misshapen brown camper, fragments of metal and twinkling glass lying scattered in its wake. Emergency-vehicle headlights illuminated the bodywork and the diagonal rain hosing the road.

It was like tourists had got themselves present in Beth's worst nightmare. She was thankful the angle didn't allow her to see Luc's face. It was turned away from the camera, but she inhaled sharply as she made out her own swollen expression. She was trying to understand him. The female paramedic stood over her, looking from side to side, and then moved away and out of shot.

She found herself frowning, appropriating the look of painful confusion she could see on her own face. Then her injured self squinted briefly out of the clip at her sitting in Jody's lounge.

It was the first time she'd registered the crowd watching them. But it felt as if she was looking directly at herself.

Cold bubbles fizzed at the base of her spine.

Her horizontal self's attention returned to Luc as he shifted on the trolley. She watched her inflated lips move as she tried to get him to lie still. She frowned harder. Beth wondered if this was the moment Luc apologised to her.

Her distended features looked out into Jody's lounge again and this time there was disbelief and anger on her face.

How can you watch this?

She swung her feet off the trolley, sat up and reached out to Luc. She clenched the balled hands at his chest, gripping them tightly.

Beth found her own fingers doing the same. Her face in the present screwed up a few seconds before the expression on the screen, however, because now she knew it didn't matter if she held on tightly to Luc. She'd already lost him. He started to convulse.

Her onscreen self yelled to nobody in particular. The mic barely picked up the words, misshapen by her swollen mouth and smashed jaw.

Beth's finger rose to hit the pause button again but she forced herself to continue watching.

She stood up from the trolley, a red blanket falling away from her. Her sapphire blue dress was soaked and clung to her trembling body and her short red curls were dark and plastered to her scalp. Her shoes had gone and her tights were both ripped at the knees, revealing raw and bloody gashes. She pitched forward and Beth winced in both moments as her body harshly struck the edge of Luc's trolley. She observed herself crawl up to Luc and tenderly touch his face. She could see from the distress in her reaction that the pain he was in made her invisible to him.

The paramedic appeared again and started to help her to her feet. "*Couchez-vous!*"

She turned to the paramedic, issuing a guttural plea for help and then looked out at Beth again, mortification and anger in her eyes.

"I will. Lie down first."

She could see the panic on the paramedic's face and registered how young the black woman was. Mid twenties? Her dreadlocks were tied in a ponytail behind her head, and it whipped about her shoulders as she supported Beth under her arms and looked for assistance.

Beth's gaze was still fixed, accusing, almost as if the censure was for her sitting watching the event from the comfort of the armchair. She broke free from the paramedic's grip and strode shakily across the road. The paramedic was about to pursue her but seemed to have second thoughts.

When she threw the first punch, the operator of the phone stepped back and briefly she could see their shoes – a pair of green trainers. A man's or a woman's? The recording didn't cease, though. It repositioned itself a few paces back from the crowd that was scattering and settled to capture Beth wildly swinging her fists at anyone within reach.

Although it repelled her, she felt strangely envious of the undiluted anger she was exhibiting on the screen. Beth wondered if she could ever be capable of such feral rage again. Since she'd woken, she knew there were components of her missing. Anger was one. It didn't feel like it was being blocked, but as if her capacity for it had been completely removed.

The sound of the helicopter distorted in the mic. Beth's hair bristled in its draught as she turned to look upwards, and leaves whirled and blasted against her. When she retrained her aggression on the crowd, she looked right into her own eyes and scarcely recognised herself.

She'd been recorded in countless clips at family gatherings, but apart from her physical appearance, no other part of her she knew was present.

She gripped the tablet tightly. More than this past desire to harm the voyeurs, Beth knew she wanted to confront the driver of the brown camper, the man who should have helped them but had instead attacked her and not called an ambulance. It was the coach driver who had alerted the emergency services. How many valuable minutes had been wasted as they'd lain there unaided? Would Luc have survived if they'd arrived sooner?

Behind her she could see a male paramedic and two police officers darting over to restrain her. The female paramedic was beyond them, leaning over Luc.

But even though she wanted to physically attack the driver who had fled, a man she knew she would never meet, she felt the compulsion only as a cold current flowing from somewhere distant. It should have consumed Beth, but the truth was that even maintaining the emotion exhausted her.

The phone operator stepped back a few more paces, the camera tilting to the grass and then focussing on Beth again just as the male paramedic and two officers reached her and she collapsed in their grip.

CHAPTER EIGHT

TWO STUDENTS KILLED WITH CLAW HAMMER

It has been revealed that the bodies of Jocelyn and Ella Dunlop, discovered on the MSU campus by fellow student Natalie Smalls on April 8th, had both been bound with fishing wire and repeatedly bludgeoned with a claw hammer. In a police statement issued yesterday Detective Ryan Mills, Deputy Chief of the Bozeman Police Department, said the extensive injuries sustained by the two students, who were both attending MSU, "had rendered initial identification impossible."

Police are still calling for witnesses or anyone who might have seen anything suspicious on or around April 8th.

Mimic examined the online news article on his iPad for the second time, but figured he'd bided his time in the car long enough. He put the device in the glove box and took off his jacket. He rolled up his powder-blue shirtsleeves and gently closed and locked his charcoal Toyota Corolla behind him.

It was past dusk and the kids he'd watched earlier sharing crank by the deserted gas station had moved on. All in the scuzzy neighbourhood was still as he ambled up the tiny incline of gravelled driveway. It bordered an unkempt garden and led down the side of the dilapidated two-storey house he'd been observing.

He didn't want to leave his car unattended for too long. It would be like a punk magnet in a shithole like Billings. There were some local places worth visiting, though. He'd done a little online research and gleaned the Pictograph Cave State Park was a must, as well as Lake Elmo and Pompey's Pillar National Landmark. It wasn't a rush job and that made a pleasant change. Normally he didn't have time to take in the scenery, but he was determined to do a little more of that while he was on the road.

He paused a third of the way along the alleyway between the vinyl sidings of the house and its neighbour. A door slammed and then bare feet slapped on concrete. Somebody had just walked from the back of the property into the yard situated through the wooden side gate to his right. There was only one person it could be.

Trip Stillman's long yard was secluded, tall conifers affording him privacy but also obscuring the back area from any windows overlooking him. He'd inherited a burglar alarm and had security lights front and back. It took Trip just under three minutes to hang out his washing, but it was two minutes and fifty seconds longer than Mimic needed. He slipped in during the gap in illumination Trip repeatedly triggered by waving his hand at the sensor as he pegged out his laundry. When Trip returned to the kitchen, Mimic was upstairs.

Trip put the empty basket on the table and locked the back door again. He knew he had to be security-conscious. It was a bad neighbourhood he'd just moved into, despite his parents' misgivings, but snapping up the foreclosed property was the only way he could afford a place of his own. He thought he'd never escape Kalispell but he'd just put over four hundred miles between him, Skylar - his psycho ex - his brain-dead band members and all the assholes of his childhood, even if the south side of Billings was where he'd landed.

Mimic waited, crouching low on the far side of his bed in the gap between it and the wall. The bed sheets were a dirty grey and smelt of stale sweat, and the carpets hadn't been vacuumed since he'd moved in. Trip couldn't afford a vacuum. He'd posted that on Facebook. Although Mimic's body exhibited the wear, tear and encroaching flab of over half a century, he was very much an ambassador of social media.

How long should he wait here, until Trip came upstairs? The houses opposite were boarded up so nobody could overlook him work. It was late and maybe time for Trip to take a shower. Naked was good. He got a waft off the bed again. Perhaps washing wasn't top of his agenda, though. Attacking him on the landing would be better. The passage between rooms was usually where people least expected to be assaulted.

He listened to the downstairs activity, looked at his hands hanging between his knees and the blue surgical gloves he'd just pulled on. Trip had the radio loud and was singing along, badly. He liked to wait. Give them a sense of all being normal; let them settle into their daily rhythm. It was when they were most vulnerable.

His breathing had slowed now but was slightly constricted by his squatting position, and his knees ached. He hadn't had any dinner and hoped Trip had something in the refrigerator. Some ham and cheese for a sandwich, maybe. His mouth watered thinking about it. His stomach gurgled a response.

That made his mind up. He heard his knees crack as he raised himself and strode back across the bedroom. He stopped at the small Heineken mirror beside the door and examined his reflection. Mimic was balding at the front but had a thick step of amber hair at the back of his pate. Most people thought he wore a toupee but, in fact, the fibrous yellow clump was all his.

He was way below average height, five foot four and shrinking. It meant he got overlooked in bars and lost in crowds, which was a real virtue in his line of work. He had an avuncular face that appeared to be tanned but was actually a mass of freckles. They usually flourished in the summer, but their reactions had slowed as much as his had lately and set up permanent camp on his weatherworn features.

His only distinguishing detail was a straight line that ran from his receding hairline and cut through his temple, stopping just above his right eyebrow. It looked like somebody had taken a blade to him, but it was a sleep wrinkle that was getting deeper. He supposed the passing years made the skin hang looser around your skull.

But he was more distracted by what was at the corners of his mouth. The little blobs of white spittle were already back even though he'd only just wiped them away. It made him look as if he were permanently eating a chicken mayo sandwich. The deposits seemed to materialise the day he turned fifty. He took his white handkerchief out of his top shirt pocket and swiped them off, and took a deep, faltering breath at the door.

People's reactions were often unpredictable, but he'd learnt to anticipate every conceivable eventuality. Flight was the usual response. But as he'd heard Trip lock the back door, he knew he had the time it would take him to try and unlock it to subdue him. Defensive counterattack was also likely, particularly with women. They seemed to respond with physical force faster than men. Males took several more seconds to realise it wasn't a joke and for their egos to recover from having been caught off guard. Those few seconds were his window of opportunity. Brute force took care of faster feminine reflexes.

He didn't need to cover up his footsteps back down the stairs. The radio and tone-deaf singing gave him ample cover. Mimic couldn't sing either, and the idea that somebody had been listening in on him in such a private moment would have mortified him. He stood outside the door to the kitchen and waited for Trip to finish murdering Chris Martin. Somebody should, he thought. When Trip started the next performance he would walk in.

But at that moment, the door opened and Mimic was face-to face-with Trip's anaemic features. He was chewing gum and his jaw halted. Mimic grinned as if he'd been caught midway through some piece of well-intentioned mischief, removed the hammer from the waistband at the back of his pants and slammed it forcefully into the left side of the kid's skull. His head sunk to the bottom stair, and the weight of it dragged the rest of his limp body down.

Mimic dumped the bloody claw hammer on the kitchen table. It was a clumsy but effective implement. A glance at the crime stats for a two hundred mile radius had soon yielded the story about the Dunlop sisters being bludgeoned with the same weapon in Bozeman last April. The perp had never been caught. Mimic had purchased the hammer and fishing wire from a hardware store before he'd entered Billings.

He opened the refrigerator door. Corned beef. OK, he could work with that. As long as there was mustard. No fucking mayo.

CHAPTER NINE

Jody shuffled into the lounge in his dressing gown and found Beth seated on the edge of the armchair. "You watched it?"

Beth nodded once but didn't look up. She heard Jody unscrew the cap from a bottle and discard it before the sound of liquid pouring into glasses. "It's nearly... It is morning."

"Not officially morning until 7." He handed her a filled glass.

She took it and sipped. She hated bourbon but the taste brought her back to the room. She watched Jody drop into the armchair opposite and balance the second glass on his paunch.

"You had to, sooner or later," he said stolidly and examined his generous measure.

"Sorry if I woke you."

He shook his head dismissively.

They drank slowly and didn't speak. Beth emptied hers before Jody. She wasn't a liquor drinker. Always drank it too quickly. She could feel her insides shrivelling against it but reached for the bottle on the coffee table. She wanted the warmth again.

Her mother and father didn't drink, and it was their teenage infractions that had united her and Jody as they'd grown up. They'd both been subjected to their parents' tag-team lectures. Being partial to the occasional spliff was their most heinous crime, but only Beth had ever been caught. When the French investigating officer, Sauveterre, made insinuations about her and Luc's substance intake prior to the accident, which were entirely untrue, her parents had deftly distanced themselves, fearing the procedure would throw up her criminal record.

It had happened thirteen years ago and she'd mistrusted law enforcement officers ever since. She'd been spot-checked outside Brixton Academy when she was eighteen and had a large amount of cannabis resin found about her person – way too much for it to be for personal use.

Ironically, she really had been holding it for someone. Granted, someone who had promised her a fraction of it for concealing it while he dealt. It had never been clear if John Dukes was really her boyfriend. All these years later and she still didn't know. John had said she had too honest a face to be searched. He'd been right, until then. The female police officer had seemed just as surprised after frisking Beth.

Bottom line, Beth was charged with possession and got a criminal record. It wasn't the beginning of her parents' disappointment in her – her first tattoo had seen to that – but it had made things nice and official.

It was why she hadn't told them about her ordeal at the station. The police hadn't thrown her in a cell, but they'd deliberately put her in a holding room with a homeless man strung out on something much harder than she'd been busted with. She'd never forgotten him. He'd looked like a walking, jaundiced corpse and had initially ignored her while his constant scratching had intensified and he'd clawed the skin on his neck raw.

His hallucinations prompted the beggar to plead with and then attempt to assault Beth. The desk officer had taken great glee in letting things play out before he'd eventually intervened. It was the first time she'd experienced their indiscriminate mishandling of civilians. It had shaken her up badly, but she hadn't let her parents see just how much when they'd picked her up from the station.

She started smoking the odd joint again with Luc, and they both did it for nostalgia's sake. If she was honest, it had never done much for her. Red wine was always a more reliable way of loosening up. Blow only seemed like something illicit to repel the sensation of being too safe.

Another thirteen years of life later, half of that spent working on the periphery of the criminal justice system, and she was still wary of the police and their methods. When they'd questioned her after the collision, she'd assured them she didn't do drugs anymore. If they'd tested her at the crash site, they would probably have found small traces of it from their nights relaxing in front of the wood burner. But she hadn't been smoking or drinking prior to the car journey to the restaurant. The police said there was no way of knowing for sure because she hadn't been breathalysed at the scene.

"You going to watch the rest?" Jody refilled his glass.

Beth shrugged her shoulders. Did she need to see them? She knew she'd have to. There was so much activity within that small frame. Would she glimpse something in the others? Perhaps the man from the camper? The police said they'd examined all the recordings and not found anyone outside of the roadside witnesses who'd made statements.

She wondered which one of them was "bloodlegend". They'd uploaded a YouTube clip and called it "nut job crash bitch goes postal". The banal description of her trauma was obscene. Why were these creeps allowed to get away with posting stuff like this? But she knew she was trying to misdirect herself from her aggression at the crash site.

She'd erupted when she should have been with Luc. She'd assaulted strangers instead of comforting him. Would he have even known she were there if she'd stayed with him? But despite the antipathy she felt towards the ghouls, Beth realised her behaviour disgusted her more than the people who had recorded them.

She found her glass empty again and looked up at Jody. He

was scanning the rack of Blu-rays as if looking for something. This had to be difficult for him, her invading his life when he hadn't seen her for so long.

"I promise I'll be out of here as soon as I can."

Jody suddenly looked at her accusingly through his bushy red eyebrows. "And I promise you're welcome to take as long as you fucking need." He seemed genuinely affronted.

Now it was Beth's turn to look elsewhere. Her gaze rested on the bottle, but she resisted the urge to pour from it again. It was already making her feel desensitised. "Thanks."

"I'm eating. You eating?" Jody was on his feet.

"No... I'm fine."

"I'll make you some breakfast and you can reheat it later."

Jody left the room and walked across the landing to the kitchen.

Beth was left looking through the bay window to the smoked panes of the newly built but vacant office block opposite. She'd spent hours watching the automated window-cleaning cradle going up and down all day. It seemed to epitomise her new existence – fruitless robotic routine maintaining emptiness.

She listened to the scrape as Jody aggressively tugged the ice-clad drawers of the freezer, and it reminded her of the snoring she'd been lying awake listening to. She was so grateful to be here, though. Momentarily, it was a neutral place. There was nothing here to remind her of the life she'd lost. There were no pictures of her or Luc on the walls as there were at her parents.

She wondered if there had been and Jody had removed them, or if her life really had no impact on her brother's for the years she'd been married. Whichever was the case, she knew she'd have to leave her detached sanctuary soon, and watching the clips had been her first step. The more she exposed herself to what was familiar, the more chance she had of remembering what had happened to her. But what did she have left now?

The bourbon suddenly tasted poisonous in her mouth, and she made her way quickly to the bathroom. She ran the tap but only stared as the water weakly coiled down the plughole. It was how she felt, as if everything that had made her Beth Jordan was slowly trickling away. She had few remnants of the life she'd previously owned. Only the family that Beth had a tenuous connection to were left. Luc was gone and someone else now occupied the familiar Edgware home they'd previously inhabited. It felt like they'd never happened.

Now she wanted to go to the new house and rifle through the boxes. Find the DVD of their wedding and the discs of digital photos to prove it had actually been genuine.

What had her last words been to Luc? She wondered if any more of the evening would ever come back to her. Would it suddenly present itself weeks, months or years from now?

She was sure they'd spoken civilly to each other after they'd made love and before they'd driven to the restaurant. Prior to that they'd had a diplomatic version of their regular argument. Both of them still opposed but politely trying to accommodate the other's perspective. But Luc had remained implacable.

Luc didn't want children. It wasn't that it was too soon. They were both in their early thirties. It wasn't that he wasn't ready or didn't want the responsibility. Luc didn't ever want children. Beth had known why, right from the early days, but she'd always figured he might change his mind.

He'd always been honest, told her he'd understand if she wanted to find somebody else who would. They'd been in their early twenties then and it had felt like a negotiable ultimatum that would be altered by time and circumstance. As years passed and their closeness deepened, however, she realised that had only been her perception of it. Luc had given her the option to leave. Had he really meant it, or had he known she would never walk away from him? The resentment had built and surfaced when she'd least expected it.

But they hadn't rowed that evening. She hadn't wanted to ruin the last night of their trip. They would have had enough to face when they returned for the move, and piling on any more stress was the last thing either of them needed. They'd got out of bed and dressed for dinner. He'd watched her in the mirror, then he was whispering "sorry" through blood.

Had their conversation been on his mind as she'd driven him for the last time?

CHAPTER TEN

Trip opened his eyes to find he was seated in the swivel chair of his den. His head still resonated with the impact of whatever had struck the left side of his skull, and he could feel the swelling there pumping like a second heart. He looked down at his wrists tied to the arms of the chair with multiple loops of clear fishing wire. It sliced into his skin as soon as he tried to raise his elbows.

His ankles were crossed and felt like they were secured by the same restraints around the trunk of the chair. The flesh there felt cold. The line was already cutting deep. He knew he had to remain motionless if he didn't want to be scored to the bone. Trip guessed he wasn't alone before he heard the mouth chewing behind him. He held his breath, but whoever it was didn't move into his field of vision.

When the hammer slammed into the right side of his face, he heard his teeth shatter and felt their fragments embed in his tongue. Hot salty blood pumped into his mouth and he couldn't breathe through his nose. He parted his lips but only a hiss emerged. A bolus of dark red saliva frothed down his chin and hung off it by a strand.

His ears screamed for him. It felt like his whole skull had fractured and his brain was rapidly lowering a dark veil over everything. Two warm hands rested firmly on his shoulders, and he flinched in anticipation of another blow. But the pressure behind the palms increased until his chair started rolling forward.

It slid awkwardly from side to side on its wheels, and the intruder thrust harder so Trip's stomach struck the edge of his desk.

A freckled male hand, with a mass of fine yellow hairs on its knuckles and up the length of its arm, reached past him and nudged the mouse so his screen came to life. Then he heard the roots of his hair tearing as the same hand twisted his head up.

"I'd like you to access your iPhone archive."

Trip could barely hear him. Aside from the blood roaring in his eardrum, the request was delivered sotto vocce.

"Then we'll take a look online. OK? Mh?" The voice reminded Trip of his doctor's bedside manner.

The grip on his hair follicles tightened and Trip bubbled "OK" through the thick liquid in his mouth. The hand released him and he leaned forward, blood and teeth dripping over the white keyboard. His red chewing gum dropped out and it held fragments of his shattered molars. The screen defined itself again through the moisture in his eyes. He heard liquid trickling and sizzling through his ear as he painstakingly tapped in his password.

"Let's delete everything there, and then I want you to go to your online channel and remove something specific."

He stabbed clumsily at the keys, a procedure that normally took him seconds now requiring every ounce of his concentration. More strands of blood dribbled onto the backs of his hands as he confirmed the final deletion of the files. There was little of his conscious thought left to wonder why he was being asked to do it. He just didn't want the pain to get any worse. He logged on and repeated the process.

His attacker whispered, close to his good left ear. "I'm sorry about this, Trip. Let me put your mind at ease; this is no random house invasion. This really did need to happen. Find some strength now, son."

Trip's thoughts of escape, his pain and cognisance ceased. The claw of the hammer pierced his scalp and tore through the top of his brain. Trip's twitching fingers gripping the mouse were the last parts of him to function.

CHAPTER ELEVEN

Beth hesitated at the top of the sloped driveway. The house was set back from the residential road, unnoticeable unless you looked down the incline and then only visible if the trees were as bare as they were now. She'd only been inside it twice, on the occasions the agent had showed them around. The rest of the time it had existed as an image on the laptop, a seemingly unattainable goal that had fallen into their hands when the previous buyer had decided to retract his offer.

The poplar trees still had some foliage when they'd viewed it. It had been a calm, unseasonably sunny day, and they'd both known they were going to make an offer on the place before they'd reached the front door. It had felt right, the undeniable setting for the next phase of their lives. How could they have shared such a potent feeling when they weren't destined to unlock the front door together?

She wondered what Luc would have wanted her to do. Keep the house they'd fantasised about? He'd thought they would be safer here. The incident with the hoodie had left him shaken, and he'd believed a new start was the answer. Beth had known there was nowhere they could move that would offer the sort of security he yearned for, though.

But he'd always been more practical than romantic and would appreciate that one income wasn't going to pay the bills here, understand she had no choice but to let it go. Beth wished she had some religious faith as she tried to decide what he'd prefer her to do. But it was just about her future now. She had to sell.

Beth looked down at the keys in the palm of her hand. They'd been sitting in the agent's drawer for a couple of months. Last year, they'd been the symbol of everything that was important to them. Now they were two irrelevant pieces of metal.

She walked down the track to the new building that now belonged only to her and recalled the conversations she'd had with Luc about the solar lights they would fit to guide vehicles to their front door in the dark. She'd been surprised when Luc had showed her the modern home he'd found online. He was usually such a traditionalist. They'd studied the spec from the agent until it was dog-eared and covered in wine and coffee stains, pored over the dimensions and made interior décor plans before they'd even had their offer accepted. Part of her had sensed it was too good to be true when they had.

She rounded the shrubbery, and the taupe stucco and white trim facade waited in silence. Beth halted a few feet from the front door and caught her sombre reflection in the blackness of the downstairs window. It felt wrong, her entering this place without Luc, and she almost turned on her heel and walked back out. But she had to locate the documents she needed, and they were stored in boxes somewhere inside.

A police car, siren blaring, shot past on the road above and barged into her thoughts. Beth stepped up to the door and slid the key into the lock.

The door opened almost soundlessly, the seal sucking slightly as she pushed in. The long hallway where she'd last stood with Luc smelt strongly of furniture polish. She remembered how he'd quietly chuckled at her spraying the radiators with it whenever someone came to their house for a viewing.

Beth left the door ajar as if she might need to make a quick getaway. The hall was longer than she remembered. All the doors to the pristine and empty rooms were sealed. She didn't want to go in any of them, just locate the place where the boxes were stacked. She tried the rear lounge.

Opening the door to the expansive space, Beth was relieved to find the crates against the back wall. Luc's neat and square handwriting was on all of them.

"IMPORTANT!"

That was the one with all their documents in it. The noise of her ripping the tape from the flaps sounded deafening as it bounced off the blank walls. She found the box file she needed inside, the one with all their insurance documents neatly collated. That was Luc's organisation, not Beth's. She'd had a turn handling the paperwork for a year, and they'd been badly penalised for late payments. Luc had taken charge of the admin after that.

She extracted the folder inside it and checked everything was in order. She had as long as she needed, but it still felt as if her visit was against the clock. Temporarily, the property was hers, but she couldn't shake the sensation she was trespassing.

When the small blue envelope fell out, she momentarily wondered what it was. She picked it up off the brand-new vellum brown carpet and recalled the contents. It was their digital legacy – online details to be passed on in the event of their deaths. Beth had thought it ludicrous, but Luc had told her that people getting locked out of their deceased family member's accounts and photo archives was a common problem. He'd asked her to make a note of her personal passwords and he'd added his before sealing them in the envelope.

Luc had meticulous contingency plans for everything. Since his father had died, Luc didn't trust the world to make adequate provision for him. It wasn't an unexpected death. His father had been hospitalised for seven long months before an eleven year-old Luc had arrived with his mother to find a new patient occupying his bed. They'd known he could no longer swallow and had been waiting out the inevitable, but watching his father reach that point had made Luc's mind up.

There had been a fifty percent genetic chance that his father would develop Huntington's disease. He'd begun to exhibit symptoms at thirty-eight. Luc had watched him degenerate for nearly two years, nineteen painful months of watching his spasms and convulsions. They'd buried him under a hazelnut tree in the family plot in Quincampoix. Fifty percent chance or not, Luc hadn't wanted to be responsible for passing on the same fate to his children. He wouldn't even consider new mitochondrial replacement IVF treatment, didn't believe children should have anything but their parents' genes.

He'd told Beth he'd understand if she didn't want to take on the spectre herself. Beth had stayed, thinking she could change his mind, but he'd remained intractable. Like his father, he'd refused to take a test to see if he'd inherited the faulty gene. He didn't want the sentence.

Beth had told him to consider how his life would change if he found out he hadn't. Luc had said she should consider how it would if he had. They'd fought frequently about it. It had been hard for her to argue without seeming selfish, but the truth was, part of her didn't really want to know if she would one day have to lose him. Now she had, and Beth wondered again how much time they'd wasted quarrelling over it

As he approached the age at which his father had died, he knew the risks became greater. But its advent only amplified his already boundless energies. And when he wasn't pouring them into the company, he was working them off on the track. Beth believed he was always trying to outrun the spectre. Luc said he forgot himself when he ran.

It was why being with him had always been so energizing. He didn't live every day as if it was his last, but he intensely respected every minute that enabled him. Trimming the fat was his philosophy. He always maintained that, even if he became a victim of his genes, cutting the corners meant he could live a life as full as anyone's.

He'd done that way before he was thirty. Like his father, his aptitude was for engineering but, unlike his father, he also had a head for business and had effortlessly spliced the two. But Avellana had been the product of his talent and other people's investment, and his rewards were still entrammelled with multiple shareholders.

It was a highly competitive and ruthless sector, but Luc had worked tirelessly to put Avellana at the cutting edge of 3-D modelling and steel detailing, and had brought in business from some of the biggest industrial-fabricating giants, internationally as well as in the UK.

The stockholders knew the organisation couldn't function without him. Luc had hated dealing with the politics. He left that to Jerome Macintyre, his partner who had provided a critical percentage of the capital that had enabled Avellana to succeed. They'd had a fractious relationship from the early days, and Beth felt that Jerome had dug his claws deep into Luc and had been clinging on for dear life ever since.

They socialised with Jerome and his wife, Lin, who also worked as the company development executive. It was a nebulous title and Beth had never really understood what her role was. They were a couple that seemed to live a lavish lifestyle disproportionate to the tangible contribution they actually made to Avellana.

Luc and Jerome had been firm friends as well as partners but, as the business had grown, the gulf between Luc's hands-on management and Jerome's constant need to expand had divided them.

It would all have to be dealt with. She was sure Jerome would attempt to make the process of handing over Luc's stake as painless for her as possible, and part of her wanted it to be just that. But she owed it to Luc to ensure that Jerome and the executive board didn't effortlessly appropriate the fruits of his ingenuity, and that meant another battle ahead.

Jerome had already phoned her mother's house to make enquiries about her well-being, but she knew exactly what his agenda was. The pressure to meet would have been mounting even before Luc's funeral.

Jerome and Lin had been in Rouen while she'd been oblivious. They'd seen Luc's coffin committed to the flames, and Beth imagined they both would have considered their livelihood being cremated inside the coffin. But she envied them. Whatever their thoughts had been, they at least had the opportunity to bid Luc farewell.

The one person who loved him the most had been absent. Her mourning had been deferred. Until when, though? Would she always feel this way, Luc's loss permanently on the periphery of her emotions?

She turned the envelope over in her fingers and then slid it back inside the folder. She looked out of the floor-to-ceiling doors at the overgrown lawn and the old teak bench from Edgware that his father had carved, still wrapped up in its cellophane packaging on the decking. She had to leave. Every corner presented her with a space they'd planned to fill.

Beth hurriedly flicked through the other papers in the box file but didn't read anything. She shut it, took the whole thing with her to the front door and only breathed when she got outside.

CHAPTER TWELVE

"Wait a minute, guys. I haven't got us both in frame."

That was the problem with having short arms – not very good for snatching iPhone shots of yourself. Spike extended his as far as he could to try to get him and Tiffany in.

"I know that's just gonna be the tops of our heads." He stretched it a little further and angled the lens down towards their faces. "How's that? Cosy?" He pressed his face against Tiffany's and spoke to the people he'd share the clip with. "Shame Tiffany's not going to remember."

Tiffany DiMarco was unconscious. Her bruised eyelids were inflated and purple, her lips were split and caked blood stuck her blonde hair to her scalp. Spike moved his shoulder and allowed her to slump to the park bench. He winced theatrically for his audience as her skull thudded against the slats.

"That's gotta hurt. See you both at the pond tonight, usual time."

Spike sent the clip to Jeb and Benny and stowed the tacky nightstick in his sports bag. His blood was still hurtling through him, and he could smell Tiffany's perfume around his face. He tied his hair back into a ponytail and secured it with a leather hoop. He at least looked respectable again. Time to head for home.

The ultimate example of recording something you shouldn't – that was Spike, Jeb and Benny's constant goal. To shoot something that would implicate them if the clip ever escaped their triangle; that could potentially land them in jail. It was about implicit trust, and it was better than a blood oath.

The three of them had hung out since first year in high school. *Jackass* had been their springboard but that had quickly become lame. They'd tired of injuring themselves on camera and had gravitated to hurting other people. They'd captured it on their iPhones and had circulated their increasingly daring attacks – first, bitch-slapping friends and enemies, then complete strangers. That's when it had become interesting.

Spike squeezed through the hole in the hedge and found himself back on the edge of the golf course. Nobody would be using this route as a shortcut after they found Tiffany. Time to scope some new territory.

The first time Spike had sent his friends the clip of him randomly bludgeoning a female tourist in Lone Pine State Park, he'd known it was the ultimate test. Stephanie Meadows had been in a coma for three weeks after the attack. Spike had pretended he hadn't cared and hadn't betrayed his relief when she'd woken from it.

He'd known the other two wouldn't talk. They were fiercely loyal, but more importantly, they were scared of him. He hadn't hooked up with them for those three nerve-racking weeks. Hadn't been able to eat. But when Stephanie had opened her eyes in hospital, he'd met them at the pond and had acted like he didn't give a fuck which way it had gone.

He'd told Jeb and Benny it was their turn then. He'd realised the sooner they'd replicated his actions the more unlikely they were to betray him. Their clips had reached his phone soon after, two muggings in the same location. The police had thought it was the same attacker. Spike had realised it gave them an alibi.

It had become a game. When one had recorded, the other two had made sure they were somewhere public. If an assault were ever pinned on one of them, it would be impossible

to implicate the others. They'd used the same weapon – a
nightstick that belonged to Spike's father. He'd stored it in the
bottom of the closet when he'd been prematurely retired from
the Kalispell PD. Spike knew his Dad was a crooked cop, and
even though his pension had been withdrawn, they still lived
in the same relative luxury they always had. His father had
some influential friends.

His mother had split a long time ago, but he'd already
chosen Dad and his philosophy:

"Nobody gives you anything. Take it when you have the
opportunity."

And Spike had. He'd taken the nightstick and had pimped it
by hammering six nine-inch nails into it. But it had only been
when he'd taken the innocence of Lauren Cassidy that he'd
realised how right his father had been.

He'd seen her around the neighbourhood, vaguely
remembered her being a few years below him in high school.
She wasn't pretty but she had that "pussy dipped in detergent"
expression that, in his mind, entitled her to be taken down a
peg or three.

He wasn't sure if he'd actually raped her. The TV news said
she'd been sexually assaulted, but the attack had been quick
because the rec area had been freezing cold. Beforehand, he'd
felt aroused by what he'd been about to do, but when he'd
whacked her with the nail club and she'd dropped insensible
to the frosty grass, he'd immediately lost his erection.

Even after he'd positioned the phone camera in the
prong of the tree and had begun his movie performance
for his two buddies, he'd felt alone. Lauren had had tight
jeans that he could only roll down to her knees. She'd also
had thermal panties on. He hadn't had time to unlace her
hiking boots so he'd squeezed his body through the tight
gap between her legs.

His exposure to the cold air hadn't helped his enjoyment
and his thrusting had been exaggerated for the lens. He'd

come into his rubber but wasn't sure if he'd penetrated her or been caught under the elasticated hem of her sweatshirt.

Spike had been angry with himself afterwards and had barely resisted the temptation to delete the clip. When he'd watched it back, however, it had looked awesome. He'd chopped off the beginning and end and had sent the money shot to his buddies. He'd certainly set the bar high for them.

CHAPTER THIRTEEN

"Positive?"

"Positive." Beth watched the anxious African features of Erica, her temporary hairdresser, reacting in the mirror. She'd already had all of her uneven brown locks cut short, and the stunted tufts jutted stiffly from her head. She felt emotion piercing the back of her throat but kept her lips tightly clamped.

"Tell me if you want me to stop." The hairdresser fumbled her long, glued-on fuchsia nails at the attachment head of the electric trimmer for a few moments and then switched it on. It didn't buzz as loudly as Beth had anticipated. She nodded at Erica to reassure her she still hadn't had second thoughts.

Its low hum resonated through her jaw as it swept from her fringe to the centre of her scalp. Erica paused, allowing them both to examine the strip of smooth, white skin.

Beth hadn't wanted to go to her regular hairdresser for this, didn't want to fence any questions about Luc. She just wanted to sit somewhere unfamiliar and not encounter any disapproval. It hadn't worked out. Teenage Erica's own multi-tonal, strawberry-blonde bob was immaculate, and Beth could see shaving everything off was going to be almost as traumatic for her.

"Should I carry on?"

Beth nodded gravely, and she knew Erica could tell there was more to her visit than a radical image change. She widened the strip with another stroke, checking Beth's set expression again before repeating the process. Beth parted her teeth slightly so they wouldn't vibrate and closed her eyes while Erica finished.

When she looked up again it was like peering at a displaced version of herself, familiar features stranded on someone else's head. The scarring about her mouth looked even more obvious now. She didn't like the person staring intently back, but was glad to feel different, relieved to have shed the remnants of the Beth she no longer was. After a glance down at the curls in her lap, she put her hand to the exposed area and felt the resistance of the short prickles there.

"OK, hon?" It didn't sound as if Erica was referring to her handiwork.

Beth moved her head, its motion effortless without the encumbrance of hair. She felt the cool atmosphere wafting around her scalp and wondered what Jody would say.

At around 4 in the morning, Cigarillo Man started to bug Beth. All the participants in the first YouTube clip she'd viewed had an explicit role, whether they were a member of the emergency services, or part of the exchange student ghouls recording the aftermath of the accident. Cigarillo Man didn't seem to fit either category.

She threw back the duvet, slipped on her robe and padded barefoot past Jody's room. Her brother had raised an incredulous ginger eyebrow when she'd walked in the door earlier that evening, but had mitigated his initial reaction to her haircut by saying he knew their mother would detest the number one look, which made it more than OK with him. He'd been sensitive enough not to question her about it further.

She turned on the light in the lounge. The tablet was still on the coffee table where she'd left it from her previous viewing. Beth quietly closed the door and turned it on. As she settled in the armchair, she questioned why she would subject herself to the ordeal again.

But although witnessing the moments at the roadside a second time had been gruelling enough, she couldn't deny that filling some of the gaps between the events made her feel she was connected to them and not just a removed victim of the consequences.

She opened YouTube and ran her fingers over the tiny spikes of her scalp. She felt brave enough to watch thatTODdude's clip full-screen this time. She skipped the commercial and waited for Cigarillo Man to make his appearance. He came into shot six seconds in, just as the camera phone was about to do its pan to the left. It only lingered on him briefly. Beth paused it.

He was in foreground, waist up and wearing a short-sleeved lemon shirt. The man was around sixty with a deep tan, even deeper crow's feet and grey tendrils of wet hair in disarray on his bald patch. She couldn't see below his waist. No glimpse of his trousers or shoes.

Beth paused the action and examined his expression. It didn't look as if he'd acknowledged that he was being recorded, was taking a toke of the slim cigar and staring at something below the camera. A piece of wreckage?

The person holding the phone had captured him a second time as they'd glided the lens briefly to the left again, sixty-seven seconds later. Cigarillo Man was still in the right-hand corner, hadn't moved and was still looking pensive. He didn't seem to be taking the same interest as everyone else. He smoked, squinted down at the ground and occasionally glanced over to where Beth was comforting Luc. This time he looked up and registered he was being recorded. His features began to change, but the person swung the camera back to the wreckage.

Even when she froze the clip, it was difficult to tell if the reaction was one of surprise or annoyance. It appeared the person shooting was eager not to be caught spying on the able-bodied and focused on the main event.

Later, at eighty-three seconds, when Beth was climbing off the trolley, the phone panned to the spot again, but Cigarillo Man had gone. Had he simply moved to a different position to get a better view?

Beth watched the remainder, right up to the helicopter taking off and the ambulance leaving, but didn't see another sign of him. Who was he, the coach driver? The police had said everyone present in the recordings had been accounted for. Would he appear in any of the other four? She scanned the related uploads down the right-hand side of the screen that, until that moment, she'd had no intention of immediately watching.

But now there were only three dark images of the roadside representing the remaining crash clips. There had been five in total but now the one title she couldn't forget – "nut job crash bitch goes postal" – was missing.

She typed it into the YouTube search, but found nothing. She opened another window, put it into a Google search and located a link to the old page but when she hit the URL, the viewer was a blank white square. She'd only seen it there yesterday. Perhaps a moderator had taken it down. She doubted that, particularly if the titles of some of the other YouTube clips were anything to go by. Had bloodlegend felt remorse and removed it? After months of it being uploaded, it seemed unlikely.

Bizarrely, Beth felt cheated. It had been withdrawn before she could view it, and it made her realise the clips felt like her property. She'd prompted their recording and one of them had been snatched from her.

The missing clip had been viewed 6,877,201 times. It had been liked 842 times and disliked only 44 times. She took in the comments below the blank square.

OMG! wot a schizo
looks like she woznt the only one injured LMAO
ROTF!
WTF? Best concussed right hook ever
Some guy recording you with their phone more important than your dying husband Who knew?
LMFAO did you need stitches yourself ????????????
bloodlegend replied to the question:
bitch would have looked like she was in another car accident if she

had got another step nearer to me

Beth swallowed hard and didn't bother clicking to the next page of comments. Instead, she watched bloodlegend's handful of other channel uploads. They were three dark recordings of an amateur death metal band shot in the same sleazy bar venue. From the drumhead Beth could see they were actually called Blood Legend. As she peered at the darkened faces of the bassist, guitarist, drummer and vocalist she wondered if she was looking at the person who had been watching her from behind the police tape.

The sound was distorted and the person shooting the band was obviously too short to see over the heads of the row of people watching them. The clips were mercifully brief and looked to be recorded during the same song, although it was hard to tell for sure.

They'd only been viewed a couple of times, but there was a link to the band's Facebook page, which she clicked through to. Blood Legend didn't have many friends other than the band members, and the page hadn't been updated for a good while. May 2013 was the last post advertising a Blood Legend gig at The Neon Idol, Kalispell.

She found photos of the band posing amongst some piles of rubble somewhere. They all appeared to be in their late teens. The drummer was an emaciated girl with multiple piercings in her eyebrows, brandishing her drumsticks amidst their guitar poses. She lingered the cursor on her and a box told Beth her name was Skylar. The others' names were Funnelweb, Trip and Mark.

The group was based in Montana, although when she Googled them, it didn't appear as if they'd had any recent gigs. She opened first a Facebook account under the name 'jawbone2014' and requested friendship, then a YouTube account with the same details. She subscribed to bloodlegend's channel and posted a message in the comments:

What happened to that awesome clip of that crash bitch? Friend me on Facebook (jawbone2014). Need to get a copy. Will part with cash!

CHAPTER FOURTEEN

"I thought it was you fucking with us," Jeb said warily, still expecting it to be a joke.

Spike was standing on the boardwalk with his back to his two gangly cohorts, looking out at the dark, weed-clogged pond soaking up the failing violet clouds. He wished he had been. "It wasn't me." He tried not to let them detect the alarm in his voice.

He knew Jeb and Benny had those dumb half-smiling, half-flinching expressions on their faces and were waiting for him to turn and tell them he'd suckered them. He'd played these games before. But Spike remained motionless.

He didn't want them to see that somebody else had the control, and if he turned around he knew they would. "Which one of you talked?" Stay in authority, he told himself. But he knew that neither of them would have let anything slip. Even they weren't that fucking stupid. He could almost hear their mortified exchange of glances and head-shaking.

"Not me."

"Or me." Benny trampled over Jeb's denial.

Had Benny been a little too eager? No, they knew they'd all be sent down if they breathed a word of what they'd been doing. However the three of them had been exposed, one fact was certain. "They know everything."

"Do you think they'll go to the police?" Benny's tone was

flat. He knew it wasn't a joke now.

"I don't know." Spike turned and their alarm intensified because, he knew, he looked as scared as them. They were all the wrong side of their eighteenth birthdays. Prison gang-rape beckoned. "We've got to stay cool." But he didn't believe that. He was just quoting something he'd seen in a movie. Jeb and Benny were shitting in their pants, and he was just about to join them.

Spike wanted to run home but knew there would be no protection there. This was hardcore and his father wasn't going to be able to smooth it over, regardless of his contacts. Somebody had intruded on the triangle and the consequences of that hadn't even begun to sink in. Spike opened the message on his phone again.

I see the three of you have been nailing the local girls. How is Tiffany DiMarco and what would you do to keep this between us?

It had been sent to all of their cells. The number had unsurprisingly been withheld.

"Who has all our numbers?"

Jeb and Benny didn't meet his eye. They'd been expecting to find reassurance there, but now they knew he was as petrified as them. They shuffled their feet and looked at their phones.

But Spike knew that the handsets they used to communicate their dark mischief to each other contained only theirs. Each of them kept this second phone locked when they weren't in touch with each other. The contents were too sensitive to include anyone else. Two were switched off while the other stalked and only switched on the next day to receive the images. How could they know about Tiffany DiMarco? She couldn't have told anybody. She was still critical in Kalispell Regional.

"Fuck!" Spike doubled over to shout it at the pond. The word echoed back, and the three of them silently studied the crescent of great pines on the other side, as if expecting to glimpse somebody within them.

When Beth checked her messages, she wasn't surprised that bloodlegend hadn't replied to her query about the clip. She returned to the band's Facebook page and clicked through to the other members. Rather than wait for one response, she planned to request friendship from all of them and try to increase her odds of contacting somebody that way.

She hit the request buttons for Funnelweb, Mark and Trip. They didn't appear to be regular users, though. She found herself on Skylar's page. She'd logged in yesterday and had 434 friends. She was her best bet, but how would she react to a faceless stranger wanting to friend her out of the blue? She was about to hit the request button when she looked down at Skylar's recent interactions:

Traumatized. RIP Trip

Several of her friends had responded with abbreviated commiserations:

STBY R U OK?

Saw it on the TV news. U must be in total shock.

Beth noticed the exchange had happened only seven hours earlier. She scrolled down to her previous comment.

An ex of mine has been murdered! Trip Stillman former rhythm guitarist of Blood Legend found dead by his folks!

There were more responses to this:

OMFG You were only dating him last summer!

Beth was chilled by the message. Instead of requesting friendship, she opened a Google page and entered:

Trip Stillman murder

She got two news results and clicked on the first, which was a website for the Billings Gazette.

New Billings resident, Trip Stillman, was discovered unconscious at his home by his mother and father early this morning following a violent assault by an unknown assailant. He was rushed to West Corner County Hospital but died soon after being admitted.

New Billings? As far as Beth knew, the handful of students on the coach had been from a college in a place called Kalispell in Montana.

A homicide investigation has now been launched by the

Billings Police Department. They are now questioning
neighbors and asking for eyewitnesses.

Beth decided to watch the remaining crash clips one after the
other. She'd initially planned to watch one a day but figured
sitting through all of them was the best way to get the ordeal
over and done with. She braced herself against the back of Jody's
armchair, touched the screen and felt the pulse pound in her
reconstructed jaw.

The second clip had been uploaded by "dustboy" and was shot
safely and steadily to the right of her attack on the crowd, then
shakily thrust forward as police and paramedics subdued her.
She could see the spittle on her chin as she sagged in their grip.

As the four of them turned and headed to the ambulance,
they staggered in the rippling draught from the overhead
helicopter. The police officers and paramedic didn't even
glance back towards the camera. What could they have done to
stop the recording? They were probably used to performing to
rows of phones at every populated crash scene they attended.

But Beth couldn't deny she'd been guilty in the past. If she
encountered an accident roadblock, she couldn't stop herself
glimpsing the wreckage when the police allowed her vehicle
to pass. What was she looking for in that momentary glance?
Was she hoping to see the people involved sitting safely on the
roadside, or something more horrific that would make her feel
grateful it hadn't been her turn that day?

Was recording it any worse than wanting to look? But to
her mind, it was inexcusable that the spectators had not only
shot it for their consumption, but with the express intention
of sharing and turning it into entertainment currency.

What was going through their heads when they were
capturing it? Watching from their position was like standing in
their shoes. Very few of them made any comment throughout.
None that was coherent, anyway. It was as if they were in awe
of what they were recording. Or were they holding their breath

in the hope of appropriating something they couldn't normally download? She could almost interpret their mood, suspense as well as boredom. If not enough was happening in front of them, they shifted from foot to foot and cast their phones about the site to try to catch something worthy of their battery power.

She saw Cigarillo Man talking to the police in the third clip that had been uploaded by "Spike666". The camera had found the coach on the grass verge and he was standing outside, answering questions. He tried to light up again but the officer cautioned him not to. She'd been right. He was the driver, Ferrand Paquet. She could see he was wearing a pair of jeans and some brown leather loafers. She mentally crossed him off the list.

As she watched the fourth, uploaded by "smilingassassin", she realised she'd become strangely detached, as if reducing what had happened to a tablet screen had somehow compressed her emotions as well. She examined the stats for it. Beth was viewer 7,133,448. All those people had seen this moment from her life long before she had, the bulk of them probably when she'd still been lying in the hospital. Her eyes were drawn to the last comment.

Boring. No guts.

But this clip did contain something the others didn't. No glimpse of any suspicious spectators but something significant while it lingered on the scene after she'd been restrained. She pulled the slider back and watched again.

The black female paramedic was gripping Luc's hand and staring intently down at him. Luc had his head lifted slightly and said something to her. She put her ear to his mouth.

Beth watched her own dark silhouette pass in front of the lens as she was led away. She barely resisted the reflex to crane around herself.

They came into view again. When Luc finished speaking, the paramedic straightened and stood motionless, whatever he'd said sinking into her abstracted features. It was only her fellow paramedic that snapped her out of it when he returned and asked for help to raise Luc's trolley.

CHAPTER FIFTEEN

"But I'm nearly nineteen." And he must have said it as many times.

Marcia O'Doole considered rising from her perch on the edge of Tyler's low bed frame. It was hardly a position of authority. He was seated higher on a swivel chair in front of his laptop. She told herself that confronting him at the scene of the crime was the best approach, but it felt as if she was kowtowing to him, and she acknowledged that that was what she usually did. Not on this occasion, though. "What else would I have found if I'd looked in some of your other files?"

"I can't believe you went snooping." He'd alternated between the two statements for the last five minutes and hadn't shifted his pout from the screen.

Marcia looked at his downy fair stubble and the acne peppering the lower half of his face. His ears glowed like they always did when he was embarrassed, jutting crimson from underneath the blue camouflage bandana that covered the remainder of his yellow curls. Her hair had been the same shade at his age, but at forty-seven, she'd long given up on calling her silver hair platinum blonde. "I understand you're at an age when you like looking at that sort of thing…" She regretted it before the words had formed on her lips.

"Mom." Tyler said in exasperation, and visibly squirmed.

"These aren't just naked ladies, though." She tried to jettison her awkwardness by recalling the material she'd discovered. "Why would you want to see women doing those sorts of things?" Her mortification started to surface. She had to remember that, despite his height, he was still just an impressionable kid. She was sure his online gamer buddy, Howie Judd, was responsible. His parents had never exerted any control over the movies he watched or the violent virtual games he played, so she was sure his files had to be brimming with the sort of clips she'd found in her son's. She hoped that was the case. Peer pressure and morbid curiosity, it had to be.

"It's an invasion of privacy," he countered petulantly.

She wondered exactly who he was quoting. "How can it be an invasion of privacy when the computer belongs to me?" She'd had that one prepared, although she knew it wasn't her best tack. But it was one of only two she had. The second was just coming and she already hated herself for playing it. "And if you're going to spend your allowance on paying lawyers to sue me for that, perhaps I should suspend that as well."

He folded his arms across his chest. "Can't believe you went snooping" was all he could muster.

This was Ted's job. But Tyler's father had fled and probably had worse on his computer. Although she did wonder if there was anything more degrading than the acts she'd glimpsed in her son's secret archive. "I'm going to put a parental lock on it."

"I'm nearly nineteen," he enunciated as if she were deaf.

"But your brother isn't. I hope you haven't exposed him to any of this."

He didn't answer, which meant he had.

She sighed. Marcia knew she was shutting the barn door after the horse had bolted but hated to think of those images being downloaded into their home. "I'm so disappointed in you." He was just a teenager. It was the equivalent of kids pulling the legs off spiders, an unwholesome compulsion that had to be curbed. "Don't you think the girls in those photos have moms and dads?"

He turned and looked at her as if it were a stupid question. "They have more than I have, then," he deflected.

Marcia ignored the retort. "How d'you think they'd feel if they saw their sons or daughters doing those things?"

"But they're porn stars. They're paid thousands of dollars."

"Thousands of dollars? Come on. A lot of them regret doing those things when they're older. If you were doing them..."

He smirked slyly then, and Marcia didn't like it.

"If you did those things because you needed the money and then regretted it, how would you feel if thousands of people were still looking at you degrading yourself years later?"

"But I won't ever do those 'things'," he said with a contempt she liked even less.

"I certainly hope not, but I don't want you to forget that those are real people who probably aren't as fortunate as you."

"People upload it all the time... Besides, porn stars have cool cribs and swimming pools."

He was right. This wasn't a good argument. Porn had become aspirational. Why would a teenager think that it was anything but cool? It was glamorous, hinged on the one thing that possessed every kid's thoughts and offered cash for no talent. What was not to like? But that's because they bought the glossy packaging and not its squalid flipside. "Don't ever download anything that could get you into trouble..."

"Of course I won't. I'm not stupid." He just sounded exasperated now.

What did she expect – contrition? "Look, I really don't want to stop you from looking at sexy girls – or boys, if that's what you like."

"Mom." He squeezed his eyelids shut as if he could hide from the humiliation there. "I'm not thirteen."

"Just get rid of the extreme stuff. I'll trust you to do this for me."

"And what do you class as extreme, Mom?" He was mocking her now. Probably for the benefit of his fifteen year-old brother, Kevin, they both knew was listening at the door. "Bukkake?"

"Facials are for health spas, Tyler."

He opened his eyes, obviously shocked that she knew what he was talking about. "So download as many bikini girls as you can this afternoon, because they'll have to sustain you until you're..."

"Twenty-one?" There was his trump card. Nobody knew if he would ever make it there.

Marcia couldn't let him use it against her. Not in this argument. She had to be a parent, not a bereaved parent in waiting. "As of this evening, I'm locking you down."

She got up from the bed and walked to the door. She could hear Kevin's footsteps along the landing before she reached the handle.

"I'm nearly nineteen..." Tyler said, but without as much ebullience.

Marcia walked out of his room without another word, locked herself in the bathroom and silently squeezed a tear. Her sons weren't the only ones who had furtive moments behind closed doors.

CHAPTER SIXTEEN

"*Parlez-vous anglais?*"

"Yes." But the weary female voice didn't sound willing to.

Beth stared through the lounge pane at the automated window-cleaner on the office block opposite and prepared for her belated enquiry to be rebuffed. She'd put the call through to the admin department of SAMU – Service d'Aide Médicale Urgente – that was the central control function for emergency services.

"I was in a traffic accident in Normandy, on the Route du Fresnay, a few months ago and have only recently been discharged from hospital here in the UK. Thing is, if I could, I'd like to personally thank one of the paramedics who attended me there…"

The woman the other end was silent.

"I obviously don't know her name. Would it be possible to find out if I give you the details of the incident?"

Beth could hear the woman's sigh boom against the mouthpiece.

"*Un moment.*"

The office atmosphere cut out and a low hiss filled her ear. Beth had just resigned herself to the fact that she'd simply put the phone down on her when it connected to a ring tone.

"*Administration?*" an effete male voice stated.

"*Parlez-vous anglais?*"

"*Un moment. Nathalie!*"

"Can I help you?" a brighter female voice said.

She hoped Nathalie would be less implacable and explained her predicament. Nathalie took the incident details from her and made no promises, but said she'd do her best. Beth was told to call back at the end of the day.

"Is there some way of editing the clips together?" Beth had been leaning outside the bathroom waiting for Jody to emerge.

He only had a faded purple towel around his waist and self-consciously knotted it tighter to his paunch. "What for?"

"To put them all in sequence."

Jody pouted his lips and theatrically examined the underside of his wet ginger eyebrows. It was his way of thinking or, at least, giving the impression he was. She'd never been able to guess which.

"Watching them separately makes me feel like I'm missing something...'

"Missing what?"

"I know it sounds ridiculous, but I think it would help if I could watch them sequentially."

"I doubt it, and I'm not sure how you would lift a clip from a YouTube page..."

Or was he not prepared to think of a way?

The constriction of the towel made him walk in short steps to his room. He looked like a geisha girl. "Let me have a think," he said over his shoulder as he quickly closed the door after him.

Kelcie Brooks was the one person you could rely on to post the most mortifying images of her friends on Facebook. In fact, her online community joked that it was so instantaneous, it was almost as if she'd uploaded them before the events had happened.

She liked that she'd been given that label of lovable infamy. Kelcie had always lacked in social skills, found it difficult to interact even with her close inner circle of school friends. But Facebook allowed her to communicate with masses of people and to present an outwardly likable persona, bolstered by her obsessive habit of bombarding them with virtual ice creams and gifts.

But it was her eye for a compromising digital still, however, and her alacrity to share it with her 1577 friends, that had brought her the renown she craved, and at parties people tended to try to get on her good side before they got drunk.

Kelcie knew she would always have a humdrum existence. But she comforted herself with the fact that all the party animals destined for greatness would live to regret their indiscretions in the future. Just as they'd achieved some semblance of professional respectability, Kelcie would be standing by to flourish the evidence.

Lying face down with their knickers bunched at their knees, exposing their breasts with their eyes rolled into their heads, collapsed on the tiles with dried vomit about their lips. It was harmless fun for them now, but she knew the images would be bargaining chips in the future. Payback would come sooner or later for Kelcie as well as the people who didn't take her seriously.

Kelcie wasn't a bad person, and she didn't mind being branded at teaching college as the requisite quiet one who might be a lesbian but nobody cared to find out. For Kelcie, dating was exclusively what she did online. She found older, married guys who used fake names and posed as singletons, and, using the promise of her sexy avatar, gradually extracted info from them so she could track them to their Facebook page and dig out photos of them with their wife and family.

It was then child's play to locate their wife's profile. How would they like to hear about what hubby was up to? She'd built up quite a database. That was the fun part, being in possession of so much damaging information.

Kelcie loved her secret agenda, was fond of the idea that behind her quiet demeanour, there was a plan she'd methodically instigated long before anyone suspected it. She'd archived everything. With one click she could open a folder with the name of one of her close friends and examine a selection of images they'd definitely want buried in the future.

But it wasn't only stills. She had hundreds of phone clips that awaited their YouTube debut. When her friends awoke the morning after and tried to remember what had happened, she knew the last person they would recall would be strait-laced and dumpy Kelcie lingering quietly out of sight.

She realised that without the slip-ups of other people's lives, her own presence was barely discernible, but she was very comfortable sitting in the margins. It was a safe place. She knew secreting herself there made it unlikely that anything exciting would ever happen to her, but that security was reward enough.

Security was very much a part of her philosophy. Earlier that evening, she'd been doing something else that nobody would ever have suspected her of: target practice at the Flathead indoor firing range. As a single girl, it was a safeguard she took seriously. She'd taken her beloved M1911 single action pistol, and as she did every week, she'd thought about all the human outlines in her sights as those she could easily shoot down in the future. She was so in love with the notion of using the pressure of her finger on an iPad screen rather than a trigger to wreak carnage.

Tonight, Kelcie was doing what she did most evenings, collating her friends' media CVs curled up on the couch with her iPad on her legs and the TV soaps turned down. She had two windows open at once – Facebook and her archive. It was quite a therapeutic process. Kelcie smiled when she happened to be exchanging "likes" and comments with one of the people she was cataloguing.

In her taskbar she noticed she'd received some mail and maximised her Outlook Express. There was some junk and a message from a "nightvisitor" via her "smilingassassin" YouTube channel. She wasn't familiar with the name.

Cool footage, LOL. I have a recording from same night. Interested in it for your channel?

The clip referred to was the one she'd captured on the exchange trip – the car crash girl who had started beating up on the crowd. It had earned Kelcie her highest hit rate: 7,133,462 and counting. She'd made quite a few bucks from advertising on that page. It had certainly reinforced her belief she could benefit financially from what she shot with her phone. When she'd agreed to chaperone the exchange students for the French trip, she'd thought there'd be rich pickings in terms of drunken indiscretions. Especially from her fellow escort, Ramiro Casales, who had mistakenly thought he was going to be knee-deep in horny sophomores before he started his medical training. But she hadn't expected hitting pay dirt at the crash site they'd encountered on the drive back from Le Mans.

Maybe she could make even more cash by posting a new clip. Must have been one of the students. She thought she'd seen all the recordings from that night uploaded. Maybe a sixth person had used their camera. Perhaps whoever it was had captured something interesting enough to make it differ from the others.

She sent a response to nightvisitor:

R U on FB?

Kelcie couldn't have known her reply appeared on an iPad less than thirty feet from her. It was inside the charcoal Toyota Corolla parked up behind the dumpster at the rear of her property.

Mimic looked up from the screen to Kelcie's illuminated lounge window, wiped at the sediment at the corners of his mouth and pocketed the handkerchief. He'd been watching her all day and was now using her WiFi. Hacking her passwords had been easy, but it wasn't just the removal of the clips that was paramount. He had to ensure that backup material was never uploaded again.

He'd confirmed she was more than happy to make money out of someone else's misfortune. Not on the scale he did, but she certainly had her head screwed on. Trip Stillman was just a stupid kid that had uploaded something he shouldn't. Kelcie Brooks had smarts.

With all of his targets now within a small area, his options were limited in terms of plausibly replicating historic homicides. It was his last contract, and the notion of dispensing with procedure was very tempting, particularly given his desire to take in the vista of the Flathead Valley from Lone Pine State Park.

Kelcie's rented Four Mile Drive cabin was remote and surrounded by scrubland. He could easily get out of the car now and put a bullet through her skull. Nobody would hear. But Mimic had a dependable system and was too long in the tooth to start changing his ways, particularly when he was in no hurry and had accessible options at his fingers.

He grazed his nail over the iPad screen and found the news story that had piqued his interest. It had happened just over a year ago and twenty-two miles away from Kalispell.

ELDERLY WOMAN MUTILATED IN BIGFORK

Police have revealed that the body of eighty-four year-old widow Virginia Greenspan, discovered at her Bigfork home in the early hours of last Sunday morning, had been extensively mutilated. The weapon used was a broken ketchup bottle found at the scene. The perpetrator forced entry and, after attacking Mrs Greenspan, had attempted to set a fire in the apartment.

The Flathead County Sheriff's Department would like to interview a teenager seen in the immediate area wearing a Billings Bulls sweatshirt.

Mimic did some further research and discovered they hadn't.

CHAPTER SEVENTEEN

"The female member of the response team that day was Rae Salomon."

Beth asked Nathalie to spell it and wrote it down. "Would there be any way of getting a message to her?"

"According to our records, she no longer works for the emergency services."

"Oh. You don't have a contact number?"

"I couldn't give out those details."

"I really do just want to send her a gift as a thank you. Have you got an address there?"

There was a pause. "I'm sorry." She genuinely sounded it. "If it were my decision I would, but I really can't."

"Is there anywhere else I could try?

"I really can't help you any further. I'm glad you've made a full recovery, Madame."

"OK, thanks for your help." She was about to replace the receiver.

"Wait, if she's actively looking for work, you may well be able to contact her through an employment website. It's an unusual name."

"Thank you, I'll try that."

Now she'd identified the paramedic, Beth hoped Nathalie was right. Perhaps she could locate her somewhere on the

Internet and local recruitment profiles were a good starting place.

She wondered why Rae had left the service, and considered her motives for pursuing her. Had Luc really said anything comprehensible to her? In the fourth clip, Beth could clearly see him uttering words into her ear while she listened intently. But the phone camera was about twenty yards away, so it was impossible to read the shapes on his lips before the recording ended.

Perhaps he'd been asking where Beth was. Maybe he'd been delirious, or even if Luc had said anything coherent, chances were Rae wouldn't remember anyway.

If Beth hadn't been attacking the crowd, perhaps the words would have been whispered in her ear. Were they an explanation for the apology he seemed compelled to impart as he lay dying? Beth suspected she was hoping for an explanation she'd never receive.

She didn't want to watch the entire clip again, so she dragged the slider to those last crucial seconds, but this time she was looking at the contemplative reaction on Rae's face. She was convinced he'd said something significant to her. Only the arrival of her colleague broke her out of it.

Rae Salomon was the last person Luc had spoken to and the one woman Beth had to find.

CHAPTER EIGHTEEN

Beth used self check-in and coasted Jody's tungsten Golf Mk7 to the allocation lanes. She'd stayed on the inside lane for the whole journey there, so it had been a long crawl. Driving made her feel jittery, and negotiating the busy traffic through the wipers and pelting rain to Folkestone had been exhausting.

It was the first time she'd been back behind the wheel of a car since the collision, and the tendons in her neck were rigid. But with the memory of the accident itself still deeply buried, turning the key in the ignition hadn't been quite as traumatic as she'd thought. She'd also had a legitimate destination, and that at least had given her a vague sense of motivation she'd not felt since waking.

She was going to attempt contact with a girl named Maryse Plourde. She lived in a small farming village called Neuf-Marché built on the banks of the river Epte in the Pays de Bray.

The village was about twenty miles from the Forêt Domaniale de Lyons. Whether she found the girl or not, Beth knew she wouldn't be able to return home without visiting the place where her old life had halted so violently.

She had to take it in, walk around the site. Perhaps not seeing the roadside through lenses of rage would alter her perception of it or jolt something loose. Maybe Beth would find the part of herself she felt had been lost there. But would standing in the backdrop of an accident long cleared of its debris do anything but amplify her acute sense of being left behind?

She'd told Jody she was visiting Luc's mother in Quincampoix for the day, but had no intention of going there. She couldn't even contemplate the idea of being in the same room as the urn. Jody had happily offered up his car keys. He'd been shut in his little recording studio, and she was glad to give him some space for a while.

Beth had been on the Eurotunnel to Calais less than three months earlier, and she thought about the different woman she'd been such a short time ago. Happily married and juggling what she thought were Herculean pressures. Now she wished for the stresses of work and moving home with Luc, instead of them being as written off as the car they'd driven onto the shuttle.

She'd thought little of the vehicle that had been transported from the crash site in the forest and scrapped soon after. The silver Nissan Pathfinder had been virtually brand new, and Beth had mocked Luc's reverence and insistence on keeping the front mats pristine.

She manoeuvred up the ramp, and as the sound of the rain on the windscreen abruptly stopped, she felt claustrophobia crawling over her. Beth had never suffered from the condition in her life, but a host of new anxieties had taken up residence as soon as she'd opened her eyes in hospital.

Jody's vanilla-scented ice-cream cone air freshener was suddenly cloying. She wanted to put the car in reverse, but there was another vehicle tight behind her. Beth had no choice but to slot into her space and sit the journey out. She was directed by an attendant to a bay and turned off her engine as soon as she was in position.

She hadn't found a trace of Rae Salomon via employment sites, but had located her dead Twitter account. Even minus the dreadlocks, the black-and-white photo of her as a child was unmistakable, but there were no details in her profile and she hadn't logged in for over two years. Beth found one follower – Maryse Plourde. She was significantly more loquacious than Rae and had over four hundred followers of her own. In Maryse's tweets, there were many references to the demands of the customers in her place of work. She was a popular waitress in a brasserie called l'Auberge du Pont.

Beth had considered contacting her via the account, but the idea of escaping the UK to locate her had been too tempting. No member of Blood Legend had bothered to contact her, but she supposed it was because they were still reeling from the murder of Trip Stillman.

Neuf-Marché was a small place. Even if Beth didn't encounter her at the restaurant, she felt sure she'd be able to find her with a few enquiries. She wondered if Rae Salomon lived in the immediate vicinity. Beth guessed she had to be nearby if she was part of the response team for the crash in the forest.

Even if she found her, Beth was preparing for inevitable disappointment. How many similar scenes had she attended? And would she remember anything that had been said to her by Luc, when she dealt with the dead and the dying on a daily basis?

But why was she no longer working for the emergency services? Perhaps she'd relocated. Maybe this whole trip would prove fruitless after all.

A female attendant in a day-glo jacket gestured to her, half smiling. Beth realised she'd left her wipers going.

As Beth's car wound its way through the tall hedges that bordered the familiar patchwork fields, it felt as if she were an interloper in a location for happy memories she could no longer lay claim to. With Luc gone, every moment they'd shared there seemed null and void. The pewter skies heightened the sensation, and as she swerved to avoid an oncoming tractor and pulled over to let it pass, the ruddy-faced driver glowered at her.

This was a silly mistake and she realised she was only there because she didn't have anywhere to run. No home and nowhere to find comfort in familiarity. Being here, in the last place she'd been the person she thought she'd be forever, seemed like her only recourse, but it was a destructive pilgrimage. If she ever wanted her life to find its balance again, she knew she had to focus on the road ahead and not the one behind her.

But if she didn't try to find Rae, she would always wonder what had been uttered to her as she'd gripped Luc's hands. A large part of her hoped the paramedic would have nothing to offer. If Rae just shrugged her shoulders and told her she had no recollection of Luc or anything he'd said, then she'd know for sure she'd reached a dead end. Her real fear, however, was being told something more significant.

CHAPTER NINETEEN

Beth saw the ivy-clad restaurant before she realised she was in Neuf-Marché. She'd been so distracted, she must have missed the sign, if there'd been one. A glance at the satnav confirmed she'd arrived.

She pulled the Golf into a quiet residential street and switched off the engine. She'd lost track of time and glanced at her watch. It was quarter past twelve in the afternoon. Sliding her leather shoulder bag up her arm, Beth got out of the car and took in her drizzly surroundings. It was chilly and she walked to the high street, pulling her tan Bella jacket tighter. The short heels of her matching suede boots crunched on the narrow gravelled pavement, and the mist of her breath hung about her face.

Her eyes settled on the steeple of the St Pierre Church. Beth had glanced at it as she and Luc had driven through the village in the past, but they'd never stopped there. She didn't want to walk straight into the restaurant. If Maryse greeted her, she hadn't decided how she would proceed.

Would she pretend she was already a friend of Rae's and ask where she could contact her? She preferred to be honest, even if she had to tell her exactly why she wanted to speak to her.

Intending to do a brief circuit of the village while she deliberated over her best approach, she headed towards the steeple, walking to the end of the side street to cross the road to where a few people were standing outside a delicatessen. She had to pause at the kerb to allow a lorry to trundle past, however, and in that moment Beth turned right and strode to the entrance of l'Auberge du Pont before she could change her mind.

Inside, the smell of coffee and pastries draped itself over her. Two overweight men in overalls were stacking crates of beer at the side of the wooden bar. Despite the large mirrors on the walls, the restaurant looked much bigger than it did from the outside, and tables stretched back to another bar at the rear. A few diners were dotted about. The lighting was subdued and a selection of musical instruments hung down from hooks in the ceiling. A muted clarinet played through a speaker somewhere.

An attractive, dark-haired and petite girl in a linen blouse and black skirt appeared from behind the two men and smiled warmly at Beth through heavy make-up. *"Puis-je vous aider, madame?"*

"Maryse Plourde?"

The girl's beam remained, but her eyes warily searched first Beth's shaved head and then the scars on her chin. *"Oui. Un moment."*

Beth had expected Maryse not to be there and to have to spend the day drinking endless cups of coffee until she arrived for her shift. She watched the waitress disappear through a door behind the bar. The two men stacking crates turned in unison and smiled perfunctorily at her before returning to their work.

Maryse emerged from behind the bar. She was much taller and athletically built than Beth had expected from her profile picture. Her crimped hair was tied up and now dyed straw blonde, but her features were unmistakable. She'd borrowed the first waitress's cagey smile. "Bonjour," she said uncertainly.

"Bonjour. Parlez-vous anglais?"

Maryse nodded quickly. "A little."

"I'm trying to find somebody. I realise your time is valuable but all I need is a contact number or address..."

Maryse's eyes glazed and she shook her head. "Slowly." She smiled again and gestured towards a nearby table.

Beth took a deep breath and followed her. As Maryse seated herself, Beth considered the best way of cutting to the chase. She remained standing and took her iPhone out of her shoulder bag. She'd been avoiding the devices since seeing the clips, but Jody had set a new one up for her and persuaded her to bring it. She recognised the irony of using it now.

Maryse looked guardedly at the device while Beth found the YouTube clip. She dragged the slider to just before the helicopter taking off and paused it on the image of Rae with Luc. Planting it in front of Maryse she pointed at the paramedic. "Rae Salomon?"

Maryse glanced up at her and her features immediately hardened. "You are police?"

"No." She pointed to Luc. "My husband. *Mon mari.*"

Maryse returned her attention to the paused clip again and Beth touched play. She didn't take her eyes from the iPhone, even when it had ended.

"Maybe you've seen this before?"

Maryse nodded.

"Can you understand why I must speak with your friend?"

Maryse looked up at Beth. "Such terrible... tragedy."

"Yes. My husband didn't survive." It still felt strange hearing herself say it. "Do you know where I can find Rae?"

"No." Maryse closed her eyes momentarily, as if she'd find the words better in the dark. She opened them again. "Tragedy after this... to Rae..." She shook her head for effect.

"Rae's... dead?"

Maryse nodded.

CHAPTER TWENTY

When Kelcie arrived home from teacher training college, she pushed the door and heard her breath snag in her throat. She surveyed the remains of the room. It looked less as if she'd been robbed and more like somebody had deliberately smashed every one of her possessions. Somebody? Looking at the destruction, it appeared as if an entire football team had stampeded through her cabin.

At her feet lay the contents of her underwear drawer and a selection of jars and tubes from the refrigerator. Mayonnaise and dark sticky syrup she couldn't identify had been used to daub all her panties. A tub of cookie ice cream was upended beside them. There was a footprint in a mound of crushed cereal that looked as if it had been left by a rubber sport sole.

All of the cheap rental property picture frames had been swiped from their hooks, their fragmented glass scattered about the rugs. The walls had been smeared and Kelcie guessed what had been used to do it. The aroma reached her then, but there were other alien scents mixed with it – cigarettes and male sweat.

She listened for signs of movement, but heard only the familiar sound of faraway traffic, louder than usual. She stepped over the ornaments that had been mashed into the carpet and peered through the buckled and split passage door to the bedroom and bathroom beyond.

The bathroom window was wide open. That was how they'd got in. Why had they targeted her shitty cabin? It trespassed on the edge of the expensive new housing complex on Four Mile Drive, but was scarcely as attractive a proposition. Surrounded by brush, she was an easy target, though. Her nearest neighbour was a good five-minute walk away.

She inched into the bathroom. The cabinet mirror was shattered and the glass and its contents lay in the sink. The shower curtain and its rail had been tugged down. She pulled her cell phone out of her bag and dialled the police. They told her they were sending a patrol car right over.

She hurried to the bedroom to get her M1911 pistol from behind the nightstand. It was gone. So were her laptop and external hard drive.

Nausea spiked and a void of dread slowly expanded in her chest.

Her world was in her laptop. But even though she had friends in every corner of the planet, all she really wanted now was somebody to hug and tell her the intruders weren't coming back. Kelcie couldn't think of anyone else to call. Her parents were visiting friends in Minnesota. Who else was there?

She cleared the debris off the couch, shakily seated herself there and waited for the cops to arrive. Should she use her trusty iPhone to snap photographs of the damage and the shit that had been smeared all over her home?

Kelcie told herself the culprits were probably just kids, opportunistic thugs with too much spare time on their hands. They wouldn't come back, not if she'd called the cops.

Then she became aware of breathing behind her.

She turned and there were three of them standing in the doorway. They'd slunk back in through the open bathroom window. Kelcie was right. None of them was older than twenty. Their faces seemed familiar.

"Don't I know you guys?" But with the question came the instantaneous realisation that they didn't care if she did.

She turned and made for the door. A club with six nine-inch nails in it was embedded in her scalp before she could reach it. The room turned blue then black as she was struck again.

CHAPTER TWENTY-ONE

Spike, Jeb and Benny watched the girl hover then topple sideways onto her underwear.

"Your turn." Spike held out the nightstick to Jeb. "She recognised us. You'll have to finish her."

He took it from him. "I told you it was Kelcie Brooks when we saw her pull up."

"Wait." Spike took his iPhone from his pocket, his hand shaking, pointed it at Jeb and activated the movie camera. "As instructed, remember."

"How come we didn't record you whacking her?" Benny piped up.

Spike knew he'd have to watch Benny. He could see exactly what Spike was up to. With all of their other handiwork deleted, this would be the only evidence left to incriminate them. He kept the iPhone trained on Jeb. He was easier to wrangle. "Hurry up, cockwad. The cops are on their way."

Jeb slammed the nail bat into the girl's head. Once, twice, three times. He laughed nervously. "She's fucking dead now." He held it out to Benny and there was blood all over his fingers.

Benny took it from him.

Jeb wiped his hands on the back of his jeans and pulled out his phone to record him.

"You can take another swing after me, OK?" Benny said to Spike. "And I'll record it with my phone."

"OK." Spike knew there was no time to argue. "Just hurry the fuck up."

Benny slugged the dead girl's indented blank expression.

"The fuck was that, jizzbubble? Do some real damage," Jeb said, coming in close with the lens.

Spike kept quiet. He didn't want to be recorded goading the other two. He'd let Benny shoot him taking a few swings, but that meant he was only captured by one phone, and he'd have no trouble taking that from him later.

Benny raised the bat and brought it down harder.

"Whoa!" Jeb said.

They'd all heard the sound of her skull breaking against the wooden floor.

"OK, your turn." Benny held the nightstick out to Spike and raised his eyebrows.

"No fucking problem." Spike snatched it from him and it felt slick in his grip. He joined the other two and looked down at the girl's caved-in head. "Awesome."

"Yeah, nice job, guys."

The three of them turned to the front doorway. A man with a toupee was standing inside it with his arm extended. At the end of it, in a hand clad in a blue surgical glove, he gripped a gun.

"I just want you boys to know there's nothing random about this. You're all part of something real important. Mh?" It was all he felt he owed them.

Mimic shot Jeb and Benny in the chest with the M1911. He'd taken it from Kelcie's nightstand earlier that day. Spike ran for the bathroom before they'd dropped, but Mimic shot him in the back of the head. Spike rammed into the door like a stunned cow and slid down it.

Mimic crossed the room and slipped the gun into Kelcie's hand. He'd found her licence details when he'd hacked her computer. She had good taste. He had a soft spot for single action firearms. At least she would come out of this scenario as the heroine. He aimed the gun at Jeb's lifeless body and made her finger pull the trigger. Another hole burst in the front of his Avenged Sevenfold sweatshirt.

He stood up and used a handkerchief to dab the corners of his mouth. Prior to his arrival, the Kalispell crime rate had been forty-six incidents per every one thousand residents. Now this brave young woman had defended herself, the community could at least look forward to safer streets.

He'd wait things out now. Let the police presence ease. He'd already scoped out his next target and was in no hurry. There were two golf courses nearby – Big Mountain and Village Greens. He'd stay off the radar and practise his swing. He looked at the bloodied, concave expression of the woman on the floor, the lifeless hand not gripping the gun open to him like a lily.

As per his instructions, the three of them had deleted every clip from their phones and Internet accounts, including the ones they'd shot of the crash. One more movie to make and he told them they wouldn't have any more worries. He hadn't lied.

There was a lesson to be learnt for Spike, but more so for Kelcie. They'd both been on that exchange trip coach, but she'd been in a position of authority. She should have known better than to record the event along with all the other rubbernecking kids, should have been setting an example. He'd remove her clips from the public domain over the next few days. The guys had left her hard drive and laptop out back as he'd told them to.

His cell chirruped and he took it from his pocket as he walked out of the cabin. He knew who it would be. Mimic confirmed that it was his employer. They were the last people he wanted to speak to. He allowed it to stop ringing and go to voicemail. It would tell them his message inbox was still full.

CHAPTER TWENTY-TWO

Beth didn't know how long she'd been standing at the side of the road, but the drizzle had now turned her tan jacket a deep brown. She was looking across from the grass to where she and Luc had been tended by Rae and the other paramedic. The silence of the forest had never unnerved her before. It had always seemed like a place of refuge and safety when she'd escaped there with Luc.

He'd introduced her to his hideaway soon after they started seeing each other. It was his special corner of the world, and she'd been touched that he wanted to share it with her. His family used to spend their summers in the region, and he knew the area better than South London.

It was where they'd taken their very first trip away together. They'd made love in the forest, had drawn up plans and had sat on the bench in front of Gîte Saint-Roch by the brick campfire grill. They'd leaned into each other, reminding themselves what stars looked like, and had let the wood smoke saturate their clothes. When they'd returned to their home under the canopy of city smog and light pollution, Beth hadn't wanted their clothes washed for weeks after, she'd preferred to inhale them and think about their next escape.

Having grown up in a buttoned-down household, the forest had been the first place where she'd felt truly uninhibited. It had always taken her a day to adjust, but the tranquillity had quickly stripped her reserve. She'd spent her time there wearing just her sunblock, a pair of cut-off jeans and one of Luc's T-shirts. She'd loved to feel the dry natural floor against the soles of her feet when they'd both run there before breakfast, and to immerse herself in the solitude that was so far removed from their daily lives.

Now, in spite of the familiar beech scents and pure air, she shivered. Beth knew she could never open herself up to it again. How could they ever have suspected the location that nurtured their relationship could wrench them apart in such a horrific way?

Rae Salomon had taken her own life. Walked into the River Epte. Had the crash been instrumental in that? Beth was still partially convinced every event had a knock-on effect. Would she and Luc even have been on this road if a hoodie hadn't tried to mug them in the car park? But Beth knew she'd drive herself insane trying to trace their fate back to anything more than their own resolve and the brown camper happening to stop dead in the path of their car.

Maryse had said nobody knew what Rae's motive had been. Her note had simply apologised to those who'd have to deal with the recovery of her body. It sounded as if she was estranged from her family and had very few friends. Had the job taken its toll on her? Whatever her reasons, like the man in the camper, she'd absented herself from the explanation Beth sought.

But what had she expected to hear, even if she had spoken to Rae? Something that would instantly disperse the numbness she felt. Luc was gone. There was nothing that would mitigate that... ever. Her journey here had been nothing but misdirection.

She looked down the road at the trees hugging the curve, their overhang recently trimmed so she had a clear view of it tapering towards the route they were never destined to complete. Beth wondered where they would be if they had.

Would they now be taking their new home and happiness for granted?

They both knew couples that had got bored with each other and had vowed that it would never happen to them. Had that been naivety? Had the accident actually drawn a line under and preserved that perfect part of their lives before domesticity drained it of its vitality?

Beth repelled the thought and inhaled the earthy aroma of wet leaves and mud. She looked down at the only remnant of the event – the coach's deep tyre tracks in the grass beneath her boots. She imagined it swerving to avoid the wreckage and Cigarillo Man finding her and calling the emergency services. He'd at least saved her life, but she had yet to feel grateful to him. But he probably had no control over the tourists he was transporting, couldn't have made them stay inside the vehicle while they waited for help to arrive.

Beth surveyed the area where their car and the camper had come to rest. Having examined it in the clips, it seemed unreal to be standing in its three dimensions. She was positioned exactly where she'd attacked the crowd; in the spot they'd watched and had recorded every moment of her distress and rage.

She waited for an emotion. If she felt nothing here, Beth knew she was broken. Part of her hadn't survived the crash. The part she could only remember now. A gentle wind agitated some leaves in the road.

She thought of Luc's body burning while she was oblivious and the faces that would have been at the crematorium – his mother, her parents, Jerome and Lin. How would he have reacted if he'd looked down and seen her missing? If there were really any sort of afterlife, surely he would have understood where she was and why she couldn't have been there.

Perhaps he would have found her and looked down at her in her hospital bed. But Beth didn't really believe in life after death, Luc had been brought up in a Christian household and, although he hadn't attended church for many years, had never entirely relinquished his beliefs. Beth had always told him that if she were fortunate enough to enjoy a full existence, she would happily take an everlasting nap at the end of it. She didn't see anything tragic in that.

But now he'd been prematurely taken from her, she found herself struggling to reconcile herself with such a pragmatic perception of death. It felt strange to imagine Luc in an urn on his mother's mantel, almost laughable. Where had Luc's sense of humour gone, his imagination, his creativity? Were they like deleted computer files? She thought of the passwords she'd recovered from the house and the residue of his existence left online.

She still couldn't bring herself to access it. Accounts had to be closed and that seemed too final. Beth knew she would have to dispose of his clothes and belongings sooner or later as well. She wouldn't be told when that was though. She imagined her mother standing over her and making her do it, telling her it was time to get on with her life and encouraging her to stuff all his things into sacks.

Would she smell his clothes before they were bagged? How long would his aroma remain on them? When it no longer did, were they just jumble? She would decide the time and now was too soon.

She didn't want to get back in the car either. Once she did, home was the only logical direction. But where was home? Her mother and father's? Jody's box room? It certainly wasn't the new house that had to be sold before she was drowning in debt. Grief and paperwork were a sickening tag team. The prospect of what lay ahead seemed suffocating.

Beth crossed the road to where she had last seen Luc, but felt nothing as she estimated exactly where they lay next to each other. She thought of him whispering sorry to her.

She could have been standing anywhere. There were no other tracks to be found, just a roadside like any other. She placed the bouquet of lemon roses and heather on the kerb, and it felt good to release their plastic wrapping from her hot palm. There was nothing to attach them to. The draught of passing cars would quickly dislodge them and probably blow them into the road. But it felt right to leave them there, even if it was for her benefit. She was a grieving widow and it was a box that had been ticked.

It was the first time she'd really considered her new label. She imagined "widow" would automatically entitle her to sympathetically knitted brows during every conceivable introduction from here on in. Until now, widows to Beth were characters in movies who dressed in black and hid behind a veil.

She looked back at the car and into the brush behind her. Briars and brambles made access to the forest on the other side of the road impossible. There were plenty of wide gaps between the trunks in the woods in front of her, however, so she stepped over the pavement and entered their cool and shady welcome. She wanted to walk away from everything the accident had turned her into, to feel the way she did when she'd been there before, even if it was a fleeting pretence.

Beth ducked under the lower branches and didn't look back. She'd left the car unlocked but didn't care. As her boots kicked up the wet leaves, the empty skeletons of the trees augmented her feeling that a once happy place had died. There was a strong scent of mould that caught in her throat, and she had to shield her eyes against the brittle points of the branches as she headed for the darkness at its denser centre.

Light drizzle that penetrated the canopy overhead became heavier and clung to her face, but she was soon loosening her pullover collar to let the moisture at her hot neck and listening to her laboured breath.

It struck Beth it was highly likely the driver of the camper had made his escape this way. He couldn't have got through the other side of the road, and this route would have been his most convenient exit. If he wanted to disappear, he certainly wouldn't have walked beside the traffic. After he'd kicked her into unconsciousness, maybe he'd done exactly as she was doing now. Perhaps she was retracing his exact steps. She looked down at the ground as if she would find some sign of his presence, but the carpet of leaves concealed everything.

As she reached what she thought would be the darkest portion of the forest, there was instantly a blacker area up ahead and, having repeated this process for some minutes, she peered back the way she'd come for the first time.

The road was no longer visible, and she was unsure of its exact direction. But it was a good feeling. For the first time since the accident, Beth felt like she was properly alone. She wasn't likely to encounter another soul and, if she did, there would be no pained expression or words of condolence. She stopped to wipe her face and listen to the silence.

How much farther should she go? Beth felt as if she could keep walking for the remainder of the day. A tiny voice said she should return to the car. It was unlocked and she didn't want to get stranded with no mode of transport to get her back to the shuttle. She ignored it and kept pumping her boots through the leaves.

Then she could hear the sound of an animal over the wet squelch of her paces and stopped to listen. It was panting and nearby. She scanned the trees around her and when her eyes halted on its seated form, it briefly stopped breathing. Then the Alsatian with the black snout snarled and sprang.

CHAPTER TWENTY-THREE

This was the price of being in the place she no longer had any right to be. Beth watched the beast coming at her, its dark jaws quickly closing the distance. She couldn't outrun it and there was no time to climb a tree. She remembered something she'd been told about disabling a vicious dog by seizing its hind legs. The animal moved as fast as the thought. Beth heard her own guttural exclamation as it reached her.

She protected her face with her hands and stumbled sideways. The Alsatian reared up on its hind legs but remained at a ninety-degree angle. A thick silver chain secured its neck and held it at bay only a few feet from her.

Despite its restraint, Beth's relief was overridden by its ferocity. Its mouth snapped at the air between them, teeth chopping and exploding spittle as it stood vertical in its attempts to reach her. She stumbled back a few more paces, anticipating the chain breaking under the strain, and met resistance against her hands.

"Kimba!"

Momentarily, Beth was too terrified to identify the source of the splenetic male voice. Each of the dog's barks seemed to burst inside her chest.

"Kimba!"

A man in a brown oilskin appeared behind the animal and

yanked it harshly backwards on the chain. His hair was tied away from his round face in a straggly ponytail and she could see his teeth gritted through his dishevelled brown beard. He dragged the Alsatian further away from her, looking for something either side of him. He located it, a peg in the ground that he wound the length of chain around.

The dog didn't stop barking, didn't take its orange eyes off her.

"Pardon." The man held up his hand in an apologetic gesture but Beth's adrenaline was still firing.

She opened her mouth to respond but no sound escaped.

Without shifting his gaze, his hand viciously slapped the beast's flank, and it squealed before falling silent.

Beth swallowed and unlocked her throat. She took a breath and smiled weakly. "Merci." But she didn't feel much safer in the man's company, particularly after he'd so brutally struck the dog.

"Votre main." The man nodded at her.

Beth followed his gaze and found her right hand was bleeding. She turned and saw the barbed-wire fence beside her that had hindered her escape. She must have grabbed one of the lethal-looking coils as she'd stepped back.

"Laissez-moi soigner votre main." He roughly shoved the animal's rear so it was sitting and stepped over it.

Beth couldn't retreat. "I'm sorry…"

He paused, aware that he was intimidating her. *"Anglais?"*

"Yes."

"My apologies. Please. My name is Roland. We need to dress your hand." He gestured for her to approach and she looked nervously at the dog. "He will not attack now. I give you my word. Come." Roland pointed behind him and, through gaps in the trees, Beth could see the red brick of a house.

The blood on her hand felt suddenly cold, and she looked at the laceration in her palm and the dark liquid flooding from it. She'd lose a lot more by the time she found her way back to the car, if she could even do that. And then there would still be a drive to the nearest village. Although she was wary of the man who had saved her, she didn't have a choice.

She looked into Roland's face and tried to find anything lurking there but a desire to help. "OK, thank you."

He indicated she should follow again and turned in the direction of the house. She clenched her bleeding hand into a ball and circled the Alsatian. Its head slowly turned with her movement but it didn't shift from its sitting position. Roland didn't look back as he led them to a gravel path running up to the overgrown garden. She could see a prominent bald patch that his ponytail clung flimsily to. How old was he, mid to late fifties?

He entered the stable door at the rear and had already passed through the tiny galley kitchen of the house when she stepped inside. A dirty frying pan was sitting on an old-fashioned, mint-green AGA, and the room was filled with the smell of fish. Condensation ran off the racks of large herb jars on the shelves that lined the right-hand wall.

The room beyond, however, was far from what she expected.

CHAPTER TWENTY-FOUR

Beth was in a large modern study with minimal leather furnishings. A long desk housing a computer monitor was mounted under a louvered window, and a second man was seated at a small dining table in front of it. He was halfway through eating a plate of sardines. The man in the oilskin was speaking to him in a low whisper, and they both turned as she entered.

The second man was wearing a burgundy towelling dressing gown and backless slippers on his feet. His wet black hair was in disarray about his boyish features, and he had a shadow of stubble that looked as if it had been applied with a sponge. He was significantly younger than the man in the oilskin, twenty-five at the most, but from their body language she could immediately tell they were a couple.

"Come. Sit," said Roland as he dragged a chair out from under the table.

The other man impassively rose and moved to a second door as soon as he saw the blood trickling out of Beth's bunched fist.

"Erik will dress your cut."

She dropped hard onto the chair and looked at the plate of sardines covered in paprika. The aroma became overpowering and Beth felt as if she were about to pass out. Now her circulation had slowed, the cut and her fright from the dog attack were vying for attention.

"Sorry about this." She allowed her head to drop to her knees so she could get some blood back into it, and saw Erik's feet return. She heard the crinkling and ripping of a wrapper and him whispering something to Roland in French.

After a few moments she looked up, and Erik was biting his lip as he waited. He gently took her hand with water-shrivelled fingers and carefully cleaned it with a disinfectant wipe. He had bloodshot eyes, but she assumed it was because he'd been in the shower. She noted his spotless nails had clear varnish on them. Then he wrapped a bandage around her palm and fingers. As he wound it, his dressing gown gaped at his hairless chest and Beth saw what looked like a white burn just below his left nipple.

Roland had his back to her while he poured a glass of brandy from a decanter on a shelf. She took in the modern décor and aubergine walls. The only items that reflected the exterior of the cottage were the three ancient but lethal-looking animal traps that were mounted on the wall over a modern fire appliance that looked like an HD TV with white coals inside. Lazy orange flames danced about them.

"Sorry about Kimba; he really wouldn't have harmed you," Roland assured her.

Beth doubted that.

"You're our first intruder in a long time. We got Kimba when some of the younger men from the village decided to call on us at night. That was some time ago, but he's still standing guard."

"Well, he terrified me."

"Did you get lost?" He handed her the balloon glass.

"Thank you. Yes." She took a sip and warmth glided into her stomach. "On purpose, though."

Roland frowned slightly. "We're used to hikers during the summer months, and make sure Kimba's in his kennel, but not many people find us at this time of year."

Beth had acknowledged Erik still hadn't spoken and

seemed happy for Roland to do the talking. She looked past his shoulder to the computer screen.

Roland saw her narrow her eyes at the document there. "I am Roland Desmoulins..." He waited, as if expecting recognition.

Beth pursed her lips and shook her head slightly. Erik looked at the floor as if he was more than used to these moments of disappointment for his partner.

"Political journalist for *Le Monde* before it became a slave to its investors. Now I find myself... freelance." He stroked his lank moustache. "If it wasn't for the bricks and mortar of my father..." He gestured around him. "I wouldn't even be that."

Beth didn't feel comfortable in their company and surprised herself by gulping the significant remainder of the brandy. "Thanks for your kindness." She looked at them both and Erik nodded slightly. "I really shouldn't waste any more of your day." She just managed to get the words out before the spirit shrivelled her throat.

Roland seemed as eager for her to leave as she was and got to his feet. "Let me direct you back to the footpath."

Beth wondered if she'd offended him by not recognising who he was. She stood unsteadily and Erik supported her arm. His grip was firm.

"Where are you staying?"

"I'm not actually staying anywhere. I had to make a stop off on my way home." Beth had seized on the casual enquiry and she knew why. "My husband was killed in a car accident near here." She lifted her arm from Erik's grip as he released the pressure of his fingers.

Roland exchanged a brief glance with Erik. Was it because neither of them knew how to respond to such a revelation?

"January the 10th."

"I'm very sorry," Erik said. His voice was more sonorous than she expected, but his commiseration was indifferent. She'd thought his previous silence was because he couldn't understand her conversation with Roland, but it was obvious they both spoke English.

"Were you also in the car?" Roland was looking at Erik.

Erik was examining her scars.

"Yes. Do you remember it?" She knew she'd wanted to ask the question before she'd entered the house.

Roland theatrically rolled his eyes up. "I do remember reading about it. Erik?"

Beth wondered if he was throwing the question to his partner because he was suddenly uncomfortable with having to talk to a recently bereaved woman.

Erik just nodded, then realised from Beth's gaze that it would be insufficient. "On the TV news."

"The driver of the car we crashed into fled the scene. He may even have come by here. That's why I was walking this way."

They both nodded and looked at the floor. It was definitely her cue to leave.

"Did the police ever question you?" She knew she would have to return if she didn't ask the other inevitable questions now.

"No. But, of course, if we'd seen anything we would have reported it."

Beth persisted. "I know it was some months ago, but do you recall seeing anyone pass through here, perhaps someone that alerted your dog? Could you think back a couple of months to anyone Kimba might have barked at? Somebody you might have rescued like you did me."

Roland was already shaking his head. "You don't seem to realise how far back we are from the road."

"We don't want any more trouble," Erik said firmly.

Beth looked at Roland and he seemed chastened. Perhaps she had the dynamic all wrong.

"I wish I could tell you something, but if we'd seen anything, we would have reported it." Roland repeated.

"If you do remember anything – and I mean anything

that may have seemed innocent at the time but you think could help me – would you contact me?" She reached inside her shoulder bag and extracted her purse. Inside were some of Luc's Avellana business cards. She handed Roland one. "Anything at all."

Erik took the card from Roland's hand and briefly examined it. "Of course." He nodded a little too earnestly.

Beth held his eye. "Thank you for the bandage... and this." She raised the brandy glass and looked around for a surface to leave it on. Roland stepped forward and relieved her of it.

He showed her through the small coat-lined hallway to the front door and quickly opened it. "There's a track through that gap in the hedge. Take a right turn at the fence. You can follow it all the way back to the road."

Beth felt relieved to be outside again and nodded thanks to Roland. She made her way to the hedge on the edge of the front garden before turning back to the house. The front door had already closed, and the bare tree reflections on the window made it impossible to see if they were watching her through it. She swivelled on her heel again and angled her body so she could pass through the overgrown opening in the hedge.

Her hand pumped in its tight bandage and she told herself she was being paranoid. With their home in the centre of the forest, it was perfectly plausible that Roland and Erik hadn't been aware of the collision. They were a good distance from the road, and even if the driver of the brown camper had made his escape into their neck of the woods, he may well have circumvented the house and the dog for obvious reasons.

Roland and Erik had seemed nervous. But then so would she if she was so isolated and a stranger turned up out of nowhere. It also sounded as if the couple had been subjected to homophobic attacks in the past. They obviously valued their privacy.

So why had she felt compelled to give them one of Luc's business cards? She could easily have jotted down her number for them. There had been a notepad and pen on the computer desk. But she'd wanted to present them with something of his, something that identified the man who had lost his life right on their doorstep.

She told herself it was being in this secluded place and having the dog attack her that had put her on edge. She would feel much better about the encounter when she was safely in the car.

Beth arrived at a high, creosoted fence and a wider, curving dirt track with trees and barbed wire either side. Crows squawked as she paused before turning right. It had to lead back to the road eventually.

She found it less than fifteen minutes later and her car five after that. Her flowers still lay on the kerb where she'd left them. She momentarily stared into the darkness and the route she'd taken into the forest. There were heavier rain droplets in the air, but she only really noticed when she was back in the driving seat and could hear them fluttering against the windscreen.

Beth put her key in the ignition and used the accident site to turn around.

CHAPTER TWENTY-FIVE

Marcia O'Doole had been pussyfooting around Tyler when it really should have been the other way round. But here she was cooking his favourite, macaroni and cheese, for breakfast. Kevin, justifiably, hated it. He loved eggs like any normal kid. Tyler detested them. Said they gave him mucus. She deferred to Tyler more than his younger brother though. God willing, Kevin would live to enjoy plenty of eggs.

Her boys were sitting at the breakfast bar engrossed in their iPhones. They both used to share the same yellow curls. Tyler's remaining hair was covered by his blue camouflage bandana but Kevin's was way out of control. He didn't let her cut his hair anymore though, so that was another new expense.

Kevin showed Tyler a clip and laughed in a way that told her it wasn't fit for their consumption and that it was even funnier because she was in the room and couldn't see it. She regretted letting Kevin have Tyler's old iPhone. But all his classmates had one and, as she'd got the latest model for Tyler, she had to be fair.

She knew she was overcompensating, trying to make it up to Tyler because his father wasn't around. And because her job as bureau events organiser at the Kalispell Chamber of Commerce meant she frequently wasn't, either. But now, of course, Kevin wanted the latest iPhone, and she was sick of telling him anything but the truth. *Your older brother gets the new one because he has chondrosarcoma.*

She knew they were in cahoots. Deciding between them which expensive gizmo they desired next and getting Tyler to ask for it. She found it difficult to refuse, and then Kevin would want the same. And why couldn't he have one, too? They all knew the truth, but it was never uttered. Marcia saw she was being played and went along with it. But all the handheld devices her overtime could provide were never going to assuage her guilt about moving the boys from their father and city friends in Auburn, Alabama, to be near her family in Big Sky Country.

She wondered if Kevin and Tyler would run rings around her if circumstances were different, if Tyler were healthy and their father hadn't fled because he couldn't face the notion of losing his son. Ted couldn't come back into her life. That was one thing she should never allow. He'd deserted her and the boys at the time they needed him the most. But what if he did want to relocate here? Would she really refuse him and deprive Tyler of being part of a complete family, for however long he had to enjoy it?

That's why she was determined to take the boys to West Glacier. Their forthcoming vacation could be the last time they all went away together.

"That's so lame, buttmonkey," Tyler said

"What are you two looking at?"

Kevin regarded her with mortification, as if she'd just broken an unuttered rule. "Nothing."

"Let me see it." She could see him consider refusal. The iPhone had a frozen image on its screen, blurred beige. She prised it from his grip. "How do I do this?"

Kevin sighed and touched the screen as if it were suddenly infectious. The clip counter rotated. What was she about to view? Was she going to give Kevin his first lecture about porno as well? She found herself swallowing as she waited for it to begin.

It appeared to be an excerpt from a wildlife show. A leopard picked off a young springbok from a herd and dragged it to the dust by its neck. The camera zoomed in for a close-up of its teeth slashing flesh and dark jets of blood staining the ground and the predator's snout. The camera lingered as the springbok's body went limp and the leopard shifted its bite so it could start gnawing with the side of its jaw. The clip ended.

The relief Marcia felt about it not being something that would corrupt Kevin, as if that were really possible anymore, stalled. It wasn't anything worse than you'd find on Nat Geo Channel, but the isolation of the kill moment and the fact that Kevin had obviously downloaded it to enjoy and share troubled her.

Marcia always tried to compensate for the fact she didn't understand the male psyche. Ted would probably say it was to be expected from boys their age. He'd always serviced their testosterone by teaching them survival skills and how to shoot. But a lot of the time, she suspected Ted's dismissals were just an excuse for the bad behaviour he'd been guilty of in the past. Did that mean she had to entertain it?

"Put it away, Kevin." She started to dish up. Marcia gave Kevin his first, but it didn't matter which order she served them in. Now it would start.

"Macaroni and cheese..." Kevin blanched.

"I'll make eggs tomorrow," she appeased.

"Eggs." Tyler mock-vomited.

They both liked anything deep-fried. It was the only food they ate without complaint. Maybe if she was giving them cheese every other morning, she may as well bite the bullet and overload them with trans fats seven days a week. But Marcia wouldn't fall into the trap so many parents did. She instead fought valiantly for a balanced, wholesome family life that maybe didn't exist.

"You'll get eggs tomorrow," she repeated when she realised Kevin hadn't picked up his fork.

"Why can't you make them for me today?" he whined.

"I'm already late for work. Just eat. I have a headache." She didn't but she knew she soon would have.

"The car's outside again," Kevin casually said, as if it were his way of punishing her for the breakfast.

Marcia crossed to the blind and looked out from the kitchen window to the other side of the street. He hadn't been teasing. The car was there. Black Toyota Corolla with a smoked windshield. It had been parked outside with someone inside the evening before. She'd gone out to the sidewalk to ask the driver if they'd needed directions, but they'd immediately driven off. Marcia thought she could see a figure at the wheel. What model was Ted driving now? She heard its engine start, as if it had been waiting for her appearance. If it were still there when she and the boys came home, she'd call the cops.

Mimic watched the window and wiped the corners of his mouth with his handkerchief. The kids had been spying on him from their bedroom the night before and had probably told Mom he was there again.

He'd parked up in the same spot in front of the freshly planted cherry trees just up from the O'Doole house yesterday and gradually got to know the lay of the lower-middle-class neighbourhood. Much more populated than Kelcie's. Family homes one side, ball park the other. The area was currently unused though, and signs warned people not to walk there, because new grass seed had been planted. The street was also the thoroughfare to the local school and so got busy around 3.30 but was otherwise quiet.

He'd get what he came for, even if it meant leaving three bodies behind for the local police department. The O'Doole mother was compact, feisty, the sort of woman who would fight him to her last breath. He'd have to stay alert with that one.

He could already visualise her incapacitated and him working on her. He would tell her it was necessary before he finished. He liked to give his targets a heads-up about their demise if he felt it was owed. To at least inform them they weren't just victims of an opportunist.

Now he'd play a few rounds of golf, go back to the hotel to grab a shower, maybe have a steak dinner, a nap and a few gin martinis to loosen him up. Then it would be time to drive back here. They would probably have all gone to bed by then and he could deal with them separately in the early hours of the morning. Wakey, wakey, eggs and bakey. One room to the next. There was no father on the scene, so he'd have a healthy amount of undisturbed hours to work.

He was about to turn into the road, but a convoy of SUVs were heading towards the school. It was the early run. While he waited for them to pass, he picked up his iPad and skated his finger over the screen. Again he found the online article about old Virginia Greenspan being mutilated with a broken bottle in Bigfork and the attempted arson afterwards.

Beth couldn't focus on the road or the signs, only knew she was driving in roughly the right direction. It was early evening; she didn't want to go back but had no reason to stay any longer. She had to concentrate and find her way to Calais, but her mind was locked on the encounter she'd had in the house in the woods. Had they been hiding something from her, or was she reading nuances into the conversation that simply weren't there?

The rain came down heavier and soon the wipers were powerless against the torrent streaming down the windscreen. The noise of the droplets on the roof was deafening. She glanced at her mobile on the dash and noticed she had a message. It was probably Jody checking up on her. She listened to it.

"Mrs Jordan, I was given this number by Maryse Plourde. My name is Rae Salomon."

CHAPTER TWENTY-SIX

Beth could scarcely hear her over the noise of the rain. She screwed up her face.

"I shouldn't be calling you, and must ask for your complete confidence. Maryse explained why you wanted to contact me. I was at the roadside with your husband. He spoke to me. I couldn't understand a lot of what he said, but one thing I definitely did." She paused. "Allegro," she whispered and then hung up.

Beth pulled the car over and stared at the phone as the weather continued to batter the car. She tried to call the number but it had been withheld. She was about to put the phone back onto the dash when it rang.

"Beth Jordan?" It was the same voice.

She was talking to a dead woman. A response stalled.

"You're not the police?"

"No. Sorry, but Maryse told me... Why did she tell me you were dead?"

"Officially, I am. And I insist it remains that way or this conversation has to end. Do I have your word?"

"Of course." But Beth was already sceptical.

"I was sorry to hear about the loss of your husband."

"Maryse showed you the clip?"

"She didn't need to. I've seen them all. It was how they located me."

"Who?"

"I moved from Luxembourg to live with my aunt in Touffreville three years ago to escape a bad scene. I got involved with the wrong man. Knew too much about his operation for him to feel secure about us breaking up."

"Operation?"

"The less you know the better. He was a people trafficker. He sees me as property as well." Her voice tapered dryly and she seemed to collect herself. "I thought I'd escaped him and took a job, but I didn't realise I'd end up in a viral clip. I knew my time was running out when it started circulating."

"You faked suicide?"

"I had to persuade them to stop looking for me for good."

"How do I know this is really you? Can we meet?"

"Out of the question." She said flatly. "I'm risking my safety even contacting you."

"Do you have a camera on your phone?"

There was a pause. "No."

"Please, if you do, could you just snap a picture of yourself and send it to me."

"I said I don't have a camera."

"I promise to delete it immediately."

"Please don't ask that of me again."

"OK. Can you at least tell me if you're still a smoker?" Beth recalled the aroma of cigarettes and mint on her breath as she'd stood over her at the roadside.

A beat. "No," she said suspiciously. "I've just given up."

She'd covered herself with that response. But why would she be trying to deceive Beth, anyway? She tried to think of a specific detail from the crash site, that couldn't have been gleaned from looking at the clips on the Internet. But Beth's own recollection was sketchy. "You remember only one word my husband said. Are you sure it was Allegro?"

There was a long pause.

"Are you still there?"

"Yes. That is all I remember. Allegro."

"Allegro?" The word had no significance for Beth. "And you don't remember anything else he said?"

Another long pause. "No. Look, this is a personal security risk I could really do without. I hope this has eased your mind. I have to hang up now." She did.

Beth stared through the water sliding down the windscreen. *Allegro*. What relevance could the word possibly have to Luc while he lay dying?

She pulled back into the driving rain. A few moments later her phone buzzed. She picked it up and found an image had been sent. It was a close-up of Rae. It was definitely her.

A couple of minutes passed and then the phone rang again. Beth snatched it up and took her foot off the accelerator. "Hello?" Nobody responded, but she could hear someone breathing on the other end. "Rae?" But she got the feeling it wasn't.

Whoever it was hung up.

CHAPTER TWENTY-SEVEN

Allegro became a one-word mantra during Beth's return journey. It was the make of a British car, but it certainly wasn't a vehicle involved in the accident. She knew it was a term for tempo, but Luc had no interest in music beyond Motown.

When she searched for it online back at Jody's using his tablet, she found a dizzying number of results – it was the name of a Polish-based auction website, a luxury restaurant in Prague, a typeface designed in 1936 and a software library for video game development. It was also a passenger train service between Helsinki and Saint Petersburg, a Mexican airline and, as well as a Rodgers and Hammerstein musical, a 2005 movie directed by Christoffer Boe. At the more obscure end, it was a cryogenic gravitational wave bar indicator – whatever that happened to be – and John Marco Allegro was a Dead Sea Scrolls scholar.

None of it had any relevance to Luc. Had Rae misheard?

But finding any trace of the word became an incentive for Beth to finally open the blue envelope containing Luc's computer passwords while Jody was still in bed and she could do it alone. Digital legacy. She pulled her robe tight around her, took a sip of her coffee and put the cup down on the table. Sliding the envelope out of the folder, she didn't give herself pause to think.

Beth messily tore it open, unfolded the first slip of paper and found her own passwords scrawled on it. She only had two. Luc had told her she shouldn't use the same passwords for all of her accounts, because if one were hacked it would be easy to access the others. She alternated between different234 and different567. If one run of numbers didn't work then she knew she simply had to enter the other. It wasn't security-conscious enough for Luc, but then she didn't have as much sensitive information to protect.

She opened Luc's to find a list of eight accounts and as many separate passwords. His handwriting was boxy and tiny and pressed through the paper, and she imagined him painstakingly penning the words. He hated writing, said it gave him hand cramps, and didn't want to scribble anything with a pen other than his signature.

She recognised some – "michaelmas2009" was a reference to their wedding day that fell on October 11th and she knew that nicolaide48131 was an amalgamation of his mother and father's names and birthdays. "Pogerola" was an Italian village they'd stayed in for their honeymoon in Amalfi and was a password they both used to access their online photo account.

The others were just sequences of what looked like random letters and numbers to her. They were for pensions and private investment funds so obviously had to be more intricate. No mention of Allegro.

She looked at the half-eaten dry bagel on the arm beside her, because its smell suddenly seemed overpowering. Beth felt clammy nausea crawl quickly over her and made a dash for the bathroom. She didn't make it in time and trailed vomit through its door to the sink.

"Are you all right?"

Beth spat into the plughole but her stomach heaved again. She could hear Jody moving about in his room. He slept naked and she knew he would be hurriedly throwing something on. "Yes," she managed before her shoulders rose to eject the little she'd recently eaten.

"Can I... get you something?" he said awkwardly from behind

her, a few moments later. "There's mouthwash in the cabinet."

"I'm sorry. I'll clean up the carpet."

"Don't worry about it."

She ran the tap and filled her mouth with water, but knew she hadn't finished. "Honestly, I'm fine. Go back to bed."

"I'll make you a cup of your mint tea." He strode off in the direction of the kitchen.

Beth heard him fill the kettle and blinked the moisture out of her eyes.

When Jody left to do some shopping, he asked her if she needed any specific groceries. Beth said no, even though she did and slipped out of the house soon after him. She was back less than ten minutes later.

She couldn't pee on the stick. It was as if her body had locked itself tight against confirming what she already knew. She tried to relax herself, then strained until her temples pounded. Placing her head in her hands and leaning forward, she repeatedly shifted her position on the seat. She hadn't passed water that morning even though she'd drunk a couple of cups of tea in readiness. After what felt like half an hour, she finally felt the warm liquid flow weakly out of her.

She'd already taken the tester stick from its foil wrapper and followed the instructions, allowing the small trickle to flow for a few seconds before holding it in the stream.

Now she had to wait another three to four minutes.

When the blue line appeared and confirmed she was carrying Luc's child, Beth felt nothing but cold inertia. What she'd thought was the sickness of expelling the trauma of the crash was the beginnings of something that had been actuated before it. It was what she'd wanted. It was why she'd stopped taking the pill and not told Luc.

CHAPTER TWENTY-EIGHT

Beth remained seated with her panties and jeans binding her ankles. She mentally calculated, remembered them making love on at least three occasions during their getaway in Gîte Saint-Roch, the last one being their final night, just before they'd got into the car and she'd driven them to the restaurant.

The stresses of the mugging and the move had meant it had been more or less off the cards for a good few months leading up to that. She'd instigated it each time, tried to get Luc to let go of what had been preoccupying him. He thought she was still taking the pill. Beth hadn't been since the previous July. She'd prepared a part of herself, girded it to have the confrontation with him should it ever lead where she wanted. But months had passed and she'd begun to believe it never would.

It looked as if the life inside her had been conceived in their most significant place. But the notion of Luc's ending in the crash there and the beginnings of someone else leaving with her was too poignant to contemplate.

How would she have felt about this news if Luc were still alive? She imagined his reaction. When he was confronted with the reality of what they'd created, would he really have been as unyielding as he'd been in the past? She imagined the embrace they would have shared. It was something they would have faced together. Now she had to alone.

She knew Jody would be supportive. He seemed to be making it his mission to look after her following the years they'd spent out of each other's company. But nobody could make the decision for her. If she had the baby, could she really live with the heartbreak of seeing Luc's likeness? Was that meant to be her recompense? Beth still hadn't begun to deal with the trauma of his death. How could she possibly be expected to face such another intensely emotional ordeal so quickly afterwards?

Perhaps it would be her redemption, but she wouldn't be respecting Luc's wishes. But if he'd known what lay ahead for him, would he have thought differently about bringing a part of himself into the world?

It was a hard truth, but what Luc wanted was no longer relevant. This was what she hadn't expected to be in possession of. She thought about all his old clothes and his digital legacy and realised it was inconsequential. A new life seemed like something she'd been gifted, however, but she still couldn't summon any emotion above her own flat assessment of the situation.

She had to be pragmatic, though. How could she possibly bring up a child if she didn't have a roof over her head? She'd already had an awkward conversation with her employer. They'd had to fill her position while she'd been out of commission. There was no guarantee the house would be sold anytime soon, and even before she could think about that, there was the long process of probate to endure. She'd barely considered how Luc's stake in his company would be disbursed. He'd invested everything in it and his wealth was tied up in its fluctuating performance. Nothing would be straightforward.

She looked down at the dirty carpet of Jody's bathroom. Again, she thought of herself lying in a coma in her hospital bed while they cremated Luc – both of them unaware of the new life that had started in their absence.

Mimic touched the boy's face and then smelt the adolescent

sweat on the tips of the blue surgical gloves he'd snapped on in the garden. Fifteen year-old Kevin slept obliviously to his presence, breath hissing from his body. The room's smell was comforting, cookies and Vaseline. It reminded Mimic of sleeping in the top bunk when he was a kid, older brother below and both sneakily watching the creature feature with the sound turned low while Mom and Dad were in bed.

The boy's eyes darted under their lids and Mimic wondered what innocent dream he was enjoying. Then his breath snagged in his throat and his head shook once, quickly. Mimic gripped the ketchup bottle tighter and waited. The boy's dried lips parted, air found exit and his frown vanished.

Mimic knew it was the sort of sleep that would make it easy to lift the boy from the bed, arm under the neck and the other behind the knees. He could be carried out to his waiting car and still not wake. No swab of ether necessary. It was something he'd done effortlessly in the past but he couldn't now, not with all his extra pounds.

Mimic turned from the boy and grimaced at the plastic-framed mirror on the drawers. The deposits at the corners of his mouth looked vivid yellow in the night light. There was no halting the incursion of age. That was something that didn't sit well. It brought Mimic back into the domain of ordinary people.

He left Kevin's room and cocked an ear to the mother's. Even under the chatter from the TV, he could hear her breathing escaping her like a hog. Mimic cracked the door with one rubber finger.

Padding to the end of the bed there was a distinct difference in aroma compared to the kid's room – perfume, body cream and halitosis. There was a spilt bowl of tortilla chips on the floor beside her Kindle. One blow to the centre of her forehead with the bottle would ensure she wouldn't even open her eyes. Mimic watched her sleeping on her back for a while, willing her to wake. Marcia didn't, not even when he rolled her onto her side to stifle the noise grazing the backs of her nostrils.

After he'd stunned and strangled them, he'd have to smash the ketchup bottle if the blows didn't break it. The Bigfork crime necessitated him defacing the bodies with the jagged glass. What a sick fuck. And he was still evading the police as well. Probably sitting at home right now, not realising the precedent he'd set.

There were plenty of crimes he could have chosen, but the perp had attempted to burn down Virginia Greenspan's apartment, and that was ideal for Mimic's needs; the less of a multiple murder scene remained, the better.

Mimic closed the door quietly and moved to the eldest child's room. Wearing only shorts, his tanned body was tangled up in the duvet. The masculine scents here were significantly more mature than Kevin's – sour sweat and cheap deodorant.

His rubber palm hovered where it was. The sensation intensified. He'd never experienced anything like this. Wasn't lockjaw something to do with tetanus? It got tighter, as if screws were being firmly turned. He couldn't open his mouth. Mimic realised he was forgetting to breathe and hissed air in through his nose. He looked at the kid to check it hadn't stirred him.

Now he felt uncomfortable about his waist and stood, shifting his paunch so it was hanging over his leather belt. Jesus, his forehead and the nape of his neck were burning cold. He needed to get some air. He lurched towards the door and tried not to stumble into the exercise bike on the way out.

This wasn't his ulcer. He was having a fucking heart attack. Of all the times to happen; he fumbled his cell out of his pocket and dialled 911.

"What is your emergency?" the female operator wearily asked.

He was standing on the landing. Didn't want to wake Mom and the kids up. Couldn't speak too loudly. Couldn't speak at all. He grunted instead.

"Sir? Are you hurt?"

Mimic managed to activate the muscles in his jaw and opened his teeth half an inch. But the action seemed to displace the pain to his stomach and his legs didn't want to be in the same neighbourhood. They started trembling at the knees and felt like they were about to give. He rigidly put one in front of the other until he reached the top of the stairs.

"Sir? You have to speak to me."

Mimic headed down the stairs, and it suddenly seemed as if moving his body was like trying to operate a faulty pedal boat. The bottom step didn't seem to get any closer. He jammed the phone closer to his ear as he tried to speak to the operator. He had to strip his gloves off, get out of the house and back to the car.

"Sir?" She hung up.

CHAPTER TWENTY-NINE

For once, Jody met her eye instead of his usual habit of examining the walls when conversation made him uncomfortable. "So, are you going to tell our guardians?" He already assumed she wouldn't have yet. "And I guess I shouldn't ply you with any more of this..." He lifted the nearly empty bottle of Gentleman Jack off the coffee table, where it had taken up residence since Beth had become his houseguest, and put it back in the cabinet.

Even though she wasn't a liquor drinker, Beth was aware she'd been responsible for polishing most of it off. What adverse effects had that had on the baby? She was suddenly spooling back through all the things she'd done that would have been harmful, but the trauma of the collision and the assault afterward seemed to eclipse everything. It was a miracle Beth was still alive, and now she'd been given a reason to believe she'd survived for a purpose. "I won't tell them until I've made my own mind up about things."

Jody turned from the cabinet, censure in his eyes. "Don't tell me you're even considering..."

She was surprised and touched by Jody's barely concealed outburst, and it wasn't until that moment that Beth knew for sure it wasn't an option. "No. I want it." It was good to hear herself say it. She saw the relief register in his eyes. "I just don't want any parental interference until I've wrapped my head around this." She seated herself on the edge of the chair and Jody settled on the arm of the couch.

"How pregnant are you?"

"Luc and I hadn't... been intimate for a while. But when we were in Normandy..."

His eyes shifted from hers.

"I was in the coma for eight weeks and convalescing for another two. I've been out of hospital for nearly three. I make that about thirteen weeks."

"So, at this stage..." He reached for words that weren't part of his vocabulary.

Until then, they hadn't been part of Beth's, either. "It's a fragile time. Anything could happen, particularly after what I've been through. I don't want to alarm anyone unnecessarily. Except for you, obviously..." She found herself smiling grimly.

"I'm glad you felt you could confide in me."

It was a very un-Jody like thing to say, but Beth realised she really had no idea who her brother was. They'd both got on with separate lives, been absent from each other's adult development. He was certainly more mature than the last occasion they'd spent any significant time together.

"Whatever you need, just let me know." He wrung his hands as if trying to get the circulation back into them.

"Any luck finding a way of splicing those clips?"

He raised his eyebrows and mouthed "clips" and then realised he should have known what she was talking about. He regarded Beth as if she were insane. "Shouldn't you make an appointment with the doctor? I can start looking up some more relevant information sites about... y'know, parenthood. I do have an expectant mother to care for." He smiled behind his beard then; it was chary and brief, but for a few seconds, she realised he hadn't been able to control his excitement.

Beth realised she hadn't made any enquiries about his relationships. She'd assumed he was a happy bachelor. Did he crave a woman to share his life with? Did he want children? It was the first time she'd seen him genuinely smile. Maybe her landing back in his life wasn't the inconvenience she'd thought it was. But she still couldn't feel even a trace of the tentative elation he'd displayed.

"Are you not just a little bit excited?" He appeared to have read her mind.

"I will be." But she didn't know if it was a promise she could keep. "Let's just take it one moment at a time."

Jody nodded and surveyed her as if looking for some physical change.

She interrupted before he could open his mouth: "Please don't tell me to put my feet up and take it easy."

Jody frowned. "However you want to do this is fine by me."

Mimic opened his eyes and was looking up at a strip light on a white-tiled ceiling. The knowledge of who he was and what he did was as instantaneous. If you were a killer, it never escaped your waking mind. It pushed to the front of the line, but that was the way it had to be – any delay in recall could have dire consequences. He'd learned that in the military.

His back throbbed, but he was instantly sitting upright and assessing his surroundings. He wasn't in a police station as he'd first suspected. He was in a section of a hospital ward segregated by a green curtain to his left and was rigged up to a monitor. His jacket had been removed and lay on top of a tall flip can to his right. He could hear plenty of activity but couldn't see anyone.

He quickly removed the sensor from his finger and slowly peeled off the velcro that held the blood cuff to his arm. Its ripping sound made him grit his teeth as he tried not to broadcast its removal. He swung his legs from the bed and found his black leather shoes on the floor. He quickly slipped his feet into them and pulled on his jacket at the same time.

He peered around the curtain. Hospital staff in blue scrubs

attended to other patients on the right side of the ward while their colleagues used a bank of pristine keyboards and monitors at the station to the left. Mimic strode as casually as he could towards the other end of the room where he assumed he'd find an exit.

He was in ER, and family members were mixed in with the staff and milled around patients that had recently been admitted. The aroma of faeces and disinfectant wafted into his nostrils, but it was the other familiar underlying scent that he could differentiate.

He encountered it all the time in his line of work. Humans didn't need to rot before he could detect it. It was the stale smell of vacated space, like a room gets when nobody visits it. The odour was instantaneous with humans. Although the hospital wing looked clean and new, the essence settled over everything like malign dew.

As he turned into the corridor and looked down the line of faces attending their loved ones on gurneys, as they waited to be allotted a space on the ward, he speculated how close he'd been to adding the bouquet of his own death to the atmosphere. He knew not everyone got a warning shot. For some it was wham-bam, keel over in the shower, ma'am.

How had he arrived there? Mimic couldn't remember anything beyond trying to leave the house. Had he got outside? He had a vague recollection of making it there, but knew he hadn't driven himself to the hospital. Someone must have rung an ambulance. It was a good job he hadn't been carrying a firearm. He had a lot to thank the sick fuck with the ketchup bottle for. Whoever had summoned the emergency services, it looked like they'd saved his life.

He wondered if they would have, if they'd known that perpetuating his would mean an end to others. And then he considered that it actually could have been his target, Marcia O'Doole, who had made the call.

CHAPTER THIRTY

When Beth returned from her first visit to the local surgery, she didn't know how she felt about being told that everything was "on track". The midwife seemed too young, but Beth had sat and nodded as she'd been lectured about the folic acid supplements she should have been taking during the time that had elapsed, and how she now needed vitamin D and why eating healthily was vital.

She'd been offered a date scan, but Beth had told her why she knew exactly how pregnant she was. The midwife had then said respectfully little as she'd checked her blood pressure and measured her BMI. Blood and urine samples had been taken, and she was then given a date to return for her sixteen week antenatal appointment. It was in three weeks' time.

She wanted to tuck it to the back of her mind. As far as she was concerned, it was something happening the other side of a barrier. Beth was still standing behind it, trying to process the remnants of the past not the future. But those seemed to be rapidly deteriorating.

Another clip had been taken down. That left only three. Is this what naturally happened? Beth assumed that once you posted something on YouTube, it was there forever. It was the sequence that captured Cigarillo Man being interviewed by the police, that had been uploaded by Spike666. It seemed very odd that two uploads of the same incident would vanish within such a short space of time.

She recalled what had happened to Trip Stillman, the drummer from Blood Legend. Attacked in his own home around the same time his recording had been removed.

She watched the one she'd cued up which showed Rae Salomon's alarm at being captured by so many phone cameras. It stopped her dead in her tracks, and Beth paused her expression. She recalled the fear in Rae's voice when she'd spoken of the man who pursued her. She'd been convinced her presence at the crash and appearance in the clips had led to her discovery.

It sounded like Rae had been caught up with some brutal people. But, even if she were, why would criminals want to remove the recordings? They were trying to locate her. What would they gain from deleting them? She was being foolish. It was just coincidence.

She was indulging her new appetite for paranoia when she had something much more immediate to concern herself with. But her encounter in the woods with Roland and Erik was needling her, too. Had the two of them been concealing something?

Beth was only torturing herself by continually watching the uploads. Shouldn't she be grateful for the fact the evidence of her ordeal was slowly dwindling? But what would be the reason for taking something down, unless there was a copyright issue or a threat of legal action?

She continued playing the "smilingassassin" clip. She'd planned to watch all of them again, volume up, to see if she could discern anything else that Luc might have said. But the noise from the crowd stepped on anything that was going on the other side of the road, and she already knew this would be the case in all of them.

She watched Luc murmuring to Rae as she held his hand. Whoever had recorded it was too far away. Even with the word firmly implanted, she couldn't really make out the shape his lips were forming.

Allegro.

There were no other uploads on smilingassassin's channel and no links to other sites. Beth sent them a message via YouTube, asking if they'd shot it themselves. She watched again, and heard Jody demonstrably slam his studio door. He was telling her it was time to stop.

When she heard the knock at Jody's front door later that day, Beth had no intention of answering. He'd said nobody of any importance would arrive on his doorstep when he was out, so it was how she dealt with all of his day callers. It certainly wouldn't be her parents, as they'd telephoned and were expecting her to visit them.

Out of duty, though, she looked down at the visitor from Jody's lounge window expecting to see a postman or delivery guy. A face was awaiting Beth's appearance, tilted upwards in readiness to intercept her. It was the dark suited figure of Jerome McIntyre.

Beth quickly leaned away from the pane as if the reflex would wipe away his obvious recognition of her. "Shit." She dipped back, smiled then indicated she was on her way down.

How the hell had he found the address? She had a strong suspicion. Her conversation with Jerome was long overdue, however. There was so much at stake, and she owed it to Luc to make sure she didn't make things too easy for him.

When she opened the door, his salt-and-pepper eyebrows had already gathered in a sympathetic cluster on the bridge of his nose. His matching beard was fuller and his hair looked longer than usual and unkempt.

"Hi, Beth. I didn't want to catch you at a bad time. But then I realised that every day is going to be a bad time, so I want to keep this as brief as possible." It sounded like he'd rehearsed it.

"Would you like to come inside?" She didn't feel comfortable saying it about someone else's home.

"No, really. I'm afraid I used the thumbscrews on your

mother, but please don't be angry with her. First of all, I wanted to say how sorry I am for what happened... personally."

It looked as if he'd put on a little more weight since she'd last seen him. And the extra wrinkle below his chin seemed to confirm this. He was standing awkwardly, an attaché case stuffed under his arm that appeared to put his whole body off balance. Or was he drunk? His red complexion seemed to suggest so, but Beth was aware he suffered from high blood pressure. But even though she knew exactly what he was doing at Jody's, she couldn't bring herself to be cold towards someone who had just lost Luc from his life as well.

"Thanks, Jerome." She waited for him to move onto the real reason for his visit.

"And I feel very uncomfortable about being here but... as you haven't returned any of my calls..." He visibly squirmed. "If it was up to me, I'd want you to take as long as you need before you have to address anything like this, but a lot of pressure is being exerted from other quarters..."

"What do you need from me, Jerome? And, for God's sake, come in."

"No, really, I know I'm imposing. Credit me with a little more sensitivity than that." For a moment he seemed genuinely hurt. "I just need you to look over this interim contract." He opened the attaché case and extracted the document. "I feel sick about this, Beth." As Jerome gulped dryly, she realised how nervous he really was. "Basically, it temporarily transfers executive responsibility to me until such time as you want to discuss matters in more depth. It just means I'm able to run things day-to-day. I simply need your signature."

She took the paper from him and his hand was shaking.

"Run it past somebody. I'd expect that." His dark blue eyes held hers for emphasis. "Just call the office when you're ready. Sorry again for this." He turned to leave.

"Jerome..."

He spun back, as if having to return his gaze to her was painful.

"Thank you for going to Rouen for Luc's funeral." It seemed like the strangest thing she'd said since waking up, but Beth was satisfied she hadn't made it sound bitter. "My mother said you were very attentive."

Jerome shook his head and blinked away her gratitude.

"Give my love to Lin." Despite her mistrust of Jerome, she'd always been conscientious about maintaining contact with his wife, even when he and Luc had been at loggerheads.

Jerome opened his mouth to say something and then didn't. He recovered quickly, though. "I certainly will."

"Something wrong?"

"Lin and I are… not really together at the moment." He looked at her waist when he said it. "I've moved out temporarily. I'm sure things will work themselves out." He didn't meet her eye as he turned back down the steps.

She watched him get into the back of the red Lexus that was waiting for him and get hastily driven off.

CHAPTER THIRTY-ONE

As Mimic strode towards the O'Doole home, he was suddenly aware of a volume of birdsong he hadn't noticed on his previous visits. The sky was an unclouded azure blue and the sun was warm on his skin. A voice at the back of his skull, usually louder than it was now, reminded him of his itinerary and the delay his health issue had already caused. The cab had dropped him off and he'd confirmed his Toyota was still parked a block away, where he'd left it the night before.

He stopped at the rows of freshly planted cherry trees that demarcated the long strip of grass at the edge of the road. There were deep wheel marks in it. Had it been his unconscious body on a gurney that had made them? He looked across the street to the green there. No house opposite. If he'd collapsed here, it must have been Mrs O'Doole who had seen him and called the ambulance.

As he ambled casually to the front door, he considered how alternative events might have precluded him from being here. He couldn't deny he owed Mrs O'Doole a debt of gratitude.

He waited for his doorbell ring to activate bumps in the house. No sound. It was Saturday morning. Maybe the whole family had gone into town. He rubbed his jaw as he waited. He felt fine now. It had been a warning. One that was significant enough to make him consider booking himself in for a private medical examination when his work was squared away, however.

He heard footfalls on carpeted stairs. One of the boys, or Mrs O'Doole? The muscles in his legs tautened. If it were her, she would surely recognise him. If she'd watched him being loaded into the ambulance, she'd know exactly who he was. He would greet her and thank her. Maybe she'd invite him in for a cup of coffee and make his job easier.

"Just a minute." A woman's voice and then scrabbling with the locks.

It was her.

The door opened and Mimic had the newly purchased ketchup bottle out of his pocket in time to slam it into the middle of her forehead. In the instant he'd heard her voice, Mimic had decided he didn't want to look her in the eye while she was still alive. The force of the blow was so great that the bottle cracked and the bottom of it dropped onto the hallway carpet as he stood over her.

It was easy to discern which was blood and which was ketchup though. Mimic quickly snapped on his blue surgical gloves.

CHAPTER THIRTY-TWO

"Hi, Lin. It's me." It was the first time Beth had picked up the telephone to call a friend since she'd been discharged from hospital.

"Beth? Oh my God." Lin swallowed loudly.

"Are you OK?"

"Am I OK?" she said incredulously. "I'm sorry, I really didn't know if I should call you there. I spoke to your parents and they said you were staying with your brother. They offered me his number, but I figured you wanted some time alone." Her words tumbled over each other.

"I have been hiding out..." Beth heard Lin take a trembling intake of breath.

"I'm so sorry about Luc." She sniffed. "I can't imagine what the past weeks have been like for you."

"Jerome was just here."

Lin sighed. "I told him not to call on you until you were ready."

"It was fine. Really. I understand. He can't allow Avellana to fall apart."

"It will now. You know that, don't you."

The statement startled Beth. On the occasions they'd dined with Jerome and Lin at their ultra-modern home, they'd always presented a united front, maintaining Luc was responsible for nothing more than half of its success. "He mentioned he'd moved out..."

"He told you?"

"Yes. Temporarily, he said."

"He might have said thát, but I don't think there's any way back for us." Lin's statement terminated in a whisper.

It was a typical Lin conversation. It entirely orbited her, even given what Beth had been through. But she was glad of it. Was happy to shift the focus from her. "I'm so sorry, Lin. It's none of my business. Just be sure."

"Of what?"

"That this can't be saved. Ask yourself if never seeing him again will be his punishment or yours."

"It wasn't Jerome's fault." Her voice thickened. "Jerome hasn't done anything wrong."

Beth was momentarily dumbstruck. Jerome had an eye for the ladies. He'd flirted with her on several occasions and made her more than a little uncomfortable. She'd assumed...

"It's my fault, Beth. I don't deserve to be forgiven."

"But it sounds as if that's exactly what Jerome wants to do."

"Jerome's forgiveness wouldn't even be the start..." Emotion spilt over.

Beth listened to her and surprised herself by how resentful she felt. Tears for a husband that was still alive, that Lin could still reach. Or was it because Beth hadn't yet shed them for the man she would never see again?

"Can we meet?" Lin's voice was suddenly clear, as if it were the product of a sudden determination.

"Lin, I'm not sure I'm ready...'

Silence on the other end.

Beth tried to pre-empt further sobs. She didn't want to hear them. "Although it would be good to see you again..."

Mimic was sitting in the car looking at the backs of his hands. They weren't shaking, but felt light, as if they'd float upwards, lifting his arms above his head. As a kid, he remembered his brother getting him to stand in a doorway and press his knuckles against both sides of the frame and count to thirty. When he let his arms slacken, they rose like they were on invisible wires. It was the sensation he was experiencing now, and Mimic wondered if it was a side effect of his attack. He anticipated the pain in his jaw again and wondered if he should still be hospitalised. He had work to do, though, and they'd only pump him full of meds. Mimic hated taking even an aspirin.

He'd followed the MO to the letter. Used the bottle on the woman exactly as the perp had at the other crime scene, and all the time he was doing it, the same thought that always occurred to him played through his head. He was giving the real guy an airtight alibi. If he was ever arrested, it was likely he'd be able to prove he'd been elsewhere when Mimic's duplication was carried out.

But while he'd used the jagged glass to deface the looks and genitals of a healthy woman, another thought had been paramount. He'd given the sick fuck an alibi and achieved nothing. Was he slacking because it was his last contract, or just turning into a doddering old fart?

The woman lying dead in the house wasn't Marcia O'Doole. He'd allowed his focus to shift. Only briefly, but while he'd considered that the target he was about to bludgeon had probably saved his life and he was about to repay her by murdering her two sons, he'd relinquished control. He'd tried to hasten a procedure he should have been a hundred percent removed from.

The woman had been the same sort of age, height and build as Marcia. It had been an understandable but still inexcusable mistake to make. Who was she? Her sister, by the looks. The sons had been absent from the house when he'd searched it as well. He'd found instructions for watering plants that had been left for the house-sitter, and there had been dust outlines on tops of the wardrobes where the suitcases had been taken down. Where had Marcia O'Doole and her family gone?

He hadn't found anything on either of their computers to indicate where they were headed. No vacation-booking emails, nothing. He'd sat on Mrs O'Doole's bed and communicated with his contact at the NCS. As an ex-operative, he still had significant currency with a lot of key staff. Accessing phones and credit card transactions was easily achieved, but they'd turned up nothing. Yet. Kevin O'Doole was a Facebook junkie, though. They were probably on the road now but it wouldn't take long for them to leave a footprint online.

He'd track them like he had so many of his other targets. His movements connected him to some of the vilest scum in twenty-three US states alone. It was rich territory for his line of work. His jigsaw personality was a global one, however, and his crimes peppered Interpol's database.

His technique not only covered his trail but also made it someone else's. He had become, amongst many identities, serial killers, random drive-by gunmen, terrorist bombers, Chechen and Namibian Mafia, Bratva, Yakuza and myriad organised and disorganised crime gangs of varying nationalities.

Whether he'd used it to kill single or multiple individuals, however, he'd only replicated another's method once. More than that meant he was stimulating his own chain of evidence and significantly threw any ongoing investigation. He was grateful for the mask he could wear, but he always handed it quickly back.

With one impersonation, either the police suspected the original perp or, if they couldn't be convicted for Mimic's crime, a one-off local copycat. And he was long gone by the time they had the right man in custody. If that ever happened.

He took an interest in those whose styles he'd adopted. If they were ever arrested, it was a chink in his armour. But it happened shockingly infrequently, and the lack of police success was breathtaking. There were only nineteen people who had been convicted of crimes that had included his.

From his position, Mimic could see the smoke curling out of the top of the house. Even though the body was downstairs, he'd set the fire in the bedroom as the perp had in the other apartment. He'd planned to tell Mrs O'Doole why it had all been necessary, and it was a conversation he still had to have with her. He started the engine and pulled the car out of its spot to make room for the fire trucks to access the street.

CHAPTER THIRTY-THREE

Lin was seated in the corner of Costa with an ivory jacquard trench coat belted around her as if she were ready to flee. Beth had never seen her slender frame looking so slouched, and her dark hair was pinned up in a messy bun. Normally confident and impeccably made up, her Chinese-Malaysian features were puffy, her eyes and pallor betraying lack of sleep. Beth wondered if she was back on the prescription medication Jerome confided she'd developed an addiction to. She rose as Lin reached the table.

"I'm so sorry." She hugged Beth tight.

Beth felt awkward and didn't know how long to maintain the embrace. She took in the abstract painting on the wall behind them as she waited to be released.

There was moisture in Lin's gaze when she finally let go. "How are you getting along with your brother?" she asked, sensing Beth's awkwardness.

"He's been a sweetheart."

Lin seated herself and Beth noticed she didn't have a cup before her. She dropped into the chair opposite.

Lin composed herself, wiped away the strands of hair that were sticking to her face and dabbed a bunched tissue at the raw edges of her wet nose. "I know you two aren't close."

How did she know that? But then, they'd had a fair share

145

of wine chats. "I seem to be getting to know him for the first time. How are you holding out?" She knew it was the question Lin had been waiting for.

"Not good." It looked as if she were about to lose control again.

Wasn't Lin meant to be consoling her? As Lin had no children or family, she usually assumed the only worthy topic of conversation was the minutiae of her middle-class universe. Had she really offered to meet Beth because she wanted to convey her condolences, or because she didn't have any other friends to talk to about her break-up with Jerome?

"I feel... like I've been emptied out."

Beth nodded and put her hand inside her shoulder bag for a fresh tissue. She extracted a packet and gave one to Lin.

She took it and pressed it against both eyelids. When she removed it, the remainder of her mascara was smudged there. But the expression on her face said even she realised how incongruous her behaviour was in front of Beth. "I'm sorry. This is the very last thing you need."

Beth didn't know what to say to her, so just shrugged her shoulders. She eyed the tissues; they'd been redundant to her since she'd woken in hospital.

A black droplet darted down Lin's face.

Beth supposed they were kind of on the same page. Even though Lin had Jerome walk out, for whatever reason, they'd both lost the man from their lives, whether it was because of death or a stupid lapse of judgement. But at least Lin still had choices. "Why do you believe it's so definitely over for you two?"

Lin fixed her, the intensity of her regard obscured by tears and her lips suddenly sealed against more words emerging. Then she rose. "I shouldn't have come here. I'm sorry." She moved past Beth and headed for the door, her jasmine scent wafting over Beth.

Beth didn't call after her but stayed in her chair looking at the abstract. A thought had already pricked the back of her

RICHARD PARKER   147

mind. It had when Lin had spoken to her on the telephone.

Jerome's forgiveness wouldn't even be the start.

She knew Luc and Lin had worked closely together. Was Lin really so upset because of her infidelity and Jerome leaving, or was it about the other man she could no longer see?

CHAPTER THIRTY-FOUR

Beth's mistrust of iPhones was further reinforced when, sitting on her single bed, she decided to turn hers on because she was waiting to receive her list of appointments from the clinic. She was just checking her messages when she found the email. It had just one word in the subject heading:

Allegro

Her heartbeat skittered. The sender's address was a long jumble of letters, symbols and numbers. It didn't have anything suspect attached to it but, even though the communication begged immediate attention, she hovered her finger over it for a few seconds. It was almost as if she knew touching it would activate something.

She tapped the screen and was asked if confirmation of her opening it could be sent. She paused momentarily before hitting "OK."

I know you're looking for answers. Please delete this email once you've read it.

Our exchanges must remain private. If they don't, I won't be in touch again.

If I can trust you, contact me on Facebook (Eileen Froley) by requesting friendship and posting the words "How did the concert go?" on my wall.

That was it. Beth noted it had been sent at 4.40 that

morning. Had the sender been waiting for her all this time? Could it be Rae? How did she get her email address? It hadn't come via the jawbone2014 Facebook or YouTube accounts she'd set up.

She logged in to Facebook and searched for Eileen Froley. There she was – a middle-aged woman with red-framed spectacles and mousy, permed hair. She was in Cape Elizabeth, Maine. There were photos of her smiling and straddling a cello. She searched the name again but that was the only result.

Beth stabbed the friend request and waited. It was immediately confirmed.

She typed: *How did the concert go?*

Beth waited but no reply came. Then another friendship request appeared. It was from "Allegro". She clicked through to the page. The account had just been created. There were no images or location details. She confirmed the friend request. A dialogue box popped up at the bottom of the screen.

I've been waiting.

Beth's jaw began to throb and she responded: *Who are you?*
Allegro.

Beth swallowed tightly.

Is this Rae?

There was a long pause before the reply came. Whoever the person was, wherever they were, they were obviously considering their response carefully.

This is the wrong channel for that discussion. We should meet.
Where are you?
I have posted details on my BriskyPix page. Look for me there.

They logged out. Beth put "BriskyPix" into a search and hit the link. It was a new image-sharing site. She searched members for Allegro and selected their account. The page opened and she found an image and a message left for her there.

The airbrushed photo was of a pier containing an illuminated big wheel against a purple night sky taken from across pale yellow sands. Below the snap it said:

Beth, Crescent Bay Oyster Shack, 1885 Appian Way, Santa Monica, CA 90401. Tell me when you're ready to meet here. No more questions answered until you do. Just post "Good luck with Beethoven 5" on Eileen's wall when you are. I will contact you to arrange a date and time.

Beth was sure she hadn't just fallen for an intricate online scam. Was this where Rae was hiding, and was she really expected to travel all the way to LA on the basis of a few online exchanges?

Whoever it was could be assured of that, however, as soon as they'd used the word Luc had uttered as he'd died at the roadside. At least, the word Rae had told her he'd uttered.

Beth studied the picture and imagined herself standing on the pier. She did a quick search for the Oyster Shack and gleaned from its website that it was a small seafood restaurant that operated near Santa Monica Pier. Smiling diners used their fingers to tuck into shellfish served on newspaper spread over tables. It was obviously a very public and family-oriented place. Was that a deliberate ploy to make her feel more secure about the rendezvous?

CHAPTER THIRTY-FIVE

Whoever had contacted her was asking her to take a massive leap of faith. But there was no question she would go. The trip to Neuf-Marché had given her direction and led her to Allegro. This was the second stage of a journey she had to make, and it didn't matter how far it took her. Besides, since her return from Normandy, she'd been itching to escape again.

Beth wanted to be anywhere but sitting in Jody's flat, calculating the volume of legal and Avellana paperwork that would have to be surmounted before she could find some space to grieve properly. Why should she delay? What had she to detain her?

She looked down at her stomach, touched it tenderly and thought about the two inches of life inside her. It was growing quickly, and soon it would take possession of her. Beth still didn't know how she felt about that. She was juggling that and the implications of what Lin had said to her, not wanting to grasp either thought for too long.

She closed the BriskyPix page, punched up Lin's number and looked at it until her iPhone went into standby. How could she possibly accuse her? It was ludicrous. Luc had never spent any time outside Avellana away from her. Their weekends had always been sacred. There wasn't one occasion she could recall when he'd made an excuse to spend a night elsewhere.

She detested herself for even entertaining the suspicion. But Luc and Lin had worked together for nine years, eight hours a day, five days a week. She touched the screen and hit the number. She would ask her outright whom she'd been seeing. She listened to it ring and it went to her answering service.

She hung up. It was ridiculous. But Beth didn't like the sense of relief she felt about not having the conversation.

"Who do you know in LA?" Jody shifted awkwardly around in his swivel chair and put his bottle of Sprite on the studio desk

"Nobody who could look after me as well as you have." Her brother's features softened, but she knew she hadn't placated him. "I think I just need to get away from everything here."

He nodded slowly, his disapproval obvious.

Beth knew what he was thinking. "OK – run away for a while," she admitted.

"I understand that, Beth..."

It was strange to hear him use her name. She wasn't sure of the last time he'd done that. Probably when they were kids. She remained in his doorway, unsure of whether he was comfortable with her venturing any further inside. It was the first time she'd invaded his cluttered workspace. There was a piano keyboard in front of two slim screens and stacks of dusty mixing desks weighing down the shelves behind him. The floor was carpeted with a mass of tangled wires. A plug-in cinnamon air freshener barely combated the smell of body odour.

"But why as far as LA? I can speak to the agency about the condo, but couldn't I just drive you somewhere here? At least then I can pick you up when you're ready."

Her emotions prickled and she felt her resolve waver. But she couldn't let Jody's obviously protective gesture deter her. "I just need a complete change of scene. Plus, all the Californian sunshine will be a good source of vitamin D." She was using the baby as an excuse and they both knew it. Beth could see he suspected she had another agenda. "Trust me. I need this trip."

He took a sip from the bottle so he could break eye contact. "Look, whatever you want. You have to tell me exactly where you go, though."

It was what she'd hoped for. Jody clearly thought she was still emotionally unstable. Probably envisaged her wandering onto a freeway. But she did want someone to be looking out for her, even from thousands of miles away.

"When was the last time you were there?"

She'd been to Universal Studios in Hollywood. Had worked her way around the major US cities when she'd been a penurious student. "Stop worrying about me. At least you'll know exactly where I am."

He seemed slightly reassured by that.

"My next antenatal appointment isn't for nearly three weeks. I'm going to spank some plastic, relax by your communal pool, and maybe go to Beverly Hills for some pamperage."

Jody nodded his disapproval again.

CHAPTER THIRTY-SIX

"Don't wave it at me!" Marcia covered her mouth with one hand and stifled a laugh.

Tyler gripped the dead raccoon using one yellow rubber glove. The bottom half of its body had rotted clean away. Only one leg remained, and that was hanging off by a sinew. "I think it's dead. What do you think?" He held it inches from her face now.

Kevin took a snap of the attack with his iPhone.

"I'm warning you, Tyler." She tried to keep her expression straight. "Take it outside."

"Want some, skidmark?" Tyler swung the raccoon carcass in Kevin's direction.

He'd been standing behind his brother, looking through his phone, but his expression turned to abject horror. He stumbled back and knocked the box of groceries off the kitchen table. Cans scattered and tomatoes rolled.

"Tyler, that's enough." But Marcia couldn't deny she'd enjoyed seeing the sadistic glee on Kevin's face evaporate. "I'm serious. Put that in the trash and help your brother clean up or we won't be going to Elkhorns."

They'd all detected the smell as soon as they'd unlocked the front door. It had happened on more than one occasion. Raccoons were great climbers. The animals got trapped in the attic crawlspace and died there. It was a familiar aroma to be greeted by. Bizarrely, it had become a "your vacation starts here" ritual.

Tyler lunged once more at Kevin with the animal, but Marcia knew it would be the last gesture of defiance. He reluctantly butted the screen with his shoulder and carried the raccoon outside.

"Kevin, they're rolling under the refrigerator."

Her youngest pocketed his iPhone and started gathering up the rogue groceries. Ted had always drilled the boys, while Marcia had concentrated on feeding them and making sure they looked presentable. Now she was responsible for all three.

She'd always thought she would be the one to buckle under the pressure of what the boys demanded from her every day, but when Ted had split, Marcia had no choice but to assume his duties. She'd been surprised at how little he'd contributed bar his salary, but she knew they still needed a father figure. Despite her being a Montana native, Ted was the one who'd used to take them hunting and out onto the river in his motorboat. He'd always filled their vacation with boys' pursuits, enjoying the fire-building, cookouts and canoeing as much as they had.

Whispering Brook, the vacation hunt lodge with the increasingly flea-bitten animal heads in the den, belonged to her folks, but they were getting more infirm, so the six-room property on the edge of the Flathead was empty most of the year. She liked to come stay in the fall or early spring. With fewer vacationers, they got the place to themselves. It wasn't exactly wilderness. West Glacier village was less than a mile away and Martin City only ten. But it was sufficiently removed from civilisation to feel like a getaway.

Despite her upbringing, Marcia never liked the idea of renting somewhere too isolated, didn't want to be far from other people. There were so many ways for the boys to endanger themselves. She couldn't think about that too much.

But, as Ted had pointed out on their first family vacation here, there were probably more immediate dangers in Auburn.

Ted was out of the equation now, though. No tree-climbing, trap-building or target practice. His guns had been locked away, and the boys weren't allowed to take the boat out without her being present. The keys to both were always in her pocket.

Marcia pushed the screen and looked down the jetty to the afternoon sun coruscating on the dirty blue water. She tried to breathe in the chilly serenity, but Tyler was scraping his gloved hand on the edge of the trashcan with a look of disgust. He glanced up at her and was obviously mortified to be found looking as repelled by the carcass as his mother.

"Raccoon fudge," he said, trying to salvage his image.

Marcia wrinkled her nose for his benefit. "Come and get washed, squirt." She didn't know why she suddenly used the term. It was Ted's and she'd always hated it.

Tyler grinned uncomfortably and it reminded her of the way he'd smirked when they'd had the conversation about the porno stars on his laptop.

He scuffed past her and into the lodge. He was nineteen next month, and Marcia was sure her parents would have been shocked to know what she had at that age. Besides, where did she get off lecturing him about exploitation? She was the one who encouraged Tyler to upload his phone clip of the British couple to his YouTube channel. Had she thought about their dignity when she'd seen an opportunity to make a fast buck?

There had been so much online interest in that woman's assault on the crowd. To begin with, she'd squared it by telling herself she'd been pissed because her son had been on the receiving end of her fists. Tyler hadn't got as much as a scratch from the episode, though. He shouldn't have used his phone to shoot something like that. But some of his friends had. Peer pressure. It was how the world operated today. Everything got recorded and sometimes it was a damn good thing. It was like another form of insurance.

Marcia had seen how one of the other YouTube clips had attracted advertisers, and decided her own family's precarious financial predicament overrode any issues of privacy the couple would have expected in that moment.

When she got Tyler to upload the clip, she certainly hadn't known the woman's husband had died. Not immediately. It had happened in France, and the couple was from the UK. It had taken weeks for that to filter back. But she still hadn't told Tyler to take it down.

She'd never been to France or Europe. It had cost her a small fortune for Tyler to go on that student exchange. Ted had said it was way too expensive. But her oldest had wanted to go so much, and she'd known he might never get another opportunity. That and Ted's opposition had made her mind up. They were still financially recovering.

And if it wasn't for the revenue generated by the clip, they wouldn't be on vacation now. Tyler liked dinner at Elkhorns, and she wanted to take him there every night if he wanted. She followed him back into the lodge and wondered how her older sister Jess was doing back home. She'd jumped at the chance to house-sit. Marcia's brother-in-law Tim was drinking again, and when he hit the bottle, looking after Marcia's place was her only safe haven from it.

CHAPTER THIRTY-SEVEN

Beth was a hopeless international flier. Time dislocation wrought weeks of bad sleep long afterwards. Her gastric and respiratory health usually deteriorated as well. She thought it might be something to do with the air con on long haul flights. It was why she and Luc had stuck to Europe for the majority of their trips.

She'd tried different approaches – sleep medication, the anti-jet-lag diet and knocking herself out by drinking copious Tanqueray-and-tonics to try to blindside her body clock. None of them worked, and she always woke in the early hours feeling oddly removed. Maybe as that feeling had attended her since opening her eyes in hospital, she would feel normal when she got to LA. She doubted it, particularly as her very reason for flying there was so surreal.

She wondered if the person who had emailed her really expected her to rise to the bait. Was it merely a piece of amusement for them? She envisaged being stood up at the Crescent Bay Oyster Shack. But there was no way she could live with herself if she didn't at least attempt to make contact with the person who called himself or herself Allegro.

She thought of Jody waving her off after he'd dropped her by departures and the uneasiness on his face as she'd left. It was the same expression he'd had when she'd arrived home with her hair shorn. He still didn't believe she was thinking straight. Had brain trauma impaired her rational thought and left her unstable? Her old logical self wouldn't have been on this flight. She'd concealed her reasons for the trip from him because she'd known exactly what he'd say. Was this what Luc used to do – running hard to forget who he was?

The stewardess arrived at her aisle seat. Thankfully, the middle one was unoccupied, so she had plenty of elbow room. A woman in her sixties slept soundly at the window. Beth had thought she was going to chat to her the whole way, but her grunting snooze started before take-off. Three hours later, she still hadn't woken. Beth felt slightly jealous.

The stewardess looked over to Beth's companion and thought better of it. "Refreshment?" she softly asked.

"Just a soda water, please."

The stewardess handed her a can and a fresh cup full of ice, and moved to the row behind her.

Beth had quickly researched flying when pregnant online and discovered that there were no major disadvantages, unless she had blood pressure issues. Her morning sickness might make the trip even more uncomfortable than usual. She was frequently nauseous on flights. Perhaps one would cancel the other out – or, more likely, join forces.

Should she really be subjecting her baby to more upheaval? It had already been exposed to enough traumas, and she dreaded that the crash, her hospitalisation and the suspended sense of bereavement she felt had already had a deep-seated effect on the fragile life inside her. But the truth was, she felt as disconnected from the child as she did from everything else. She hoped that would change soon.

She didn't want to countenance the idea that a new life would replace Luc's, but considered how its arrival would shift the spotlight from her. She wanted that more than anything else. But was it fair to give a person a life that could be wrenched away – in a manner she could already envisage?

If the baby arrived safely, she knew she'd be asking herself the same question thousands of times in the future. But life would throw up plenty of other obstacles and dangers from the moment it left her womb. She couldn't safeguard against any of those, and that wouldn't be an argument for not going through with the pregnancy.

When would be the right time to tell them? Luc's parents had kept the condition from him until he'd been eleven years old. He'd resented them for that, said he felt he would have handled it better had they sat him down when he'd been a much younger child. That he would have been more receptive to the revelation when he didn't fully understand it. If he'd grown with the knowledge, Luc said he would have been better equipped to gradually accept it.

As it was, his mother had dropped the bomb just after his father had died. Barely had he got to grips with the concept of losing him when he was told he might suffer the same protracted agony he'd witnessed first-hand.

But Beth felt like she already understood why she'd waited. When was the best time to present a ticking clock, to remove innocence from your child like that? Would she persuade them to take the test when they were eighteen? Not knowing had acted like a spur with Luc. He'd achieved so much in his life because of the potential restraint that had been put on it.

She imagined herself sitting with her son, his arms folded. Sitting with her daughter, Beth's hand on hers. Whoever was waiting to fill that moment, she couldn't allow their father to become obscure to them – or her. She wanted to be able to tell them everything about who he was, and until he'd whispered things she didn't understand at the roadside, she thought she could. Now Beth had questions she had to answer.

She kept her hands where they were, palms resting gently on her stomach, and slowly breathed the cooled, processed air in through her nostrils. Sickness lurked on the fringes of sleep, so she kept her eyes on the screen in front of her and watched the plane's progress across the Atlantic.

Then it struck her. She'd been so seduced by the idea of escape and chasing one word, so misdirected by packing and booking the flights, she hadn't stopped to consider how much of a coincidence it was that the place they'd asked to meet her happened to be where Jody had his condo.

Beth remembered the phone call she'd received immediately after Rae had rung her in the car and the person hanging up. Was she being monitored? After all the Facebook subterfuge, she wondered if they were they capable of accessing the details of Jody's timeshare via his computer.

Whoever had arranged the meeting had certainly made it very easy for her to be lured from the UK.

CHAPTER THIRTY-EIGHT

The air in LAX airport didn't feel any warmer than the climate Beth had left behind her in the UK. As she passed along the blue rat-runs of passport control, she felt oddly alert. The other passengers shuffled through the process in a zombified state, and she was able to examine the faces around her without any fear of them meeting her eye.

It was almost as if she'd woken from a refreshing sleep, which couldn't have been further from the truth. She'd remained awake for the entire flight, abstractedly staring through the latest Ryan Gosling movie, only eventually realising she'd watched it twice as it completed its loop.

She retrieved her single Samsonite case from the carousel and wheeled it to arrivals. She wouldn't post on Eileen Froley's Facebook wall yet. Beth wanted to check things out first. Then she would alert whoever it was to her presence. Even though she had the gate code details, she'd already decided to bypass Jody's condo in Woodland Hills and book into a hotel.

Warmer air blasted at her through the open window of the yellow cab she picked up outside the airport. Beth told her driver to take her to Santa Monica Boulevard. As the car turned off Century Boulevard and hit the San Diego Freeway Beth looked up at the tall green signs and glimpsed faraway palms between the buildings. It gave Beth the sensation of

being in a Martian landscape. From her closeted life at Jody's
to suddenly being in the middle of such an unfamiliar urban
expanse made her feel completely vulnerable. As they reached
their destination, she asked the rodent-featured cabbie with
the nicotine stripe through his silver moustache to drop her at
the first hotel she spotted.

The extra couple of dollars' tip were scarcely in his palm
before the vehicle drew away and left her standing in front of
the sliding reception doors of the Francisquito Boutique Hotel.

The place clearly operated behind a thin veneer of
respectability, but the warm welcome of the receptionist in the
metallic purple bikini top at the desk dispelled her temptation
to turn around and find somewhere else.

"Checking in?" The words squeezed around the peroxide
beam, but Beth noticed her dark green eyes looked exhausted.
As she moved closer she realised that, even though the
woman's henna hair was braided in a circle around her head,
she was probably in her late fifties. Beth said she hadn't made
a reservation and the receptionist consulted the computer
for a vacancy. She squinted, put on her half glasses and then
positioned her face almost flat against the screen.

The low sucking noise of a filter directed Beth's gaze
beyond the desk to the tiny swimming pool set into the raised
concrete platform in the cramped back courtyard. Nobody
was using the two loungers positioned there, and two faded
inflatable animals buffeting against each other took up most
of the water space.

As she blinked at the system Beth noticed the silver roots
bisecting the centre of the receptionist's scalp as well as scars
on her deeply tanned arms. They looked like notches on a
post, and Beth wondered what sort of trauma each one
represented. She tried not to speculate if she was a self-harmer
or if someone else had carved them there. The woman seemed
to personify the place she was booking into. She looked up
with relief to say she had a room for her, and her smile didn't

falter as her eyes briefly lingered on the flaws around the left side of Beth's mouth. Looked like she was right at home.

The receptionist got Beth a swipe key from a drawer. "You're in room 234, one floor above ground; the elevator's to your right. Sorry, left."

Beth thanked the receptionist and examined the cracked key. The hotel didn't look big enough to have 23 rooms, let alone 234. She picked up her luggage and got into a tiny clattering metal crate when it eventually arrived. She had to straddle her small case to fit inside.

Her room was dated but spotlessly clean. The air con sounded as if it had emphysema. She scraped the mushroom curtains along the rail and looked down at the inflatables in the pool. A few potted orange trees surrounded it, and their small dark leaves covered the surface.

After a shower and a change, she left the hotel and used her iPhone to navigate her way to the pier. Beth made her way downtown via Colorado Avenue, looking for a cab or bus, but decided to walk all the way. The day was heating up, but there was still a pleasant breeze along the sidewalk. She had on a mauve sweatshirt, cut-off jeans and a pair of purple All Stars, and felt completely conspicuous. The air smelt like marijuana as she walked past a row of homeless people sharing cold pizza from a box.

Nobody in the street paid her any heed, but she had the sensation of being exactly where she shouldn't. She jaywalked, crossing between the traffic and anticipating the sound of a police siren. She felt suddenly exhausted but told herself she wouldn't stop until she found the Oyster Shack. Exhaustion could play catch up later.

She turned left into Ocean Avenue and then cut down Seaside Terrace and found herself in the International Chess Park. The sand area with the wooden benches of fixed, green-chequered boards was quiet, with only a handful of children playing amongst them. From there she walked to the beach.

Even though it looked inviting, she didn't want to explore it. This wasn't a pleasure trip, and to Beth even stepping onto it seemed wrong.

The sun was breaking through the clouds, and she put her hand above her eyes to observe the tiny people moving along the pier towards the big wheel with the twinkling blue ocean beyond it. She wasn't a million miles away from where the BriskyPix image had been taken.

She inhaled the salty, sunblock-scented air, and the wind blasted at her eardrums, muffling the sounds of the people on the sand. Frisbees were being tossed, dogs were being walked and everything seemed slightly staged.

Beth consulted her iPhone again, crossed the oceanfront walk and found Appian Way. She could see the red, switched-off neon half-shell logo of the restaurant jutting out on the right-hand side and suddenly stopped in her tracks.

She looked back the way she'd come, expecting to see someone following at a discreet distance. It was ridiculous. Nobody knew she was here yet. But if they did have access to her phone or computer, they would certainly know she'd booked the tickets and had checked in online.

Lynyrd Skynyrd's "That Smell" eventually disentangled itself from the bass thud pouring out of the open door. She stood outside, the aroma of broiling shellfish and butter in her nostrils. A sign outside proclaimed:

Beware! Shuck Attack! Oysters $20/dozen Mon-Thurs!!

Looked like the lunch shift was just finishing; only a few tables were occupied by diners within the dingy interior. Three waitresses stood against the back counter with stoical expressions that said they were waiting for them to leave so they could close up. Beth took a step inside and three hostile sets of eyes regarded her.

Smiles simultaneously appeared and one of them, Chinese and looking barely sixteen, stepped forward to intercept. "Sorry, ma'am. We're closed until this evening."

Beth quickly absorbed her surroundings. Louisiana theme. Lots of framed retro ads for shrimp, clams and gumbo. The family nearest to her were finishing ice creams in enormous glasses. "No problem. What time do you open then?"

The girl's features softened with relief. "Five o'clock for happy hour."

"Thanks." She turned, grabbed a card from the stand at the waitress station and left. She was parched but decided to find a coffee bar in a different street, somewhere she could think about what to do next. She looked up and down Appian Way before making her way back to the beach.

She walked onto the pier and paced out past the big wheel and towards the ocean. It felt like only a minute later that she had gone as far as she could. The wind was keen and goose-pimpled her exposed head. She could feel the sun's heat starting to burn her scalp. Being exposed like this was foolish. She had to get into the shade.

But Beth remained where she was, leaning on the warm wooden balustrade and looking out into the blue void.

CHAPTER THIRTY-NINE

After stopping off for a chilled coffee, Beth walked back to the Francisquito and was sticky with perspiration by the time she got there. She showered again, slipped on the scratchy white hotel robe that had seen one wash too many, set her iPhone to wake her in two hours and slept fitfully.

When she woke, it felt like the gravity in the room had changed. She rose heavily, took some deep breaths to bring herself around and couldn't think of a reason to delay any longer. She seated herself cross-legged on the bed and used the iPhone to post "Good luck with Beethoven 5" on Eileen Froley's Facebook wall. She waited. Less than a minute later, a message appeared in the dialogue box.

Feeling hungry?

Am nearby. How soon can you be?

She expected her reply to momentarily startle them, but theirs was instantaneous: *10.30 reservation already made for tonight.*

She was fully awake now. They already knew she was here. Had they watched her checking out the Oyster Shack? Had they followed her back to the hotel? She glanced over to the door and then quickly typed: *How did you know?*

When she'd waited for two minutes and there was no response, she climbed off the bed and quickly locked the door. Beth thought about the receptionist downstairs and how the lobby had zero security but her. Anybody could walk in. She listened at the panel. Somebody padded past, footsteps muffled by the thick carpet. They carried on along the corridor, and she heard them descend in the elevator.

Beth picked up her shoulder bag from the back of the chair and took out the card for the Oyster Shack. It was gone 5, and when the phone was picked up, a mature female drawl shouted the name of the restaurant over the commotion of happy hour.

"Hi. I'm just calling to enquire about a booking made for tonight."

"A reservation?"

"Yes, do you have a table for 10.30?"

"Just a sec, honey."

Beth heard the phone drop onto the bar and fingers rattling a keyboard.

"We have six reservations for 10.30. Do you want to add some people to your party? What's the name?"

"That's my problem. Someone I don't know made the reservation. Can you tell me which names you have?"

"OK – I've got a party of six for Palmer…"

"No."

"Then we have a party of two for Jordan."

Beth felt like an insect had scuttled across her shoulders. "OK. Do you know when that reservation was made?"

"Sorry, couldn't tell you. I've only just come on my shift. Do you want a bigger table?"

"No, thanks. I just needed to contact the person who made the booking. I don't suppose you have their number."

"We don't take bookings without a number."

"Can you tell me what it is?"

"Sorry. I can't give out those details."

"I do really need to get in touch with them." She improvised. "I really don't want to leave him sitting there on his own."

"I see." The waitress obviously thought she did. "Letting him down gently and you don't know his surname. I shouldn't really, but as it's your table, I guess it can't hurt." The waitress read the number out. "Are you still there?"

Beth realised she hadn't responded. It was her mobile number.

"Shall I cancel this table now?"

"No. That's OK."

"Good luck then. You're not going to stand him up now, are you?"

Ramiro's cell wasn't loud, but strident enough to drag him back to the land of the living. He usually turned the ringer down before he slept, but after a long shift at the hospital, he'd just slipped into bed and unconsciousness. He tried to keep his eyes shut and stay half asleep but scrabbled for the phone on the nightstand.

"Hello?" He anticipated a familiar voice from the ward pleading for him to return earlier.

No response.

"Hello?" If this was his phone company trying to sell him a more expensive package... There was still no reply, but he was relieved not to hear the bustle of the ward. He could discern breathing, though. Then they hung up.

Ramiro switched on the lamp and tried to squint at the number. It had been withheld. He dumped the phone down on the duvet, sat up and rubbed his face. 5.33 in the afternoon. He'd only been asleep for five hours. But now he was wide awake. Once he opened his eyes, his brain immediately switched on. No gradual re-engagement, just the immediate spectre of all the study he still had to do. He might as well just catch the bus back to the hospital and go to one of the quiet recovery rooms to use the time constructively.

He spent most of his waking hours there. Ramiro only had three months left at Spring Valley and couldn't wait to finish his radiology training and settle somewhere more permanent. He'd been careful with the money he'd expended on his temporary apartment and hoped to have saved for somewhere decent by fall. Unfortunately, that meant his current accommodation wasn't in any way conducive to study or sleep.

His ears had already homed in on the kitchen fan of the Lebanese diner opposite and the daytime traffic on the freeway. And very soon the young couple upstairs would begin their physical assault of each other, whether it was fighting or another screw-a-thon.

Ramiro considered logging in and spending an hour chatting with one of his online girl friends. One of the five would surely be available. Things were getting pretty intense with his thirty-something girl from Thailand. She was becoming a fatal distraction. Plus, he hadn't been to confession for over three weeks and he'd lied to his mother about it. He would go the following weekend for absolution.

He trudged into the bathroom and looked at his pasty complexion and his normally dark, spiky hair plastered to one side of his head. Ramiro thought of what he'd do if he ever met the person who had crank-called him. It wasn't very often that aggressive thoughts came into his head, but back-to-back shifts and sleep deprivation left him in short supply of his usual good humour. If he could just have a couple of minutes with them...

He trickled some water over his fingers and scrubbed his face, not realising that very shortly he would get his wish.

CHAPTER FORTY

Why was the table booked so late? Perhaps whoever it was had to travel some distance to make the rendezvous. But any fears Beth had about the time being arranged to ensure the restaurant had emptied out for their meeting were allayed as soon as she arrived. The place was packed and the air heavy with aroma of hot seashells and garlic. Waitresses weaved between the raucous tables with trays of drinks, and a band was just finishing setting up in the corner to the right of the bar.

"I hope you have a reservation," the waitress with grey pinned up hair said over Steve Miller singing "Going To The Country".

Beth immediately recognised her voice from her earlier phone call. "Yes – table for two – Jordan."

The waitress gave her a reassuring smile. "I'm Lauren, your waitress for the evening. This way, hon."

Beth followed her weaving path through the diners and was shown to a small table only a few feet from the band. She hung her suede jacket and shoulder bag on the back of her chair.

"What can I get you to drink?"

"Just a soda water and lime, thanks."

"All righty, I'll be right back with that and some menus. Hope he's worth it."

The waitress shimmied past and Beth looked around. She

hadn't expected to find anyone waiting for her. Was the person she was meeting hidden in the drinkers seated at the bar or maybe watching her from a corner of the restaurant?

As she scanned the room, she anticipated a pair of eyes locking with hers. Rae Salomon's? But big parties filled the rest of the tables, and they were too engrossed in their seafood, precipitous stacks of onion rings and conversations to notice her.

Her drink arrived with some menus, so Beth pretended to be engrossed in the entrees. The lights dimmed so it was impossible to discern anyone's face amongst the cheering and whooping diners behind her. The band introduced themselves as Gatorbait and launched into a non-stop barrage of zydeco. A drunken couple got up and started dancing, and Beth had to lean away to avoid being whipped by the black leather tassels of the girl's jacket.

After twenty minutes had elapsed, she knew nobody was going to show. But she remained where she was until the band's first break another twenty minutes later. The lights went up and she looked at her watch for the hundredth time. Just gone 11.20. She waited until half past and left just before the band kicked off again.

"Son of a bitch." The waitress said as she handed the menus back to her at the station.

"Can I just settle up for the drink?"

"On the house, hon. If he calls, give him hell from me."

She smiled, thanked Lauren and walked out of the Oyster Shack into the cool night air. The door closed behind her and, as Beth passed the dimly lit alleyway beside the restaurant, somebody ran at her out of the darkness.

CHAPTER FORTY-ONE

An orange streetlight glow was cast over the panicked features of the diminutive but paunchy man as he emerged. Beth estimated him to be in his fifties. He was wearing a blue shirt rolled to the elbows and a toupee.

"Do you have a cell phone I can borrow?" American accent. He extended his shaky hand and gestured with his fingers.

Beth took a step back, her grip tightening on her shoulder bag.

"Sorry, I didn't mean to startle you, but there's two women back there who've been attacked. Do you know CPR?"

Beth did but, like a lot of people, everything learnt evaporated in the face of a situation that demanded it. She pulled her phone out of her bag and handed it to the man, still wary of his motives.

He put it to his face and began walking away. Beth wondered whether she'd been the victim of a devious mugging, but he turned back to her as he was connected.

"Ambulance and police, there's two women here losing a lot of blood. They've been attacked. Crescent Bay Oyster Shack, Appian and Arcadia. Yeah. I'll stay with them." He rang off and handed the phone back to Beth. "Thank you." He turned and was swallowed by shadows as he trotted back into the alleyway. She could hear a woman's low moan and then panting.

"Try not to move. Ambulance is on its way," he soothed.

Beth entered the alleyway and the darkness smelt of rotting food and disinfectant. As her eyes adjusted, she discerned the man stooping over a homeless woman. She was lying on her back in a pool of black blood that reflected the blue neon sign above the restaurant's side entrance. The sound of the band filtered through the closed door, but over it was the woman's hisses of breath as the man gripped her hands at her chest.

"Breathe slow, now. Won't be long." There was a slight southern twang there.

The woman, who was somewhere in her seventies, coughed up a dark bubble that burst over her chin. Momentarily, Beth was at the roadside again, looking at Luc bleeding and whispering to her. Syrupy blood soaked through the newspapers that were wrapped around the old woman's legs. She searched the alleyway for sign of the second victim.

The man stood and turned. "Can you stay with her while I see to the other lady?"

She nodded and knelt beside the old woman, whose eyes were bulging from her skull. Beth recoiled as she saw a deep laceration at her throat. Then she realised the hands that the man had been holding were bound together at the wrists with black plastic cable ties

"She wouldn't let me alone when I was waiting on you."

Momentarily, she didn't register what the man had said, and the delay meant Beth barely turned her head before his hand clasped her chin. She arched away from him, her body skewing sideways as his fingers lost their grip. She was on her back, her palms in front of her face to repel an attack. Briefly, she thought he'd already injured her because of the dark splashes over the backs of her hands, but Beth realised she was lying in the old woman's blood.

The man didn't seem to be in a rush with the hunting blade that he held in his hand. "Do me one small favour?" he asked politely, as if whatever it was would be trivial.

Beth used her elbows to crawl backwards through the cold blood, but her head struck the bottom of a dumpster.

"You're going to die now. Don't make it any more traumatic than it has to be." He nodded reassuringly at the woman beside her. "She embraced it. Barely struggled. I suggest you do the same."

"Don't fucking touch me!"

He took a pace forward and displayed the blade sideways, not menacingly, but as if he were offering its size for approval. "Now, Beth..." He shut his eyes, a barrier against any more noisy objections. "Just take a couple of breaths. Compose yourself. Mh?"

CHAPTER FORTY-TWO

Her name on the lips of the stranger only momentarily paralysed her. "Help!"

A dog barked a response over Gatorbait and their appreciative audience. She felt her scream vibrate through her temples.

"Nobody's going to venture down here." His body tautened in readiness for his lunge forward.

"Help!"

But the music from the Oyster Shack seemed to get louder, as if it were in league with him.

"I could reassure you this isn't some random act of senseless violence. And I wouldn't be lying," he soothed. "But in the short time we have together, there's something more important to tell you. Not a second-hand message; this comes straight from the horse's mouth."

"Who is Allegro?"

He gritted his capped teeth at her in the blue neon as if he were in pain and shook his head like it was the wrong question. White spittle glowed at the corners of his mouth. Then the fire exit door swung hard into his spine and he stumbled forward, before turning to confront the person who had opened it.

It was Lauren, the waitress that had served Beth, wearing a

dark overcoat. She casually walked into the alleyway, puffing on a cigarette with a slightly nettled look on her face, as she squinted through smoke and scanned the darkness for the source of the obstruction.

The man stood further back in the shadows and briefly slid the knife behind his back to conceal it while he assessed the situation.

"He's got a knife!" Beth cried, trying to stand while the heels of her hands skated in clammy blood.

But the man had already stepped forward, elbow quickly drawn back.

He reversed his steps as swiftly, staggering with blue smoke billowing about him in the yellow light through the door. The waitress remained where she was, the exhalation still pouring from her mouth.

The man collapsed backwards and landed hard on his spine, two curled red wires connecting his chest to the plastic gun in the waitress's hand. She'd tasered him, and his one arm jerked as breath whistled in through his nostrils.

The waitress opened the fire exit wider, so more light could spill into the alleyway. It slammed into the wall.

"There's someone dying here!" Beth skidded and thudded into the dumpster behind her as she found her feet. The blood felt slick on her hands.

"Jesus. Let me get Francis."

Momentarily, Beth was alone with the homeless woman and her attacker's paralysed and twitching body. Keeping one eye on the man's prostrate form, she knelt and held the old lady's bunched hands. They felt like cold leather, and her matte eyes looked straight through Beth. The music stopped and suddenly she could hear the sounds of the neighbourhood – cars, people on the beach.

"Police have been called, hon." The waitress was at the fire exit again, a tall man silhouetted behind her. He stepped past and briefly examined the dead woman. "Fuck."

In the light, Beth could see he was a black man in his forties, his square-cut hair greying at the sideburns. He knelt his considerable weight on the chest of the man on the floor. "This motherfucker ain't going nowhere." He turned to Lauren. "How long you been packing a taser?"

"Since they found those kids trussed up with their throats slit under the pier." The waitress looked down at the woman, the light from the door illuminating her pale blue features. "It's Maggie. Is she dead?"

Beth nodded.

The waitress took a step nearer to the body but didn't appear to want to get any closer. "Maggie?"

The woman remained motionless.

Francis looked over at her. "Maggie never did nobody no harm." He held the man's head firmly against the floor by his neck. "You sick fuck. Looks like we may have the Butcher."

"He was waiting for me." She could feel her suede jacket was heavier.

"Is this the guy that stood you up?" The waitress took the cigarette out of her mouth as if its taste suddenly disgusted her.

Beth didn't react. She knew it was. Her name had been on his lips. He'd lured her there and had waited for her in the alleyway.

The waitress dropped the cigarette.

"Chrissakes, Lauren. This is a crime scene now."

The waitress quickly retrieved it and gripped it like she was holding it for someone else. "Be careful, Francis. He's still got a knife here somewhere."

Beth saw it glint blue on the other side of the alleyway. "It's here." She stood and walked over to it.

"Don't touch it! Jesus, don't either of you watch *CSI*?" Francis shifted his position on the man and shook his head. "Just be ready to kick it away if he tries to make a move."

Two men that she recognised as members of the band joined Francis and helped restrain the man.

"Come on, hon. He ain't going nowhere now. Step inside."

As she entered, the waitress turned and Beth saw an expression of revulsion solidify her features. She looked down at her suede jacket and held her arms up to examine the dark blood on the backs of her sleeves.

"Don't bring that in here. Drop it outside."

"Help me," Beth said, a tremor of panic in her voice. "Get it off." She couldn't manoeuvre it from herself without getting more chilled blood on her hands. The waitress was behind her, pulling at the collar to drag it down her back so it would slide off her arms.

"Quickly." Her ordeal in the alleyway suddenly impacted and she felt her blood draining to her feet. "I'm not feeling good." Beth could hear the sound of police sirens and more people pushed past her to get to the alleyway.

"Lean against the wall, hon." The waitress continued to yank at the jacket.

Beth slid down the wall on her side, the blood greasing her descent. As she bent her knees, she looked back out of the fire exit. She could no longer see her attacker; he was surrounded by a ring of men all telling each other how best to disable him.

"Stay with me, hon. I'll get you some water."

The jacket came off her and she looked at it piled in a sticky mess of the old woman's congealing blood. It should have been hers.

CHAPTER FORTY-THREE

Mimic bided his time as he was driven to the precinct on Olympic Drive. His neck throbbed and the back of his head still buzzed from being forced against the floor in the alleyway. His ribcage was bruised from the taser and being knelt on by the owner and several other men. Not good for a man with his health issues. He'd requested they cuff his hands in front of him, as he was experiencing tightness in his chest. He hadn't been kidding.

His arresting officers were both thickset Latino men, and he looked sideways out of the back passenger window at the nightlife, knowing they'd be nervously and repeatedly checking their big arrest in the mirror. The vehicle smelt of shampoo, like it had just been valeted, but he could discern their tart sweat wafting back at him through the metal grill.

They entered a half-empty parking lot at the rear of a grey cinder block building with Police Department in silver letters across the front. The two officers got out, the vehicle tipping and rising as they shifted their considerable weight off the suspension. His door was opened.

"Follow," one officer said, and led the way purposefully up a ramp to the rear entrance. The other was behind Mimic. Three uniformed officers sharing a joke were coming down it. They passed them, as they were a third of the way to the doors.

At the top, the first officer yanked the door and held it open.

Mimic stepped through and found himself in a small entrance area between the door he'd just entered and the next set that led to the desk lobby. Both officers were now behind him, and he waited a couple of seconds, estimating they were all inside the same space. He knew it was his only window of opportunity.

Mimic interlocked the fingers of both hands and pivoted his body, bringing his cuffed wrists up and feeling the metal halt against the first officer's skull. The second was drawing his weapon just as Mimic swung them back the other way and found his temple.

The first officer slammed unconscious against the wall, his bleeding head streaking the plaster. The second remained upright. Mimic slugged his dazed expression again, the metal clunking hard as it cut through layers of skin to find bone. The officer's spine banged noisily into the door behind him.

Mimic darted a look through the glass to the lobby and saw two officers leaning against the counter talking to the female behind it. As the second officer slid down the pane, he quickly retrieved the keys to the cuffs from his belt, but didn't hang around to unlock them. He opened the door with his shoulder, trotted back down the ramp and around the side of the building from view.

Finally back at the Francisquito, Beth stood in the shower cubicle under the sunflower head, eyelids closed and letting the warm water blast harshly against them. It made her hold her breath and blocked out the sound in her ears as she tried to let the spume wash away the smell of the alleyway. She wanted to stay there until morning. Having been given two cups of black coffee by Lauren, while a softly spoken Italian detective named Cabrini had taken her statement, she suddenly felt light-headed and queasy. Her jet lag had been waiting in line but now wanted its turn.

It was only she and Lauren who had witnessed the attack in the alleyway. None of the other customers had seen the man in the vicinity of the Oyster Shack or had heard any noise or cries for help. The zydeco band had done for that. The diners had been dismissed quickly, and Beth and Lauren had been told they would have to make themselves available for further questioning. That meant she had to stay in LA until they'd finished with her.

Beth hadn't told them exactly what she'd been doing in the restaurant, simply that she'd been stood up by a date and had then been attacked by the stranger outside. She hadn't said she'd first made contact with him online, or that he'd lured her there with one word. Why had she withheld that from the police? Was it her old mistrust resurfacing, or because she suspected revealing it might compromise Luc in some way?

But Luc was dead. Her internal retort chilled the acid already washing around in her stomach. She would have to tell the police. There was no way of finding out what her attacker knew about it otherwise. Or maybe he didn't. Had it just been a ploy? She couldn't work out how he'd deceived her. If he had, it seemed so intricate.

Lauren had said the attack on the old woman was identical to a murder that had happened the previous December. Two students, boyfriend and girlfriend, had been discovered bound with plastic cable ties and their throats cut under the Santa Monica Pier. Another woman had been slain in the same way the previous April in Palisades Park. The media had dubbed the killer the Beachfront Butcher. If it was the same man, why had he targeted her and not another local?

After towelling herself down and putting on the scratchy robe, she started to tremble. Even as she turned it down, Beth knew it wasn't the overwrought air con unit. She didn't feel remotely hungry but knew she'd have to eat soon. She'd had nothing since the plane. Beth rang down to the desk.

"Yes?" The receptionist sounded out of breath.

"This is 234. Really sorry to ask, but is there any chance of getting something to eat sent up?"

"Sure, no problem. There's an all-night deli next door. What can I get you?"

"Anything. A sandwich? I just need solids."

Even though she sounded more exhausted than Beth, she laughed. "OK. I'll see what they've got left. Coffee with that?"

"No thanks."

She hung up and opened the tiny safe to double-check her passport was still there. When she'd been dropped at the hotel, the officer had told her they'd need her to report to the precinct the next day with her ID. She gripped it for reassurance. As soon as they were finished with her, she would be gone. She slipped it into her robe pocket and seated herself on the edge of the bed. She wanted to be back in her tiny bedroom at Jody's, listening to him snore through the wall. Beth badly needed to call him, to hear his voice, but she didn't want to have to explain why she'd been in the Oyster Shack. Not yet. She didn't have the energy for that conversation.

She picked up her iPhone from the bed. 1.44am. She didn't know how long she'd been in the shower, but her fingertips and the heels of her feet were wrinkled deep.

After applying some cream to both, she grabbed the remote, but the TV wouldn't come on. She checked it was plugged in. It was, but none of the buttons responded. She had to distract herself, not think about the old woman and the man standing over her telling her to calmly accept his murder of both of them. That disturbed her more than anything else.

Did they really have the Beachfront Butcher in custody? If so, she wondered again why he'd singled her out. She thought about the other murder that had recently impacted her life. Trip Stillman, a guy who had recorded her at the roadside, had been attacked in his home. She used her iPhone to search for more details online and found them. They chilled her stomach.

The killer had used a claw hammer. No cable ties, no hunting knife. But it hadn't been in the place where the other students went to college. She put Kalispell into a search and looked for recent local news stories. She skated over one but having found little else, read it in more detail. One name immediately stuck out.

LOCAL GIRL DIES DEFENDING HOME AGAINST THUGS

After responding to a 911 call, Kalispell police found the dead body of trainee teacher, Kelcie Brooks, in her home on Four Mile Drive. Miss Brooks, 22, had been repeatedly bludgeoned but had discharged a firearm resulting in the deaths of three men who have been identified as Jebediah Lindsay, Spike Freeman and Benjamin Wright.

Police say the weapon used in the attack on Kelcie Brooks ties the three deceased males to a spate of recent attacks in Lone Pine State Park and the surrounding area.

Spike Freeman. One of the clip uploaders was Spike666. His was the last one to have been removed. Beth went to his YouTube, but there were no other links to click through to. She searched for him online and found Freeman's sparse Facebook page. Nobody had posted anything there yet. Was it the same Spike?

Calculating it would only be late morning in France, she found the number for the Normandy Gendarmerie and spoke to the secretary of the investigating officer, Sauveterre, asking if she could be given the list of the witnesses' names from the crash site. The woman reluctantly agreed to speak to him about it and took her number.

She waited, trying to sleep but seeing the old woman's leaden eyes. She went to smilingassassin's YouTube page to watch the clip of Luc speaking to Rae Salomon again. She was disappointed that she hadn't got a reply to the message she'd sent them. It was the recording that gave her the most uninterrupted view of that moment

Allegro. She was becoming obsessed.

The clip was no longer there.

Before she could react her phone rang.

"Mrs Jordan?" A breathless American accent, not French.

She didn't recognise the voice but guessed it was the police. "Speaking."

"This is Officer Rimes from the LAPD. Detective Cabrini gave me your cell number. Now, please try not to panic."

Which, to Beth, meant exactly the opposite. "What is it?"

"The man who attacked you tonight, he's... no longer in police custody."

"What?"

"He escaped as he was being escorted to interrogation."

"Escaped, how?"

"We're doing all we can to locate him..."

Four knuckles rapped on her door.

"Ma'am?"

CHAPTER FORTY-FOUR

The circulation in Beth's ear pumped against the screen of her iPhone. She took one pace to the door. "Who is it?" She waited, expecting the receptionist's cheery response. None came.

"Mrs Jordan?" the officer's tiny voice said as she lowered the handset and let it hang beside her.

"Who is it?" she repeated.

Still no reply.

Beth returned the phone to her face and whispered. "There's somebody at my hotel room door and they're not answering me." She walked backwards in the direction of the bathroom.

The officer seemed as suddenly breathless as Beth. "OK, try not to panic." It sounded like he was calming himself more than her. "It's unlikely he would have been able to locate you."

She thought about how he'd reserved the table in the restaurant using her number. Was he tracking her phone? Beth had just been using it. "What should I do?" She wondered how old the officer was. He sounded as if he'd scarcely started shaving.

"Stay on this line. Do you have a phone in your room?"

"Yes."

"OK – use it to call reception."

But she knew that if it wasn't the receptionist at the door, she was probably away from the desk buying her sandwich. Beth had given whoever was outside the perfect opportunity to enter the hotel. Taking her eyes briefly off the panel to locate the phone next to the bed, she then whipped her gaze back to the inch of wood that separated her from somebody who was very possibly the Beachfront Butcher. "Please stay on the phone..."

"Of course, tell me what's going on. Can you do that for me, Mrs Jordan?"

She was too scared to be irked by his sudden reversion to whatever script he'd been taught to use.

"Is the door locked?"

"I think so."

"I have a situation here." He was addressing someone nearby. "Mrs Jordan, you're staying at the Francisquito?"

"Yes."

"An officer's on their way now."

"An officer's on their way now?" She repeated loud enough for the person standing outside to hear. "Thank you."

"Mrs Jordan, are you calling reception?"

Beth put his voice in her robe pocket, gently lifted the handset of the bedside phone and gingerly pressed the button to dial down.

"Reception?" Beth recognised the woman's voice. "Don't worry. Dinner's on its way up."

"Wait." But the receptionist had hung up.

Even though no obvious gunshot or explosion preceded it, the door cracked and burst. Beth instinctively crouched as varnished splinters blasted into the room. There was a large hole where the lock mechanism used to be, and the handle was now barely attached. She heard several loud thuds as someone kicked at it.

Beth quickly fled to the bathroom, slammed the door, locked it and immediately turned to the tiny window over the bath. There was no way she could fit through it. Footsteps pounded across the bedroom floor.

"Beth Jordan." The pacific voice said from the other side of the door.

"Get the fuck away from me! The police are on their way!"

Beth knew the handle of this door could be just as easily obliterated.

"You coming out? Mh?" he asked, as if he were a father addressing a moody teenager.

"And let you kill me."

"We can do it out here or in there. Your decision."

His casual pragmatism was terrifying. "Why are you doing this?"

"I wish I had a few moments to explain. I tried earlier tonight, but you'll understand time is something of an issue now."

The handle exploded and the door started juddering violently in its frame.

Beth looked around for a weapon. Just plastic bottles and tubes unpacked from her bag on the sink. She swept a vase of dried flowers off the top of the toilet tank. She gripped the heavy lid of the cistern with both hands and lifted it off, just as the door burst open and slammed against the opposite wall.

Beth swung the lid in the direction of the doorway and its impetus slid it through her fingers. Its brief ascent coincided with her attacker's entrance, its edge striking him hard below his earlobe. As it thudded to the tiles, the man staggered against the wall and slid down it, hands at his neck and body shrinking into the pain.

Beth stayed crouched where she was, momentarily alarmed by the injury she may have caused him. But the sight of the gun still clutched in his hand shook away any doubts he meant to take her life. A silencer was attached to the barrel. She considered trying to wrestle it from his grip while he was still stunned, but she didn't want to touch it or him and took advantage of the gap between his body and the doorframe.

She angled herself past him, crossed the room and was out

through the shattered doorway onto the landing. The receptionist was coming the other way, carrying a plastic tray containing a covered sandwich, her brief smile halting at Beth's obvious alarm.

"Run!" Beth shoved her back towards the elevator, the tray and food flying from her hand. "He's got a gun!"

The receptionist could see the panic in her eyes and didn't argue. She turned and fled, already a few paces in front of Beth and running as fast as she could in her sarong and cork heels.

Beth felt her bare foot connect with something soft and wet. The elevator doors had not yet closed but had started to. She anticipated a bullet in her spine as she pumped her legs towards the shrinking aperture. She didn't dare turn back. Perhaps he was still stunned. Beth focused on the buttons beside the elevator, willing the receptionist to reach them in time. Then she heard the sound of movement behind them, the thud of heavier footfalls.

"Help us!" Beth yelled at the other hotel room doors as they passed them. None of them opened.

The receptionist reached the elevator doors as they closed, and slammed the heel of her hand at the button. The doors parted and Beth followed her inside. She turned and they both panted as they waited for the doors to finish opening, the sound of footsteps slapping nearer. The receptionist banged her fist at the shut button.

The doors began their slow journey back to the middle, a barrier between them and harm gradually sealing itself. The receptionist flattened herself against the left buttons in an attempt to shield herself at the side of the doors from anyone who might appear at the shrinking gap. She turned and hissed, "Get on the floor."

Beth slid down the wall and pushed her body into the corner of the elevator. They both waited as the footsteps reached them. Beth closed her eyes and screamed, thinking only of the tiny life that would die inside her.

Time, the elevator and Beth's stomach hovered uncertainly before they plunged.

As they settled in reception a few seconds later, there was no time for relief. The gunman would be now taking the stairway down to intercept them. Beth opened her eyes and scrambled to her feet, waiting for the doors to part so they could sprint for the front entrance and raise the alarm on the street. As they began opening, she turned to the receptionist.

She was leaning against the buttons, braided henna coil over one eye. Beth could see the extinguished light in the other eye before she noticed the bullet hole punched through the centre of the receptionist's chest.

CHAPTER FORTY-FIVE

The elevator had stopped but felt as if it were repeatedly lurching to a standstill. Beth reached out to the receptionist's body where it leant against the buttons. Her fingers tentatively touched a tanned bare shoulder. It was warm but she knew there would be no response. As if to confirm this, the receptionist's head slid sideways and thudded heavily against the cubicle wall.

The doors had opened into an empty lobby but Beth couldn't leave her like this.

She was dead, though, and there was nothing more the gunman could do to her. It was Beth he was after, and he was probably descending the last flight of steps.

She scrambled to the sliding lobby doors and waited in front of them as they glided sluggishly open. Her bare feet sprinted across the small faux-cobbled courtyard until Beth found herself standing on the warm concrete of the boulevard. It was still dark, and sporadic traffic zipped by.

Walking to the edge of the sidewalk, she was about to make a dash to the other side when she saw a line of three cabs, two yellow and one blue, moving in a group towards her. It was too good to be true. Beth waved her arms frantically, her robe lifting up her body with the action. She didn't care what she was exposing.

The front yellow transit slowed, so the others had to as

well. Beth continued to wildly signal and heard her own cries for help as she discerned the bemused driver's face through the glass.

He seemed to have made his mind up about the manic spectre trying to hail his vehicle and accelerated away. The yellow taxi behind him followed suit, but the blue sedan slid over to her.

Beth turned back to the hotel and saw the gunman appearing through the sliding doors. Her hand scrabbled and found the handle of the back seat door and quickly yanked it open. She backed herself into the smell of citrus air freshener and the sound of Johnny Tillotson singing "Poetry In Motion".

The gunman's arm lifted like a lever from his side and trained the gun on Beth as he continued striding steadily towards her. Surely he wouldn't try to shoot her out here, on a public street. She quickly slammed the car door shut behind her, and its glass evaporated.

Beth was on her back, shards raining over her. She hadn't even heard the shot. The cab was still motionless, and over the sound of the settling fragments she could hear his footsteps.

"Drive. Fucking drive!"

The engine gunned and the vehicle slid her hard against the back seat as it took off. She stayed where she was, spine flat to the leather and the soles of her feet against the door. Wind rushed over her, and she gritted her teeth and closed her eyes, urging the taxi to find an extra gear.

But as a second shower of glass sprinkled her face, the engine suddenly slowed and the cab struck something solid. The impact rolled Beth off the seat, a family's smiles enlarging as her face rammed an ad for Six Flags Magic Mountain on the back of the front seat.

The vehicle settled, but over her jaw singing she could now hear police sirens. How much distance had they put between themselves and the gunman? It couldn't even have been a hundred feet.

Then she registered the side driver's window was missing as well. The cabby's head was no longer skull-shaped; one half of it had been blown out, flaps of his skin and bone opened like petals. His blood was sprayed over the front window. It was all over her as well.

She clamped a hand over her mouth and turned away, her eye line just above the back seat and looking down the boulevard. Cars were surging quickly past and she could see why. He was walking down the sidewalk, his gun arm still rigid.

Beth ducked just as the back windshield erupted over her.

She shook the glass off her head and knew she couldn't stay in the cab. Looking out of the space where the side window used to be, she saw the sedan was skewed against a concrete bench. If there had been any pedestrians nearby, there weren't now.

Beth was alone and had to get out of the car. Her fingers trembled against the handle, but the right door wouldn't open. Maybe the impact had warped the frame?

She was at the roadside again. Would she make it out of a second wreck?

Beth prayed there wasn't some sort of lock mechanism that was controlled by the driver, and slid quickly over the prickles of broken glass to the other door. She yanked the handle and slammed her shoulder against it for good measure.

The breath was forced from Beth as she dropped harshly onto the road, car tyres screeching as they swerved around her. Nobody was going to stop. Using the blue taxi to shield herself, she looked back towards the gunman. He was about twenty yards away and closing. Tillotson continued obliviously.

She could either try to negotiate the moving traffic and risk him shooting her in the back, or attempt to cross the sidewalk in front of him and head through the double doors of Pageant Kids. There were lights on and she could see a squat man with his back to her vacuuming the dirty yellow aisle carpet between the rows of children's wear.

She knew she stood more chance there than dodging cars and bullets. Beth ducked and circled around to the front of the cab, concealing herself at the side of the concrete bench. The closer he got, the easier it would be to catch her at the doors. She took one breath and then sprinted across the sidewalk and started banging on the entrance with her fists.

Now she could see the vacuuming man clearly through the glass, she realised he had a pair of earphones on. She beat it harder; feeling her bones bashing the pane and hoping it would break.

She didn't dare turn around. The gunman knew she was here. He was closing on her, could be running by now. She had a matter of seconds.

Beth could hear her voice shredding in her throat as she screamed at the man inside. "Turn around! Turn around!"

CHAPTER FORTY-SIX

Either her yells or the vibrations of her pounding the doors alerted the man in the store. When he turned, Beth could see he was Japanese and in his sixties – deep brown tanned baldness, beer pot and drooping grey moustache. It didn't look as if he was going to reach her in a hurry.

"Let me in!"

He shed his earphones and frowned, a request for her to repeat it.

"Open up!" She could hear the gunman's steady footfalls on the sidewalk.

He didn't move but did make a small gesture. At first Beth didn't understand, but then realised what it meant. He was aping a pulling action with his hand.

She'd assumed the doors were locked. She yanked on one handle. It was solid. She tried the other and it swung towards her.

"Hide! He's got a gun!"

The man with the vacuum took Beth at her word and had scurried between some racks of clothes to her right before she reached him. She looked down his escape route. The polythene-covered miniature dresses and dungarees had already closed up behind him. Beth took a similar exit to her left, ducking down but padding quickly forward over carpet, until she reached the end of the rack and was looking across another aisle.

She stopped, turned and listened. A muted radio ad whispered indiscernibly over the speakers in the store, and she tried to zone it out and distinguish any other sounds. The sirens suddenly seemed miles away. The door must have closed. Had the gunman followed her in before it had?

Her pulse thudded at the base of her neck, and as she knelt down to look under the rows of clothes, it worked its way up her throat to the top of her skull. Beth held her breath, put her cheek against the coarse carpet and craned to see back to the entrance.

His feet were standing just inside the doorway, motionless. Beth froze in her uncomfortable position; eyelids peeled back and mouth closed to seal the sound of her heart in her head. Had he seen her hide as he'd reached the entrance?

The shoes started moving quickly down the aisle. Even if he didn't already know where she was, he only had to crouch down to locate her. Beth examined the rack she was cowering behind. It had a crossbar between its legs. If she could climb up onto it so she was clear of the carpet, he might not be able to spot her. But would she give her position away when she did?

She could hear the swish of his sleeves as he moved closer. Beth put the palms of her hands against the floor, hardly registering the fine spray of blood over the backs of them, and crawled to the rack. She blinked then and could feel her eyelids were sticky.

"Mrs Jordan?" a tiny voice said from nearby.

Startled, she looked around her.

"Mrs Jordan, are you still there?"

The iPhone in her pocket. The officer she'd been talking to in the hotel was still on the line. He was about to give away her hiding place. She clamped her hand tight against her robe in an attempt to stifle him.

Polythene crinkled and parted above her.

"Ma'am?" A female uniformed police officer was looking down.

As Beth was led out of Pageant Kids, her insides quaked and she clasped her bloody hands at her chest as if she were holding a fragile butterfly.

"This way," the female officer who had found her said, like the straight aisle leading to the door wasn't an obvious route.

She was glad of the firm hand on her elbow and the smoky-voiced reassurance, though. She'd given Beth some time to compose herself before helping her gently to her feet.

As Beth reached the door, she could see the man with the vacuum stood with another officer outside. He turned to look at her as she stopped there. Did he think she'd saved him or led the gunman straight into his shift? Looked like the latter.

Her guide had requested a blanket from one of her colleagues, and it was draped around her shoulders as they walked back onto the boulevard. Beth looked nervously up and down the sidewalk.

"You're perfectly safe now, ma'am."

She didn't believe her.

"We're going to get you checked out before we take you to the station. Are your clothes at the hotel? Can we get you some stuff brought down? Which room were you in?"

Beth just nodded.

"I'm just going to sit you in the car until the paramedic arrives."

The only bystander was a grubby-faced old woman wearing a balaclava and an orange day-glo jacket. She stood to Beth's right, another uniformed officer blocking her with his arm as if she were a crowd. It was hard to tell if she was a street cleaner or a hobo. The old woman stared expectantly at Beth as she passed, disappointment registering as if she'd hoped her to be famous... or more injured.

CHAPTER FORTY-SEVEN

Holding the flimsy brown plastic cup of black coffee seemed to take all of Beth's concentration as she sat numbed in the small aseptic station office of Detective Sal Cabrini. She'd been loaned some loose-fitting grey sweats and sneakers and had just relayed her ordeal to him for the second time.

Beth absorbed him more than she had at the Oyster Shack, distracting herself from the memory of the receptionist's dead expression. She hadn't even seen the cab driver's face, but couldn't shift the spectacle of his collapsed head. They'd made her wait almost an hour before she'd been allowed to shower off the blood. Cabrini's mop of matte black hair looked like it had been given a helping hand to hide the grey hairs, and she wondered if the same dye had been applied to his thick, dark eyebrows.

She analysed the few props scattered around the sparse office. A squash racquet leaned against the wall and grubby-soled white socks protruded from a sports bag shoved in the corner. There were no framed family photographs in evidence. He was probably mid-thirties, and she could see how everything in his life orbited his job. Glancing briefly through the blinds, she was surprised to see the daylight outside. The night had felt like it would never end.

He looked up at her from his notes like he was disappointed to find she'd stopped talking. "Nothing else to add?"

"I just want to know when I can get out of here."

"Back to the UK?"

She nodded.

"Not right away," he said categorically. "Once I've digested this, I'll probably need to interview you again. You're sure you haven't had any prior dealings with this man before your encounter at the Oyster Shack?"

"No." He'd asked her this three times already. Did he know she was lying?

The gunman wanted her dead and had gone to great lengths to finish the job. There was every chance he would try again. The police were Beth's best recourse, to locate him and protect her. Why then, if she was still in such obvious danger, was she withholding?

But Beth had made her mind up. Allowing the police to know her visit to the Oyster Shack had been far from casual was something she wasn't prepared to impart yet. She was aware this made any eventual revelation more incriminating, but knew her real motive for concealing it was because of Luc.

How could the gunman possibly be connected to him? Had the man she loved and trusted been involved with something that completely contradicted who she thought he was? And would an admission to the police be the beginning of an investigation that would reveal more about him than she wanted them to know?

Did the gunman know why Luc had said what he had at the roadside? She was sure he'd been about to tell her something significant in the alleyway, before Lauren had interrupted him at the fire exit.

She found it impossible to displace the night's events and think clearly. It was Rae who had told her about Allegro. The gunman hadn't planted the word, but if he'd used it to draw her to the US, why? Were the other people who had witnessed the crash part of what was happening, or was it just coincidence? Why had smilingassassin's clip also vanished?

She was still waiting to hear from Sauveterre's secretary.

Since she'd woken in hospital, she'd been a helpless victim of circumstances. Beth had to feebly accept that Luc and her previous existence were gone. Now one word was the only key to her old life, and she wasn't prepared to give it up.

Why should she trust it in the hands of the police? If she offered the information, told them why she'd made the trip to the US, it became their official property and her own journey had ended. She'd have to stop running. Would she be able to return to the UK, put her trust in an investigation happening on the other side of the Atlantic?

The detective was writing something on the yellow page in front of him. Was he making a note of his scepticism?

"Nothing else to add?" he repeated, and still didn't look up, as if he were giving her the opportunity to reflect on what she'd told him.

She shook her head.

He nodded and met her eye. "Can you give me any more details about the man you were meant to meet in the Oyster Shack? What's his name?"

"What for?" She should have known this was coming. Beth hastily attempted to concoct one.

Cabrini waved one hand mock dismissively. "Just so we can eliminate him. How well do you know him?"

"As I said, he's just somebody I've been chatting with online. I don't know his real name."

Cabrini raised a bushy eyebrow. "You've been communicating with someone anonymous in the States and you agreed to meet them the first night of your vacation? Sounds like you enjoy living dangerously, Beth."

"It was why I chose somewhere public."

"The waitress there said you almost cancelled."

He'd looked into it more than he was letting on. Beth knew she had to tread carefully. "Yes. I did get cold feet. I changed my mind, though."

"How long have you been chatting with him?"

"Not very long. Are you saying he could be the same man?" She thought it best not to play too dumb.

"It's a possibility. I'd like his details."

"I don't have them with me."

"Just call me with them then." He handed her a card. "As soon as possible. Now, I appreciate you've had quite an ordeal, so I'm assigning an officer to protect you. Your room at the Francisquito is now a crime scene, but there's a hotel only a block away from here. The Grand. No great shakes, but it's homely. Maybe you'd feel more comfortable staying nearby."

It sounded like it was Cabrini who wanted her nearby. She clearly didn't have any choice in the matter.

CHAPTER FORTY-EIGHT

Mimic found a small square of garden tucked inside the parking lot of a tiny modern Quaker chapel. He seated himself on the wooden bench at its edge. The tall hedgerow around its perimeter effectively silenced the traffic passing by on the freeway, but he didn't experience the inner calm the surroundings were meant to solicit. He took out his handkerchief and dabbed the corners of his mouth.

Beth Jordan would be dead soon. Wherever she went, he would find and kill her. She was likely to be in police custody now. They might even offer her protection until she'd safely left the state. It didn't matter. Only limited time separated her from dispatch at his hands, and he had others to attend to in the meantime. What really vexed him, however, was how she'd disrupted his rigid system.

As a SEAL, he'd had seventeen confirmed kills as a sniper prior to the Israeli army withdrawal from Beirut in '83 and twelve as an officer for SAD. He'd always killed under the auspices of someone else. It was how he removed himself.

When he'd become unaffiliated, he'd been able to continue by adopting the homicidal regimens of established criminals. Every contract had a local precedent. They set the bar. He'd researched the Beachfront Butcher's methods before orchestrating his meeting with Beth Jordan, but circumstances had forced him to step outside the killer's identity.

He'd dropped the ball at the Oyster Shack and had underestimated Beth Jordan in the hotel. His neck was bruising from where she'd struck him with the tank lid. It was another sign that age was catching up to him.

His cell rang and he knew who it would be. He looked at the screen to confirm it was his employer and let it go to his answering service.

He used to analyse the rationale of the people he worked for, took an active interest in the identities, political or otherwise, that dictated his workload. That was when he'd seen the process of extinguishing human lives as something symbolic.

The reality, however, was that they'd become less and less significant to him. Not only those of his targets, but those of his employers. As the years had passed, they'd come and gone, and the faces in his portfolio had become just a continuous procession of features attached to the same clichéd machinations.

The designs he'd understood implicitly before, he took less and less interest in. It had become work and nothing more. Mimic had thought only of the real estate it could accrue for him. He'd recognised this was the case with any occupation. Blue collar to exec, the repetition of doing the thing you were good at eroded the spirit, so that eventually the reward was all you thought of. It was how good people ended up fucking over their friends.

At least he'd never fucked anybody over. He knew it would be only that which would make him lose sleep now. His had been a solitary and easy freelance existence, because he'd developed a rarely found talent. He wasn't a sociopath but, using his background, he'd been able to adopt their traits. As he'd always done, Mimic used the homicidal ambition of others to entirely excuse himself from considering the implications of killing.

People had to find a reason for continuing, though. Something that raised them from their bed every morning and made them clamber up the hill again. And when he was far from the trappings his job had earned him, he wasn't afraid to admit it was the actual moment of taking life.

It wasn't a sexual thing. He didn't even get the adrenaline spike that he used to. It was a kind of peace. Not a feeling of power, but a period of internal silence. Right or wrong, his was an action that couldn't be undone. It was pure truth. Whatever his kill meant for the people connected to the individual, his existence alone had created it.

A lanky forty-something woman in jade sweats and a headband interrupted Mimic's timeout. She was being pulled up the steps and through the open gate by her teacup chihuahua and seemed surprised to discover his presence. Perhaps this was her special morning place. He smirked reassuringly at her as she allowed the animal to nose at the flower border between the chapel wall and the lawn. She grinned nervously, and it didn't look like she was going to stay long.

Having been spotted by the O'Doole household, he'd decided to use the time he had to dump the Corolla and pick up a different ride. They might have taken note of the plates, and he wasn't sure if they'd returned home during his detour. His vehicles changed constantly throughout the year, depending on his itinerary. He opened his iPhone and did a quick search for the nearest rent-a-car. He'd choose another pedestrian model, something that would meld with the run-of-the-mill traffic. Mimic squinted at the small screen and wished he had his iPad with him.

The lanky woman stood patiently and examined the middle distance while her dog defecated over the border flowers.

His finger paused on the screen as he awaited the outcome of the episode. The woman appeared as if she was frozen in her own time zone while an event that was clearly nothing to do with her came to its trembling finale. Would she?

Whether it was because of his presence or that she was a conscientious dog owner, the woman produced a small green plastic bag from the pocket of her sweats and pulled it over her hand. She looked in any direction other than down at her feet while she scooped it up and quickly pulled the bag back over her knuckles so the animal's hot package was trapped inside.

"Come on, Anthony," she said to the creature, and pulled him back towards the gate they'd entered by, his little legs scampering to keep up with her long strides.

What a fucking strange name to give a dog. He was about to return to his iPhone screen when he watched the woman knot and dump the little package. Not only that, but she dropped it in front of the trashcan by the gate. It came to rest against the base of it.

"Excuse me, Miss?"

She ignored him.

Mimic was already on his feet. "You dropped something."

She started to descend as he crossed the lawn.

"Miss!"

The volume in his voice made her halt.

As he caught up with them, she looked back at him, a mask of lethargy on her face. The teacup Chihuahua regarded Mimic with its head cocked to one side.

"You dropped this. Mh?" He picked the bag up in his hand and weighed its warm contents.

The woman turned her back on him and walked down the steps.

Mimic still had his SIG Sauer P226 in the holster. He put his fingertips on the clip. Having failed in his attempts with Beth Jordan, he could certainly do with the low-key harmony he should have experienced at the Oyster Shack or the Francisquito.

Instead, he satisfied himself with exerting some self-control. It would be so easy for him to drill the back of her head and push the bag of shit inside the hole he made. Maybe leave the dog witness tied to the hedge. It was his last tour of duty, but not pulling the trigger, even though the rich homicide tapestry of LA would effortlessly absorb her death, meant he was respecting the system and was firmly back on track. And that was where he was most comfortable.

He watched the woman drag the dog down the street.

CHAPTER FORTY-NINE

Beth was lying against the propped-up pillows of her bed in the Grand, swallowing repeatedly but convinced the migraine pills she'd taken were no longer on their way back up. Dislocated morning sickness and jet lag had decided to get together with the trauma of the last hours, and her feet hung over the side of the mattress, ready to make a dash for the bathroom. It came in waves and she'd just ridden the last one out.

Her suitcase was part of a crime scene and she'd been informed she would only get it back when forensics was satisfied. She'd used the phone in her room to call her bank and been told she could use her credit card account number to withdraw cash. At least she could buy some new clothes.

Her hotel was indeed only a block away from the precinct, and there was a young uniformed police officer perched on a seat outside the door of her frowzy new room. Cabrini had promised to keep her posted, but she'd already been in the Grand for two hours and was getting increasingly nervous about providing specific details of the man she was meant to have met at the Oyster Shack.

She'd already attempted to buy the pills and a mineral water herself, but the officer had sent down for them. She may as well be in a cell. Beth guessed it was better than being held at the station but knew it was because they wanted her to be easily accessible.

She was just surfing the news channels again, looking for reports of the shooting on the boulevard, when her iPhone rang. Jody? It wasn't his number and not one she recognised. Nausea briefly halted. Could it be the gunman trying to make contact? Should she even pick up? Surely he wouldn't try anything under the nose of the police? Beth locked the door.

To her relief, it was Sauveterre. His voice exhibited an aloof mistrust, but he gave her the thirteen names of the witnesses on the coach. She quickly scribbled them down, immediately recognising Ferrand Paquet (the driver/Cigarillo Man), Trip Stillman and two others.

Spike Freeman and Kelcie Brooks.

Not only was it the same Spike who had been shot in the property in Kalispell, but it looked as if the woman who had defended her home had been on the coach as well. What the hell had gone on in that house? She found Kelcie Brooks' Facebook page. Lots of photos of drunken college kids displayed there. Beth looked back through her old posts until she came to a blank square with a familiar name in the link below it.

If you still haven't watched this crazy bitch yet please do so and make your contribution to the Kelcie Brooks retirement fund. Ker-ching!

To double-check Beth clicked the link and was taken to the empty YouTube page. Kelcie Brooks was smilingassassin.

Kelcie, Spike Freeman and Trip Stillman had all been murdered. That left her with another nine witnesses on the coach bar Cigarillo Man. None of the names matched the other two intruders Kelcie had shot that had been mentioned in the online news story. Out of the five clips, it meant two people remaining had uploaded them. She had to warn them and find out why they might be being systematically hunted down, but which two were they?

One of the names on the list was Tyler O'Doole. A YouTube clip had been uploaded by thatTODdude. She located seven Tyler O'Doole Facebook pages, but only one of them lived in Kalispell. He hadn't posted since 2013. She noted one of his friends was Kevin O'Doole. It had to be his brother. She clicked to his page and saw that he'd posted that day. She requested friendship.

Should she be doing this on her iPhone? Maybe she was getting paranoid, but she could be showing the gunman exactly what she knew. He did have the number. She was surprised the Grand even had WiFi, but there was no computer in her room and she needed anonymous access. That was another reason to get out of the hotel.

What was the gunman doing in the meantime? Was Beth prepared to wait until he arrived? She thought of the receptionist with the hole in her chest and considered the young sentry outside her room. If he did come looking for Beth, did she really want to put anyone else in his sights?

She was still dizzy but climbed off the bed and let the room adjust before walking into the bathroom and looking around for inspiration. Her gaze halted on the sink. She turned the cold tap on and kept rotating until it started to unscrew. She twisted the metal grip all the way off and slid it into her sweats pocket. Beth tried to turn the metal pin of the tap but it was rigid. A pair of pliers would be required.

She walked to her door, unlocked and opened it. The gangly sentry using his Blackberry on a low padded stool outside immediately stood up, turned and smiled. He looked to be seven feet tall to Beth and his hat seemed too small for his head. His long eyelashes were fine filaments that matched his wispy blonde moustache.

"Ma'am?"

"I'm sorry. I would call room service but as you're so handy..."

He raised his feint eyebrows.

"Bit of an emergency, the cold tap's broken. D'you think you could have a look?"

The officer seemed relieved it was something he could handle and nodded emphatically.

Beth led him to the bathroom door and stood back. Hopefully, the gushing water would misdirect him from asking how the tap got turned on in the first place. He entered and tried gripping the pin of the tap firmly between his fingers and turning it. His face contorted and he grunted. No luck. He grabbed a towel from the rail to give him some more purchase and tried again. Beth hoped he didn't have too much strength in his wrist.

"I'll see if there's anything in the desk we can use." She walked away from the bathroom and strode faster as she left his line of vision. Beth kept padding through the door out into the corridor and headed for the elevator.

CHAPTER FIFTY

Beth walked a couple of blocks, ducked into a busy Internet café and seated herself at one of the stools away from the window. She decided to keep her iPhone switched off as long as possible. Logging into Facebook, she left the gunman a message on Eileen Froley's wall.

When's your next performance?

She waited, but there was no response. Beth found Allegro's page and posted there as well.

I want to talk. I promise not to involve the police.

No dialogue box opened. Was he already searching for her? He could easily be in the neighbourhood. Could he have been watching when she was escorted to the hotel? Beth looked back to the window and the human conveyor belt passing by.

She didn't want to wait for him to find her. Where would she feel safe? Even though she'd found her passport in the pocket of her robe, Beth couldn't go home. She would probably be stopped before she got on any flight out of LA.

Beth found Kevin O'Doole's Facebook page again and examined the recent posts there more closely.

Short work of ribs in Elkhorns!

Above the comment was an image of stripped, sauce-covered bones in a bowl. The photo below it was a little more arresting.

Tyler slapping Mom with dead raccoon! Shame Dad is not around to protect her. We are officially on vacation in West Glacier!

So that's what Mom looked like. Through the window behind her was an expanse of grubby blue water. Beth studied the mock horror on her face as a hand held the decomposed animal out to her.

West Glacier? Where was that? Beth Wiki'd it. It was a small, unincorporated village community in Flathead County, Montana, and the west entrance to the Glacier National Park. It had a small population that relied on tourism. Surely the O'Doole family wouldn't be that difficult to find if they were staying there. But if she'd seen the photo, so had the gunman.

Beth opened Google Maps. It was 1,349 miles away from her. She was in no fit state to get on a plane again. By road, it would take her nearly a day. That was madness. Drive all that way to track down two young boys and their mother. What would she say, even if she found them?

Her friendship request hadn't been accepted. Why would it be? Beth had only posted it twenty minutes ago. She had to warn them. But, even if they had time to notice it, what would she post? *"You don't know me but just thought I'd let you know there might be an assassin stalking you."*

She found three commercial sites that rented out lodges in West Glacier and a handful of others that were privately owned. Beth cut and pasted the same message to all of them.

This is an emergency. I desperately need to contact the O'Doole family who may be staying in your lodge in West Glacier Village. If this is the case, or you know of their whereabouts, please reply to this email as soon as possible.

Beth355@hotmail.co.uk

She reread the words underneath the stripped bowl of rib bones that had been photographed.

Short work of ribs in Elkhorns!

It had been posted today. She put "Elkhorns, West Glacier" in a search and found a basic site for "Elkhorns Smokery,

Beer & Bar-B-Q Pit". Beth borrowed a pen and scribbled down the phone number. She also found a number for the West Glacier general store and took both to the payphone outside the bathroom.

"Elkhorns?" A shrill female voice said over the lunchtime drone.

"Hi, I know this may sound odd, but I'm trying to locate a family, the O'Dooles, who are staying in West Glacier..." She could almost feel a current of indifference wafting against her ear. "A mother and two sons; it's really important I contact them... it's an emergency."

"We get a lot of families in here."

"I think they may have had dinner there in the last couple of nights."

"Like I say, we seat sixty most evenings."

"Can you think a little harder? This is really important."

"I wasn't working last night. I had an ear infection."

"Is there somebody else there I can talk to?" Beth instantly regretted asking.

"I'm the head waitress." The girl was obviously affronted.

"I mean, somebody who may have been working the past few nights who might have seen them. Perhaps they reserved a table and left their number."

"We don't make reservations." There were some extra ice crystals in her voice now.

"I appreciate that, but this is vital. I need to get in touch about something very urgent. Life or death."

"I can keep an eye out for them. Who shall I tell them is trying to get in touch?"

"I'm... just a friend."

"And it's a Mrs O'Toole?"

"O'Doole."

"And her son?"

"Two sons."

"What's her first name?"

This was going badly and nowhere. Beth hung up, called the number for the West Glacier general store and got an answering service. She left a message asking if an O'Doole family came into the store, could they please call her iPhone number. She could always pick up any messages when she felt safer about using it.

Beth seated herself back at the monitor and found a dialogue box had popped up at the bottom of the screen.

I've just attempted to kill you twice. Why would you want to talk?

CHAPTER FIFTY-ONE

Beth checked the window again before typing.

You were going to tell me something outside the Oyster Shack.

There was a few seconds pause before his reply appeared.

First, I need an assurance that there aren't any cops at your shoulder. Believe me, they really can't help you.

Perhaps he didn't know where she was. Or did he just want her to think that? She tapped in a response.

I've just left police custody.

She felt even more exposed as soon as she hit enter.

If you haven't and value Jody's life, I suggest you do so right now.

Seeing her brother's name become part of their dialogue sent a new dread reverberating through Beth.

Why are you doing this?

I'm meeting with Allegro tomorrow afternoon in Las Vegas. Maybe you'd like to join us.

So you can kill me?

I have a different agenda to pursue first.

First? Every part of her knew it was a trap.

Besides – how could I kill an expectant mother?

Revulsion trickled like powder between her shoulder blades. How had he known?

As if allowing her to absorb this, he continued. *I have a schedule to maintain and I'm running behind. You can catch me in*

Vegas tomorrow afternoon. It's your choice. Maybe we can have a dialogue about the meeting with Allegro when you get there.

Beth's fingers remained poised over the keys.

Deal? I have to hit the road now. I'll be watching. If there's a sign of any cops, I don't need to reiterate the consequences – and not just for you.

If he had access to her personal emails, he must have already known she was pregnant when he tried to kill her at the Oyster Shack and again at the hotel. But she still didn't want to sever their dialogue.

Contact me here as soon as you're in town.

He logged out. Maybe it was another game. Perhaps he was only feet away from Beth and the Vegas dialogue was a way of misdirecting her. But if he knew exactly where she was, wouldn't he have already disposed of her instead of engaging her online?

Beth had to work on the assumption he didn't and was reeling her in to Vegas so he could track her there and finish the job. Could she refuse if he was now threatening Jody's life?

She searched the remaining names Sauveterre had given her, looking for their Facebook pages. When she located one for the sixth person, Ramiro Casales, Beth found he'd posted only nine days ago. In his profile she could see he was studying radiology at Spring Valley Hospital, Las Vegas.

Beth looked at the black-and-white still of his youthful features and him squinting through the smoke of a cigar he held in his fingers. Spikes of dark hair were gelled into a ridge down the middle of his scalp. Was he dustboy? Allegro? Or did the gunman just want her to believe that?

She used the payphone to call the hospital and asked to be connected to the radiology department. The receptionist had never heard of him but put someone on that had. It was another trainee who said Ramiro wasn't on duty, but might be on site, studying. Beth asked if she had an address for him. The trainee said she didn't. She left her iPhone number, stressed the urgency and asked her to pass it on as soon as she saw him.

Beth put Las Vegas into Google Maps. It told her it was 278 miles away and that it would take over four hours to get there. She stared at the route and another wave of nausea crashed over her.

Outside, Beth hailed a yellow cab. She felt a little safer once they were moving.

"Where to?" the head wearing the knitted blue yarmulke asked.

Good question. Now was the time to make up her mind. "What's the best way to get to Vegas?" She watched the cab driver's shoulders tense. "It's OK, I don't want you to drive me there; I'm going to rent a car."

The cab driver turned his craggy berry nose in her direction. "Don't follow your GPS. Take 405 and head up to Lancaster. Go through the Antelope Valley. I travel to Vegas a couple of times a year and I never have any problems that way."

"Thanks." She sat back, not knowing what the hell she would do when she got there.

"You afraid of flying?"

"No..." But she couldn't deny she was afraid. "Can you drop me off at the nearest car rental?"

"You're in luck. My brother-in-law has got a place. He'll do you a good deal... and he won't rip you off."

"OK." She looked at the meter. What choice did she have? "Where do you recommend staying when I get there?"

The cab driver slitted his wet blue eyes at her in his mirror. "Business or pleasure?"

"Unfinished business."

The cab driver nodded, as if he understood the place generated plenty of it. "I usually stay in Fremont Street. It's cheaper than the Strip, but it may be a little seedy for a girl on her own. You are on your own?"

She nodded at the reflection of his eyes. That was the truth. She'd never felt more alone. No Luc on the end of a phone to reassure her. Beth thought about Jody. Wondered if he was worrying about her or just relieved to have his personal space back for a while. It felt like such a long time since she'd seen him but it had barely been two days.

"I stay at the Golden Nugget. It's a bit old-school but I kinda like that. I think I've still got some two-for-one cocktail coupons here in the glove box." He started rifling with one hand while keeping his other arm rigid to the wheel.

Beth didn't hear him. She was questioning the insanity of what she was about to do. Why follow the gunman, especially given his acknowledgement of her child? Beth and the baby were now intertwined, but the more her instincts told her the man who had left a part of himself inside her was a stranger, the more desensitised she became to what she yearned to have before. She remembered Jody's reaction and how relieved he'd been that she hadn't been considering a termination.

A mother and baby both with a grim truth to face in their futures – her empty life without Luc, and her son or daughter's fate dictated by their father's genes. How easy could one of the gunman's bullets make it for both of them?

She quickly chased the thought away, disgusted with herself for letting it out. But Beth knew it had been waiting to be released for some time.

CHAPTER FIFTY-TWO

Marcia O'Doole was sitting in her grandmother's rocking chair on the decking at the back of the lodge and watching the darkening blood-orange sky being reflected in the Flathead River. She'd rescued the piece of furniture from the attic and brought it to West Glacier the summer before last. One of the runners was split – courtesy of Tyler – so you couldn't actually rock, but she was glad to be using it. She didn't often get the chance to sit still without immediately falling asleep. Like her mother, she dropped when she stopped.

It was an unusually warm night for mid-April, and Tyler and Kevin were stripped to their boxers and wrestling each other on the edge of the jetty. The water was freezing and whoever was pushed in – usually Kevin – semi-feigned hyperventilation when they broke the surface. Their commotion echoed off the other bank.

She watched Tyler as he tussled with his brother. He had Ted's muscle tone and skin colouring. Marcia never tanned and, despite nagging everyone to smear on sunblock, was usually the one who ended up getting burnt.

Tyler's condition had made him lose a little weight, but he looked like any kid his age. The doctors had said the cancer cells in his cartilage didn't respond well to radio or chemotherapy, but they'd put him through it anyway. Surgery on his pelvis was the next step, and he was booked in for June. Tyler had had a few months to regain his strength and, bar some dizzy spells and bladder complaints, was miraculously back to his old self. She knew appearances were deceptive, though. They had to make the most of his break from treatment, and it was good to be away from the usual distractions – no Internet or landline connection, and she'd confiscated the boys' iPhones for the whole fortnight. Marcia only kept her cell switched on in case her sister needed to contact her. Kevin was finding it hard. He'd sneaked off and spent an hour in an Internet café updating his Facebook page when they'd gone into Martin City for extra provisions that morning.

Some harlequin ducks barked eerily. They were early this year. She breathed the earthy air in and took a swig of her third Blue Moon beer. She couldn't relax, didn't like to take Kevin out of school, but they had to work around the time she could get off. Tyler wasn't trying with college, and there was only so far she wanted to push him. He'd figured he might not need an education. It was a regular argument, and Marcia didn't know if she yelled at him because he was so dismissive of his future, or because she wondered if he was right.

She still hadn't made her mind up if every day should be more precious, or if they should carry on as any normal one-parent family would, despite the prospect of what could be waiting for them at the next doctor's appointment. Marcia had opted for the latter, but that didn't mean she didn't question the decision every time she had a screaming match with him.

Both the boys missed Ted, and she knew they were suspicious she'd been responsible for his absence from their lives. Fact was, their father was a coward, and how could she tell them that?

Kevin lost his balance again and fell in. As he clambered out it sounded as if he was exhausted.

"Tyler, let your brother catch his breath!"

Tyler ignored her and pushed down on Kevin's head. Kevin

was halfway out and resisted, his shoulders trembling with the exertion.

"You're going down, cockwad." Tyler wouldn't let him up.

Kevin slipped back underneath the water.

"Tyler!"

He didn't turn but helped his brother out this time.

She knew that, even though he tormented him, Tyler looked out for Kevin. During one of their scraps, she'd overheard him tell his little brother he had to toughen up because he might not always be around to protect his ass.

Marcia finished her beer and put the bottle between her feet on the deck. Maybe a glass of merlot would relax her a little more. Why couldn't she enjoy these moments? Was it being back in this place without Ted? There wasn't a snowball's chance of him turning up. But something else was disquieting her, and she couldn't put her finger on it.

She could see a couple of brown bats circling on the far bank, hear their squeaks piercing her eardrums when they swooped close. She always got itchy before a storm. But as Marcia surveyed the vista before her, there were only a few flattened wisps of cloud in the orange sky.

CHAPTER FIFTY-THREE

Beth's journey to Vegas made her feel even more disengaged. For brief stretches, she was the only car within the voluminous darkness of the desert. She'd been expecting to travel through the classic American panorama – layers of deep blue sky, red mountains, grey scrub and blacktop. However, the cabby's brother-in-law had advised her to avoid the traffic and drive at night. She'd been glad of the suggestion, as when he'd shown her around the SUVs, she'd felt dead on her feet.

The smallest model on the forecourt had been the "Atlantis Blue" Chevrolet Equinox she was now seated in. She felt dwarfed by its cabin, but the elevation made her feel safer. It was like guiding a bus along a monotonous reflective chain.

He'd recommended a stop off at the Barstow station and had told her to try the Cuban snacks there, but hunger was the last thing on her mind. The only clothing store she'd spotted en route to the freeway was a Timberland. She'd quickly stopped off and had bought a tan leather jacket, some plaid shirts, jeans and Chelsea boots.

The yellow line to her left and the white to her right illuminated by the car's lights became hypnotic. Her brain skimmed sleep. Luc was beside her in the passenger seat. She turned but he didn't, just stared intently ahead before his profile addressed her.

"Sorry," he whispered, his lips motionless and features impassive.

Beth blinked him away and hit the button for the window. The icy breeze buffeted her left eardrum as she drove with the window half down. The side of her face was soon numb but it kept her awake. She wondered if the gunman was sharing the same highway as her, peered in the mirror and scrutinised every driver that passed.

The sun rose just as she reached Vegas, the city silhouetted and spread out in a thin band of lights beneath strata of sky shades: cerulean blue, pink and yellow. She'd expected to see a conglomeration of the major Strip hotels spring up in front of her, but it looked more like a crouching desert encampment. As she approached, its coloured neon started to wink at her from within the glitter ribbon, delineating its different buildings. She remembered once joking with Luc about them getting a quickie Elvis wedding here. But other than seeing it in the movies, it had never really been on her radar.

It wasn't a place she'd ever wanted to come to. Heading towards such an unfamiliar environment in the rented vehicle, Beth felt like the last of the girl who had got into the car with Luc had trickled away.

She waggled her buttocks in her seat and sat up in readiness to negotiate the traffic. Quickly checking her messages, she found none from Ramiro's fellow trainee. Beth switched off her iPhone again and knew exactly where to head first.

She used the satnav to negotiate her way to the sandstone façade of Spring Valley Hospital and parked. From the plaque on the wall in reception, Beth could see it had recently celebrated its tenth anniversary. She followed the signs in the pristine air-conditioned corridors to the radiology department, but none of the blue-smocked staff on duty knew where Ramiro Casales or his temporary apartment was.

In the absence of any other place to go, Beth drove to Fremont Street and found the gilded canopies of the Golden

Nugget. She walked in and waited in line, detecting the faint aroma of steak and looking up at the ornate chandeliers before checking into a Carson Tower room.

The bed there looked like it could sleep six and probably had. Beth collapsed onto it and painfully wrenched off her boots. It felt like they'd grafted themselves to her feet. She lay back on the soft mattress and stared upwards, her mind as blank as the plastered ceiling. Her eyes half closed, and the weight of sleep drove them the rest of the way. When Beth sat up again, she realised she'd been out for over four hours.

It was just before midday. Beth felt panicky, didn't know what window of opportunity she had with the gunman. She wasn't about to use her iPhone to contact him and decided against using the hotel Internet. Electing to find a café and try to establish a dialogue, Beth considered exactly what she was going to do when she did.

She quickly showered and put on her new clothes. Leaving her room, she made her way over the garish carpets, past the rows of pensioners feeding gaming machines and onto Fremont Street. A canopy of tiny lights switched off for daytime and a zip wire awaiting its first passenger ran the length of it. A sign for it demanded a passport for each rider. For identification in case of death? Hers was still in her pocket and felt as if it was about to serve the same purpose. The go-go bars were being wiped down, and she recognised the famous waving cowboy cut-out at the far end.

Beth found an Internet café with a gaudy Aztec theme further along.

You're here?

Beth could almost sense incredulity in the response to her Facebook message. It was almost immediate, which she assumed was because his alerts went straight through to his phone.

I don't want to interfere with your schedule. Am happy to exchange dialogue here. Beth waited and imagined the gritted smile he'd given her in the alleyway on his face as he deliberately delayed a reply.

I still feel a face 2 face dialogue would be better.

She typed quickly. *That would certainly be convenient for you. Have your unfinished work follow you here so you can kill two birds with one stone.*

It's a risk you'll have to take.

Beth bit her lip and looked instinctively around, as if expecting to find him seated nearby. She didn't want to remain in the café any longer than she had to.

I'm meeting Allegro at 3 o'clock by the concierge desk in the lobby of the Luxor. It's nice and populated.

He logged out.

CHAPTER FIFTY-FOUR

Tired of navigating the human traffic and the groups of guys snapping cards with hookers' numbers on them at her, Beth hailed a cab but didn't return to the Golden Nugget. She got the driver to take her up the Strip towards the Luxor, but asked to be dropped at the MGM Grand. She would lose herself in the people there, where she could feel relatively safe, and decide what to do.

She left the glare of the sun and, for a moment, couldn't see as she entered the subdued bustle around the rows of jabbering machines. A few dowdy waitresses ferried trays of drinks to gamblers who barely glanced up, and the whole place had a burnt-out feel. There was something unsettling about the people feeding dollar bills into the slots, almost as if it were a joyless, robotic compulsion.

Feeling dizzy, Beth walked unsteadily and glanced the faces passing by. She recognised a set of features there and stumbled back, walking onto the bare, sandaled toes of a man behind her.

"Jesus!" He sounded British.

She turned to look at him and apologised. There was pain on the pockmarked features above her, and his rigid smile said it was OK but not really. Had she seen the gunman watching her? As she scrutinised the crowd there wasn't any trace of

him, no face she could have mistaken for his. Had her drowsy
mind inserted him amongst them?

He could easily have slipped back into the crowd. If it had
been him, why wait before pulling the trigger? Perhaps his
barrel was trained on her right now.

Beth spun round, feeling suddenly exposed.

"Ma'am?" It was the voice of a black, thickset security guard.

She couldn't work out if he was concerned for her well-
being or considering escorting her off the premises. He'd
obviously reacted to the mini disturbance she'd made. "I'm
fine." But even though she knew it made no odds to the
gunman, she was glad of his presence at her side. "Just feeling
a bit sick." She wasn't lying. Oh God, not here, not now. She
vomited onto the carpet and several passing pensioners leapt
out of the way as if she were a terrorist. Beth braced herself
for another wave, her hands gripping her knees. She felt the
security guard's fingers gently skim her back.

"She's OK," he reassured the crowds. "You OK, ma'am?
Don't worry. We'll have someone right along to clean that up."

She threw up again onto the patterned carpet. Through the
moisture in her eyes, it actually seemed to blend in.

CHAPTER FIFTY-FIVE

Beth's straw rattled in her ice as she sucked the last of the lime and soda out of the frosted glass. She felt dehydrated and wanted to get rid of the acid taste in her mouth. Ordering another, she looked at her wan reflection in the mirror beyond the rows of spirits. She was tucked at the end of the Centrifuge bar in the MGM, and it was 2.35. The gunman was probably already in position.

How could she even contemplate meeting him? He'd not made any attempt to conceal the fact he wanted to kill her. What did she really expect? That he'd put her mind at rest before he pulled the trigger?

Beth didn't have any edge or advantage. She was just a dumb tourist, and it was mainly luck that had kept her alive until now. Perhaps that's why she'd caught him off guard. Maybe he'd thought she was such an easy target that her reactions had surprised him. Or was he just toying with her?

She knew she had to stop running and using any reason not to go home, even following a killer. But was she really safe, even if she got on a plane back to the UK? If the gunman failed when he'd lured her to LA and Vegas, would he then come looking for her? Was home any more secure, and did she want to endanger the lives of her family? Beth considered the threat he'd made against Jody's life. The police, on whichever side of the Atlantic, weren't going to be able to protect them indefinitely.

Or was she convincing herself to continue her own death wish? Beth wondered if she would have believed where she was now if she'd told herself only a handful of months ago. How had she arrived here? The only person who could definitively give her an answer was now a pile of ashes.

What had Luc been mixed up in that could have provoked this outcome? Maybe it was something Jerome had got him embroiled in. He was the more ambitious partner and was always pushing Luc to expand their remit. Perhaps he'd been socialising with some less-than-savoury clients. It all seemed so unlikely.

But if somebody wanted her dead, she should at least take the opportunity to find out why, rather than wait for a bullet. Was this her only chance to discover who Allegro was? Ramiro Casales?

The other drink arrived, but she was already off her stool and dumping dollar bills on the bar.

Beth entered the Luxor via the medieval-themed Excalibur hotel, wearing a mint-green baseball cap she'd bought in a souvenir store. She could at least make it difficult for him to spot her shaved scalp, but knew it was barely a disguise.

She walked down the ramp into the Luxor and found a floor map. Striding straight on, Beth studiously examined the features of everyone she passed and skirted the long wall of the Liquidity nightclub. The giant Egyptian pyramid interior of the Luxor was cool and welcoming, and the aroma of coconut oil was being piped through the air con. She stopped by the stairs outside the Tender steak restaurant that led down to the "All You Can Eat" buffet area, her knees wobbling.

The food smells wafting up made her throat spasm. Not again. Beyond her were a security post, the LAX nightclub and escalators up to the next level. She checked her watch – 2.59 – and, again, the faces of the people passing her. If he weren't going to wait in the lobby, where would he be? She imagined the balconies overlooking the reception were way too obvious.

Where would he think she'd go to observe from a safe distance? Right where she was? Nowhere in the hotel was going to be safe. Her best recourse was to leave right now. She could attempt to contact him during his meeting via the Facebook page.

Beth was about to turn on her heel when she noticed the exposed screens of a security booth that was under maintenance. The front of the booth had been removed exposing board and wires but she could see the three screens at the back of the booth as they shifted through different sectors of the Luxor lower floor. A bleary-eyed security guard with a braided ginger beard, grey uniform and peaked hat was seated on a swivel chair below reading his Nook. She looked around for signs of anyone else loitering nearby, but the area was clear.

Beth walked left until she was parallel with the booth. She couldn't approach the security guard and try and make idle conversation while watching the images, so she walked to the sidewall of Liquidity and leaned there.

Beth got out her iPhone and pretended to be busy with it. She was too far away to see the images, so she opened the camera and used her fingers to zoom it on the security booth. Her hand was shaking as she tried to steady it. The lens picked up the deadpan features of the security guard. He hadn't acknowledged her observation of him.

Beth turned her iPhone on its side so she was focused on all three screens and their shifting perspectives. She waited, trying to slow her breath so the circulation in her arm didn't keep wobbling the image. The black-and-white screens shuffled through other sectors on the lower level. There were about eight seconds between each angle change.

If she got a quick glimpse of reception, however brief, she could at least ascertain if the gunman was actually waiting for

her. Beth took the opportunity to glance up and around. The
security guard still hadn't registered her presence, and apart
from an old couple hobbling past, there was nobody else in
the immediate vicinity.

She studied her iPhone again. One of the images was of
the lobby, and her hand shook as she rapidly tried to assess
the people there. Where was the concierge desk? Beth didn't
have long. There was a man in a Hawaiian shirt with a small
rucksack on his back standing at the desk, about two feet
away. It looked like the spiky head of Ramiro Casales.

CHAPTER FIFTY-SIX

The shot changed, and Beth bit her lip hard while she waited for the cycle of images to return to the lobby. If this was the perfect way for her to observe the concierge desk without being there, had the same thought occurred to the gunman?

She glimpsed quickly around her again but couldn't see anyone in evidence. Maybe he was watching similar screens elsewhere.

That's if he wasn't hidden somewhere near Ramiro. Would he assume his threats were sufficient enough that she wouldn't call the police and have them arrest him?

Beth gulped audibly as she waited for the shuffle back, expecting Ramiro to be gone when the angle returned. She checked her watch. It was 3.02. How long would he wait there?

Then she was looking at herself on her iPhone, leaning against the wall of the nightclub.

She darted her head left and spotted the spherical white camera that was trained on her. As she looked up at her figure isolated on the screen above him, the sudden movement brought her to the attention of the security guard.

Beth tried not to look as stricken as she felt when she met his gaze. Returning her attention to her iPhone, she tried to hold it solidly by clenching the tendons in her wrist. Her hand was shaking too much. She was still in her viewer. Surely it had been longer than eight seconds. It felt like a minute already – a minute the gunman would have to register and locate her if he was watching on the security screens nearby.

At last the image changed to people at a bar with their backs to the camera. If he'd been searching for her on monitors, she'd pinpointed herself nicely within the shot. She had to get out of there, trot quickly back the way she came. Not too fast or he'd easily spot her amongst the crowds via the other cameras. But she had to see Ramiro in the lobby again first. Should she warn him now?

Beth kept the lens of her phone trained on the security screens.

Another carpeted area and more people playing the slots. How much longer was it going to take to return to the concierge desk? Every second put her in danger. But she remained rooted, gritting her teeth as another eight-second scene and another presented themselves. The lobby perspective finally appeared again.

Ramiro was still there. But she was looking at the top of his head. He was crouching over. What had happened?

Beth realised his rucksack was on the floor. Had he dropped it? She held her iPhone steady. Ramiro's arm pumped.

He was rifling through it, looked like he was searching for something. He withdrew his hand from the recess. It was holding a revolver. Ramiro placed it into his mouth and immediately pulled the trigger.

Beth saw the dark cloud erupt through the back of his skull and screamed as the sound of the shot bounced back at her.

CHAPTER FIFTY-SEVEN

Again, Beth's eyes locked briefly with the security guard's. Then he turned in the direction of the shot, frowning as if he'd misheard. She tilted her gaze to the screen above him. The image of Ramiro's collapsed body changed, as if she'd already been shown enough. Then another woman's scream, coming from beyond the escalators, broke the silence.

The security guard quickly ditched his reading and jumped off his chair. Another yell quickened his pace as he headed towards the lobby. Beth retreated in the opposite direction.

The screams swelled and rebounded off the balconies. People emerged from the bars and cafés to investigate, but she trotted dazed and robotically past them and back to the ramp that led to Excalibur. Ramiro's bursting head played on a loop in hers.

Mimic remained to one side of the large potted palm tree opposite the concierge desk.

Ramiro's body had slammed against the champagne floor about twenty yards away from him. Briefly, confusion allowed him the temporary freedom of the scene so he could examine his handiwork. Besides, a sudden departure would draw attention. He moulded his own features into horror, duplicating those around him. More people screamed.

He allowed the security cameras to capture his presence as

he walked falteringly towards the body. He'd gone for a coffee in the Starbucks opposite and had taken his position minutes before Casales had arrived. Now he stepped out from it so he was centre stage. It didn't matter. The kid had taken his own life. No suspects.

"Jesus fucking Christ." His whispered words vocalised the expressions of the young family of vacationers checking in who had turned to look at the mess behind them.

Although his legs and arms were in disarray, Ramiro was still alive. But Mimic knew, despite the fact Ramiro was lying on his back with the worst of his head wound against the floor, the fragments of bone and flesh scattered around him meant his scrambled brains were likely to drop out if anyone tried to lift him up.

Even though his eyes were open, Ramiro wasn't seeing anything. His nostrils pumped as he breathed erratically. Looked like the kid's ruined cortex hadn't had time to tell his lungs what happened. They were operating on their own, but they'd close down soon enough.

It was his best work. He'd replicated not a local but a globally trending crime and got the kid to do it for him. Was he really ready to retire? It was better than the Kelcie Brooks set-up, and his removal from the process certainly hadn't robbed him of his inner mellow.

He turned and ambled back in the direction of Starbucks. "Somebody call the cops. He's been shot." People were emerging, rearing up like meerkats to see what the commotion was. "Call them!" he addressed a young black couple clutching their cells and staring dumbly past him. Everyone was momentarily stunned.

But it would only be fleeting. Soon, those iPhones would be activated as cameras and there would be no blind spots. Mimic's exit had to be legit. He didn't have time to be a witness and so had to surf out of there on a wave of natural distress. He moved to a bright orange girl in a turquoise halter neck clutching her phone against her cleavage and craning to see past him.

"Call the cops!" he reiterated, but she looked at him through ridiculous eyelash extensions as if he were a distraction to the main event. It was his best cover.

He pushed past her and strode briskly down the side of Starbucks, passing the restrooms, Luxor Essentials and Spirits. He could hear sirens already. More people were coming to investigate, but they didn't see him. He hung a right and exited the pyramid via the ramp into Excalibur.

A pyramid, he considered, was the perfect place to leave a body.

CHAPTER FIFTY-EIGHT

Beth reached the moving sidewalk to Excalibur twenty seconds before Mimic. Her whole frame trembled and she had to concentrate on staying upright. Would there be two bodies lying in the lobby if she'd been foolish enough to try and warn Ramiro? She turned right into the hotel. More "All You Can Eat" buffet signs and gift liquor stores. It felt like she was trapped in a maze of the same place.

She eventually made it out onto the bustling, hot Strip. The sky was clear blue and the desert breeze warm like a hair-dryer. She sidestepped Elvis and the Disney and Pixar characters selling their poses for a gaggle of Japanese tourists. An enterprising man in a wheelchair dressed like Tom Cruise from *Born on the Fourth of July* was doing equally good business.

Beth wandered into the first Internet café she found and waited, anaesthetised, for a terminal to become available, finally seating herself on a dank hot leather chair vacated by a huge man in sweaty black lycra.

There was no question of where Beth was going next. They were already over two hundred and fifty miles nearer to West Glacier Village. It would be much less than a day's drive now.

Against agency policy to release details of guests was the response from OutwardlyBoundVacations.com

Sorry. Nobody of that name staying in our lodge. Will ask around,

Scott and Margaret Gellar apologised.

They were the only responses she'd had to her email. Maybe the O'Dooles weren't staying in rented accommodation. Perhaps it was a private cabin. So it didn't matter if every company she'd emailed did get back to her – which was unlikely.

Whatever remained of her logical self told her to call Cabrini. But she'd already fled the protection of the LAPD. What about law enforcement in West Glacier? She'd already been warned about who was really in danger if she involved the police.

The gunman was relying on her needing the answers he said he had, and seemed happy to string her along in the meantime. But Beth knew it was only because he wanted to keep her close until it was her turn.

Why?

She left it on Eileen Froley and Allegro's walls. Beth guessed he'd get the alert and respond. She sat back, the line of people waiting glaring at her while she remained idle in front of the monitor. A couple of minutes passed. Perhaps he was packing or heading to the airport. It had sounded as if he'd driven to Vegas, though.

Beth checked the YouTube clips. Dustboy's had been removed. That only left the one Tyler O'Doole had uploaded.

Physically looking for the family was her only remaining option. Would the gunman leave immediately or try to locate her in Vegas before he left? That was if he was actually heading to Montana. Beth guessed if she'd found them online so easily, though, he'd know exactly where they were as well.

She looked up flight details from Vegas to Glacier Park International. Allegiance Airlines operated limited flights out of Vegas to Kalispell. There was one flight that day, but it didn't leave until 5. There was another at 6.15 to Bozeman, but then she would have a four-hour drive to West Glacier Village.

Looks like dustboy has bitten it.

Beth shuddered inwardly as she straightened in the clammy

chair and typed a response to his in the dialogue box.

Why did Ramiro kill himself?

You guessed he wasn't Allegro? Ramiro was a good Catholic boy. I left the gun for him in the bathroom and told him to do it publicly; otherwise I'd send the webcam jerk-off performances he thought he was swapping with a Thai girl direct to his family members. Tragically, this is happening to so many young folks nowadays.

Repulsion swelled and Beth was just as sickened by the gunman's flippancy as the suicide she'd just witnessed. *Why are you killing the people who witnessed the accident and deleting their clips?* If she'd revealed she knew who Ramiro was, there was little point withholding the question.

I knew you were a sharp girl, Beth. Ramiro made it easy. He works long hours at the hospital and I was able to remove his recording using his home laptop. Found the password that he uses for all of his accounts. We didn't need to meet but I like to oversee things.

Her fingers trembled on the keys. *Stop this.*

Say pretty please.

Beth looked at her watch. It was 3.32. She knew he had to be leaving for West Glacier. She anticipated him logging out, and rapidly typed. *Are you protecting Allegro?*

How about dinner at Tony Roma's? We can talk it out over surf and turf and go see a show afterwards. The Elvis Cirque Du Soleil is a hot ticket. My treat.

His invitation froze her blood cells. Another decoy? *If I refuse?*

Just don't stand me up again. See you around 7.

Beth pushed her way out of the café and hailed a cab. If the gunman had driven to Vegas and left immediately, she could still overtake him on a flight, even if it didn't leave for another couple of hours.

But he had to know she would try to find the O'Dooles. They were the last clip that had to be erased.

CHAPTER FIFTY-NINE

When he'd got the message from Beth Jordan, Mimic had pulled his white Nissan Murano SUV over and sat on the hood. He'd closed the Facebook page on his iPad and had opened a Google search.

Nothing but blacktop and dry wilderness stretched ahead. He briefly closed his golden eyelashes against the breeze skimming across the desert prospect in front of him. He opened them again. Interstate 15 disappeared into the haze. It felt like the hottest part of the day, and he was eager to get back into the air con even though it gave him cottonmouth. He inhaled some real and tepid air and dabbed at the sour cream at the corners of his lips with a napkin he'd taken from Starbucks.

Beth Jordan had given him a run for his money and so had the O'Dooles. Both parties had to be silenced, Jordan because, as suspected, she knew what united his targets. He'd told Ramiro Casales to shoot anyone in the Luxor lobby answering her description before he turned the gun on himself, but Mimic had guessed she wouldn't show. He still had Allegro to reel her in with, but the threats to her family were no guarantee she wouldn't ruin everything he'd painstakingly orchestrated. He wondered how he would finish her, Mrs O'Doole and her children. Google told him.

He found some more details to ponder, and then slid off the hot metal and dumped his iPad back through the driver's door. This route was alien to him, but the enjoyable part of his work was when it took him to new territory. He removed his jacket and rolled up his sleeves. He'd always wanted to visit the Moapa Valley, and decided to stop off on the way. They had a renowned wildlife preserve there. He'd let Beth Jordan locate the O'Dooles. Mimic had over fifteen hours of driving ahead, so he figured, by the time he arrived, he'd have them all in one place.

CHAPTER SIXTY

Belted in and rolling back, Beth took shallow breaths over lurching sickness and tried to convince herself she was a step ahead. Hers was the first flight to leave. She'd waited in a different departure lounge until the plane had boarded, and she was positive he hadn't checked in. The flight after hers went to Bozeman, so he'd have a four-hour drive from the airport there to West Glacier. Whether he got on that or was in his car, she still had a decent enough window to find the O'Dooles before he did.

The flight was just under three hours, and all she could think about was the desert road below. Even if he'd left immediately after she'd communicated with him, by the time she'd got to the airport and the plane had taken off, he would only have had a two-hour head start. When she got to West Glacier, he would have been on the road for five hours. Google Maps driving time told her he would still be about ten hours behind her.

If he got the next flight to Bozeman at 6.15, it was an hour longer than hers because it stopped in Salt Lake City. He still then had to drive four hours to West Glacier. That meant it would take him nine and a quarter hours from the time she took off. That gave her six and a quarter hours extra to play with. Depending on how long it took her to get out of the airport. Wait, was that right?

She spent the flight turning the times over and over in her head, coming to the same conclusion but doubting her mental calculations and convincing herself she was missing some other way he could be there before her. He had to know where she was headed, and when she arrived, Beth still had to locate the family. Perhaps he knew exactly where they were staying. That would seriously shrink her time advantage.

Beth doubted the gunman had left anything to chance and was convinced she would be putting herself exactly where he wanted. She looked out of the half-shuttered window and watched the clouds turn coral pink and then darken, dirty blue to black.

CHAPTER SIXTY-ONE

The plane began its descent just before 8, Vegas time. Kalispell was just an hour ahead. What would the O'Dooles be doing now? Was there somewhere near their lodge they'd go for the evening, or would they pick this night to stay put and make matters even harder? Beth knew where she'd try first.

With no baggage, she was clear of the airport in less than twenty minutes and at the front of the taxi line in the freezing cold rain. It was fortunate, as there were only two white SUVs waiting there.

"Any bags?" The cabby half opened his door but didn't look like he wanted to emerge.

"No. It's fine."

w

"Been to Montana before?"

"Never." She was in no mood to be treated like a tourist.

"We have a saying here – if you don't like the weather, just wait five minutes."

Beth didn't respond, only pulled her leather jacket tighter around her and used the weak yellow streetlight to squint at the time on her watch: 8.23 Vegas time. Nothing stopped there. Everyone would probably be in bed here.

Her cabby remained silent for the remainder of the thirty-five-minute journey to West Glacier. She wondered if it was because she'd been rude, or if he was picking up on her agitation. She sat rigidly back in the seat, occasionally glanced at the dipped peak of his cap in the mirror and clasped her hands in her lap.

Their journey revealed little of her surroundings, the headlights picking up the dark wet asphalt and yellow lines of the expansive road, and occasionally catching tall pines and the green reflective signs on US 2. The scenery skulked within the darkness and it felt like they were hissing down a black tunnel. She could have been anywhere but Flathead County. She wished she were.

"You staying at the Belton?"

"No. Could you just drop me off when we get to the centre of town."

"The centre?" the driver said incredulously.

She wasn't sure what he meant by it until the wooden buildings of West Glacier started to appear at the sides of the road. There didn't appear to be anyone on the street. She spied an inn and the general store and saw old signs for the railway. She was about to ask him about Elkhorns restaurant when its carved sign illuminated by tiny yellow bulbs appeared to their left.

"Here's just fine. How much do I owe you?" He told her and she gave him a generous tip, but he said nothing as he turned the taxi and headed back the way they'd just come.

She could hear Bob Dylan getting "Tangled Up In Blue" inside Elkhorns and smell mesquite and burgers. The rain fell harder and Beth trotted quickly across the road to the cedar-wood-panelled building, and pushed on the heavy glass swing door.

The aroma and music became overpowering inside. A fibreglass grizzly greeted her. It held a sign that said: *Today's saying – "You look like you've been chewed up by a wolf and shit over a cliff."* It looked like a staff joke to relieve the boredom. Most of the wooden chairs were stacked upside down on the dining tables.

"Help you?" But it sounded like the last thing the girl at the waitress station wanted to do. Was she the one Beth had spoken to on the telephone? She was diminutive and compact, her solid bust too big for the crimson shirt she was wearing. A dyed black bob cupped her canine features.

"I'm looking for some friends of mine. The O'Dooles."

The girl's eyes went dead. "Only a few regulars in tonight, so we're closing early, so unless you want to order right away..."

"I called here recently..."

"I know, and I told you I don't know them."

Beth opened her mouth.

"And as we don't take reservations, I can't help you any further. Now, Chef is about to turn the grill off so..." She raised her eyebrows and chewed something invisible.

"Thanks a lot for your help." Beth found herself back in the street, pulling her leather jacket over her head. She turned left and headed along the sidewalk in the direction the cab would have taken her if they'd carried on. The music was quickly gulped by the darkness, and the impacts of her boots on the wet paving stone and her own breathing inside the tent of leather were the only sounds. Not even a solitary dog barked. Where the hell would she try next?

She suddenly stopped by a parked car and braced herself by putting her palm against its cool, wet metal. Another surge of nausea. Not again. Probably brought on by the aroma of food. Was her sense of smell becoming oversensitive? Her legs wobbled and felt suddenly fragile. She tried to remember the last time she'd had solids. Apart from a tiny bag of pretzels she'd consumed on the plane, Beth knew she hadn't eaten properly since LA. How long ago was that?

Beth waited for her ears to stop burning and the sensation to pass, but it felt like an hour. Eventually, she straightened and sniffed the night air. The rain was just drizzling now, but it was getting cold fast, probably because they were near water.

Near water. Beth recalled the water through the window in the photo of Mrs O'Doole that Kevin had posted on the Facebook page.

CHAPTER SIXTY-TWO

The lodge was beside the water. It was a start. She saw a sign for the "Alberta Visitor Center" and followed it, passing West Glacier Mercantile until she came to a brick building that looked like a miniature Alamo with a triangular wood and glass roof, flanked by four motionless flags on poles. Beth climbed the five steps to its courtyard and made for the faintly illuminated windows at the front.

She tried the door but already knew it was locked. Taped inside the pane was a map of West Glacier, however. Beth wiped the cold vapour from her eyes with her fingertips and found the building and its relation to the Middle Fork Flathead River.

She passed West Glacier Mercantile again and headed down Going-To-The-Sun Road. It led to the nearest stretch of the river. The sign told her it was closed winters.

Beth smelt the cold soil aroma of the water before she saw it. She left the road and walked onto the grass of a clearing. Her boots squeaked on the wet blades as she moved carefully towards the river's edge. A gang of dark clouds was restraining the moon and she couldn't tell where the land ended and the Flathead began. The ground became softer underfoot and she stopped as she reached a fence of tall reeds.

A cool draught hit her face and she briefly closed her eyes against it. But when the wind dropped, she could hear the fizz of the water. She looked right to where the river bent around into the distance, but couldn't make out the shape of any cabins. When she gazed the other way, she could see a faint yellow light through the trees. A streetlight? It seemed too high up.

She strode back to the road, keeping her eye on the light as the branches between it and her made it wink. It disappeared as she reached the asphalt again, and suddenly Beth felt as if she wasn't alone. Halting and holding her breath, she could hear nothing but the odd gurgle from the sizzling river. She headed in the direction of the light via the track curving around the cedar trees.

Beth swivelled back to the clearing when she heard the scuff. Her circulation knocked in her ears as she strained to listen again. It was ridiculous. He couldn't be here. Not yet. No other sound. Perhaps it was an animal, or somebody out walking. She tried to focus on the different shades of darkness within the trees but couldn't discern any movement or figure.

Beth paced quickly along the track and found it becoming a steep incline of loose stones. Her boot slipped on its uneven surface as she tautened the muscles in the backs of her legs to push herself upward. Beth turned again and peered back down the track, expecting to see someone furtively pursuing her. There was nobody. She was just getting jittery in the dark of an unfamiliar place.

Beth followed the curving edge of the trees and thought about the crash site. Everything must have seemed harmless there too, until they'd rounded the corner.

She thought about the clips and her at the roadside staring out into Jody's lounge through someone's iPhone. She wished she were viewing this from the comfort and safety of the armchair. The track levelled off, then the yellow light winked into view again, lower this time. It couldn't be a streetlight; if it was, it seemed odd that a single one would be positioned in the forest.

As she progressed further around the bend, Beth realised it was a spherical lamp over a wooden sign. She made for it, reading the words carved into it.

FLATHEAD BEND

The sign was positioned atop a flight of wooden steps leading down to a hunting lodge perched on the edge of the river. A fishing jetty extended from the back of the property, disappearing into the blackness of the water.

As she reached the bottom of the steps, she was suddenly illuminated by motion detector lights positioned on the gables. Simultaneously, a window rattled and opened below them.

"And just what the hell can I do for you?" a hostile male voice.

Beth couldn't see the man through the glare of the overhead bulb. She shaded her eyes with the edge of her hand. She could see he had grey muttonchops and whiskers. "I'm sorry. I'm looking for someone. A family called the O'Dooles. They're staying along the river here somewhere."

"There are no O'Dooles in this house and I have a hunting rifle already loaded right here."

"You haven't seen a mother and two teenage boys?"

"You'd better scram before I call the cops."

But there was another incoherent voice now, a woman's whispering, placatory tone.

The man paused while he listened, then it sounded as if he'd turned to address them. "OK, OK." His voice got loud again. "Apparently, there's a mother and two teenage boys staying at Whispering Brook."

"Could you tell me where that is?"

"Go back down the track you came up and make for the footbridge. It's a good ways along there on the left."

"Thank you."

"There's a couple of other family places along there. Try not to terrify anyone else."

"Thank you again. I'm sorry if I–"

But the window closing cut her off. Beth turned and headed back up the steps, feeling his eyes on her back all the way.

CHAPTER SIXTY-THREE

Beth stumbled back down the track and quickly found herself at the clearing again. She strode quickly, surveying the woods to her left, and soon reached a dilapidated covered wood footbridge held up by scaffolding. It groaned with her slight weight before she was heading down another dark tunnel of trees. Thankfully, the clouds relinquished the moon and spilled some extra light through the branches.

It was a long time before she reached the next lit sign.

BLUE PONTOON

She kept walking and passed BEAR BECK and SAW CREEK before WHISPERING BROOK finally materialised out of the overhang of trees.

Beth could easily have missed it. The sign was barely visible from the track, and no lamp illuminated it. She approached to double-check. It didn't look as new as the others, and she guessed a letting company didn't maintain it.

She was looking down another flight of wooden steps cut into the bank that led to the front of the house, but couldn't see any motion detector lights positioned anywhere on its cedar cladding. A dull glow of yellow light emanated from the back of the property and died halfway up its jetty. There was also smoke weakly emerging from its chimney, being blown at her from the direction of the river.

The aroma of beech ash wafted over her. What the hell was she going to do now? Even if it were the right family, where would she begin to tell them why she was there? But ascertaining it was the O'Dooles had to be her first priority. If it wasn't, she only had a matter of hours left to find them.

Beth descended the steps, her palm grazing the rough, green-stained wood handrail as she decided what to say. The truth seemed to be the only option, however unlikely. She hit the walkway that led down the side of the lodge and to the jetty. Her thudding footfalls along it would alert anyone inside she was approaching.

She turned the corner and was standing at the back of the house. In front of the double-glazed window were a narrow seating deck and a balustrade. A table with its parasol folded had four metallic seats collapsed and leaning against it.

Looking in through the window, she saw a spacious lounge illuminated by ceiling spotlights. There were animal heads on the wall, a huge circular wooden table dominated the polished tiles and some skewed mats in front of three chairs were at the far side. A wood-burning stove was to her right, and there was still a log glowing orange inside.

She moved to the frosted glass door at the side. There were a couple of garbage cans beside it with elasticated rope threaded through the top and side handles. She remembered the photo of the raccoon that had been posted on Facebook.

Were they still up? She resisted trying the handle. Beth knocked on the frame of the screen and stood back; trying to decide what sort of expression she should have on her face for whoever opened it. She opted for neutral.

"Mom!" It was a boy's voice.

Beth swallowed and cleared her throat. She could hear footsteps on stairs and then a distorted face peered at her through the glass. The door opened.

It was Mrs O'Doole. Beth recognised her from the photo. Her eyes looked puffy. "Can I help you?" There was no suspicion in the question but plenty on her face.

"I've come a long way to find you. This may sound ridiculous, but I've reason to believe you and your boys are in danger."

Now suspicion morphed into something else. Mrs O'Doole's gaze hardened, and she seemed to be using all her effort to keep her head steady.

"Are you all right?"

"I'm fine." But she definitely didn't look it. Her face began to tremble, and the vibration travelled down her body. "Come inside." She turned her back on Beth and walked into the kitchen.

Beth followed. The kitchen was retro-look, traditional fixtures but modern appliances; wheelback chairs around the table and old-fashioned cabinets housing equipment with digital displays. It smelt of damp and stale coffee grounds.

"Go through to the living room." Mrs O'Doole's voice was close behind her, and there was hardly a gap between it and the heavy and sharp object that slammed into the back of Beth's skull.

CHAPTER SIXTY-FOUR

When Beth awoke, she was suffocating. Something was pressing against her eyes and nose, and when she tried to move her head clear of it, she felt the same pressure on the back of her skull forcing her face harder against a tensed skin of plastic. Its intense aroma filled her nostrils and she tried to lift her hands to push it away. But her arms were tight against her sides, and Beth couldn't feel any sensation below her wrists. With a supreme effort, she managed to crack her eyelids only for her vision to be flooded white.

She focused on texture within the glare, tiny wrinkles in the plastic. There were white airbags closing in on her from all sides, creaking and inflating to bursting point while her body was squeezed tighter between them. Beth couldn't breathe, but still the weight on her ribs and lungs increased. She gulped air into her constricted chest and heard the crack of bone.

Suddenly, the airbags parted to reveal Luc upside down in the car. He turned to her as the blood started pouring from his nose and up into the ceiling. "Sorry."

Turning to look through the windscreen, she saw the vehicle looming around the bend. The brown camper was only feet away.

Beth heard her teeth squeak as she gritted them in anticipation of the crash. Her chin was against her chest and her eyes were squeezed closed, but no sound came except for a low grumble. The plastic smell had gone and was replaced by a new one – timber and damp.

She lifted her eyelids and raised her head, immediately striking something solid behind her. The impact, a hundred times more agonizing than it should have been, unstuck her dry lips. Her cry ricocheted deafeningly around her cranium and her whole scalp throbbed, the swelling behind her skull pounding out of sync with her circulation.

Beth quickly gleaned she was sitting on a low, red-leather stool about six feet away from the foot of some bare narrow wooden stairs. Looking up and squinting against the low-energy bulb in the red tassel shade above her, she could make out a closed door through the darkness at the top of them.

Glancing right to the gas boiler churning away, she caught her reflection in a dress mirror that was leaning on its side against the peeling brickwork. Beth could see the bottom half of her body. She had been positioned against the black stained support pillar, and some yellow elasticated ropes bound her hands behind it. Her ankles were secured by white, plastic-coated curtain wire

The walls of the room in the large cellar area to the left of the stairs were rough concrete painted white. An air hockey table was set up on the threadbare blue carpet. Beyond that, a crippled tennis table, missing one leg and bowing precariously, looked just as neglected. At the far end, two orange canoes were mounted on the wall. The air was cool and stale. Her leather jacket had been removed to allow her to be restrained. Beth shivered.

She tried to lean forward but could instantly feel how tightly she'd been tied up. As she waggled her wrists, the exertion pressed her head harder against the support and a yellow kaleidoscope of pain momentarily blinded her. She felt like she was about to pass out again.

There was no leeway in her bonds, and the curtain wire

cut into her ankles when she tried to move them. She tried to locate any tool nearby she could possibly use. On top of the gas boiler she could see a meat-tenderising hammer. Its spiked head was dark red, and she could see small traces of her skin on the points. Realising what she'd been struck with suddenly made her perspective of the cellar fluctuate. She couldn't pass out again. There was no way she would be able to reach the hammer. Perhaps it had been left there as a threat.

Mrs O'Doole had invited her in without even hearing her story. Why hadn't that rung any alarm bells? And how long had she been out? She opened her mouth to shout up the stairs. What would she say? "Mrs O'Doole!" The words reanimated the pain at the back of her head, but when there was no response, she shouted the name louder. "You don't have to release me, but please... just listen to what I have to say!" Beth waited.

Footsteps on the floorboards above her. The handle at the top of the stairs rattled and daylight briefly bisected the wooden steps from above. The door slammed closed again. The person descended and entered the circle of light from the shade. It was the gunman.

CHAPTER SIXTY-FIVE

His claret shirt was rolled to his elbows, and he finished wiping at his mouth with a brown napkin before pocketing it. The gunman covered the carpet between the stairs and Beth, and clamped her Adam's apple between his thumb and forefinger.

"They might expect you to yell at me, but if you do I'll crush this. Mh?" His tone was amicable, the threat lurking behind it all the more convincing.

Beth felt his grip tighten on it and nodded as much as she could.

He looked at his watch. "Told you I'd pick you up around 7, even if it is the morning. Now, for the purposes of this conversation, I'm Special Agent MacDonald. I don't have much of an imagination – I rely on the creativity of others – but I'd stopped off to grab an Egg White Delight McMuffin when I made the call to Mrs O'Doole. I've also chosen the name Harry, my father's. Ronald would have been too much of a giveaway."

Beth fought to swallow and felt the solidity of his fingers as her Adam's apple struggled to bounce in her throat.

"I called Mrs O'Doole and told her about her sister's murder. Jess had been looking after her place while she was on vacation. The likeness was unnerving. Very unfortunate but there's always an element of natural wastage. I told her it was a federal matter and that I needed her to examine a photo of the suspect. It's a good one of you from your Facebook page. Tyler immediately recognised you as the woman from the crash site who attacked him. They all figure you still have a score to settle. It would be very expedient for me to make you responsible for the deaths of the people upstairs, but that might lead any subsequent investigation too close to what I've been doing. I'll have to keep things partitioned. There's a lot of wilderness hereabouts, though. I can make you disappear, bury you somewhere deep in the National Park."

The gunman's face blurred as Beth's eyes began to water.

"I told her to stay put in West Glacier, keep her boys out of danger. Said she was in the safest place. Then she calls me up and tells me you'd come looking for her and she had you tied up. The three of them are up there shakily making pancakes for me now. Quite an experience for the O'Dooles. I'm going to kill you, and then I'm going to eat another hot breakfast with the family. I'll need my strength to handle the three of them."

She shook her head, tried to scream but his fingers completely restrained her. Just beyond her view of his paunch protruding through his shirt, she knew the meat tenderiser lay way out of her reach.

"There was a grizzly attack in West Glacier seven years ago. A family's remains were discovered in a picnic spot. The park wardens used beaver meat to snare a rogue bear and shot it dead. But the coroner's office proved a human had been responsible for the attack. The bodies had been mutilated to make it look like a grizzly. The bear died for nothing and they never caught anyone. It's all online, although it wasn't very high-profile. I suppose that's understandable; bit of a tourism killer. It was an ideal cover story for me, though. Decomposition would complicate matters for the cops, and Mrs O'Doole said they're going to be here two weeks. Their bodies wouldn't have been discovered for some time. Trouble is, I've already used someone else's MO to dispose of Jess.

Would seem a coincidence if the entire family fell afoul of two different human predators. Highly unlikely."

His fingers pinched harder, and Beth's shoulders jerked as she used up her last reserves of oxygen.

"So I'm going to have to improvise. I'll tie them up and drive them downriver, hold their heads under and leave one of their boats adrift. A plausible accident, but still too much of a coincidence. It's not ideal, but it's where we are. Scarcely leaves me any time to pick up on the conversation we were about to have at the Oyster Shack."

Beth couldn't see him now; his face was just a pink blob. She felt him shift his body though, redistribute his weight on both feet as his grasp tightened and squeezed, and she bucked against the support pillar. The blood churned in her eardrums.

CHAPTER SIXTY-SIX

The gunman's whole mass was suddenly against her, and Beth could smell his stale odour. His bulk ground the wound at the back of her head against the support. White pain momentarily bleached out everything, but his grip on her throat loosened, and she quickly scraped in some air.

His body slid over and past her and she blinked water out of her eyes to see him sprawled on the cellar carpet. Mrs O'Doole was standing in front of her holding a wok and assessing his prostrate form. She shot Beth a glance and then returned her attention to the gunman, gripping the handle as if she would strike him again.

"I heard enough," she said flatly.

"Please…" The word felt like it had sharp edges. "Untie me."

Mrs O'Doole scurried to the other side of the cellar. She heaved a red metallic toolbox off the shelf and allowed its weight to slam it to the floor.

The gunman rolled onto his side and looked up at Beth with confusion.

"He's waking up!"

Keeping hold of her weapon, Mrs O'Doole opened the toolbox and produced a small pair of bolt cutters. She scrambled back over to Beth and quickly snipped the curtain wire coiled around her legs.

Beth felt the blood pump back into them as they parted. But she didn't take her attention off the gunman. His eyes were open but emptied out. It looked as if he didn't know who or where he was, but Beth knew he'd regain his senses soon. Mrs O'Doole was behind her now, working the blades against the elasticated rope.

"He's conscious. Hit him again!"

But her hands were freed and she was on her feet. Beth's legs trembled and her knees immediately gave. Mrs O'Doole caught her under the elbow and helped her stumble around the gunman towards the stairs. The flight was narrow and would only allow one person to ascend at a time. Beth grabbed the meat tenderiser off the top of the gas boiler on her way past and glanced back.

The gunman was on his front, arching his spine to push himself up. Beth shoved Mrs O'Doole up the stairs first and gripped the metal handle in her hand tight as she turned to repel any attack. He was on his feet and she could see from his expression that he'd caught up with the situation.

She pivoted and ran up the stairs, watching the back of Mrs O'Doole's yellow-socked feet pumping the steps above her. The door was ajar and blue daylight was only seconds away.

Beth felt the impact of the gunman's weight on the stairs behind her and heard their creaking as he pounded up in pursuit. Mrs O'Doole was through the door and turning around to face her, features pleading to her to make it. She clasped the handle in readiness to seal it. Beth felt a hand on the back of her calf, fingers gripping tighter and restraining her from taking the last two steps.

She kicked back but the hand only released its grip to secure a firmer one behind her knee. His palm was hot. Beth turned with the meat tenderiser and smashed it onto the crown of his baldness. She felt the impact resonate through the bone of her arm as if she'd brought it down against a block of solid wood. But it sounded softer. She let go of the handle.

The spikes held the tenderiser in place, and his body

wavered as if he were surfing. Beth turned and took the last few paces through the door.

Mrs O'Doole quickly slammed and locked it. "I'll call the cops." She leaned against it, as if her slight frame would act as an extra barrier.

"Where are the boys?"

"I told them to run." She sucked in the last word as the gunman's bulk battered against the door, the impact flicking up her silver fringe.

"Get away from there. He's armed!" Beth dragged Mrs O'Doole from the panel by her shoulders. "Where's your phone?"

"In here."

Beth followed Mrs O'Doole into the living room.

"My cell." She ran over to the dining table, ditched her wok and rifled through her handbag. "Where the hell…"

"Has he been in here? Could he have taken it?"

"We were in the kitchen…" Grim realisation. "I gave Tyler and Kevin their iPhones to take with them, though."

Beth's fingers fumbled with the lock of the double-glazed door. "Let's catch up with them." She recognised the sound of the gunman's bullet shooting out the lock. "Go!" She slid the glazed door open and gestured Mrs O'Doole through.

They both sprinted out and Beth quickly closed the door behind them. As they crossed the deck and headed around the side of the house, the gunman emerged through the kitchen screen.

"Stop!"

Beth gritted her teeth, waited for the bullet in her back, but they'd just turned the corner and were pelting down the side of the lodge. Their frantic breath echoed back at them as they headed towards the steps. But the gunman only had a few feet to cover before he had them in his sights again.

She looked back briefly as they reached the bottom of the steps. The gunman still hadn't appeared at the corner. Beth followed Mrs O'Doole, hauling her weak legs up using the rough wooden handrail to drag herself higher. There were about fifteen to climb and she expected to hear a gunshot on each one. They neared the top and Mrs O'Doole exclaimed: "I told you to get out of here!"

When Beth reached her, Mrs O'Doole's sons were standing there, faces tightened by fear. Beth recognised the eldest with the blue camouflage bandana and the green trainers.

He looked to be on the brink of tears. "We couldn't leave you."

"Fucking run!" Beth broke up the reunion, and they all headed towards the path, ducking and getting struck by the low branches of the trees.

"Tyler, call the police!" his mother instructed him.

"Spread out!" Beth yelled. Tyler was ahead of her. She saw him pull his iPhone out of his back pocket and then heard the shout behind her. It was the other boy.

Beth turned to find Mrs O'Doole had halted. Just beyond her, the gunman was standing. He had Kevin, his arm locked firmly around the boy's neck and the barrel of his revolver rammed against his cheek.

CHAPTER SIXTY-SEVEN

The iPhone clip the boys had gloated over flashed momentarily through Marcia O'Doole's head. The leopard attacking the weakest, youngest member of the springbok herd. "Kevin!"

The man who had claimed to be an FBI officer whispered something in his ear, like a father or an uncle might. Kevin immediately stopped screaming.

"Let him go!" Tyler dryly shrieked from behind her.

"Kevin, do exactly as he says!" She held up her palms to both of them.

"Let him go, motherfucker!"

"Shut up, Tyler!" Marcia didn't take her eyes off them.

"I've got the police on the line, Mom!"

"Hang it up, Tyler. Now!"

"But, Mom–"

"Now!"

For a moment the sound of birds filled out the silence. Kevin trembled against the barrel, his cheek indented by its pressure.

"OK. Everyone walk back with me to the house. Mh?"

He didn't need to catch them all. Only one.

Mimic watched Mrs O'Doole and Beth Jordan pass him. Neither of them met his eye. Tyler O'Doole did. Poor kid. He probably thought his withering look could change the course of events. The ladies understood they couldn't. "Show me your phone, son."

Tyler halted and held it up, still holding his gaze.

Mimic examined the screen to make sure he'd hung it up. "Drop it at your brother's feet." He blinked the warm blood from the tenderiser wound out of his eyes.

Tyler released it and looked at it lying on the dead grass. Now he wouldn't meet Mimic's eye.

"Go and join your mom, and let's have no more of this 'motherfucker' monkey business."

He swivelled Kevin, lifting him off his feet and setting him down again, so he could watch Tyler catch up and the three of them approach the steps. He whispered again into Kevin's ear. "If you have a phone, just take it out of your pocket and leave it with your brother's."

Kevin wrenched it out and let it drop.

He eased the pressure on his cheek. "Just stay calm. This will all be over if you do exactly as you're told." He'd initially told him he'd shoot his mother and brother in the face if he didn't stop crying, and he'd responded appropriately.

The women and teenager turned at the top of the steps.

"Go into the dining room and stand by the mantel. Don't be tempted by any impulse to escape."

"I'm not going anywhere without Kevin." Mrs O'Doole's voice trembled behind her defiance.

"You are. Back to the dining room or I shoot both your boys in front of you."

"Mom..." said Tyler, although Mimic was unsure whether it was a caution or just a child's demand for her to make what was happening stop.

Mrs O'Doole gripped him firmly by his arm and moved him towards the steps. Beth Jordan followed. What was turning over in that brain? He'd be watching her closer than anyone else.

Mimic watched their three heads disappear below the edge

of the bank and then marched the boy across to the handrail. "Walk slowly in front of me; don't run, or I'll put a bullet in your spine and then one in your brother and Mom." He released the boy's clammy body.

Kevin looked as if his legs might give out as he gripped the wood and descended. Mimic watched the adults looking back at his progress as they moved slowly down the side of the lodge. "Eyes front, all of you. Dining room mantel."

When Mimic reached the bottom of the steps, the others had turned the corner. He'd have to be wary of an attack here. The adults knew it would be their last opportunity. "Kevin."

The younger boy immediately halted and Mimic secured his arm around his throat and pushed the barrel back into the circular impression in his cheek. "Walk."

They hit the corner but Mimic saw the adults had already entered the dining room via the double-glazed door. Perhaps they still thought they might be able to plead for some of their lives to be spared. That wasn't going to happen. Killing them was the least of his worries, and the sooner he got started and had space and time to think about how to dispose of the bodies, the better. He briefly looked out across the river and sniffed in the clean air.

"That's it, one more step."

When he saw the other three standing in front of the mantel, Mimic released Kevin. He ran to his mother and she wrapped her arms around his head as he crooked it into her shoulder. He was taller than her, and Mimic allowed the awkward hug a few seconds before stepping into the room, keeping his gun pointed at the boy's back. He dragged the door shut behind him. He wouldn't need the suppressor. Their isolation meant concealing the shots wasn't going to be necessary.

CHAPTER SIXTY-EIGHT

Beth looked directly down the barrel of the gunman's revolver for the third time.

"Why are you doing this?" Mrs O'Doole's eyes were firmly closed.

The gunman wiped at the corners of his mouth with his Starbucks napkin and pocketed it. "Everyone down into the cellar."

The two boys started crying then, but a series of solid knocks immediately halted them. All five of them were suddenly holding their breath.

"Not a word," he warned them, narrowing his eyes as if it would focus his hearing.

They waited for further sound. The knocks on the front door came again. Silence. Then pounding, heavy footsteps. Somebody was walking down the side of the lodge. The gunman swivelled to the double-glazing and waited for their arrival. "Any noise and I shoot our visitor and then the kids." He didn't even turn to them as he issued the threat.

Beth recognised the man who appeared on the deck outside. It was the grey-whiskered resident of the property she'd visited further up the track. He was dressed in fishing gear.

"Help you?" the gunman said cordially as he slid the door open a crack. He kept his revolver hand behind his back where they could all see it.

"Name's Ned Hollis. I'm staying at Flathead Bend. Just a

heads-up; were you expecting a visitor here last night?"

"There's a bunch of us assembling here. Family vacation. Why?"

"We had a girl come onto our property last night. Said she was looking for a woman and two young boys. My wife directed her here. Just wanted to know if she arrived."

"Yeah. She did. Safe and sound."

"It would put our minds at rest. If she was just an opportunist thief trying her luck around the area..."

"As I say, she got here last night," the gunman said firmly.

"What time was that? Pardon me, but I'd like to make sure we're talking about the same lady."

The gunman was briefly struck dumb. "Let me think, now."

"Just to confirm... this was a young lady with a shaved head. We didn't know–"

"Tell you what. Beth!" the gunman called her as if she might be in another room. He turned. "Oh, here she is. This your night caller?" He angled his body towards her, using his empty hand to gesture her to the door. "Beth, you scared this man half to death."

As she reached the double-glazing, the man smiled warmly. "I wouldn't say that. Just gave us a rude awakening is all."

Beth tried to return the man's smile but found the muscles around her lips had seized up. "Sorry again."

"No trouble; I won't disturb you good folks any longer."

"Thanks for stopping by. Appreciate it." The gunman was already sliding the door shut. He returned his attention to his hostages, training his revolver on them while they all listened to Ned's waders clumping slowly back around the side of the lodge.

"OK, everyone down into the cellar." He motioned them towards the hall. Kevin started to weep again as the O'Dooles complied. He gestured Beth to follow.

She fell in behind them, wondering what the hell she could do, but knowing that the barrel was pointed at her back. As soon as they were in the cellar, they were out of time.

Kevin clung onto the edge of the door and she could see his knuckles whiten.

"Kevin." Mrs O'Doole tried to lift him away.

"No delays. We can do this up here if you want. Mh? Or I can give you some options downstairs."

Beth knew there was only one option and they were about twenty paces from it.

CHAPTER SIXTY-NINE

Marcia O'Doole put her arms around Kevin's shoulders, her own sobs threatening to break through. She smelt the shampoo scent in his hair as his body shook in her embrace, and whispered into his hot ear. "Take my hand, Kevin. I won't let go of it."

"There's no time for this. Move him downstairs."

She ignored his instruction, screwed her eyes shut against it and gripped him tighter. "Got to be brave now." Attack was pointless. How could she disarm him? But she knew he wasn't going to let any of them walk out of the house alive and that this moment was the last she'd have to protect her sons.

Maybe if she launched herself at him, Beth Jordan would follow suit... and then maybe the boys. Perhaps the four of them could overpower him, even if he pulled the trigger.

"Do you want me to move his fingers from there?"

She didn't want to open her eyes again. Wanted to be suspended in this moment. But now was the time to act. Marcia tensed herself and opened them. She saw their executioner first and then the deer head.

Mimic saw it a second after the pain of its antler piercing just below his waist. His back arched against it and he fell onto his side. While he'd been distracted by the kid clinging to the door, the little fucker Tyler had dropped behind him and swiped it off the wall.

"Run!" Tyler yelled.

Mimic felt the sharp edge of something strike the wound already in the top of his skull, and the room flashed yellow then black as his brain momentarily disconnected. Sound was briefly muffled, but he maintained a grip on the gun. Sharp nails dug into the back of his hand, but the new pain was no match for the cold burn below his spine. He swung his free fist at whichever woman was trying to prise the revolver out of his fingers and rolled onto his back. He waved the gun at anyone who might be stood over him.

"Mom!" Sounded like Kevin.

"Out the back!" Tyler again. Like he was underwater.

"He'll catch us out there." Beth's voice was the same.

"He will if we don't go now!" Mrs O'Doole's vibration in the soup.

Mimic used the barrel of the gun to shakily push himself up, the yellow film clearing as the sharper sounds of their frantic footsteps crashed back.

"Upstairs!" Beth again. Clear as day.

They were running back past the dining room doorway and scrambling up the stairs before he could rise properly. Mimic looked down at the benign features of the deer head and the blood on one of its antlers. He staggered out into the passage and walked past the cellar door to the foot of the stairs in time to hear an upstairs door slam and lock.

Beth had been right. He would have used the suppressor and gunned them down as they climbed the steps or ran along the jetty. Even if they'd made it into the water, he could easily have picked them off. They were safer locked away from him, for now.

He didn't have to panic. When he'd arrived and used the upstairs bathroom, he'd ascertained there weren't any telephones or computers up there, no way of them communicating with anyone outside the lodge. Tyler and Kevin's iPhones were outside, and Mrs O'Doole's was safely in his pocket.

They'd done him a favour. He could now consider how to deal with them as a group without being distracted. Now he didn't have to hold a gun on two unpredictable adults and two teenagers; he could focus on the easiest way to dispose of them.

He slowly climbed the stairs and heard something heavy sliding across the floor as he reached the bedroom door they were behind.

Beth and Mrs O'Doole shunted the old chest of drawers as flush with the door as they could. The room was in darkness as the wooden shutters were closed over the window.

Beth dragged Mrs O'Doole low and hissed at the boys. "Get down on the other side of the bed."

The boys took cover between it and the window just as a shot rang out and the handle splintered, wood flakes and dust flying. Beth and Mrs O'Doole crouched in the cover behind the drawers and put their body weight against it, panting as they waited for him to try and bulldoze his way through.

No attempt was made, but as they exchanged eye contact, both their jaws remained clenched in readiness.

CHAPTER SEVENTY

Mimic lowered his gun arm and stepped back one pace from the door. That should keep them immobile for a while, and he intended to exploit the time. He quickly slid his shoes off and hooked them up with his free hand before padding downstairs in his socked feet. Stepping on the sides of the steps meant they only creaked slightly as he made his way down them and back into the kitchen. Not knowing where he was in the house would keep them afraid.

They wouldn't unlock the door for a good while, but he had to check any other exits they had. He left his shoes on the counter and quietly opened the back door. He limped a few paces along the deck and noticed a small utility hut further along the riverbank. Perhaps there were some tools there that might be useful.

The pain at his waist intensified with each step. He stopped to put his fingers gingerly against the wound and felt a jolt as he touched it. His mouth filled with saliva as he looked at the blood caking his fingertips. Little shit. He wiped them on his claret shirt.

He turned the corner and slunk down the side of the lodge, stopping at the next corner to look upwards at the windows to the bedrooms. They were all covered with white slatted wooden shutters, so no attempt had been made to open them... yet.

There was no drainpipe beside any of them, so if they did try to exit that way, they would have quite a drop to the concrete and probably break their ankles. The bank that the steps were cut into was too far from the lodge to jump to it.

Maybe they'd try to tie some sheets together and climb down, but he'd let them know they should reconsider that. Mimic aimed his gun at the slatted window and put three bullets into it. He could hear them scream as the bullets pierced the wood and glass.

He strolled back around the house and into the kitchen. There was a stack of thick pancakes on a plate. He peeled one off and it was still slightly warm. He stuffed it into his mouth. They were good and rich. Mom obviously used extra eggs in the batter. His head throbbed as his jaw pumped. He tentatively touched the tender area on his scalp and winced.

Mimic turned things over while he painfully ate two more pancakes, and then went down to the cellar.

CHAPTER SEVENTY-ONE

Beth strained her ears for sounds of movement in and around the lodge over the rapid breathing in the room. She was still crouching with Mrs O'Doole at the base of the chest against the door, both of them on their knees. Directly after the potshots at the window, Tyler and Kevin had come over to their side of the bed and were lying on their stomachs next to each other. Three rods of daylight penetrated the wooden blinds and distressed glass, and Beth watched motes of dust rapidly moving through them.

Mrs O'Doole swallowed loudly and whispered. "I haven't heard him come back up the stairs."

"We didn't hear him go down them, either. I don't think we should move until we know where he is." Her throat felt bruised when she spoke, and the tenderiser wound Mrs O'Doole had inflicted still pumped under the flow of adrenaline.

"Who the hell is he?" She looked squarely at Beth as if she were responsible for his presence. "I heard what he said to you in the cellar. I came down because Kevin said he was sure he was the man we saw collapsed in the park and I'd called an ambulance for the morning we left."

"He's been murdering every person who used their phones to record the crash site." It felt like the first time she'd made eye contact with Tyler. He looked down at the carpet. "I came here to warn you."

"Why is he killing them?"

"I wish I knew. But you're the last people left."

Mrs O'Doole closed her eyes briefly, as if silently remonstrating with herself.

"Maybe he's gone." Kevin hissed hopefully. The imprint from the gunman's barrel was still in his cheek.

"Don't be a cock. He's not going to let us leave," Tyler growled

"Tyler." Mrs O'Doole shot him a barbed look.

Tyler realised his big-brother default setting wasn't helping matters. "Maybe if he thinks he can't get to us, he will, though," he added lamely.

But it was too late. Kevin looked petrified.

"If he can't get through the door then the window's his only other way in." Beth nodded towards it.

Tyler and Kevin started to raise their heads above the mattress to take a look.

"Keep down," Mrs O'Doole snarled through her teeth.

"The shutters are sealed." Beth could still see the hooks in place.

"Until he shoots off the locks."

"He'll need a ladder to get in. Is there one around?"

Mrs O'Doole rolled her eyes up briefly. "The cellar."

"If he tries that, we'll at least have warning and can pull these drawers away and escape down the stairs."

"And go where?" Mrs O'Doole raised her eyebrows. "He'll meet us coming up the side of the lodge or use us for target practice if we try to swim for it."

"We could split up," Beth said. "Some of us could try getting back onto the track while the others jump in the water. He can't chase us all at once. It might be the only chance we have."

Mrs O'Doole lowered her voice. "I'm not letting the boys out of my sight. Besides, he could chase anybody to the track and still have time to return to the jetty before we'd gotten to the other side."

Beth looked up at the ceiling. Over the bed, next to a smoke detector, was an attic door. "Can we get out through there?"

Mrs O'Doole followed her gaze. "There's no window in the roof. It's just for storage."

"Is that the only door to it?"

"No. The second one is over the landing."

"And that's the only other one?"

Mrs O'Doole nodded.

"What about Dad's hunting rifle?" Tyler interjected.

Beth turned to him and then looked back at his mother.

Mrs O'Doole didn't reflect the hope in the three sets of eyes suddenly on her. "It hasn't been fired for a long time. And we don't have any ammo for it."

"Um. We do," Tyler said, semi-contrite.

Mrs O'Doole narrowed her eyes at her older son. "I threw the ammo away."

"We found some of Dad's old stash at home and brought a box the last time we were here."

"You've been firing that thing unsupervised?" Her whisper could barely contain her mortification.

"You didn't really think we were fishing, did you, Mom?"

Mrs O'Doole's gaze panned to Kevin, and he looked shamefully down at the carpet.

"I don't believe this. What did I tell you, Tyler?"

Beth held up her hand. "Forget the discipline. Where is it?"

"Locked up in the gun cupboard in the back den." He avoided his mother's glare.

"You're sure?"

Tyler nodded. "It's the only one in the rack."

"At least we could use that to defend ourselves with. Who's got the key?"

Mrs O'Doole fumbled in her jeans pocket and extracted a bunch. She started looking through them. "It's missing."

Tyler produced his own set and held up the key for Beth.

"Tyler. I should..."

"Kill me?"

CHAPTER SEVENTY-TWO

Tyler's defiance forbade a response. Mrs O'Doole opened her mouth to admonish him but thought better of it.

Beth cut through the family stand-off. "The gun's definitely locked away?"

"Yeah. We put it back there after the last time we used it."

"And there's ammo?"

"In the bottom drawer of the desk," Kevin chimed in. "Right at the back, behind all the fishing reels." He evaded the heat of his mother's gaze as well.

"Tyler, how long do you think it would take to open the gun cupboard and load it?" Beth asked.

"He's not going down there," Mrs O'Doole interjected.

"I'm not saying he should. I'm just asking, if we did make a run for it, how long it would take to arm ourselves."

Mrs O'Doole bit her lip as she resigned herself to their limited options. "I can load the gun."

"Not as fast as me," Tyler butted in.

"Tyler, no."

"It's sticky. You haven't got the knack."

"I won't hear of it."

"Mom," Tyler said firmly, and waited for her eyes to engage his. His voice softened. "It's not like I have a whole bunch of time left to play with..."

"Tyler, enough."

He continued regardless. "But you and Kevin do."

Mrs O'Doole shook her head rapidly.

"You know it makes sense. You could never handle Dad's guns. Let me do it."

Beth sensed there was something more significant than a mother/son feud being aired and kept quiet.

"Out of the question." Mrs O'Doole bit her lip harder to compose herself. "End of discussion."

A sound at the window. All their heads turned towards it. It was barely discernible; four sharp scrapes in quick succession as if something were scratching the wood.

"What's that?" Kevin's eyes were suddenly bulging.

"Quiet," Mrs O'Doole whispered.

Four chests halted as they waited.

"I thought you were going fishing," Mrs Hollis responded to the sound of the kitchen door opening. She'd just settled herself in front of an old *Law and Order* rerun in the lounge with a plate of microwaved cinnamon cream hotcakes. Caught in the act. It was the sort of nightclothes brunch that Ned had outlawed because of her hypertension. She waited for a response but none came. "Ned?" She quickly slid the plate under the chair and walked into the kitchen. He was leaning on the counter with the receiver of the wall-mounted telephone to his ear. "What is it?"

He didn't look at her. "Police."

"What's going on?"

He still didn't respond, just blinked his eyes while he waited to be connected.

Mrs Hollis hated her husband when he kept her out of the loop. She'd recovered from almost being discovered with the hotcakes, but maybe he could smell them in the kitchen. Why the hell didn't he just go fishing and let her have her day? "Ned, tell me. Did you stop by Whispering Brook?"

Ned turned to her and she could see the gravity of the situation in his eyes. "The girl was there... and a guy. He seemed anxious to get rid of me, virtually shut the door in my face. When he turned from the window, though, I saw he had a gun behind his back."

Nobody wanted to breathe first. No further sound had come, but none of them shifted their gaze from the window.

Beth was the first to briefly exhale. "He's going to try something soon."

"Maybe he'll wait for us to make a move." Mrs O'Doole swung her weight from knee to knee to stop her legs going to sleep.

"I don't think he'll wait. We've got to be prepared. Is there anything in here we can use as a weapon?"

The four of them cast their eyes about the room, but another sound at the window magnetised them to it again. It was the same as before. They waited a second time. It came again, more insistent. Something was at the shutters and it wasn't a bird. It was making a concerted effort now, the scratching accelerating. Was a part of the blind being filed or sawed?

"He's trying to get in." Fear gave Kevin's words volume.

Beth put her finger to her lips and crawled slowly across to the window on her hands and knees.

"Stay here," Mrs O'Doole whispered behind her.

As she approached them, Beth kept focused on the shutters. If he were on a ladder trying to open them, there would still be glass between them but he could very easily shoot her through it. She scuttled faster and pressed herself against the wall below the window to find Mrs O'Doole crossing the oatmeal carpet.

"Mom." Tyler grabbed her leg as she passed him.

From Beth's position, the boys were entirely concealed by the bed. At least they would be safe if he started shooting into the room.

"Let it go." Mrs O'Doole didn't look back at her son. "I have to help."

"No, you don't."

"Stay there out of sight with your brother. I'll be safer under the window if he opens it." She blinked a few times as she waited, and then moved quickly forward as he released her. When she reached Beth, they exchanged a glance before the sound drew their eyes upwards again. It was becoming more frantic.

"We'll stand either side, I'll open the window and we'll push the shutters out. If he's there, they'll hit him."

Mrs O'Doole nodded, and they both slid their backs along the wall and then stood either side of the window. Mrs O'Doole carefully shifted a lightweight dressing room stool with clothes heaped on it to one side and took up position at the edge of the frame.

Beth looked up and tried to spot any movement through the three holes in the glass and wood but thought it unlikely he'd give away his presence so obviously. Maybe he was crouching below it while he worked. Perhaps opening the shutters was exactly what he wanted them to do. Once they were wide, she and Mrs O'Doole wouldn't dare reach out to close them again, which would leave the room accessible.

The scratching came again. Maybe he was about to break open the shutters. If he did, they'd have to shift the chest away from the door before they could escape, and he could shoot all of them through the glass in that time.

As if in answer to the thought, Beth heard a sliding noise behind her. She turned to see Tyler prising the drawers back from the door.

"Tyler." Mrs O'Doole's alarm grated in her throat.

Her son whispered back, "I can get Dad's gun while he's at the window."

"Stay where you are."

Beth waved her hands to halt him as well.

The scratching was frenzied now.

Mrs O'Doole took a step forward. "Get back behind the bed."

Tyler looked down at Kevin. "Shut this after me and be ready to open it again." He tugged the busted handle and slid through the tight gap.

"Tyler!" Mrs O'Doole shrieked.

CHAPTER SEVENTY-THREE

Tyler darted quickly along the landing to the top of the stairs and stopped briefly to look down at the patch of floor visible at the bottom. Once there, he'd have to walk about eight paces to the end of the passage and slip into the den.

He listened for signs of movement below. Had his argument with Mom been overheard through the window? Was the guy now on his way back around the side of the lodge?

He put his right toes on the top stair and stopped, his creaking weight teetering on the front of his green sneaker. He had to go now. Had to do this and get it right. Tyler put all his weight on the foot, moved the other one past it and quickly pounded down the stairs.

The whole staircase creaked with his descent. He attempted to tread lightly, but every step seemed deafening.

Marcia O'Doole reached the door and opened it as far as it would against the chest. She put her face to the gap and peered along the landing just in time to see the top of his head disappear below floor level. "Tyler." Her voice was dehydrated, but she knew it was useless trying to call him back. She prayed he was quick.

"Wait, wait, wait." It was Beth, and when Marcia turned back to the bedroom, Beth was holding her hand up for silence. She hadn't opened the window. Kevin was standing on his knees, and Marcia gestured for him to get back on his stomach. He complied, and she stopped halfway back to the shutters as the scratching recommenced.

Beth looked upwards to the ceiling. "It's coming from above."

Marcia joined her and looked hard at the spot in the plaster above the window, as if it would enable her to see through it to the source of the sound.

"Could he be in the attic?"

Marcia nodded. "Although it sounds more like..." Her words butted into realisation.

"What?"

"Raccoon."

The word immediately demystified the sound. Paws scratching at wood beams above.

The revelation drained the blood out of Marcia's frozen expression. "It's a raccoon." She was running back to the door. Tyler was downstairs and so was the man who wanted to kill them. She peered back through the gap, her mouth open.

Marcia wanted to scream his name but stopped herself. If she shouted a warning, would that alert the killer to her son's presence?

Tyler shut the door to the musty den as quietly as he could and tiptoed to his father's desk. He quietly rolled the leather chair back, his stomach muscles clenching against every sound, gently sat down and leaned to the bottom drawer. He lifted the metal ring out of its mounting and half closed his eyes as he slid it slowly outwards so he wouldn't disturb the clutter inside.

He silently blew out short blasts of breath as his shaking fingers carefully dragged back the fishing reels and spools of line and he sought the bullets he'd positioned in a hiding place at the back.

Tyler's hand settled on the box, and the bullets rattled slightly as he drew it clear. He delicately stood and then crossed the rug to the gun cupboard on the opposite wall above his father's old music system.

Marcia O'Doole was almost through the door when she felt Beth's hand firmly clasp her shoulder.

"Stay here," Beth whispered at her ear.

Marcia tried to struggle free.

"Stay here," Beth said again firmly. "Someone needs to look after Kevin."

Marcia felt drawn to the stairs and the situation at the bottom but knew she had to protect her youngest as well. How could she warn Tyler? If she screamed his name, it would telegraph his having left the room. If she didn't, he wouldn't know the killer could be in the house.

Tyler's fingers slid over the cool metal of the keys as he slipped the correct one into the lock and opened the wooden door. The hinge groaned a little as he swung it wide and grabbed his father's Merkel RX Helix hunting rifle. He'd introduced Tyler to it when he was thirteen, extolling its close-range virtues. It was a straight-pull, bolt-action weapon designed for rapid follow-up shots. Tyler fumbled the shells out of the box and quickly loaded up the detachable box magazine.

He remembered to slide the safety button back on the tang, then stopped at the door and listened. Tyler expected to hear a commotion from the bedroom, but all was quiet. He gulped and it felt like a rock bouncing in his throat. He put his fingers on the handle and opened the den door a crack to peer into the passage; nobody in evidence. He hadn't looked back as he came down the stairs, but could see through the screen that the back door was hanging open. Tyler cycled the bolt so he had a round in the chamber, and opened the door.

The weapon felt unwieldy in his clammy hands. He and Kevin had taken shots at rabbits but had never hit anything but his father's Miller cans. Tyler had no doubt he could pull the trigger on the fucker who had put a gun to his brother's head, though. He gripped it tighter and grazed the trigger with the pad of his sweaty forefinger. The wall clock ticked in the kitchen.

He pointed the rifle down the passage as he crept back to the bottom of the stairs. Still no sound from above. Perhaps he'd given up on trying to get in through the window, which meant he definitely was on his way back into the lodge. He decided to sprint up the stairs and not worry about how much noise he made.

He'd just braced himself to make the dash when the screen creaked and the man he'd stabbed with the antlers entered the kitchen, holding a sledgehammer.

CHAPTER SEVENTY-FOUR

Tyler's finger jerked against the trigger, but the shot slammed into the wooden floor of the passage, fragments of fibre bursting from the corner of the coconut mat at the kitchen doorway. His target didn't falter and marched steadily towards him, swinging the sledge to shoulder height in readiness.

Tyler's hand gripped the bolt but he estimated the sledgehammer would be arcing down on him before he'd ejected the spent case. He tore up the stairs and felt heavy footfalls behind him. He didn't look back, just had to get the gun to his mother. Get back to the room and safety so he could reload.

He saw her terrified face at the gap in the door.

"Tyler!" She pulled herself out of the way so he could squeeze back in.

Halfway through, he could feel fingers on his T-shirt collar dragging him back. A hot, solid fist bunched the material on his bare shoulder to secure its grip, and he could hear it stretching as he tried to tug his body clear. Mom and Beth were digging their nails into him, gripping and yanking on him as the fist wrenched Tyler back towards the landing.

"Kevin!" he shouted to his brother who was lying with his hands over his head next to the bed. Tyler lobbed the rifle at him. He looked down at it as it skidded to a halt in front of him. "You know how to load it!"

But Kevin didn't move from his position.

"Kevin!"

Beth hooked her fingers over his belt and yanked him at the waist.

"Let go of him!" Mom screamed as she frantically jabbed at the man's hand with a pair of nail scissors.

Tyler heard the T-shirt rip and grunted to propel himself forward. He heard a male howl and the hot fist briefly lost its grip. But the fingers quickly reattached themselves, first to the knot of his bandana and then, when that was dragged off, the few curls he had left at the nape of his neck. His head was bent backwards as Tyler gripped the edge of the chest and attempted to use its weight to lever himself inside.

"Mom!"

She was still lunging at the hand holding him.

Tyler could hear the hairs being torn from the roots. He heaved his shoulders forward so he couldn't snap his neck all the way back, and his whole body shook with the exertion.

"Let him go!" Mom's hand flashed past him again and again.

Another growl from the landing and Tyler was released. He staggered a few paces into the room and then fell onto his knees in front of Kevin. The door slammed.

Without exchanging eye contact with his brother, Tyler scooped up the rifle and cycled the bolt as he turned. The spent case was ejected and pinged across the floor, and a new one was locked in the chamber. Mom and Beth were pushing the chest of drawers up against the door again and he ran to their aid, leaning against it as they all anticipated a further assault.

For a few seconds, their panting was the only sound. Tyler looked at his mother's hands against the chest. Her right was a fist of blood. The pair of nail scissors blades poked bent out of her grip.

The room shook with the impact of something heavy. The two women put their shoulders against the chest to hold it in place.

"He's got a sledgehammer." Tyler stood back and aimed the

rifle at the door. "I've got a full magazine! I'll fucking shoot you if you come in here!"

Another impact; a picture fell from the wall beside the door and smashed.

Beth yanked Mom back from the door. "If he punches a hole in the door, we'd better take cover. Sure you know how to fire that thing?"

Tyler nodded but didn't take his eyes off the panel. "Might take him some time to work through that. It's solid."

"But that's not." Beth pointed to a fissure that had appeared in the plaster beside the door. With the next swing, the head of the hammer poked through the wall.

CHAPTER SEVENTY-FIVE

Beth watched the hammer disappear from the crack and then slam back harder, the metal waggling as the handle was twisted to open the gap. He just needed an aperture wide enough to shoot them through.

"It's a stud wall." Mrs O'Doole gripped Tyler's ragged T-shirt and tried to drag him back towards Kevin. "Just drywall."

Tyler, minus his bandana, the back of his bald skull raked and scratched by fingernails, stood his ground.

"Let's not wait for him." Beth gripped Tyler's arm tight. "Can you shoot him through that?"

He nodded, aiming the rifle at the crack as the hammer was extracted again. He fired once, and his whole body jerked with the recoil. The gun had done its best to dislocate his shoulder, but he quickly reloaded and pulled the trigger again.

The noise in their enclosed space was deafening. Beth's ears hissed as they waited for a sound from the landing. The head didn't return. Daylight was seeping in through the crack.

The same thought occurred to everyone at once.

"Down!" Beth reached Kevin first and dragged him around to the other side of the bed. The four of them crouched there in the three spotlights from the holes that had been punched in the shutters.

A different ear-piercing shot rang out. The bullet

thumped into the wall above them. Beth put her arms around the O'Dooles and pulled their heads as far down as they would go.

Another quickly followed, and she watched a column of holes working its way down the smashed wall. Only the angle of the end of the bed protected them, and his bullets would easily puncture it as soon as his shot was aimed a foot further down. He was quickly working his way towards that. Either they'd be dead by then or he could just kick out the perforations he was making and finish the job.

Beth watched another hole appear the same time she felt something buzz past her head. "Tyler!"

He was lying against her lap, his fingers still shakily reloading the rifle. Beth waited for the next shot and wondered whose it would be. But another sound beat them both. A police siren.

Dust and plaster floated about the room. As Beth's eardrums still throbbed from the gunshots, she watched Tyler's hands frozen on the rifle. It got louder until they could hear the car's engine. They held their breath and knew the gunman had to be doing the same.

Soft footfalls on the stairs. He was on his way down them. Beth struggled to her feet and scrambled to the window.

A hiss of gravel as the car and siren halted.

Knowing he was downstairs, she felt safe enough to peer through the bullet holes in the glass.

"Let me look." Tyler was behind her.

"Get back here, Tyler."

"Do as she says." Beth squinted through the holes but, after her eyes accustomed themselves to the bright daylight, saw only the trees at the top of the bank. She quickly unlocked one window. She swung it in and then released the eye-and-hook catch on the shutter. Even if he was walking fast, he could still only be on his way around the side of the lodge. She gently pushed on the slats.

A police car, lights revolving, was parked at the top of the bank and two officers with buzz cuts in black zip-up jackets and matching potbellies were concentrating on the wooden steps as they made their way down them.

"Help! Up here!" Beth shouted.

They looked up in unison, pausing a few steps from the bottom.

"I'm Officer Breslin. One of the residents called us and reported a man with a firearm."

"There's a man coming to meet you and he's dangerous."

"Are you being held against your will?"

"He's on his way to you now!"

Both officers put their hands to their holsters.

"Just get us out of here!" Tyler shouted at her ear.

Beth watched the gunman emerge from the side of the lodge in his socks, his arm extended. The officers turned from the window, their guns swiftly drawn.

The gunman's weapon discharged first and one officer slammed back against the steps, his hand still gripping the wooden rail. The second officer loosed off a shot, and Beth saw the gunman's left shoulder dragged back by the bullet. His right arm remained rigid as he fired a second time.

The second officer's elbow shattered in a cloud of red, and then the material of his dark jacket jumped against his chest as another bullet pounded into it. He slid down the steps, his trousers riding up his white legs.

The first officer was still trying to get to his feet. As he pulled himself back up by the rail, his neck burst, dark blood spattering his face and the steps, before the top half of his agonised expression was obliterated.

The second officer came to rest at the bottom of the steps while the first finally released his hold on the handrail. His lifeless hand slapped against his waist and slid beside him. The sound of the gunfire still bounced around the trees.

"No!" Tyler screamed.

Without faltering, the gunman turned and shot at the window. Beth turned and threw herself against Tyler. The glass lampshade exploded above their heads and showered them with frosted fragments as they hit the floor.

CHAPTER SEVENTY-SIX

Mimic lowered his gun and turned from the window. Nobody would appear there for a good few seconds. He looked at the two officers' bodies sprawled on the steps. No movement.

He knew the pain in his shoulder was biding its time, and kept his arm rigid at his side. The situation was escalating out of his control, and time was now much more an issue. Mimic had as long as it took for the station to get suspicious about them not checking in. He strode to the dead officer at the bottom of the steps and unclipped the radio from his belt.

Mimic knew he now had to resort to the only other option open to him. They'd acquired a rifle, and trying to enter the room would be too risky. Even if they barely knew how to fire it, he didn't want to be on the receiving end of any more stray bullets. It was time to implement the plan he'd suspected was inevitable the moment they'd locked themselves in the bedroom.

He made his way back down the side of the lodge, listening to dispatch. It was a woman's sleepy, sexy voice, Carolina accent. She'd want a report soon, and then she'd wake up. Maybe he could be all finished up before it was needed. He turned the corner, walked down the back of the property and headed to the utility hut. Amongst the weed killer, detergent and barbecue tools, he found a black bottle of charcoal lighter fluid. He also found an oversize lighter with "License To Grill" written on it. As he shook it, he noticed the tiny bloody slits in his freckled hand that Mrs O'Doole had inflicted with her nail scissors.

On his way through the kitchen, he resisted the temptation to eat any more of her pancakes and slipped back up the stairs. He still had to be quiet or they might take their chances through the window.

Mimic stopped four steps from the top. He could see along the landing floor, and the bedroom door was still sealed. He put the bottle on the stair, pushed down on and opened the childproof lid with his good hand then picked it up and aimed it. There was a stand further down with a bowl of potpourri in it. He squeezed and arced the jet so it landed there and soaked it. He had to be careful not to use the last drops of fluid, because the bottle was going to squeak and give him away.

He stopped and shook it gently. Still a decent weight left. Mimic squirted it all over the runner rug and then at the wall, and doused it and the bullet holes there. The drywall would go up, no problem. The only thing he couldn't be sure of was which exit they'd use.

Mimic guessed the adults would test the water either way and tell the kids to leave via the route that seemed safest. He needed to start the fire as soon as possible. Get them panicked while he took up position. Perhaps he should seat himself in the patrol car and wait for them there. Back down to the cellar first, though. He played the jet over the door and then across the gap at the bottom, watched the liquid trickling underneath it.

The bottle was nearly empty. He rolled it up the rug and it came to rest just outside the door. Mimic sparked the lighter and held it against the edge of the doused runner. A blue sheen rose from the fibres and travelled the length of it to the wooden stand. Damage limitation was the most he could achieve now. He had to secure one of the O'Doole boys to extract his password, burn the whole family in their lodge and remove Beth Jordan to dispose of elsewhere.

Mimic turned to walk back down the stairs and stopped. He reached up to the smoke detector attached to the angled ceiling above him and unscrewed it from its position.

Beth lay on her stomach, the breeze from the open window wafting in fresh pine air and birdsong. Was he still training his gun on the window? The four of them were motionless as they listened. Tyler was lying in the same position beside her, staring at the backs of his hands. Mrs O'Doole was still against the bed, cradling Kevin.

"Are they dead?" Mrs O'Doole mouthed.

Beth nodded and tried to halt the replay of the officers' bodies exploding on the steps. "Do you think they left the keys in the car?" she said to Tyler, unsure of how the deaths of the men outside had affected him. He suddenly moved and grabbed the rifle.

Mrs O'Doole sat up and whispered. "Where is it?"

"Top of the steps." Tyler loaded the rifle, his third spent shell rolling and pinging against the wall. "If we can't find the keys, we can hotwire it."

Mrs O'Doole blinked once but dismissed the temptation to quiz him further about this ability.

Beth sat up. "We could see if the officers have them on our way up the steps, but we might not have time."

"The car will at least give us some cover." Tyler moved on his buttocks back to the wall beside his mother.

Mrs O'Doole shook her head. "We shouldn't even think about trying to reach the car while he's still out there. Here we have a weapon and walls to protect us. This is the safest place."

Mimic took his napkin out of his pocket and wiped at the edges of his mouth.

"Unit 22, where the hell are you?" It was the sleepy female voice on the police radio.

He placed his mouth against it so his response would be distorted. "Unit 22."

"What is your position?"

He repeated the process. "We're clear."

"Say again?"

"We're clear." It wasn't going to work.

"Unit 22, is that you?"

"Who else?"

No response.

He belched and tasted Mrs O'Doole's pancakes. Time was running out. But the fire was about to precipitate their upstairs escape, and as soon as he heard movement, he would be ready to respond. He waited, listening for vibrations in the lodge.

CHAPTER SEVENTY-SEVEN

Kevin was the first to spot the smoke. He pointed at the wisps crawling up the wall from the bullet holes.

"Jesus. He's set a fire." Tyler sat bolt upright.

Beth exchanged a look of resignation with Mrs O'Doole. "He's going to expect us to escape through the window and will probably be waiting for us to climb down."

"If he's lit a fire on the stairs, it's going to be our only way out." Mrs O'Doole lifted Kevin away from her so she could uncoil her legs. She knelt in front of him, took him by the shoulders and addressed his terror-stricken expression. "We have to be ready to run."

He shook his head.

"Listen, Kevin, we have no choice. This whole room will be on fire soon."

Beth tugged the duvet off the bed and started removing its cover. "Don't stand in line with the window. We can tie this and the bottom sheet together and dangle it out."

"So he can shoot us off it."

"Tyler!" Mrs O'Doole narrowed her eyes at him.

"It's exactly what he's expecting us to do," Beth said grimly. "Let me take a look in the attic."

Mrs O'Doole yanked at the bottom sheet. "If there's fire below, we don't want to get trapped up there."

"Didn't you say there's another hatch over the landing."

"Yeah. But what good is that going to do us?"

"At least we could get out onto the landing without having to open that door. If we move the chest now, he'll know we're making a run for it down the stairs."

Mrs O'Doole started knotting the sheet to the duvet cover. "He's probably made sure we can't get down that way, anyway."

"Let me check. If there's a way out up here–"

"I've told you there isn't."

"At least let us try, Mom. I'll take a look."

Mrs O'Doole gripped Tyler's arm as he went to get on the mattress. "You stay here with the gun. He still might come through that wall."

He turned to Beth. "Come on, I'll boost you."

They both got on the bed and Beth slid her foot into his interlinked fingers.

"One, two..."

On three, he raised her to the ceiling, and she punched her palms against the hatch. It slid sideways, and Tyler teetered as she scrabbled for the edge.

"OK?"

She felt him push against the soles of her boots and crawled into the darkness. There was a strong aroma of wood lacquer. Beth looked down into the bedroom at Tyler.

"There's a pull-cord for the light above the hatch." Mrs O'Doole leaned in and gestured.

"I should go up there, Mom."

"Stay where you are."

Beth half straightened until she felt the beams against her scalp. Cobwebs stroked her face. She waved her hands about until she touched the string. The end of the pull struck her in the chest and she trapped it there, gripping the plastic and quickly yanking it down.

Strip lights flickered on. Mrs O'Doole was right. The roof was made of solid beams. No window or hatch. Only a small amount of daylight coming through a grille that was no bigger than a place mat. There were a few crates skulking in one corner, but otherwise the considerable space was empty. Beth headed towards the landing side, padding carefully across the floorboards. She found the hatch with a telescopic ladder clipped to the top of it and, as she slid her finger into the ring, felt a warm draught from below.

Marcia O'Doole looked at the wall behind her. Black patches were blistering the ivory wallpaper and rapidly spreading upwards to the coving. The blaze on the landing had to be intense. She looked at the open window and the sunshine outside.

Sooner or later, they'd have to lower the sheets and take their chances. Maybe Tyler could cover them with gunfire from the window while she took Kevin down. But even if they reached the ground, they still had to make it up the steps to the patrol car.

Beth still hadn't opened the hatch. What if he'd pre-empted this move and was waiting on the stairs with his gun trained on it? She ran back to the opening she'd entered by and looked down at the two faces there. "Drop the sheets from the window and let me know when you've done it. Then I'll open the other hatch."

Mrs O'Doole and Tyler nodded uncertainly.

"Maybe we can distract him. Be careful."

They left her looking at the stripped mattress. Suddenly it was slid out of view leaving a square of darker oatmeal carpet. She assumed they'd moved it nearer the window so they could secure the sheet around the slats in the end.

Beth waited, crouching and bracing herself for gunfire, but none came. Their two faces returned and nodded again. Beth crept over to the second hatch. He hadn't started taking shots at the window. Was he in position on the bank? If he was, he wouldn't give away his presence there yet, wouldn't start firing until at least one of them tried to climb down. Or perhaps he was still in the house.

She knew she didn't have time to delay any further. Beth grabbed the ring and heaved the door, leaning swiftly back from the opening as it hinged up. Fire found fresh oxygen; a thick streamer of orange flame sucked through, scorching the ceiling above. She waited for it to ignite the beams. To her relief, the column quickly weakened to short spikes at the aperture before it dropped completely out of sight again. Acrid grey smoke poured upwards and started to fill the attic, though. Beth clamped her hand over her mouth and fought back a cough. She couldn't give her presence away if the gunman was nearby.

Beth leaned slowly over the opening, the draught of heat almost unbearable, and looked down at the blazing carpet runner below. The house popped and cracked amidst the heavy rumble of the fire. From her angle, she couldn't see down the stairs. She moved to the other side of the hatch and quickly dipped her head over the edge so she could get an upside-down view of the landing.

She squinted against the fumes, felt her scalp and eyelids tighten. Huge flames covered the wall of the bedroom, their tips gradually creeping across the ceiling. The stairs were clear and the other side of the landing hadn't yet caught fire. Beth quickly and quietly sealed the hatch to prevent any further smoke filling the space and ran over to the bedroom side where two faces were waiting for her.

She waved away the smoke so she could see them and allowed herself to splutter. "I couldn't see him on the landing. Which rooms are on the opposite side?"

"That's the boys' bedrooms and the bathroom," Mrs O'Doole said, and looked behind her nervously.

She blinked the water out of her eyes. "Do they all have windows?"

Mrs O'Doole nodded.

"We could try to climb out the other side of the house."

"If he hasn't locked them..." Tyler thought aloud. "It's got to be better than trying our luck out this window, though."

"I won't use the telescopic ladder. He might hear me. I'll drop down on the landing and try the handles. If it's safe, I'll bang on the door twice. You can cover yourself with blankets and cross the landing into the other room."

"Let's do it," Mrs O'Doole said. "But what if they *are* locked?"

"I'll have to make a run for it downstairs."

"No. We'll try to open this door."

"If you do that, the fire will quickly spread into the room."

"It's not going to matter. We'll all have to leave by the window then."

"No. If you don't hear my knocks, I'm heading downstairs. The fire hasn't spread down them yet."

"He could be waiting for you."

"If he's in the house… I'll bang once. That'll be your signal to climb out of the window."

"If you're able to." Mrs O'Doole paused. "Take the rifle."

Even though she'd offered it, Beth knew from her hesitation that Mrs O'Doole didn't want to give it up. She couldn't blame her. It would be the only thing she'd have to defend her children with. "I can't carry it and climb down from the hatch."

Tyler held it aloft. "It has a shoulder strap."

"No. Just listen for two bangs on the opposite door. As soon as you hear them, pull the chest away and be ready to make a break for it."

The two faces below shared the same pursed expression, as if they knew it would be the last time they'd see her.

CHAPTER SEVENTY-EIGHT

Beth returned to the second hatch. The ladder was red hot and so was the ring. Tugging the door back and briefly standing back from the intensified updraft, she estimated she could quickly turn her body in the opening, hang from the edge and only be about two feet from the floor. Her impact wouldn't be too heavy, and it made up her mind that it would be quicker than trying to use the ladder. She would be dropping onto the blazing carpet, but hopefully she could hit the ground running and quickly open one of the doors on the other side and barge into the room. Then it would be a case of banging it to signal the O'Dooles.

For a brief second, the reality of what she was about to do froze her there. The logistics of the task had briefly misdirected her from the notion of dropping into flames and the likelihood of having to face the gunman alone. But the increasingly black smoke rolling up at her told Beth she had little time for second thoughts. She couldn't even take a breath before dropping down. Beth wouldn't get a lungful of fresh air until she made it into one of the other bedrooms, and even that wasn't guaranteed.

But as she turned her back to the hatch, knelt and then allowed her bottom half to drop through the hole, she felt as if something else was driving her. An inner power Beth didn't know she possessed.

She felt the flames heating her legs through her jeans as she extended them and her belly being scorched as her shirt rode up her body. Beth slid out of the hatch, straightened her arms and briefly looked down at what she would land on.

The conflagration was being drawn to the air in the attic above, and the yellow peaks rose steadily to meet her. She could see the fumes immediately emanating black from the rubber soles of her boots and knew her feet would combust if she remained there for more than a few seconds longer.

Beth released her grip on the attic above and landed softly in the fire, the flames curling around her legs before she jumped sideways to the door on her left. She pulled down on the handle and it was blistering hot, but her scream was lost above the roar of the blaze. The door didn't budge. Maybe the heat had warped it in the frame. She pulled her sleeve over her hand and tried it again. No movement inwards. Beth rammed her shoulder against it and felt the panel scorch her skin.

She moved quickly to the next but she was moving away from her exit down the stairs, and chances were, if one door had been locked, so had the others. Her lips sealed shut and her lungs strained for oxygen. She could barely see the landing through the black vapour and scrabbled her hands along the bubbling wall, her fingertips hissing and her exclamations of pain locked tight in her head. As she tried to estimate the handle's position, she felt the skin shrink tight to her skull.

Beth couldn't open her eyes; they were clenched tight against the caustic chemicals radiating from the smouldering wood, so she remained motionless while she tried to locate the door and the flames ate through the clothes on her right side. Her fingers found the handle, and although she gripped it through the material of her shirt, she felt it sticking to the palm of her hand. She grunted inwardly again, feeling the heat shrivelling her right ear. The door didn't move. He'd locked that one as well.

Beth couldn't bear it any longer, and if smoke inhalation

didn't make her black out, she was about to pass out from the intensity of the flames. Should she try the last door? If she ventured any farther away from the stairs, trapped herself where the flames were hottest, she knew she wouldn't make it. The third door was sure to be locked. She thought of the O'Dooles waiting for her signal, but had no choice.

Beth turned and bolted for the top of the stairs, her circulation pounding at her core as she stamped her way through the fire and tried to estimate where the landing finished. She waved her arms at the churning smoke, cracked her watering eyes and tried to discern anything that would let her know how much farther she had to go.

The floor ended and she was running into thin air.

CHAPTER SEVENTY-NINE

Beth's knees bashed the edges of the wooden stairs, her hands reaching for something to break her fall. She didn't manage to grab the rail until she was three from the bottom, her wrist snapping back hard as it became lodged between the slats. Her stomach struck the step, winding her. Her first breath was asthmatic, her body hastily tugging in what it needed to stop her losing consciousness. But overriding it was the horrible notion that the baby had just been harmed.

The smoke about her was thinner, the air cooler. Her head felt suddenly cold. She was quickly on her feet though, yanking her hand from the rail and ignoring the pain that pumped through her frame. Beth supported herself by gripping the wooden globe of the banister and swung carefully around it to look down the passage.

Already disoriented, Beth jumped as country music blared loudly from behind the door of the den. There were noises from the kitchen, too. Radio voices under whirring sounds. She wiped the water from her eyes and peered up and down the passage.

Beth guessed he was trying to spook her, throw her off balance. She had to remain focused. He'd turned off the electricity, turned on all the appliances. Now he'd turned it back on. Where was the switch? He must be in the cellar. Even if he wasn't, he had to still be inside the house.

Beth leaned back so she was standing at the bottom of the stairs again. She bunched her fist and struck the panelled wall to her left once, as hard as she could.

Marcia O'Doole and her two sons were standing at the chest, ready to heave it back. She knew Beth hadn't been successful.

"Did you hear that?" Tyler whispered.

They all waited for the second impact but it didn't come.

"Does that mean she's found him?" Marcia's voice cracked.

They waited and then the door exploded into flames. They shrank back from it.

Tyler hustled his mother and brother over to the window. "We have to go while we can! That was her signal!"

Marcia shouted above the rush of flames and the smoke detector on the ceiling that had just activated. "It might not have been. It could have just been something collapsing!"

"We have to go now anyway!"

She momentarily looked out of the window. Tyler was right. Better to take their chances outside than be burnt alive in the bedroom. "I'll go first. Stay away from the window until I'm halfway down, and then send your brother down."

Kevin shook his head violently.

She put her hands either side of his face and looked deep into his eyes. Was this the last time they'd ever look at each other? Marcia kept her own emotions in check. "I'll be there to catch you! I won't let anything happen to you!" They both knew it was a lie. Like when Tyler had told him Santa Claus didn't exist but Kevin had chosen to continue believing. She knew he nodded now for the same reason.

The door and the portion of wall above it collapsed and flames blasted through the opening. Marcia released Kevin and clambered out. She hooked her hands over the sill and allowed her body to hang down. She waited for the bullets to slam into her but retained eye contact with Kevin. "I won't let anything happen to you!"

"Climb out after, Mom!" Tyler was at the window pointing the rifle out of it in all directions.

"Get away from the window, Tyler!"

"I can't see anybody." He swung it left and right. "I'm going to see if I can help her!"

"What?"

"She might be lying on the landing. It should have been me going up there!"

Tyler slung the rifle on his shoulder.

"Tyler!"

Marcia watched him drag the stool over to the floor below the hatch opening. Her weight was dragging her down. She couldn't pull herself back in. Kevin stood between them, eyes wide with terror.

"Tyler!"

She watched her eldest son jump up, swing at the hatch opening and crawl into the smoke above.

EIGHTY

Tyler's eyelids clamped tight against the smoke. His body shook as he hooked his right elbow onto the edge of the hatch, his stomach muscles quivering as he hoisted his weight inside the broiling attic.

Should he be back at the window, covering Mom and Kevin's descent? If the noise they'd heard had been Beth's signal, it meant they could climb down in safety. It should have been him that had clambered up here in the first place. He had the gun, knew how to use it and shouldn't have let her come alone. Tyler thought about Beth Jordan swinging her fists at him at the roadside and how he'd hid behind his iPhone.

He got to his feet, crouched low and cupped his hand over his mouth and nostrils. Through the rolling waves of smoke, he could locate the other hatch by the orange fire jetting through it. Maybe it was too late. He would just take a look; see if she was below. Maybe she'd passed out. If the flames were too intense, he would return to the bedroom and follow his family out the lodge that way.

His stomach pumped, retching against the fumes. He'd already breathed some in through his nostrils. Tyler reached the hatch and leaned over the opening, the blazing current forcing him back.

"Beth!" He leaned over before being repelled again. The

billowing smoke made it impossible for him to see anything below. She said the fire hadn't spread to the stairs. If he dropped down he could head straight for them, have the rifle ready to shoot. But the flames could have blocked that exit by now, in which case he'd be trapped on the landing.

Beth was halfway down the passage. She knew the gunman was waiting for her just before the kitchen door, concealed at the entrance to the cellar. Black vapour surged past her and was sucked through the screen of the open back door. The smoke alarm joined the cacophony in the kitchen. Was a sprint her best option? Try to run past him and close the inner kitchen door?

It would give her a few valuable seconds to ram the screen and dive over the balustrade into the river, swim down so he couldn't get a clear shot and hold her breath as long as she could. She couldn't think beyond that. Beth hoped the O'Dooles had heard the signal and were getting out of the house. Perhaps they were already at the patrol car.

If she started her run up here, it would alert him of her approach, however. She had to get as close to him as possible before she made a break for it. Beth flattened herself to the staircase panel and crouched low, sliding her back towards the right turning to the cellar where he was waiting for her.

Tyler realised it was foolish. But the woman had come to warn them, and his mother had locked her up in the cellar. Now it looked like she was alone with the maniac. Could they leave her without a weapon? Tyler knew he couldn't live with himself if they waited outside while she lay unconscious and the lodge burnt down.

But how long would he have to live with it? And if he dropped through the hatch, he was likely to be roasted alive.

Tyler wasn't ready to die. Even though he was always so gung-ho about his condition for everyone else's benefit and knew he might not see Kevin's sixteenth, he wasn't ready to die down there.

"Fuck," he said into his palm and turned back to the bedroom hatch.

Marcia O'Doole stood on the concrete in front of the lodge, clasping Kevin to her and watching the smoke gushing from the bedroom window. She couldn't have stopped Tyler. She'd already dangled out of the window and had to make sure Kevin got down safely. She'd thought she wouldn't be able to climb back and that Kevin would remain frozen there, but, to her relief he'd quickly followed her out, and she'd talked him down until it was time to drop the few feet from the end of their makeshift rope.

It flailed gently in the breeze, and Marcia knew they couldn't wait for Tyler. She had to bottle her anger, concentrate on getting Kevin to safety before she came back for him. They still had to make it up the steps. If they did, they wouldn't stop at the patrol car; she'd drag Kevin to Saw Creek and call the police from there.

There was a scrabbling above them, and Mrs O'Doole looked up. Tyler's leg cocked over the ledge, and soon his entire body was sliding down the sheets. He dropped to join them and unshouldered the rifle. She hugged him. He was rigid.

"I couldn't get through. Couldn't reach her," he said emotionlessly.

"We have to go." She grabbed both her sons and hurried them to the steps.

Beth was covering her mouth, stifling her fear and her need to cough against the smoke that had filled the hallway. Its curtain was now only a foot from the floor, and it wouldn't be long until the gunman would be overcome as well. She was about three feet from the turning to the cellar entrance and edging nearer. He must have heard her come down the stairs, knew she was working her way towards him. Perhaps he thought she had the rifle. She wished she had.

It was time to make her move. If the smoke forced the gunman to make his presence known, she was an easy target.

Mrs O'Doole and her boys reached the top of the steps and the patrol car. Its red-and-blues were still switched on.

"This way." She led them along the bank. They would skirt it under cover of the trees until they reached the next lodge.

Tyler headed for the vehicle. "Let's see if they've left the keys in it."

"Tyler, no! He'll hear the engine."

He was nearly at the driver's door. "Just let me look. We could use the radio."

"Tyler, stay with me!"

He opened it.

CHAPTER EIGHTY-ONE

Beth had reached the edge of the panelling, her eyes slitting and throat trembling with the effort of holding back a hack to expel the fumes. Daylight through the kitchen door was eight feet away. How shallow the river would be, she had no idea. She could be diving straight onto jagged rocks and, in a few seconds, she'd know. Beth tensed the muscles in her calves.

The square of daylight was blocked as the figure of the gunman stepped into the passage. Through the smoke she could see his weapon arm out straight, aiming above her crouched position. He hadn't heard her approach. Beth sprang upright and forward.

She aimed the crown of her head at his paunch, struck him solidly in the stomach and heard the wind escape his body. Beth kept on going, trampling him as he fell backwards.

He thudded onto his back and she was crouched over him, trying to get upright again. Beth kneed him hard in the face, stamped at his injured shoulder, but his hand grabbed her right arm and she cried out, dragging smoke into her mouth as his fingers locked painfully hard around bone.

He pulled her down towards him so she couldn't use her legs. Beth tried to jab her left fist into his face, but he caught it by the wrist. She was immobilised, but so was he. Their linked arms trembled with the exertion of Beth trying to get free and him trying to hold onto her.

She put her entire weight behind her left fist, tried to force it towards his face and extend her fingers so she could push them into his eye socket. He twisted his head away and grunted as he tried to lever his shoulders off the floor.

Beth realised if both his hands were restraining her, he must have released the gun. Where was it? As his strength forced her back, she could barely see his gritted expression below her. A fresh gust of smoke completely obscured his features. Beth felt the passage invert as the dizzy overture of a blackout seized her. She hacked against the fumes, but its exertion made her weaken in his grip. She knew he would release her soon – momentarily. Then his hands would be about her throat and he could throttle her while she was barely conscious.

Beth was still crouching over him, the bottom half of her body across his waist. She straightened her knees, stood up and then leaned back so she could aim her melting boot at his face. She stamped where she thought it was and felt her sole connect with something hard. Beth stamped it again, using it to push back from his grip. She screamed and slammed her boot down as hard as she could, wrenching his arms up with the action. His fingers released her and she stood up straight, recovered her balance and jammed her boot downwards again. It struck the floor. He'd rolled out of her way.

Beth headed for the fading daylight, stumbling over his bulk and grasping fingers and staggering into the kitchen where the smoke alarm shrieked, radio blared and coffee grinder and food mixers buzzed. Was there a knife block nearby? But she could barely see the floor. Lying on the tiles to her right, however, was a small black shape. She reached for the gun and turned, waving it in all directions as she reversed towards the doorway.

She banged her spine against the screen and stumbled out backwards, gun trained on the kitchen. She stopped at the wooden balustrade and waited as the screen swung back into the smoking frame.

It slammed quickly outwards again as the gunman emerged, his hand holding his burst nose, blood cascading down his chin. His left eye was closed and his right rolled up at her as he took a faltering step forward.

"I'll shoot." The smoke in her throat shrivelled the warning to a whisper. She knew she'd have to anyway.

The gunman came at her and her finger hooked hard on the trigger. It stuck there.

He smiled through burst lips, a film of red on his crowns. "You really don't know how to use that thing, do you. Mh?" He came at her.

Beth's finger instinctively flicked against the solid trigger again. The gunman halted midstep and grabbed his arm.

There had been no shot. Beth knew she hadn't fired the gun.

"Jesus..." the gunman said breathlessly. He bunched his body around the arm and gripped it tighter.

Beth took a step back as he lurched diagonally to the balustrade.

"Call an ambulance."

He said it clearly enough, but she couldn't believe he had. Beth barked more smoke out of her lungs and spat. Then she put her boot against his side and shoved hard. He hinged over the balustrade and dropped into the Flathead.

CHAPTER EIGHTY-TWO

Beth didn't know how long she stood motionless on the deck, but eventually she looked over the balustrade. If she'd dived in headfirst, she would have been fine. The water was pretty deep the other side. Driftwood churned. She waited for him to surface, but he didn't. It looked like the trauma of their struggle had brought on a heart attack. The river was flowing fast. Strong undercurrents had probably already dragged him away. Behind her, the lodge boomed. Smoke skimmed over her and out across the river where the cloudless blue sky was reflected. It was still only early morning.

Her adrenaline started to ebb. A few seconds later, Beth's pain and exhaustion followed her out of the back door. Her body started to buzz and harmonise with the high-pitched whistle in her ears. She put one hand on the balustrade to support herself and the other gently on her stomach as her whole frame started to quake.

Two armed officers found her in the same position and quickly guided her around the side of the burning property and up the steps to safety. A fire engine was on the scene, parked at the edge of the bank, water already jetting from it onto the smoking roof of the lodge.

Mrs O'Doole was waiting at the top, talking to a female police officer, a blue blanket draped about her. Beth realised she was now wearing one, too.

The lines in Mrs O'Doole's features momentarily evaporated.

She shrugged off the blanket and walked to meet her. She seemed to consider an embrace but instead put her fingers lightly on the side of her arm and tugged in a faltering breath. Her brown eyes steadily held Beth's.

"The boys?" Beth couldn't see any sign of them.

"They've been taken to the hospital. They want to check them for smoke inhalation. I said I wanted to hang back here."

Suddenly, the blanket felt heavy around Beth's shoulders. "Kevin's OK?"

Mrs O'Doole nodded. "Tyler tried to come back for you. The heat was too intense. What happened to the... Is he...?"

Beth coughed and nodded. She spat onto the floor and threw up. When she stood, two medics had joined them. The medics told the officers they wanted to examine Beth before they interviewed her.

"Ma'am, are you OK to walk to the ambulance?"

Beth nodded, and they led her and Mrs O'Doole over to the vehicle. The back doors were open, and they were both taken inside, told to sit on the gurneys. Neither of them spoke. Then the medic treated Beth, and she answered his questions while he dressed her ear.

The two women looked out of the open back doors, their shared ordeal making the frantic activities of the emergency services seem insignificant. Beth's seared ear prickled as the medic moisturised it. She looked at his sandy moustache but focused on the sound of the trees rustling overhead.

Minutes passed before Beth eventually asked, "When Tyler said he didn't have much time..." But she already knew why he'd been wearing the bandana. Mrs O'Doole didn't answer. Eventually, Beth turned to gauge her expression.

She was still looking out of the doors, her expression composed. "He has grade three chondrosarcoma, cartilage cancer."

Beth's pain momentarily halted. The medic stepped between them again, but when he shifted, Mrs O'Doole's expression hadn't altered. Beth could see just how exhausted she was.

"Doesn't make him any less a monumental pain in the ass, though." Her eyes glistened. "Trying not to treat them differently is the hardest thing. Trying to remind them they're special and ordinary at the same time... and giving them the life they should have, however long it is."

Four days of questioning followed. On the second day, Agent Scott Morales, a softly spoken FBI suit whose sideburns had been painstakingly shaved to razor points, commandeered the cross-examination.

The connection between the gunman's victims was incontrovertible, but it was obvious from the direction of inquiry that the motive for the murders was as unclear to them as it was to her. She couldn't offer them any theory as to what the clips contained that warranted the immediate removal of them and their owners. She'd given them the few remaining online remnants of her communication with the gunman and explained how he'd threatened Jody's life and why she'd been afraid of involving the police. Morales said they'd run a background check on her and asked her about the accident and Luc's business dealings. She waited, drank endless cups of coffee and wondered what they'd find.

They'd hinted Beth would have to remain in the States pending further investigation, but by Wednesday, they'd given her the all-clear to fly back to the UK. She agreed to return if they needed her further. Beth booked a ticket before they could change their minds.

"I'm parking out front." Marcia O'Doole put her cell on the dash.

It was early evening when she pulled her car into the front lot of the Overton Motel. It was just off Stillwater and not far from home, but nobody wanted to go back there. The FBI had said they'd be in touch.

The boys were staying in the motel with her mom and dad.

They'd driven up from Spokane. She thanked God for them. Her sister was gone, and she knew the reality of that hadn't even begun to soak in for any of them.

The doors at the front of the motel slid open, and they all came out to meet her. Tyler, Kevin, Mom and Dad. Ted was there, too. He stood behind the boys, a hand on each one's shoulder, and she could see how pleased they were to have him there. He would use that as cover, she knew. They were all smiling a little awkwardly, happy to be welcoming her back safe but not knowing what her frame of mind would be.

She'd vowed never to let Ted back into their lives, but now wasn't the time. She climbed down from the car, and while she got her bags out of the trunk, they crossed the lot to meet her.

She hugged the boys and her mom and dad. Ted didn't wait for her permission. He squeezed the air out of her, and she briefly inhaled the smell of him from the collar of his sweatshirt. The tears started to well, but she held them back. He released her and took her bag. Dad took the other.

CHAPTER EIGHTY-THREE

Jody picked Beth up from the airport but only answered her questions in monosyllables during the drive back. She knew he was furious with her for putting herself and the baby at risk. She slept part of the way.

When she walked into his place, it actually felt like home. It was early morning and she felt completely spaced, but Beth made an appointment with her midwife for the following afternoon. During her medical examination, immediately after the incident at West Glacier, the US doctor had confirmed that, despite the ordeal, her child was still very much healthy. But she didn't want to take any chances.

Then she sat down with Jody and a pot of decaf and told him everything she hadn't via the phone calls she'd made to him during questioning.

While she'd been in the States, he'd reassured her time and time again that she was safe and that the gunman wouldn't come knocking on her door. The police hadn't recovered the body but had said the currents would make it very unlikely that he would ever be found. Beth knew she wouldn't rest easy until he was, even now she was back home.

She took a long shower. Standing in Jody's heavy towelling dressing gown afterwards, she felt the exhaustion she'd kept at bay filtering through, and surveyed her defects in the toothpaste-dappled mirror. With heavy lids, she examined the scars around her mouth from the car accident and her shrunken right ear and burnt shoulder from the fire. The dressing had been removed before her flight, and she'd been given cream to apply, as well as a course of analgesics. Beth touched the top of her ear where the skin was dead. Much longer in the flaming lodge, and it would have withered to nothing.

Her hair had grown considerably and her brown spikes had softened into a boyish cut. Was this her new face? The person who had got into the car with Luc felt almost fictional, the chasm between her life and the harrowing experiences of the new Beth so vast that it was hard to believe she'd ever enjoyed a life of reassuring mundanity. Did she ever want to return to being that woman?

Beth ran her fingers over her stomach. Her touch was blunted because of the dead layer on the tips, but she'd been reassured the skin there would regenerate. She looked at the smooth pads. Would her prints, her identity, ever re-establish?

Having gone to bed at midday, she awoke just after 3 feeling fully awake and elected to get up for a few hours. She headed to the lounge in her nightshirt to find Jody but heard activity from his recording studio. Beth put her head around the door but recognised the sounds before she did.

"What's this?"

He clicked his mouse and the sound of the roadside ceased. "If they're having problems locating the recordings, I thought the FBI would be interested in these…"

Beth stood behind him and examined the two monitors on his desk. On the right hand screen one of the clips was paused. "But this has all been removed."

"I recorded them from YouTube."

"How?"

"Off the screen with my iPhone." He sounded coy. "It's why they're not great quality. Then I ripped them into my

FleetSuite editing software."

"You stitched them together?"

"Minus the one that had been removed before I could record it…"

Beth bit her lip.

"You did ask me to."

"I should call them straight away about this."

"By using the people moving through the frame I've been able to put together a rough timeline. There are gaps but they're only a matter seconds."

"Show me it," she said, after a few moments consideration.

"You sure?"

She reached down, used the mouse to drag the slider back to the start of the clip and played it.

A phone camera panned from the front of the stationary ambulance at the right hand side of the screen to the crash site. The gendarmes were securing the road. Suddenly the angle, lighting and quality of the clip changed.

"What happened there?"

"The clip jumped because they stopped recording for a few seconds and picked up further along the road. This is a different clip cut into the same timeline."

"How do you know for sure?"

"Watch the police." Jody dragged the slider back so the clip reversed slightly.

Beth watched the officers as they moved about the roadside. When the screen quality changed, their progress didn't alter.

"I was able to assemble the clips in the right order by navigating via the movement of the emergency personnel. And when the cameras aren't focused on them, I used the other ghouls in foreground. Like this guy…" Jody pulled the slider along to reveal the clip with Cigarillo Man/Ferrand Paquet in his lemon shirt. "Remember him? He's actually turned out to be an invaluable marker during the edit."

"How long did this take you to put together?"

Jody shrugged his shoulders. "I had to occupy myself with something while you were putting your life in jeopardy."

Beth ignored his rebuke. "How many times have you watched it?"

"So many times, I don't see it anymore. The patchwork is just over nine minutes long. It does give you a bigger perspective watching it. There's a lot of overlap. I used the clearest clips, but you can click in the bar at the bottom to switch between the alternate footage." He rose from the chair to allow her to sit there.

Beth felt cold pins and needles across the top of her shoulders. "I've changed my mind. I don't know if I can watch it just now."

Jody paused it. "I'm sorry. I'm a dick. This has just been a project for me..."

"I do appreciate this, Jody."

"It didn't take me that long."

"I don't mean just this...'

Jody looked uncomfortable and glanced at the door. "I'm going to hunt out something to eat. What do you fancy for dinner?"

"I'm good, thanks. Can you zip this edit and email it to me?"

"Sure."

"I'll forward it to Agent Morales. I think it'll save them a lot of time."

"You've seen it enough, but it's there when you feel ready. If you ever want to look at it again."

Beth didn't, but when Jody headed to the kitchen, she seated herself, inhaled slowly and viewed Jody's assembly of the crash site footage from start to finish.

CHAPTER EIGHTY-FOUR

Beth found Jody in the kitchen, trying to turn an eight egg omelette in a pan. He picked up on her distracted expression.

"You watched it all the way through?"

Beth nodded. "Twice."

"You OK?" He took the pan off the heat.

"There's something odd."

He frowned.

"I only noticed it second time round."

"Show me." He turned off the gas and followed Beth back to the studio.

Beth seated herself again and moved the slider to the end of the clip as the helicopter containing her and Luc took off. "Nine minutes and seven seconds in, there." She paused it. At the far left-hand side of the screen was the back of a white vehicle pulling out of shot around the darkened bend of the forest. "It's only there for four seconds, but that's definitely an ambulance."

"It must have left as soon as the helicopter lifted you out."

"I'd spotted it before and assumed it was the one at the scene. But now you've stitched them all together, I can see it doesn't pass through the shot at any point." Beth dragged the slider slowly back through the edit and halted it at the start of the sequence. At one second, the ambulance was stationary.

Beth accelerated the slider back the other way, the road in

the shot throughout. No ambulance passed through any of the clips. She paused it on the ambulance leaving at nine minutes and seven seconds.

Jody frowned. "So there are two ambulances."

"The accident report said only one ambulance attended the site. And that was sent back after the helicopter arrived. Look, the one that leaves shot after the helicopter took off has a thick blue band across the back doors and..." she moved the slider slightly so they could see it turning out of shot "...down its side. This one..." Beth dragged the slider back so they were looking at the first ambulance stationary at one second "... hasn't any of those markings."

"So if there were two ambulances, is that much of a revelation? It could be a private or volunteer ambulance that was first to the scene and left when they weren't required. That would explain the different markings."

"But where does it come from? There's no sign of it until this moment." She slid the slider back to the end of the edit. "And why weren't they attending us? There are only ever two paramedics in shot: Rae and the man who helped her wheel us to the helicopter when it arrived. There's no sign of any other ambulance crew. You'd expect them to appear at some point, especially earlier on in the footage. Why wasn't it mentioned in the report?"

Jody looked pensively at the image on the screen. "Did you check this moment in the alternate clips?" He clicked the bar at the bottom of the edit window and found the same moment in the three other clips. All of them contained brief glimpses of the other ambulance that had been captured as each member of the coach party had directed their phones at the helicopter taking off.

Jody paused the clearest shot and enlarged it. They could make out the licence plate.

"Can you get it any bigger?"

Jody tried with each of the clips, but magnifying the image only obscured the dark numbers there.

"I recorded them with my phone from phone clips. The resolution is useless."

After emailing the clips to Agent Morales, Beth found a variety of images of French ambulances via Google. She thought maybe she could try and find a website for the private response companies, but then remembered the conversation she'd had with the hospital. They hadn't mentioned an additional ambulance, but then she'd been trying to track down Rae and not another vehicle. Maybe they could quickly clear this up. It wasn't the presence of the ambulance that bothered her; it was why nobody from it had appeared on the scene.

Beth made the call to Service d'Aide Medicale Urgente from the lounge and was told somebody would get back to her in half an hour. Jody brought her some cold omelette and ate his while she poked at hers. He switched on the TV and they both stared through it while they waited for the phone to ring. Fifteen minutes later, it did, and Beth snatched up the receiver.

"Hello?"

"Turn and look out of the window. Mh?" The placatory tone halted the blood in her veins.

CHAPTER EIGHTY-FIVE

"And do it slowly. I have you and your brother in my sights and can drop you both if you respond to any foolish impulses."

Beth turned and peered through the dismal afternoon light at the new office block on the other side of the street.

"Up there. See the open window?"

Beth saw the tiny square of darkness within the smoked glass opposite, vertical blinds bunched beside it.

"Now, alert Jody to the situation. If he tries to stand or dive to the floor, I'll put a hole through his brain. Turn and do it."

Beth felt the muscles in her neck tremble as she swivelled on her feet to face him. "Jody."

He looked distractedly up from the TV and then reacted to her expression.

"Stay seated and listen. There's a gun on us, the window – other side of the street. We have to do exactly as we're told…"

"Good." She heard the gunman swallow in her ear.

Jody cracked his mouth to speak but, knowing of his sister's recent ordeal, thought better of it. The cushion resting against the back of the sofa beside him exploded, the white stuffing bursting as two more shots sliced through it.

"Stop!" Jody's hands were in the air, his rigid features

anticipating another bullet an inch nearer. "Fuck, stop!" He spat at the fibres of stuffing drifting over his face.

"Precision hardware this time, I'm hunkered down and I have all night. I can see the remote on the arm of the chair. Tell Jody to switch off the TV so I can hear you properly."

Beth relayed the instruction to Jody and he quickly obeyed. She turned back to the window, gripping the receiver tight. "Don't hurt him; he isn't a part of this."

"He's as much a part of this as you. Granted, he hasn't caused as much inconvenience. He's a loose end, though. Especially given the little package he assembled that you just sent to Agent Morales."

Beth felt her leg shudder and waited for the spark in the black space she could see through the holes in the cracked glass.

"I've been hacking you from the moment you offered to buy the clip that Trip Stillman recorded. You brought yourself into play. You weren't even part of my contract until then. I extracted the details of Jody's LA condo from his computer. It was how I made your decision to take a trip to the States so easy. I broke in and waited for you there. You stood me up, first. Things would have been so much easier if you'd shown up. The outcome was always going to be the same, so you could have saved both of us a trip back here."

Beth remembered how neatly the hole had been silently drilled in the forehead of the receptionist in the LA hotel.

"I'm a completionist, like to serve my indentures. But before I finish the job, I wanted to give you something."

Beth waited, her heart kicking at her chest.

"When I can, I prefer to offer my guiltless targets the benefit of knowing why they're about to die. To at least inform them their termination isn't arbitrary..."

Beth swallowed hard, peeling her tongue from the roof of her mouth.

"I know you're probably hoping I can clear up the whole Allegro business, but honestly, I can't. I found the message from Rae Salomon on your cell when I hacked into it and then your searches for it online. I assumed it was something you needed to figure out. I used it as a way to lure you to LA via the Facebook page."

Beth darted her eyes around the room, looking for a place they might take cover.

"Keep 'em on the window, mh?"

She realised how clearly she was in his sights.

"I'm sorry there won't be that closure for you, but there is one pertinent piece of information I can offer, seeing as I was one of the few people who saw everything the day your car went off the road."

CHAPTER EIGHTY-SIX

Mimic subtly rolled the muscles of his shoulders, relaxing but maintaining his frame around the lightweight titanium sniper rifle. He'd turned the desk he was seated at lengthways towards the open window. The AS50 semi-automatic resting on its top wasn't his first choice, but it was the weapon the East Hill Sniper had used to kill three people and injure two from a nearby apartment block. Mimic had achieved satisfactory results with British manufactured firearms before. The adjustable bipod and rear support grip would allow him accuracy up to 1,500 yards.

The perspiration on his fingers adhered him to it, made it an extension of him. He'd slowed his circulation before calling Beth with his Bluetooth. "Last year, my services were secured by individuals within the current French administration. A second reactor at the Degarmo Nuclear Power Plant, to the northwest of Dieppe, had been proposed and the public consultation had gone well. The multinational, Vpower, had the contract. But a radioactive water leak at the station rapidly changed opinion, and the Ecology Minster, Christiane Vipond, was suddenly aggressively opposing the commission of the second reactor. The UMP is wet behind the ears when it comes to covert resolution, so I was asked to remove rather than terminate Vipond, convince her to withdraw before she could damage the party's relationship with Vpower, as well as their chances in the general election."

Mimic slightly clenched and unclenched each of his buttocks and watched Beth's unblinking eyes. Beyond her he could see her brother's Adam's apple bob in his throat.

"She was in her sixties and had a well-documented history of seizures. I was to orchestrate her ill health publicly and ensure she took a permanent sabbatical from politics. I had her prescription history, so it was easy to select the corresponding medication to slip into her food. The Ecological Forum dinner being hosted by Vpower at the Hôtel Le Grand was the ideal venue. Even though security services issued an assurance the paramedics had been summoned, my associate and I quickly arrived and picked her up in a decommissioned ambulance so we could drive her to a secure location. There we were to use various methods to dissuade her from further involvement in the debate. She could make up her own mind if I'd been in the employ of Vpower or her own party. Comfort deprivation and threats to her grandchildren proved to be more than sufficient. But she didn't soil herself as quickly as your brother..."

He saw Beth turn to where Jody had closed his eyes against the dark patch spreading from the crotch of his jeans.

"Unfortunately for you, my associate hadn't secured the gurney properly in the back of the ambulance, and on the way to the location, it got loose and started slamming against the sides. We pulled over in the middle of the Forêt Domaniale to secure it. My associate got out and was just opening the back doors when a camper came around the corner. You know how narrow the road was at the curve. I heard it braking, but he swerved to avoid us and struck a tree."

He pressed the pad of his forefinger against the trigger. One more tiny increment of pressure would burst her head apart.

"We got out and found the car had rolled back into the road. The driver was semi-conscious. Then Christiane starts screaming through the gag and struggling to get herself free of the straps we'd restrained her with. I opened the doors and threatened her with a scalpel, and she piped down. But when I got back down from the ambulance, my associate was dealing with the driver of the trashed vehicle. He'd gotten out and had seen Christiane all trussed up. I told him I could explain everything and immobilised him by pushing the scalpel into his eye."

Jody wouldn't look up at Beth as the liquid spread out from his lap. He had every right to be petrified. She knew his terror was more than justified. The gunman's account wasn't something that could be repeated.

She swallowed, his connection to her briefly cutting out and then vibrating the hairs in her ear again. "Even though it was raining, I didn't want his blood on the roadside. He was still alive when we dragged him into the ambulance, so I slit his throat there. We secured Christiane, shut the doors and were just about to drive off, when we heard your car hit the camper. Bam! I assessed the damage and made sure you and your husband couldn't compromise us. Afterwards, we decided to leave with our two passengers, but as we pulled out, we could see the bus coming the other way. We pulled off into the trees and waited there, watched it stop at the side of the road and all the college kids get out with their iPhones."

Beth tried to estimate which one of them he would target first. Jody was semi-paralysed, so it was likely the first bullet was hers.

"The only way out of the forest was to pull back onto the same road in an opening a little further down. We couldn't be spotted, so we waited, but then the cops and ambulance turned up. I knew it wouldn't be long until they worked out the driver of the camper was missing and searched the forest. We slipped back out while the helicopter taking off distracted the crowd. Just before we did, two men walking a dog strolled by us. It had to be a suspicious sight, an ambulance pulled into the forest and the two of us sitting up front, doing nothing. We drove by them and left."

Was he talking about Roland and Erik?

"I located them. There weren't many residences nearby they could have walked a dog from. Discovered one was an ex-journalist."

Beth saw a movement in the periphery of her vision. She knew what it was, but she didn't raise her eyes to acknowledge it.

"The driver of the camper was an illegal Bulgarian immigrant, which made disposing of his body easy. I dumped it in a storm drain along with my associate's. I successfully concluded my business. Vipond announced her resignation two months before the election."

The movement continued gradually downward. It was the automated window-cleaning cradle and Beth knew she couldn't allow him to see her register its presence.

"I told my employers about the complications, attempted to extract remuneration, but they weren't interested in prolonging our association."

She estimated it would reach the gunman's window in a matter of minutes. He had to be using a telescopic sight. Would he have one eye closed against it? She recalled how his left had been injured in their struggle. He might not see the cradle until it had obscured his view.

"Unfortunately, Vipond's heart gave out and she died less than a week after my powwow with her. But she'd had a bedside meeting with her biographer beforehand. Nobody knew what was said. People started to get nervous. A month later, a document questioning the presence of a decommissioned ambulance at a crash site viewed by the entire Internet community winds up on the desk of the French Minister of the Interior. Suddenly, they're trying to re-establish relations with me, entreating me to do whatever was necessary to suppress the party's connection to the vehicle, because God only knew what else was lurking in the files of all those iPhone witnesses."

Beth's curiosity overrode the situation. "Roland sent the document?"

"No. I sent it. I gave Roland ample opportunity to break the story. I monitored his emails, hacked into his computer and was ready to inform my employers as soon as he started writing the story. But I got sick of waiting for him to climb off his lazy, has-been ass. Recently, I contacted him to let him know if they come forward as witnesses, they'd end up as meat for their dog. Regardless, I'm on my way there to make that happen as soon as I'm done here."

"Why leak the information yourself?"

"Because it gave me the extended contract I wanted. It's not in my interests to tie up loose ends unless they point to me or I'm being paid to do so. The party needed it to go away, whatever was necessary. I'm on the brink of retirement, so I needed to be retained by an administration that not only had access to generous donations but was completely running scared. And when my services have been secured, not even my clients can pull the plug. Although I know several attempts have already been made."

The cradle had reached the top edge of the gunman's window.

Beth had to keep him talking. When his view through the sight was blocked, she would know. "But the FBI already know what connects the people you've murdered."

"But not the reason why. Besides, it's no longer my concern. And while my clients try and extricate themselves, I'll have already disappeared. And you and your brother will be two more victims of the East Hill Sniper."

The cradle dropped farther down towards the lower open window. Could he hear its motor, or would it get lost in the noise of the traffic from the road below?

"But I want to step back to the middle of events, to the moment that has the most relevance to you. I knew it would when I started tracking you via your social networking and found your little Facebook memorial to your husband. Luc, mh?"

Beth kept her eyes fixed on the open window, tried not to let them flick up at the cradle. "Yes." But she wasn't just trying to extend his dialogue now.

"After your car had struck the camper, we deliberated whether or not to leave immediately, which in retrospect would have been the correct decision. But I got back out of the ambulance and walked along the road to see if I had to deal with any more witnesses."

She listened, fighting her eyeballs' instinct to roll upwards.

"One vanished driver was going to arouse enough suspicion, so I was hoping to find corpses. The crash sounded like nobody would have survived, but when I walked around the curve, there you were, having crawled out of your car, face down in a puddle of water and barely conscious. That's when Luc staggered out of the wreckage."

The cradle was at the edge of the open window, but Beth wasn't seeing it.

"His nose was bleeding and he appeared to be delirious, but he had real purpose. You lifted your head out of the puddle just in time for him to kick you so hard in the face I heard your jaw break from twenty yards away."

CHAPTER EIGHTY-SEVEN

Beth shook her head, almost imperceptibly at first.

"He'd done me a favour, put you out before you even knew I was there. But he'd seen me. I pulled my gun on him and told him to crawl back inside the car. He sat there on the ceiling and I told him to lie back. Then I reached in and broke his neck. It was awkward; he was barely breathing when I returned to the ambulance, but I knew he wouldn't make it to the hospital alive."

The cradle must have been moving over the aperture now, but Beth was still processing what she was being told.

"I thought he'd finished you, was surprised to find you'd survived his attack. When I wanted to find out who had contacted Trip Stillman, I was even more surprised when I saw what you'd said on Facebook about the man who tried to kill you. I realised you didn't even know it was your husband who put you in a coma."

"You're lying."

"Why would I? I'm about to pull the trigger on you. It makes no odds to me."

"You're punishing me." But Beth didn't have any memory that could disprove his story. It was inconceivable.

"Don't shoot the messenger, Beth. But then Brits love irony, and this is definitely an irony worth…"

When he paused, Beth didn't even look at the window but

turned to Jody, knowing the cradle had briefly obscured his shot. "Move!"

She darted towards her brother. It would probably only take the gunman seconds to realise what had happened and reposition himself. Jody opened his eyes but didn't budge. "Now!" Beth grabbed him by his T-shirt and tried to heave his bulk up off the couch. He looked at her if she were mad, but she was relieved to feel his frame respond, his weight reducing as he tensed his legs and pushed himself up.

She anticipated the bullets as they ran to the lounge door. Had she mistimed it? Maybe he would allow them to reach it before he pulled the trigger.

They staggered into the passage. Jody was in front of her as she heard the bullet hiss through the doorway and thud into the wall beside them. She locked her arms around his waist and dragged him down, quickly twisting onto her back, flattening herself and looking back through the doorway. She could see the smoked windows of the office block through the fractured glass of the bay but no sign of the cradle. She was looking at a higher floor. They were out of his line of fire.

Another two bullets puffed plaster out of the wall farther along, the pane of glass in the lounge collapsing and shattering onto the carpet. If they stayed down and crawled the length of the landing, they would drop down two steps to the kitchen level. "Keep moving." She hissed back to Jody. But he didn't. "Just a few more feet." She used her heels to push herself back against him.

A fourth bullet embedded itself into the wall inches above their heads.

"Go!" She felt Jody move as she rammed him.

He squirmed away on his front and slid his body down the two stairs to the lower landing. Beth came down backwards and followed him on all fours around the corner of the kitchen wall.

Once they were inside, Beth grabbed a small knife from the magnetic strip on the tiles.

"What are you doing?" Jody was crouching by the fridge.

"He can't shoot us here." She had second thoughts and swapped the small blade for the carving knife.

Jody got uncertainly to his feet and snatched the receiver from the unit on the wall. "I'll call the police."

Beth was already heading for the stairs.

"Beth, stay here!"

As her bare feet slapped the steps, she told herself she had to intercept him. If she didn't, Beth knew she'd always be anticipating his bullet. She couldn't allow him to sow that fear again.

Having failed to kill them, it was unlikely he would linger very long. Could she reach the ground floor before he did? Maybe the rifle was the only weapon he thought he needed. If it was, she had a chance to put the knife in him.

Beth was out of the front door and descending the stone steps to the street. The road was busy with traffic. She looked up at the open window expecting to see him there with the barrel trained on her, but the frame was empty. He wouldn't be expecting her to come out of the house so soon. Probably thought she was still taking cover inside. He had to be on his way down.

Beth ran into the road, tyres squealing and cars swerving as she weaved between them. She scarcely realised she was only wearing her nightshirt and leapt up onto the opposite kerb in front of the building. The doors were propped open and fine dust floated out. A young woman dragged two children back behind her as they saw the blade in Beth's hand. Men in facemasks were working inside, the soon-to-be reception area draped with polythene sheeting.

Beth didn't doubt she could push the knife into him. But it wasn't just the spectre of him stalking her beyond today that drove her through the open doors. It was what he'd said about Luc, the notion he'd implanted that she knew she'd never be able to refute.

Standing in reception, the carving knife gripped firmly in her fist, Beth counted three workmen obliviously sanding down the newly plastered walls. The elevator doors were propped open and out of action. She could already feel the dust in her throat. Squinting through it, she deliberated whether to take the door to the car park or the one to the stairs.

Beth yanked open the door to the stairs and found an expression of surprise waiting the other side. It was a young man in a business suit with cropped silver hair. She pushed past him and headed up the first flight, turning and looking up the stairwell for movement above. There was no sign of the gunman's descent, but she flattened herself to the wall and raised the knife in readiness as she hastily climbed.

CHAPTER EIGHTY-EIGHT

Beth reached the top of the first flight and halted, listening – just the vibration of the sanders below and still no footfalls. Perhaps he'd already gone. Maybe he was, at that moment, screeching out of the underground car park. Had a man his age really managed to clear these stairs in the time it took her to cross the road from the house?

She padded up the second slowly, the steps cold against the soles of her bare feet. When she reached the double doors leading to the first floor, she ducked to one side and briefly peered through the glass panels into the corridor beyond. No sign of movement. Whitening her knuckles around the knife, she cautiously tugged the door handle with her other hand, and it squealed as she eased it back. If the gunman were still here, he would certainly know somebody else was.

Beth stepped into the pristine and sterile corridor. The air smelt of resin, the floor was covered with large institutional blue carpet tiles and, ahead of her, two doors were locked open.

She inched towards them, slowing at the edge of the daylight spilling through the frame. The sound of the workmen was muffled here, but she could hear traffic through the open window. Beth gulped her fear and walked through them.

She was standing in an expansive, open-plan office space.

Bunches of coiled grey wires hung from the ceiling, and ceiling panels were stacked in one corner. She was alone. But Beth had already seen the doors leading to two smaller private offices on the other side of the floor and knew that that was where the gunman had been, or was still, positioned.

She listened again, not breathing, for what felt like minutes. If he had made it down to the car park, there was no way she would catch up with him now. But her instinct told her somebody was in the office. Beth moved forward, brandishing the knife beside her cheek. Would he have the rifle trained on the door when she opened it? She put her fingers on the handle and strained her ear for sounds from the other side. Beth stood to the right of it and quickly yanked down, allowing it to swing inward.

No gunshot. No movement.

She peered slowly around the jamb and choked. The gunman was seated at the table, his rifle positioned on a stand in front of him and his finger still on the trigger.

From behind him, she could see that his head was bowed. There was a small smudgy hole in his bald scalp. She couldn't see his face. Most of it lay in fragments over the tabletop.

As she clenched her fingers over her mouth, she thought of the man she'd run into at the bottom of the stairs. The gunman had been wrong. It appeared the French government knew much more about covert resolution than he'd given them credit for.

CHAPTER EIGHTY-NINE

"I'm just waiting for her so I can finish for the day." Karina, the harried domestic help, opened the door to Beth with a coat and furry hat on.

"What time do you expect her home?"

"Oh, she's here, but she's in the garden. If you like I can–"

But Beth was already striding away from the doorway and across the front of the house. She knew the way. It was dark and only a few lights illuminated the carport and the vapour of hot breath about her. She vaguely heard Karina call after her, but everything around Beth was a tunnel that led to the conversation ahead.

She opened the gate and walked into the landscaped area at the side. Lin was talking to her gardener in the top tier. A bonfire was burning there, sparks soaring from the peaks of the tall flames. She considered the inferno she'd jumped into through the attic hatch and the scars she'd emerged with. As she strode up the steps, Lin spotted her, conversation cut short as she waited for Beth to enter the orange glow.

Lin's puzzled smile quickly vanished. "OK, thanks, Paul. I'll see you next week."

The gardener passed Beth on the steps, but she didn't acknowledge him. As she reached Lin, she was still hoping she was wrong. But when she saw her expression illuminated by the intensity of the fire, she could see the fear Lin had barely kept hidden when they'd last met immediately betray itself.

For a moment, there was only their breath clouds and popping wood between them.

Beth examined the shadows dancing on her face, distorting her into someone different. "Don't make this worse by pretending you don't know why I'm here."

"Mrs McIntyre?"

They both looked back to the house where Karina was standing.

"Is everything OK?"

"Yes. Fine."

"Pete's outside in the car. Can I slope off?"

Beth turned back to Lin when she didn't answer.

Lin seemed to be in two minds about being left alone but met Beth's eye and replied without shifting her gaze. "Yes. Go," she said with resignation.

"Sure everything's OK?"

"Go!"

"OK." Karina didn't sound certain.

They both waited for the noise of the door slam.

Beth sniffed. "Does Jerome know?"

"No. He knows I was seeing somebody but not that it was…"

"Luc."

Lin nodded and went to turn.

"Don't fucking walk away from me."

Beth's tone halted her. "So what are we supposed to do now?" Lin sighed.

"What does that mean?"

"Exactly what I said, Beth. What are we supposed to do now?"

"Not that. The sigh. Was that a 'we're grown ups and beyond making a scene' sigh?"

The beginnings of panic started to register in Lin's expression.

"Or was that a 'Luc is dead, so what does it matter anymore' sigh?"

"Hit me, Beth. Do what you want. Luc's been taken from both of us."

But it was clear when Beth stepped forward and Lin flinched that she didn't expect Beth to strike her. "Maybe as I had to suffer an assault, we should even things out."

Now Lin's features shifted to horror. "That was Luc's idea."

Beth began to tremble. How premeditated had it been and how long had Luc been waiting for an opportunity? When he staggered out of the wreckage, had Lin really been the catalyst for him to finish her; to stamp her out and make her look like a casualty of the collision? "So when was it decided you'd attack me? And why? You'd have plenty of money if you divorced Jerome."

"Jerome's ruined." Lin held Beth's eye again, as if it were an admission that was relevant.

Beth realised that Lin truly believed the revelation would elicit sympathy. Her universe was herself. She'd never wanted children with Jerome. Was that why Luc had been so drawn to her?

"He's made a lot of bad choices that have caught up with us."

"Luc never..." But Beth stopped herself. Of course he hadn't told her. Because Luc had been lying to her. She gritted her teeth against the heat of tears building. Not here. Not in front of this woman. "So you thought you'd hop over into my life. And you didn't want a divorce to deprive you two of half Luc's share of Avellana."

Lin said nothing.

"You conniving cunt."

Lin blinked as if she'd been slapped, like it had never occurred to her she'd have to answer to what she'd done. "I told Luc it was a bad idea."

"Because you were both scared of doing it or scared of getting caught?"

Aggression flared in Lin's features. "Because I knew Luc wouldn't have the balls. I did exactly what I had to and waited for you in the car park. I had to hit you once with the baseball bat in front of the security camera and push you into the blind spot. Luc was meant to take care of the rest. Then he'd hand it back to me and I'd run. I knew he wasn't capable. He still could have done it though, even when you hit me. We were out of view behind the pillar."

The impact of Lin's words seemed harder than the moment the car had spun off the road. "You were the hoodie?"

"Of course." Lin nodded vehemently, but when Beth's reaction halted her, a new abhorrence supplanted her anger. Not for what she'd done but for the mistake she'd just made.

Beth thought about the night they'd been mugged and how she'd fought back. She was meant to have died that night. She shouldn't even have been in the car in France.

She recalled how easily Luc had thrown away all of their postcards and photographs from the memory chest when they were moving. He'd been preparing to dispose of her.

"You must have had such great plans together, but now Luc's dead, his wealth is out of your reach and you'll never get Jerome back. You should be thankful he couldn't bash my brains in, Lin; otherwise, these scars would be yours." Beth falteringly drew breath and considered the gunman and his commitment to closure for the people whose lives he was about to end. "I suppose I owe it to you to let you know Luc did finally find his courage. After we crashed the car, he took his chance to try and finish me there. Which is what I was actually talking about."

Beth turned and walked down the steps, shaking and sick and hating herself more than Lin. Hating herself for how she'd nursed Luc through his depression after the mugging. She wondered who he was and how he could possibly have allowed her to do that when his abjection was purely because he hadn't had the guts to go through with his plan to kill her.

She remembered her last meeting with Lin in the coffee shop and her hugging Beth and saying how sorry she was.

Sorry that Luc was dead? Sorry for trying to kill her? Sorry their plan had misfired? It struck her how much Lin's ultra-modern home was similar to the one she was meant to move into with Luc. The house Luc had found online that was so unlike anything she imagined he'd want. Luc's genetic sentence meant he'd lived his life by cutting corners. She'd never, ever conceived she could be one of them.

"It was me he texted before he died," Lin said through tears behind her. "Minutes before he died. He was sitting next to you in the car, but he was talking to me."

CHAPTER NINETY

"Are you coming?" Jody shouted up from downstairs.

Beth Lucas knew she'd kept him waiting too long, but that he wouldn't let it show when she joined him there. He was finding it difficult helping her move out. There was no way she and Theo could continue living with him, even though he'd told her they were welcome to stay and she would have been happy to. He'd helped her through the aftermath of her ordeal and had been as supportive as she'd reached full term.

She'd finished changing Theo and made sure he was tucked and warm in the carrier before she hefted the handles. Beth looked into his four week-old expression of exasperation and waited for the tears to start. They didn't, so she headed for the door.

They were moving into the new house tomorrow but had got the keys a day early. Now the house in Wandsworth and Luc's stake in Avellana had been sold, she had at last been able to get a place of her own. It was less than ten minutes from Jody's. Just as she reached the top of the stairs, her iPhone rang. Beth considered ignoring it, but put Theo down on the landing and scrabbled it out of her handbag.

"Hello?"

"Beth?"

She immediately recognised the voice. "Rae?"

It sounded like she was in a busy thoroughfare and didn't answer.

"Are you staying safe?"

"I'm still moving around."

"Is he still looking for you?"

"I don't know for sure. And it's probably better that I don't."

Beth knew what it was like to live in the indeterminate shadow of a man, but at least, as the months had passed, Luc's had gradually begun to fade. "Why are you calling me?"

"I heard about what happened to you on TV."

As soon as Beth had the baby, there'd been a resurgence of interest in her story. The previous morning, she'd seen Lin's face next to hers on the front of the newspapers. After confessing to being an accomplice in Beth's attempted murder, she was awaiting sentencing. "I'm trying to put everything behind me now."

"I wish you good luck. How is your newborn?"

Beth looked down at him. His eyes were half closed.

"He's perfect."

Tyler, the boy she'd attacked at the crash site, had made her consider the limited life he had. She'd thought a lot about her conversation with Mrs O'Doole as they'd sat in the ambulance.

Trying not to treat them differently is the hardest thing.

But something else Marcia said had more resonance.

Give them the life they should have, however long it is.

She thought about the immediate future, was already making provision for it. Whatever lay further than tomorrow, however, they would face together when it arrived. Beth didn't want to look too far around the corner or consider what might be lurking there.

"I'm sorry for what you came to learn about your husband. But I am relieved. I couldn't be personally responsible for destroying your memory of him."

"What are you saying?"

"At the roadside, he already knew he wouldn't make it to the hospital. He told me he'd done something terrible to you. That he didn't deserve forgiveness."

The phone felt hot against Beth's ear.

Rae's voice was suddenly louder. "I couldn't have told you that. It wasn't my place."

"What about Allegro?"

"Allegro... is my daughter. I was leaving the voicemail for you. I was going to tell you everything but decided I couldn't do that in a recorded message. At that moment, my daughter came into the room. I was asking her to leave."

Beth remembered her whispering the name. Rae had been scolding her child

"I hung up, but I had to call back and speak to you personally. I was going to tell you exactly what he'd said, but you already believed Allegro was the word. I realised you would have been consumed if you'd never known what his last words had been, but when I heard the desperation in your voice, I changed my mind. Better that it was Allegro than what he'd whispered to me. A mystery and not an admission of guilt. I let it be Allegro."

A child's name. It was what had driven Beth to find the truth. And in the flames, she knew it had been protecting her own that had made her jump through the attic hatch and escape to safety.

"Then I saw the news and knew the secret of his guilt was no longer mine."

Beth shook her head.

"Are you still there?"

"How old is your daughter, Rae?"

"She's seven in three weeks."

Beth understood how Rae could go on, even with the spectre of what she'd left behind threatening to impact her present. "Thank you, Rae; stay safe and look after her."

"I will." Rae hung up.

"Beth, I'm double-parked!" There was a distinct trace of irritation in Jody's voice.

It was time to go. "Coming." Beth gently picked up Theo in the carrier, briefly regarded the bullet holes in the wall of the landing then headed outside.

ACKNOWLEDGMENTS

As always, everlasting love and thanks to my long-suffering missus, Anne-Marie, and the support she gives me along with my enthusiastic Mum and Dad who particularly liked this one and exhausted their Kindle batteries reading an early draft. A debt of gratitude to my editor, the indefatigable Emlyn Rees, for not making me pull my punches or go down the well trodden path. All hail the book bloggers who took the time to read and enthuse about *Scare Me* as well as Caroline Lambe and all at Team Robot. Kudos to the passionate members of GoodReads and Shelfari for their kind words and cheers to the denizens of Twitterland for all the generous tweets and RTs. Extra special thanks also to Richard Shealy, Cécile Bondaletoff, Dave Carr, Nate Matteson, Marc Gascoigne, Joanna Sharland, Suzannah Brooksbank, Mike Underwood and all the members of The Beefsteak Club.

ABOUT THE AUTHOR

Richard Parker has been a professional TV writer for twenty-two years and started by submitting material to the BBC. After contributing to a wide variety of TV shows, he became a head writer, script editor then producer. His first novel, *Stop Me*, was shortlisted for the prestigious UK Crime Writers Association John Creasey Dagger Award. His second novel, *Scare Me*, has been optioned by major Hollywood studio Relativity Media. He has now moved from London to Salisbury, but in no way hates London, and divides his time between reading, writing, cooking and visiting old English pubs.

richard-parker.com
twitter.com/bookwalter

When did you last google yourself?

When did you last google yourself?

SCARE ME

RICHARD PARKER

Shortlisted for the CWA Dagger Award